学术顾问
（以姓氏笔画为序）

王　宏　冯智文　李正栓　李丽生　原一川

Academic Advisors

Wang Hong　Feng Zhiwen　Li Zhengshuan

Li Lisheng　Yuan Yichuan

主　编

李昌银

副主编

黄　瑛　彭庆华

General Editor

Li Changyin

Professor of English　Yunnan Normal University

Associate General Editors

Huang Ying

Professor of English　Yunnan Normal University

Peng Qinghua

Professor of English　Yunnan Normal University

云南少数民族经典作品英译文库
Classics of Yunnan Ethnic Groups in English Translation

主编 李昌银　General Editor　Li Changyin
副主编 黄瑛 彭庆华　Associate General Editors　Huang Ying & Peng Qinghua

Li Feng
厘俸

汉译整理◎刀永明　薛贤　周凤祥
英译◎杨燕
译校◎[美]包琼

Edited & Translated into Chinese by
Dao Yongming, Xue Xian & Zhou Fengxiang
Translated into English by Yang Yan
Revised by Joan Cecile Boulerice

云南出版集团
云南人民出版社

图书在版编目（CIP）数据

厘俸：汉、英 / 刀永明,薛贤,周凤祥汉译整理；
杨燕英译. -- 昆明：云南人民出版社,2020.2
（云南少数民族经典作品英译文库 / 李昌银主编）
ISBN 978-7-222-19072-6

Ⅰ.①厘… Ⅱ.①刀… ②薛… ③周… ④杨… Ⅲ.
①傣族—史诗—中国—汉、英 Ⅳ.①I222.7

中国版本图书馆CIP数据核字(2020)第028256号

出 品 人	李 维	赵石定	
项目统筹	周 祥	殷筱钊	
项目组稿	郭木玉		
责任编辑	郭木玉	明 珍	
装帧设计	马 滨	石 斌	
责任校对	王琳淇	溥 思	费 珺
责任印制	陆卫华	代隆参	

云南少数民族经典作品英译文库
Classics of Yunnan Ethnic Groups in English Translation

厘　俸
Li Feng

汉译整理◎刀永明　薛贤　周凤祥
英译◎杨燕
译校◎［美］包琼

Edited & Translated into Chinese by Dao Yongming, Xue Xian & Zhou Fengxiang
Translated into English by Yang Yan
Revised by Joan Cecile Boulerice

出　　版	云南出版集团　云南人民出版社
发　　行	云南人民出版社
社　　址	昆明市环城西路609号
邮　　编	650034
网　　址	www.ynpph.com.cn
E-mail	ynrms@sina.com
开　　本	787mm×1092mm　1/16
印　　张	24.5
字　　数	390千
版　　次	2020年2月第1版第1次印刷
印　　刷	云南出版印刷集团有限责任公司　云南新华印刷一厂
书　　号	ISBN 978-7-222-19072-6
定　　价	135.00元

云南人民出版社
微信公众号

序 一

◎李正栓

民族典籍英译是传播中国文化、文学和文明的重要途径，是中华文化走出去的重要组成部分。文化与文学的传播，是一个国家提高文化软实力的重要方式，在文化交流和文明建设中起着不可或缺的作用，对提高国家对外话语权、构建国家对外话语体系以及对建设世界文学都有积极意义。

中国各少数民族拥有许多优秀的典籍，具有很高的文物价值、文学价值和文化价值。各民族的先人们通过口头流传或用文字记述了他们各具特色的文化。各少数民族几乎都有自己民族的创世史、史诗和神话传说。

中国民族典籍独具特色，不可替代。重视民族典籍的翻译和研究工作，对于挖掘各民族优秀文化，保护各民族文明，增强各民族之间的沟通和了解，进一步向世界其他地区传播各少数民族优秀文化，乃至提高我国文化软实力都有着重要意义。不少少数民族聚居地处于祖国边疆，有的处在"一带一路"建设关键部位，有的处在与周边国家进行各种交流的重要位置。

中国民族典籍是世界多元文化的有机组成部分，与其他文化共同造就了世界文化的绚丽多姿。世界正因为其文化多样性才变得缤纷多彩。我国各民族典籍中包含的文化多样性极大地丰富了世界多元、特色鲜明的文化。人们对多样性形成全新的认识角度和思维方式。多样性开阔了人们的视野，丰富了人们思考问题的角度。挖掘这些典籍中所蕴含的教育价值和文化价值，对世界其他民族都有指导和借鉴意义，并且有助于建设我国的文化自信。

民族典籍本身蕴含的特殊价值对加强民族文化了解、促进中外文化交流具有重大意义。民族典籍英译具有文学翻译和文化传递之功能，有对外宣传作用，还是一种文学外交。因此，民族典籍翻译和研究对于维护祖国统一、促进民族团结、稳定边疆以及增强国内各民族和中外文化之间的交流都起着极为重要的作用。

中华人民共和国成立以后，中央政府一直十分重视民族典籍翻译和研究工作，提供了强有力的政策支持，并采取了一系列有效措施，加快了各少数民族典籍的抢救、整理、翻译和研究的进程。中央政府多次召开西藏工作会议和新疆工作会议。近年来，国际和国内对于多元文化高度关注，少数民族文学典籍的翻译已然成为业内研究的热点。

近年来，民族典籍翻译和研究迅猛发展，势头良好。国家大力支持，发放国家社科基金课题，教育部和国家民委也发放课题，扶持了一大批研究者。很多民族典籍翻译课题得以立项并顺利开展；为数不少的民族典籍被翻译成汉语、英语和其他语言并出版发行；越来越多的业界人士致力于这个满富生机的学术领域。

在中国文化走出去的国家战略下，全国少数民族典籍英译学术研讨会陆续召开，已经召开三次。

云南是中国民族最多的省份。人口在5000人以上的少数民族有25个，其中有15个民族为云南所特有，分别是：白族、哈尼族、傣族、傈僳族、佤族、拉祜族、纳西族、景颇族、布朗族、普米族、阿昌族、基诺族、怒族、德昂族、独龙族。其中除白族人口占全国白族人口总数的84%以上外，其他14个民族95%居住在云南。

云南还是我国跨境民族最多的省份。在云南的25个少数民族中，有16个民族跨境而居，分别是：傣族、壮族、苗族、景颇族、瑶族、哈尼族、德昂族、佤族、拉祜族、彝族、阿昌族、傈僳族、布依族、怒族、布朗族、独龙族。

云南少数民族创造了辉煌的文化。据不完全统计，云南少数民族文字文献古籍蕴藏量达10万余册（卷），口传古籍4万余种。云南省民委少数民族古籍整理出版规划办公室为了挽救和保护这些古籍，计划在5年内编纂出版100卷《云南少数民族古籍珍本集成》。这是一个令人瞩目的庞大计划。将这些古籍中的珍品翻译介绍给世界，不仅能够弘扬云南省丰富多彩的民族文化，而且有助于增进与南亚东南亚国家的理解与交流，为"一带一路"倡议的实施做出贡献。

云南师范大学外国语学院很重视这一领域的工作。在外国语学院领导支持下，李昌银教授带领一个由教授和中青年学者组成的团队对精选出来的17部云南少数民族经典作品进行英译，计划在5年内（"十三五"期间）翻译出版。这是一项十分有意义的宏大工程。

这17部民族典籍，内容全部为各民族的英雄史诗或神话传说，具有很高的历史意义和文学价值。这些作品涉及阿昌族、白族、傣族、德昂族、哈尼族、景颇族、拉祜族、苗族、纳西族、普米族、彝族等11个少数民族。

云南师范大学这支翻译队伍实力强大，主要由一些多年从事翻译教学、研究和实践的教授和副教授组成，他们是李昌银、黄瑛、彭庆华、孙兴文、吴相如、刘德周、杨慧芳、郜菊、陈萍、包琼（Joan Cecile Boulerice）等国内外专家学者。他们在云南翻译界都是风云人物。

在民族典籍英译中，这支队伍异军突起，为我国民族典籍英译壮大了声势，必将为中国民族典籍走向世界而成为世界文学的一部分做出新贡献。

民族典籍翻译与研究事业关乎国家的稳定统一，关乎民族关系的和谐发展，关乎世界多元文化的实现。在中国，民族典籍资源极为丰富，有待进一步挖掘、翻译。因此，民族典籍英译前景光明。同时，我们也应意识到，仍有许多濒临消失的少数民族典籍亟待拯救，民族典籍翻译与研究工作任重而道远。

（李正栓，中国英汉语比较研究会典籍英译专业委员会常务副会长兼秘书长、河北师范大学博士生导师）

Foreword by Li Zhengshuan

The translation of Chinese ethnic classics is an important approach in spreading Chinese culture, literature and civilization. It is a crucial component of Chinese culture going global. The spreading of Chinese culture and literature is a national policy and an important way to improve the cultural soft power of China. It plays an indispensable role in the cultural exchange between China and other countries and the development of world literature.

The ethnic groups in China have countless excellent classics with high anthropological, literary and cultural value. The ancestors of each ethnic group have passed down their distinctive culture orally or in writing. Almost all the ethnic groups have their own story of creation, epics, myths and legends.

Chinese ethnic classics are unique and irreplaceable. It is imperative to attach importance to the translation and research of ethnic classics; to explore the excellent ethnic cultures; to protect the civilization of ethnic groups; to enhance the communication and understanding among ethnic groups; to further spread the outstanding culture of ethnic groups to other parts of the world; and to build the cultural strength of China. Many ethnic groups live in the border areas and thus play an important role in the cultural and economic cooperation between China and its neighbors in the context of the Belt and Road Initiative.

Chinese ethnic classics are an important component of the magnificence and diversity of world culture. It is diversity that makes the world so colorful. The cultural diversity of Chinese ethnic classics has greatly enriched the world's pluralism and its distinctive features. People around the world have formed a new understanding of diversity. This diversity has expanded people's horizon and enriched their way of thinking. Digging out the educational and cultural value in these classics can contribute to the construction of China's self-confidence in culture.

The special value of the ethnic classics itself is of great significance to the strengthening of national culture and intercultural communication between China and foreign countries. The translation of ethnic classics is not just a literary exchange, but also a form of cultural communication. It is diplomacy through literature in that it consolidates the cultural ties between China and other countries.

After the founding of the People's Republic of China, the central government attached great importance to the translation and research of ethnic classics, provided a great deal of policy support, and adopted a series of effective measures to speed up the process of rescuing, collating, translating and studying ethnic classics. The central government has convened several working conferences on Tibet and Xinjiang. In recent years, both China and other countries have paid close attention to multiculture. The translation of ethnic classics has become a hot topic.

In recent years, the translation and research of ethnic classics have progressed rapidly and have shown good prospects. The government strongly supports and grants the research projects of the national social science fund. The Ministry of Education and the State Ethnic Affairs Commission are also issuing research projects and giving funding to a large number of researchers. Many research projects on ethnic classics have been approved and carried out. Many ethnic classics have been translated into Chinese, English and other languages and published. More and more professionals have dedicated themselves to this new sphere of learning.

In this context, the academic conferences on translation of ethnic classics are held one after another all around the country. And up to now three have been held.

Yunnan is the province which has the most ethnic groups in China. Besides the Han people, there are 25 ethnic groups, each with a population of more than 5,000. Among them, 15 ethnic groups are unique to Yunnan, which are the Bai, the Hani, the Dai, the Lisu, the Wa, the Lahu, the Naxi, the Jingpo, the Bulang, the Pumi, the Achang, the Jinuo, the Nu, the De'ang and the Dulong. Among these, 84% of the total number of the Bai people in China and 95% of the other 14 ethnic groups are living in Yunnan.

Yunnan is also the province which has the most cross-border ethnic groups. Of the 25 ethnic groups, 16 live across the border, namely: the Dai, the Zhuang, the Miao, the Jingpo, the Yao, the Hani, the De'ang, the Wa, the Lahu, the Yi, the Achang, the Lisu, the Buyi, the Nu, the Bulang and the Dulong.

The ethnic groups in Yunnan have created splendid cultures. According to statistics, the number of classics of Yunnan ethnic groups is more than 100 thousand volumes and classics in oral tradition are more than 40 thousand. In order to save and protect these ancient books, the Office of Classics Collation and Publishing of Yunnan Ethnic Groups Affairs Commission planned to compile and publish 100 volumes of *A Collection of Yunnan Ethnic Group Rare Books* in five years, which is an ambitious plan. The introduction of the ancient classics via translation can not only promote and develop the colorful ethnic cultures of Yunnan, but also contribute to the understanding and exchange between China and countries in South Asia and Southeast Asia and to the implementation of the Belt and Road Initiative as well.

The School of Foreign Languages and Literature of Yunnan Normal University is paying close attention to this field. With the support of the School and the University,

Professor Li Changyin is leading a group of professors and young scholars to do the project of *Classics of Yunnan Ethnic Groups in English Translation*, which includes 17 ethnic classics selected carefully from Yunnan's bountiful ethnic classics. These books are the heroic epics or myths and legends of each ethnic groups with great historical significance and literary value. They will finish the translation in five years (during the Thirteenth Five-Year Plan). After that, all the works will be published by Yunnan People's Publishing House.

The 17 works cover 11 ethnic groups: the Achang, the Bai, the Dai, the De'ang, the Hani, the Jingpo, the Lahu, the Miao, the Naxi, the Pumi and the Yi. All of these groups except the Miao and the Yi are unique to Yunnan.

The translation team of Yunnan Normal University is full of strength and vitality, composed of professors and associate professors who have been occupied in translation teaching, research, and practice for a long time. They are Li Changyin, Huang Ying, Peng Qinghua, Sun Xingwen, Wu Xiangru, Liu Dezhou, Yang Huifang, Gao Ju, Chen Ping, Joan Boulerice and other experts and scholars who are representative figures in the translation field in Yunnan province.

This team is a new force that has suddenly arisen in terms of translating ethnic classics. It is expanding the momentum of ethnic classics translation in China and has made a new contribution for China's ethnic classics to go global and become a part of world literature.

The translation and research of ethnic classics are related to the development of Chinese culture and the realization of multiculturalism in the world. In China, ethnic classics are extremely rich in resources, which require us to make further exploration and research and translate them into other languages. Therefore, the future of translating ethnic classics is bright. At the same time, we should also realize that there are still many ethnic works which are close to extinction and urgently need to be rescued. We still have a long way to go in the fields of translation and research in ethnic classics.

(Li Zhengshuan, Standing Vice Chairman and Secretary General, Classics Translation Committee of CACSEC, PhD supervisor at Hebei Normal University)

序 二

◎王 宏

好友云南师范大学外国语学院李昌银教授来电嘱托我为"云南少数民族经典作品英译文库"的出版写一序言,并随即发来该文库的背景资料,让我"不着急,慢慢写"。我本人从事中国典籍英译及研究,深知少数民族典籍对外传译的重要性,但又是少数民族典籍翻译的门外汉。因此,我是怀着虚心学习的态度来写此序言的。近年来,在中国文化"走出去"战略工程大背景下,在中央和地方各级政府的大力支持下,我国少数民族典籍的对外传译及研究工作顺利开展,取得了很大的进步。请看以下数据:

2008年,广西百色学院韩家权教授获批国家社科基金项目《布洛陀史诗》(壮汉英对照)。该项目已顺利结项,并于2013年12月获得中国民间文艺最高奖"山花奖"。

2012年,广西百色学院外语系翻译团队翻译的国家级非物质文化遗产《壮族嘹歌》(英文版)由广西师范大学出版社正式出版。

2012年,东北大学秦皇岛分校吴松林教授主编的《蒙古族系列:江格尔(汉英对照)》(上下册)由吉林大学出版社出版。

2013年,河北师范大学李正栓教授英译《藏族格言诗》

由长春出版社出版发行。

2013年，云南财经大学崔晓霞教授撰写的《〈阿诗玛〉英译研究》收入由王宏印教授主编、民族出版社出版的"民族典籍翻译研究丛书"。

2014年，东北大学秦皇岛分校吴松林教授撰写的《满族档案文献研究》申请到国家社科后期资助，他英译的《英雄格斯尔可汗》由吉林大学出版社出版。

2014年，中南民族大学张立玉教授主持的"土家族主要典籍英译及研究"获批国家社科基金项目。

2015年，西安外国语大学梁真惠副教授撰写的《〈玛纳斯〉翻译传播研究》收入由王宏印教授主编、民族出版社出版的"民族典籍翻译研究丛书"。

与此同时，第一届和第二届全国少数民族典籍英译学术研讨会分别于2012年和2014年在广西民族大学和大连民族学院举行，参加会议的院校分布之广、与会代表数量之众、提交论文数量之多和涉及研究话题之细，十分可喜。2016年还将在中南民族大学举行第三届全国少数民族典籍英译学术研讨会。

为什么少数民族典籍的对外传译及研究工作在短短几年就受到译界的青睐，取得众多成果？我认为，这在很大程度上归于典籍翻译界乃至翻译界同仁对"中国典籍"的重新思考和认识。中国典籍浩如烟海，卷帙浩繁，举世瞩目，是全人类共同的精神财富。但对于中国典籍的理解，我们以前较多限于汉民族的重要文献和书籍，而对少数民族多有忽略。在讨论中国典籍时，也较多关注古代文学作品。其实，中国典籍指"中国清代末年1911年以前的重要文献和书籍",这就要求我们从事典籍翻译时,不但要翻译古代文学典籍作品,还要翻译古代哲学、科技、法律、医学、经济、军事、天文、地理等诸多方面的典籍作品,不但要翻译汉民族的典籍作品,也要翻译各少数民族的典籍作品。

民族典籍具有该民族的原型符号的特质,蕴藏着能够"遗传"并不断"再生"的文化基因。民族典籍是中华传统文化的内核,同时还是中华传统文化的符号构成规则。中国是具有56个民族的多民族国家,少数民族典籍是我国少数民族勤劳与智慧的结晶,是中华文明、也是世界文明不可或缺的一部分。少数民族典籍对外传译具有跨文化交流的作用,它不但有助于更多的人了解少数民族的独特文化,而且还有助于保护少数民族文化的独特性、维持少数民族文化多样性、促进各民族团结、提升中华文化软实力等。

中国少数民族典籍涉及宗教、文学、历史、语言、医学、天文历算等领域,内容丰富,版本多样,载体特殊,传承奇特。仅以《中国少数民族古籍总目提要》为例,该书于1997年正式立项,全书总体设计约60卷、110册,目前已出版23个民族卷共20册:纳西族卷、白族卷、东乡族卷·裕固族卷·保安族卷、土族卷·撒拉族卷、锡伯族卷、哈尼族卷、回族卷·铭刻、柯尔克孜族卷、羌族卷、毛南族卷·京族卷、仫佬族卷、达斡尔族卷、土家族卷、鄂温克族卷、鄂伦春族卷、赫哲族卷、苗族卷、侗族卷、黎族卷、朝鲜族卷。该书真实地反映了我国各少数民族古籍赋存的全面情况,充实了中国的历史和文化内容,为后人探索各种文化形式的源流、揭示中国社会文化发展的轨迹提供了极为珍贵的资料，为我国乃至世界各国人文科学研究提供了一套新颖而全面的资料，对于弘扬中华民族传统文化具有深远的历史意义和现实意义。

少数民族典籍的对外传译是一项艰巨的工作，涉及将少数民族语言译成汉语、少数民族语言之间的互译和少数民族语言译成外语（主要是英语）。前两类翻译历史源远流长，最早可追溯到春秋战国时代《越人歌》的翻译，即汉、壮语之间的翻译。少数民族典籍译成外语的时间则要晚一些。据考证，维吾尔族古典长诗《福乐智慧》成书于1069年或1070年，目前尚未发现完整的原稿，只存留下来三个抄本，分别为赫拉特抄本、费尔干纳抄本与埃及抄本，其中费尔干纳抄本于12~13世纪用阿拉伯文纳斯赫体抄写，1914年发现于今中亚乌孜别克斯坦纳曼干城，现存于该共和国科学院东方研究所。这是少数民族典籍译介到国外的最早纪录。少数民族典籍外译在现代有了较快发展。一些少数民族典籍，如藏族的《格萨尔王传》、蒙古族的《江格尔》和柯尔克孜族的《玛纳斯》等英雄史诗，云南彝族的《阿诗玛》、维吾尔族的《艾里甫和赛乃姆》等民间叙事长诗已先后被翻译成英语及其他外国文字，为世人所知。这对传承少数民族经典，推动中外文化交流起到了不可替代的作用。然而，还有大量的中国少数民族典籍等待我们去翻译和研究。

云南省少数民族典籍资源十分丰富。据不完全统计，云南少数民族文字文献古籍蕴藏量达10万余册（卷），口传古籍4万余种。"云南少数民族经典作品英译文库"正是依托云南省丰富的少数民族典籍资源，借助云南师范大学外国语学院强大的翻译师资队伍，在云南人民出版社的有力支持下，首次将云南少数民族经典作品成系列对外译介的大力举措。云南师范大学外国语学院对"云南少数民族经典作品英译文库"十分重视，他们首先邀请省内外少数民族语言文化研究专家对云南民族典籍和民族文化经典作品进行筛选，做到"好中选好，优中选优"，同时调配最强的翻译力量承担文库的翻译任务。我粗略看了该文库的选题，发现选题面广，覆盖范围宽，收入了云南省阿昌族、白族、傣族、纳西族、德昂族、哈尼族、景颇族、拉祜族、苗族、普米族和彝族等民族的典籍作品。云南共有25个少数民族，其中11个少数民族的典籍作品都覆盖到了，不少作品还是首次译成英文。这将彻底改变云南少数民族典籍由于对外译介数量较少，不为世界了解的尴尬局面。

对于云南师范大学外国语学院而言，把少数民族典籍英译作为翻译专业的优势特色进行建设，这将对该院的学科建设起到助推作用。"云南少数民族经典作品英译文库"所产生的翻译成果和研究成果将培养出一批优秀的典籍翻译和研究团队，凸显该院在全国的学术特色和学术影响，同时还能将翻译能力和研究能力转化为教学能力，提高云南师范大学外国语学院翻译专业研究生的培养质量，为社会输送高水平的翻译人才，有力地支撑学院翻译专业学科的建设和发展。我对云南师范大学外国语学院的翻译师资队伍较为熟悉。作为云南省唯一获得省级高校优势特色学科建设项目的外国语学院，该院具有雄厚的翻译师资力量，在云南省各高校中当属第一。多年来，该院翻译与跨文化研究团队一直承担着对外交流与合作的各种口笔译项目及任务。由外国语学院精心挑选和确定的"云南少数民族经典作品英译文库"翻译人员绝大多数都是云南省翻译领域里的知名教授或专家,有国外留学经历,且具有扎实的英汉双语语言功底,曾翻译出版多部译著和翻译作品,并且主持和参与过多项翻译项目的研究。我阅读李昌银教授发来的文库翻译人员名单,发现多名我所熟悉的知名教授、博士也在其中,感到格外放心。

"云南少数民族经典作品英译文库"的出版发行是云南省翻译界的一件大事,也是我国少数民族典籍翻译传来的又一佳音。想当年,我和"大中华文库"总协调人李林老师曾在参加全国典籍英译学术研讨会之余一起找到李昌银教授,敦促李教授向学校和同事呼吁,少数民族典籍翻译及研究是富矿,值得快挖、深挖,能早出成果,出大成果。今天,我们当年的心愿变成了美好的现实,心里感到特别高兴。再次热烈祝贺"云南少数民族经典作品英译文库"的顺利出版!

(王宏,中国典籍翻译研究会副会长、苏州大学博士生导师)

Foreword by Wang Hong

My friend Professor Li Changyin of Yunnan Normal University asked me to write a few words for the publication of *Classics of Yunnan Ethnic Groups in English Translation*. I am more than delighted to do it. As I have been doing research in English translation of Chinese classics, I know how important this work is. In recent years, substantial progress has been made in translating Chinese ethnic classics into English and introducing them to the world. Let's look at the following accomplishments.

First of all, several projects in the English translation of ethnic classics have received funding from the National Planning Office of Philosophy and Social Science. The first of these projects is *The Epic of Baeuqloxgdoh* (Zhuang-Chinese-English trilingual version), given funding in 2008 and headed by Professor Han Jiaquan of Baise University in Guangxi Zhuang Autonomous Region. In December 2013, this translation won the Shanhua Award, the most prestigious prize for folk literature and art in China. The second project is *A Study of the Manchu Archives*, written by Professor Wu Songlin of Northeastern University at Qinhuangdao and which was given funding in 2014. The third is *English*

Translation and Study of the Major Classics of the Tujia Ethnic Group, headed by Professor Zhang Liyu of the South-Central University for Nationalities, also granted in 2014.

Secondly, several English translations have been published. In 2012, *Liao Songs of Pingguo Zhuang*, has been listed as one of China's national intangible cultural heritages. It was translated by the School of Foreign Languages, Baise University, and published by Guangxi Normal University Press. Also in 2012, *Jangar* (a Chinese-English bilingual edition), edited by Professor Wu Songlin of Northeastern University at Qinhuangdao, was published by Jilin University Press. In 2013, *Tibetan Gnomic Verses Translated into English*, translated by Professor Li Zhengshuan of Hebei Normal University, was published by Changchun Press. And in 2014, *Heroic Geser Khan*, translated by Professor Wu Songlin of Northeastern University at Qinhuangdao, was published by Jilin University Press.

And thirdly, two important monographs have been published by The Ethnic Publishing House in the *Ethnic Classics Translation Research Series* edited by Professor Wang Hongyin of Nankai University. One is *A Study on the English Translation of* Ashima *by Gladys Taylor* (2013), which was the PhD dissertation of Professor Cui Xiaoxia of Yunnan University of Finance and Economics. The other is *Translation and Dissemination of the Oral Epic Manas* (2015) written by Associate Professor Liang Zhenhui of Xi'an International

Studies University.

Meanwhile, it is encouraging to see that the first conferences on English translation of ethnic classics in China have been held in Guangxi Nationalities University and Dalian Nationalities Institute respectively. Participants were both many and enthusiastic. Many papers were presented and a lot of topics discussed. The third conference will be hosted by South Central Nationalities University in 2016.

Why, then, has this field attracted so much attention from translators and scholars alike and accomplished so much in just a few years? The answer, I believe, lies in a rethinking of what constitutes Chinese classics as an indispensable part of human heritage. We used to see Chinese classics as more or less equal to the classics of the Han people, excluding works by other ethnic groups. Moreover, when we talk about Chinese classics, we focus too much on the literary works of ancient times. Yet Chinese classics actually refer to "important works and books before 1911, the year when the Qing dynasty fell, bringing an end to imperial rule". This definition requires us to pay attention not just to literary works, but also writings in other subjects, such as philosophy, science, law, medicine, economics, military affairs, astronomy, and geography, not only Han works, but writings by other ethnic groups as well.

The classical works of a nation are its archetypal symbols, the major carriers of its cultural genes. Chinese classics make up the core of Chinese tradition. The Chinese nation consists of 56 ethnic groups. Ethnic classics are an important part of not only Chinese traditional culture, but also world civilization. The translation of these works into other languages is important in that it helps to promote cross-cultural communications between China and other countries and to protect and preserve the uniqueness and diversity of ethnic cultures by making them accessible to foreign readers.

Chinese ethnic classics cover a variety of areas, such as religion, literature, history, language, medicine, astrology, and calendar, with numerous editions, special media and unique ways of transmission from generation to generation. Take, for example, *An Anthology of Chinese Ethnic Classics*, a colossal project that includes 110 volumes, 20 of which, from 23 ethnic groups, have been published. The anthology reflects the variety and quantity of China's ethnic classics and provides valuable material and resources for studying, understanding and developing Chinese culture and history in a more comprehensive and sustainable way.

The translation of Chinese ethnic classics into foreign languages is a very demanding job, involving rendering from ethnic languages to Chinese, between ethnic languages, and from ethnic languages (often via Chinese) to foreign languages. The first two types of translation can be traced back to the Spring and Autumn Period, when *The Song of the Yue People* was translated from their mother tongue into Chinese. The earliest translation of ethnic classics into a foreign language is *Wisdom of Royal Glory*, a long poem of the Uygurs, which was rendered from the source language into Arabic and is now in the Oriental Institute of Uzbekistan at Namangan. But it was not until modern times that the translation of ethnic classics into foreign languages accelerated. Noticeably, ethnic epics, such as *The Story of Prince Geser* of the Tibetans, *The Story of Jianggeer* of the Mongolians, *Manas* of the Kyrgyz, and narrative poems such as *Ashima* of the Yi people, *Alip and Salam* of the Uygurs, etc., have been published. These translations have contributed to acquainting the world with Chinese ethnic classics, but many remain to be translated.

Yunnan is rich in ethnic classics, boasting more than 100,000 volumes of written classics and over 40,000 pieces of oral literature. Relying on such bountiful resources, as a collective endeavor of the translation team of the School of Foreign Languages and Literature, Yunnan Normal University and with the help of Yunnan People's Publishing House, *Classics of Yunnan Ethnic Groups in English Translation* is the first project to translate Yunnan ethnic classics into English on a large scale. The School adheres to a professional spirit and academic standard in carrying out the project by selecting the most authoritative texts in the source language (Chinese) and recruiting the best translators from its huge faculty. The selection of the works, covering eleven of the twenty-five ethnic groups of the province, indicates expertise and insight. The implementation of the project will change the embarrassing obscurity of Yunnan ethnic classics by making them known to the world, many of them for the first time.

In light of disciplinary development, the project is of great importance, too. Participating in the translation will strengthen the academic foundation of the teachers, enrich their experience and enhance their translation skills and research ability. This in turn will help them become better teachers and thus able to educate students with higher quality. The publication of the books will add greatly to the faculty accomplishments of the School and raise the academic standing of Yunnan Normal University by taking the first step in this direction among the universities of Yunnan province.

This publication project is a great event not only for Yunnan itself, but also for China. Looking back, I remember that Professor Li Changyin, our friend Li Lin, editor of the *Library of Chinese Classics*, and I talked enthusiastically about initiating something like this in Yunnan when we attended a conference on the translation of ethnic classics in Soochow. Lin and I strongly suggested that Professor Li do it as soon as possible. Now I am very pleased to see our talk becoming reality. Again, my congratulations on the publication of *Classics of Yunnan Ethnic Groups in English Translation*!

(Wang Hong, Vice Chairman of Classics Translation Committee of CACSEC, PhD supervisor at Soochow University)

导　言

"云南少数民族经典作品英译文库"旨在将云南少数民族的经典作品翻译介绍给国外对其感兴趣的英文读者大众。随着以古代汉文经典构成的"大中华文库"的出版发行，学界正将注意力转移到民族典籍的翻译上来。民族典籍是指由民族作家创作的反应民族历史和文化的经典作品。广西、贵州、辽宁、新疆、西藏等省区的大学已经捷足先登。我们云南也理应有所作为。云南拥有全国最多的少数民族。全省25个少数民族中，有15个为云南特有民族，即阿昌族、白族、布朗族、傣族、德昂族、独龙族、哈尼族、景颇族、基诺族、拉祜族、傈僳族、纳西族、怒族、普米族、佤族。这些民族的典籍，有的是原作，有的是汉译本，构成了一个巨大的宝库，我们有义务将其介绍给国外的英语读者和学术界。问题是，先译什么？

云南所有的25个少数民族都创造了自己的经典作品，包括史诗、神话、创世故事、民谣、戏曲、山歌和丧歌，以各种形式流传于各地，总数不下10万卷，这还不包括口传文体。经过调查研究，并征求民族学专家的建议后，我们决定重点翻译史诗和神话。史诗和神话叙述的是民族起源故事，最能反映各民族哲学、历史、文化等的概貌、渊源。我们从汗牛充栋的民族史诗与神话中精选了云南阿昌族、白族、傣族、德昂族、哈尼族、景颇族、拉祜族、苗族、纳西族、普米族、彝族等11个少数民族的17部最具有代表性的经典作品。这些作品全部都是汉语译本，由既会讲母语又精通汉语的双语学者整理、翻译而成。其中有的是在节庆仪式和表演时从口语录制而来。我们没有选择用民族语言写成的文本，首先是因为很难寻找到民族语和英语俱佳的译者；其次是因为一部分典籍的民族语言文本在民间以多种方言形式流传，情节五花八门。汉语文本系专家仔细整理、翻译而成，因而更具权威性。接下来的问题是：如何译？

在我们选定的17部作品中，除了《白国因由》为散文体之外，其余全部为民歌韵文体，诗行长度大致相当，行末有松散押韵，无格律。译诗为诗是最起码的要求。我们遵循的原则有如下几点。

一、若原文为诗歌，译文也必须为诗歌。

二、译文尽可能完整地再现原文的思想内容和意象。

三、译文尽可能再现原文的修辞手段。

四、不改变原文每一节诗的行数，除非万不得已。

五、不使用英文的标准格律，因为原文并不是标准的格律体。采用英文的自然节奏，但诗行长短应大体一致。

六、不用韵，除非符合英文表达习惯且不损害原文内容。

我们所追求的，用苏珊·巴斯奈特的话来说就是"异地播种"，而不是直接移栽树木。关于原文的形式特征，尤其是尾韵，能再现时再现，不能再现时果断放弃。

那谁来翻译呢？本文库是云南师范大学外国语学院的集体项目，因此我们的翻译团队由本院十几位同行加上两位在职攻读翻译专业硕士学位的高校教师组成。所有译者都在高校教授翻译课程，从事翻译研究，不仅发表了翻译论文，也出版了译著。

  传统上，人们通常是将外语译为母语，而不是将母语译为外语。但是这种情况正在发生改变。现在许多译者都将母语译为外语。根据耐克·帕科恩[①]和斯图亚特·坎贝尔[②]的论证，将母语译入非母语，能够达到相当高的水平。中国的情形为他们的观点提供了新的论据。中国典籍英译在19世纪由英国汉学家理雅各和翟理斯发起，20世纪在亚瑟·伟利、戴维·霍克思、波顿·沃森、约翰·闵福德、宇文所安等英美汉学家的推动下继续发展。值得注意的是，在这一过程中，旅居西方的华人学者迅速加入到了中国典籍英译的行列中。其中最著名的是辜鸿铭和林语堂。他们主动承担这个任务，因为他们认为西方汉学家的母语并非汉语，其译文往往误读汉语原文本，误解中国文化，自己义不容辞，必须为英语读者提供更忠实的英文翻译。自20世纪50年代开始，越来越多的中国大陆译者投身于典籍英译或重译。在杨宪益、许渊冲、汪榕培、王宏印、王宏、李正栓等当代翻译家和翻译理论家的积极倡导和引领下，典籍英译蔚然成风，势头强劲。许渊冲、王宏、李正栓等都在西方出版社出版了英文译著，这表明他们的英文水平达到了国际上的出版标准。

  就本文库而言，我们采取了一系列保障译文质量的措施。我们要求译者尽最大努力拿出代表自己最高水平的译文。文

[①] 挑战公理：译入非母语. 阿姆斯特丹：约翰·本杰明斯出版公司，2005.
[②] 译入第二语言. 纽约：劳特里奇出版社，2013.

库的主编们对译文进行仔细研读，纠正理解偏差、语法错误以及格式上的问题。在此基础上，我们采取了一个不可或缺的步骤，请长期在我院从事英语教学工作的美国老师包琼（Joan Cecile Boulerice）对每一个译本进行逐字逐句的修改，使之更自然流畅，更符合英文表达习惯。我们尽了最大的努力。如果译文还存在什么问题，皆由我们负责，与包琼老师无关。

在这里，我们对所有给予我们宝贵帮助和支持的专家学者深表谢忱。感谢云南人民出版社的领导为文库成功申报为"十三五"国家重点出版物出版规划项目和国家出版基金项目给予的大力支持。感谢文库责编、东南亚南亚读物编辑部主任郭木玉，她的严谨和敬业令我们动容。感谢云南师范大学为文库提供了出版资金支持，使译者们不被"眼前的苟且"干扰，能够一心一意地追求"诗和远方"。感谢李正栓教授和王宏教授不仅一直鼓励我们前进，而且欣然为文库作序，从全球视野对其意义进行肯定，极大地提振了我们的信心。感谢包琼老师，她的修改保证了译文的流畅性。最后要特别感谢王宏教授和湖南人民出版社的资深编辑李林先生，是他们的建议促成了本文库的构想。

云南师范大学外国语学院
"云南少数民族经典作品英译文库"编委会

General Introduction

This publication project, *Classics of Yunnan Ethnic Groups in English Translation*, aims at introducing Yunnan ethnic classical works to the world by making them available to native speakers of English who might be interested in them. With the publication of the *Library of Chinese Classics*, which consists only of books written by Han authors in classical Chinese, attention now is being turned to the English translation and publication of ethnic classics, books produced by ethnic writers about their history and culture. Universities in provinces such as Guangxi, Guizhou, Liaoning, Xinjiang, and Xizang, have taken the initiative. We in Yunnan must do something, because Yunnan has the largest number of ethnic groups in China. 15 of the 25 ethnic groups in the province, the Achang, the Bai, the Bulang, the Dai, the De'ang, the Dulong, the Hani, the Jingpo, the Jinuo, the Lahu, the Lisu, the Naxi, the Nu, the Pumi, and the Wa, live in no other place but Yunnan. The classics of these people, either in their own language or in Chinese translations, are a great treasure house, which should be accessible to English readers and scholars. But what works should be translated first?

All the 25 ethnic groups in Yunnan have their classics,

epics, mythology, creation stories, folksongs, folk drama, mountain songs, and funeral lament lyrics, most of which exist in different versions in different places. According to one estimation, there are more than 100,000 volumes of them, excluding those in oral form. After a thorough survey and extensive consultations with experts of ethnic studies, we concluded that priority must be given to epics and mythologies, as they reflect an ethnic people's philosophy, history and culture more than anything else by narrating the stories of where and how they think they came from. From many epics and mythologies, we selected 17 of the most authoritative and popular classics representing 11 Yunnan ethnic groups, the Achang, the Bai, the Dai, the De'ang, the Hani, the Jingpo, the Lahu, the Miao, the Naxi, the Pumi, and the Yi. These works are all in Chinese, translated from the original by bilingual scholars whose mother tongue is their own ethnic language and who are fluent and proficient in Chinese. Some were recorded from their oral form at rituals and performances. We did not choose texts written in the ethnic language, not least because it is very hard to find a translator who is skilled in both the ethnic language and English. Moreover, some of the classics in the ethnic language were circulated in various oral forms and fragments. The published Chinese versions have been carefully edited and translated, hence they are more reliable. The next question is: how to translate them?

It happens that all of the 17 works except one are in verse form, with lines more or less the same length and loose rhymes, but no regular meter. A poem must be rendered into a poem; anything less is unacceptable. So here are the general rules we follow when doing the translation.

One. If the original is verse, the translated text must be verse, too.

Two. Reproduce the ideas and the images of the original as completely as possible.

Three. Reproduce the figures of speech of the original as much as possible.

Four. Do not change the number of lines in a stanza unless absolutely necessary.

Five. Do not use standard meters in English, because the Chinese original does not follow any regular meter. Use the natural rhythm of English instead, but most of the lines should look more or less the same length.

Six. Do not use rhyme unless it comes naturally and is faithful to the content of the original.

What we try to do is, to use Susan Bassnett's words, "transplant the seed", not the tree itself. As for the various aspects of form, particularly meter and end rhyme, we reproduce them when it is possible and abandon them when it is necessary.

Who will do the translations? As this is a collective project of the School of Foreign Languages and Literature of Yunnan Normal University, our team consists of a dozen faculty members and two students from our MA translation program who are already teachers in other universities. All the translators have been teaching translation and doing translation research for a long time. They have published not just academic articles on translation, but also translated books from English to Chinese or vice versa.

Traditionally, people translate into their mother tongue, not into a foreign language. But the situation is changing. Many translators today are translating from their mother tongue into a foreign language. The quality can be good, as Nike K. Pokorn and Stuart Campbell prove in *Challenging the Traditional Axioms: Translation into a non-mother tongue* (Amsterdam: John Benjamins Publishing Company, 2005) and *Translation into the Second Language* (New York: Routledge, 2013) respectively. The case of China provides further evidence for their argument. The translation of Chinese classics into English was initiated by James Legge and Herbert Allen Giles in the 19th century and carried on in the 20th century by Arthur Waley, David Hawkes, Burton Watson, John Minford, Stephen Owen and others. It is noticeable that these English and American sinologists were soon joined by Chinese scholars residing in the West, such as Hongming (Tomson) Gu and Lin Yutang, among others. They took up the job because they thought it was their obligation to give English readers more faithful translations than Western sinologists could, who, as their target language is their mother tongue, often misinterpret the original text and misrepresent Chinese culture. Since the 1950s, there has been an increasingly powerful trend for Mainland Chinese translators to render or re-render Chinese classics into foreign languages, English in particular. In our time, this work is gathering momentum, enthusiastically advocated and actively practiced by such well-known translation experts as Yang Xianyi of Beijing Foreign Language Press, Xu Yuanchong of Beijing University, Wang Rongpei of Dalian Foreign Language Institute, Wang Hongyin of Nankai University, Wang Hong of Soochow University, Li Zhengshuan of Hebei Normal University, and many more. These professors are not just translators, but also scholars in translation studies. More importantly, some of them, Xu Yuanchong, Wang Hong and Li Zhengshuan, for example, have had their translations published by Western publishers, which suggests that their English meets the international standard.

In the case of our project, we request that the translators do their best to produce good translations. When they submit them to us, they should represent the highest level that they can attain. Then the general editors appointed by the School read the translated texts and remove inaccurate renderings and grammar mistakes if there are any. On top of that, we've taken an indispensable measure to ensure that our English is readable. We asked Ms. Joan Cecile Boulerice, an American teacher who has been teaching English in our school since 2009, to read every text that we've translated and improve the English by making it more natural and idiomatic. This is the best we can do. Of course any problems that still remain in the translations are ours. They have nothing to do with our American teacher.

As the project is well under way, we would like to thank all those who have helped to make it possible. Ms. Guo Muyu, director of the South and Southeast Asia Editorial Department, Yunnan People's Publishing House, has been most helpful in our cooperation. In addition, she has added importance to the project by turning it into a national publication project. Yunnan Normal University has supported us by paying the publication fees so that the translators won't have to be burdened with the financial responsibilities for this project. Professor Li Zhengshuan and Professor Wang Hong not only have always encouraged us to go on but have also written the forewords for the project, putting it in a global perspective. Ms. Joan Cecile Boulerice's revision has ensured the fluency of the translated texts. Finally, special thanks must be given to Professor Wang Hong, again, and Mr. Li Lin of Hunan People's Press for their suggestion that has helped us conceive the project from the very beginning.

The General Editors
School of Foreign Languages & Literature
Yunnan Normal University, Kunming

厘俸

目录

一 // 2

二 // 17

三 // 26

四 // 35

五 // 41

六 // 113

七 // 185

八 // 242

九 // 304

译后记 // 350

Contents

Li Feng

I // 2

II // 17

III // 26

IV // 35

V // 41

VI // 113

VII // 185

VIII // 242

IX // 304

Translators' Afterword // 352

厘 俸 Li Feng

故事讲述两个古代傣族部落之间的战争。

It is about the war between two ancient Dai tribes.

厘俸 // Li Feng

一

清晨的太阳刚刚升起，
海罕已起床洗漱完毕。
匆忙吃罢早饭，
敲响震耳的鼓声。

鼓声咚咚传向天空大地，
宫廷的大门迅速开启。
文武百官急忙骑着大象，
进入宫廷聚集。
银色的象牙闪闪发亮，
悦耳的铃声清脆无比。
混①海罕端坐在宫殿中央，
象牙雕刻的龙椅光滑富丽，
宝石镶嵌的金幡幢悬吊在头
　　顶上。
他的弟弟桑本、桑温入朝
　　参拜，
忠诚的老军师布冈伴、布冈戈
　　也入廷敬贺，

---

① 混：官的统称，与官家有亲属
　　关系者也称混。

I

When the sun rose in the morning,
Haihan got up and washed.
Having finished his breakfast in haste,
He beat the drum with a deafening sound.

With the drum beats spreading far and wide,
The royal court gate opened promptly.
Riding on their elephants,
The officials surged into the court.
The silver tusks of the elephants were sparkling,
And the bells were ringing melodiously.
Hun① Haihan sat in the middle of the palace
On a splendid dragon throne carved from ivory.
Above him hung a golden prayer flag embellished with
　　　　jewels and gems.
Coming into the court were his younger brothers Sangben
　　　　and Sangwen,
His loyal military counselors Bugang Ban and Bugang Ge,
Hundreds of civil and military officials, a thousand

---

① Hun: a general designation for all the official titles. The
　　relatives of the officials can also be addressed as "Hun".

还有数百文武官员和一千个勐
　　的首领登堂入席，
勇猛的武将艾召生①也来到
　　这里。
当他步入朝廷，
百官纷纷欢呼起立，
他用目光向人们频频致意。
百官坐定朝廷肃静，
海罕在龙椅上发布命令：
"我的忠臣们！
面对凶恶的敌人，
骑上你们的大象，
拔出你们的利刃，
挥舞你们的长矛，
勇敢地夺取全胜。
我的将官啊，
胜利就依靠你们！"
朝廷肃静，百官屏息。
海罕面对着无数忠诚的目光说：
"去年到今年一年之际，

chiefs from different *mengs*[①],
And the brave and valiant General Ai Zhaosheng[②] as well.
When Haihan strode in,
The officials all rose to their feet and cheered.
He looked around at them.
Seeing that the officials had all taken their seats in solemn silence,
Haihan began to issue a decree:
"My loyal officials!
Facing the vicious enemy,
Please mount your elephants,
Pull out your swords,
Wield your spears,
And march bravely for victory!
My generals!
It's on you that our victory relies!"
Silence hung over the court and the officials all held their breath.
Meeting the eyes of the many loyal officials, Haihan said:
"Right on New Year's Day this year,

---

① 艾召生：又名冈晓。艾：老大。召生：一勐之主。

---

① Meng: a Dai word which means "district".
② Ai Zhaosheng: another name for Gangxiao. "Ai" means "the eldest son". "Zhaosheng" means "chief of a *meng*".

厘俸 // Li Feng

就像阿巫戛①一样能飞的艾哈腊②,	Aihala①, able to fly like Awu Ga②,
来到我们勐景哈③,	Came to our kingdom Mengjingha③.
看见我和妻子坐在宫廷里,	Seeing my wife and I sitting in the court,
他摇身一变,	He turned into a stranger,
变成一个陌生人来到宫里,	Holding a fierce fighting cock.
抱着一只凶猛的斗鸡,	He challenged me
来和我的斗鸡相战相比。	To a cockfight
他运用法术,暗中使计,	And defeated me
打败了我的斗鸡。	By means of dirty magic and tactics.
他忽然又变成了一只美丽的马鹿,	Then he changed into a beautiful deer,
越过斗鸡场,	Crossed the cockfighting ring
向远处奔跑而去。	And ran off.
我骑上一匹没有鞍子的快马,	I mounted a fast horse without a saddle
向神秘的马鹿追击。	And chased after the mysterious deer.
鹿像飞箭一样,	The deer was running as fast as a flying arrow,
马像狂风一般。	And my horse was chasing it as quickly as a fierce wind.
追啊,追!	I chased and chased
马鹿忽然不知去向。	Till the deer suddenly vanished into the blue.
我失望地回到宫廷,	Disappointed, I returned to the court
发现妻子已不在原来的地方。	Only to find that my wife was no longer there.

---

① 阿巫戛:叔叔,名叫戛,此人能往来于天上和人间。
② 艾哈腊:对俸改的贬称,其意为野蛮残忍。
③ 勐景哈:海罕治理的王国。

① Aihala: a disparaging term for Fenggai to indicate his ruthlessness and atrocity.
② Awu Ga: an uncle by the name of "Ga". He could travel freely between heaven and earth.
③ Mengjingha: the kingdom ruled by Haihan.

艾哈腊抢走了我的婻崩，	Aihala had abducted my wife Nanbeng.
他变鹿是为了调虎离山。	The deer was just part of a "lure and distraction plot".
不见妻子，	Losing my wife
我的心如刀绞，	Wrenched my heart.
万分悲伤！	How sorrowful and grief-stricken I was!
百官们啊，	My dear officials!
如今我只能孤零零地独坐，	Nowadays I can
孤零零地吃饭。	Only sit alone and eat alone.
我真想孤零零地进入森林，	How I wish I could walk into the forest lonely
孤零零地一死了之！	And die there lonely!
为了寻找婻崩，	In order to find Nanbeng,
我宁愿用生命相换。	I'd rather sacrifice my life.
我的混俸①啊，	My dear hunfengs①,
我希望得到你们的帮助！"	I really need your help!"
朝廷肃静，百官屏息，	Silence hung over the court and the officials all held their breath.
你看看我，我看看你，	They looked at each other,
大家都沉默无言。	Not knowing what to say.
忽然艾召生捋袖拍桌，	Suddenly Ai Zhaosheng rolled up his sleeves, pounded the table
应声而起说：	And stood up to respond:
"召②供养我们尽心尽意，	"Zhao② provides for us with all his might,
希望人人都是一员猛将。	

---

① 混俸：文武百官的统称。
② 召：官，还有尊敬之意。

① Hunfeng: a general designation for all the civil and military officials.
② Zhao: a respectful way to address an official. Here it refers to Haihan.

厘俸 // Li Feng

旧衣未破又给新衣，
战袍未磨又给新装，
绫罗绸缎在所不惜。
如今海罕失去爱妻，
天大的悲伤织在心里。
他的不幸就是我们的不幸，
他的仇敌就是我们的仇敌。
百官们啊，
让我们骑上大象，
为海罕夺回婻崩爱妻。"
他的话响亮有力，
震动了整个宫廷。
话音刚落冈晓话音又起：
　"我们一千个勐的首领，
已经在宫廷内外齐集。
我们要找回婻崩，
让她和海罕永远在一起。
让幸福和富裕与他们相伴，
让她做我们的皇后，
是大家的心意。
百官们啊，
我们应该为海罕出力。"

Hoping for each of us to become a valiant fighter.
We are given new clothes when the old ones are not worn out yet.
We are armed with new suits of armors when the old ones are not damaged yet.
He never hesitates to give us silk and satin as rewards.
Now Haihan has lost his beloved wife,
Weaving the greatest sorrow inside his heart.
His misfortune is our misfortune,
And his enemy is our enemy.
Dear officials,
Let us mount our elephants
And help Haihan take his wife back."
His words were so powerful
That everyone in the court was deeply impressed and astonished.
Then Gangxiao said more:
"A thousand chiefs
Are now gathering inside and outside the court.
We are all determined to take Nanbeng back.
Let Nanbeng be with Haihan forever.
Let happiness and well-being always accompany them.
Let her continue to be our queen.
This is our will.

他转身又对召海法①说：	Dear officials,
"尊敬的召海法呀，	We should lead a hand to Haihan."
面对大事我们不能性急，	He then turned to Zhao Haifa① and said:
狗一般的慌乱不能夺取胜利。	"Our respectable Zhao Haifa,
人人都知道天上有天堂，	Facing such a big problem we should not be hasty.
地上有个勐景罕②。	Dog-like panic will be no good to win a victory.
那里的土地宽广无边，	Everybody knows that up above there is Paradise,
那里的人多如蚂蚁一般。	And down here there is Mengjinghan②.
我们怎能将它团团包围？	Mengjinghan has a vast land
因为我们没有足够的兵将。	And people as numerous as ants.
如果我们不能取胜，	How can we besiege Mengjinghan
布领暖③的指责就要从天而降。	When we do not have enough soldiers and generals?
我记得你在勐准果做召的时候，	If we cannot win the war,
布领暖送了一只仙鼓与你为伴，	God Bulingnuan③ will put blame on us.
用来保护你免灾免难。	I remember that when you served as an official in Mengzhunguo,
一旦发生危急的事情，	Bulingnuan sent you a magic drum
就把仙鼓敲响。	To protect you from disasters and catastrophes.
或者派阿巫戛上天去见布领暖，	Once a crisis develops,
布领暖就会给我们帮助和力量。	You are supposed to beat the drum.
这次进攻勐景罕，	

---

① 海：即海罕。法：天。意为海罕与天一般高。
② 勐景罕：俸改治理的王国。
③ 布领暖：天神名。

① Zhao Haifa refers to Haihan. Hai: Haihan. Fa: heaven. It suggests that "Haihan has the same prestige and power as heaven".
② Mengjinghan: the kingdom ruled by Fenggai.
③ Bulingnuan: name of a god.

厘俸 // Li Feng

需要布领暖的许诺和天兵的
　　　帮助。
只有这样，
才能攻下勐景罕，
婻崩才能回到你的身旁。
我的召海法啊，
请你认真地想一想。"
海罕点点头表示同意，
然后向宫廷台阶走去。
面对仙鼓跪下叩头，
　"仙鼓呀，仙鼓，
我从未作恶多端把人计算，
也从未侵占过别人的土地，
艾哈腊为什么抢走我的妻子？
使我每时每刻把她思念，
独坐吃饭我泪珠不断。
虽然她还活在世上，
但我却成了鳏夫一样。
我要率领我的兵马，
立即出征勐景罕。
我的力量不够强大，
请布领暖派给我天兵天将。
请让我把仙鼓击响！"
他起来敲响了仙鼓，

Or you may send Awu Ga to see Bulingnuan in heaven
And seek help and power from him.
When planning to attack Mengjinghan we must depend on
　　　a promise from Bulingnuan and help from heavenly
　　　soldiers.
Only in this way
Can we occupy Mengjinghan.
Only in this way can you have Nanbeng back.
My respectable Zhao Haifa,
Please think it over."
Haihan nodded his head in approval
And then walked towards the court steps.
Facing the magic drum he knelt down:
"Magic drum! Oh, magic drum!
I have never done evils,
Nor have I invaded other people's lands.
For what reason has Aihala taken away my wife?
This makes me miss her all the time at every moment.
This makes my tear drops roll down my cheek when
　　　eating alone.
Though she is still alive,
I have in fact become a widower.
I will command my army
To attack Mengjinghan promptly.

鼓声洪亮如雷传向四方，
也惊动了上天。
睡在床上的布领暖被鼓声惊醒，
生气地起身说话：
"仙鼓本用来保护海罕，
为什么突然把它敲响？"
布尚色、布尚勐①立即打开
    天门，
俯身观看人间大地，
只见勐景哈的周围遍布战马
    战象。
他们急忙报告布领暖：
"海罕的仙鼓不是无故敲响，
请派阿巫戛下凡了解查看。"
阿巫戛得令后马上下凡，
转眼来到勐景哈这个地方，
果然到处是战马战象。
他急忙走进宫廷刻不容缓，
只见海罕哭泣坐在床上。
海罕见了阿巫戛更加哭得悲伤：
"我的阿巫啊，阿巫啊，
当年推我做召的时候，
是你将婻崩匹配给我做了皇后，

---

① 布尚色、布尚勐：天神名。

But my army is not powerful enough.
So please, Bulingnuan, send me more heavenly soldiers
    and generals.
So please, Bulingnuan, allow me to beat the magic
    drum!"
Rising to his feet he hit the drum.
The thunder-like sound spread in all the directions
And shocked heaven as well.
Bulingnuan was awakened by the drum sound,
And was quite annoyed about that:
"The magic drum is supposed to protect Haihan every
    critical moment.
Why is it suddenly beaten?"
Bushangse and Bushangmeng① then quickly opened
    the gate of heaven,
Bending over to see what was happening in the world below.
They saw war horses and war elephants all around
    Mengjingha.
Very quickly they reported to Bulingnuan:
"The magic drum is not beaten for no reason.
Please send Awu Ga to have a look."
Awu Ga then descended to the earth,
And very soon arrived at Mengjingha.

---

① Bushangse and Bushangmeng: names of two gods.

厘俸 // Li Feng

可是俸改现在已将她抢走。
我失去了心爱的婻崩，
为了婻崩我心神不宁茶饭难进。
我要报仇，
要夺回失去的皇后。
可是我的力量不够，
因此我敲响了仙鼓，
请求天神给予帮助。
阿巫戛啊，
我是多么的痛苦！"
阿巫戛听完，
也落下了同情的泪珠。
他拉起海罕的双手，
愤怒的话语涌出：
"该死的俸改啊，
多次把别人的妻子儿女抢夺，
特别是美丽的女人他从不放过，
对他的痛恨来自四面八方。
只要我们一声号召，
各个勐的兵马都会赶来援助。
该死的俸改啊，
过去我没有成仙的当初，
为了生活我做起了生意。
有一次买了三百头公猪，

There were war horses and war elephants everywhere.
With no delay he walked into the palace,
Where Haihan was weeping on his bed.
Haihan became even more grieved when he saw Awu Ga.
"Awu! Oh Awu!
When you chose me to be a Zhao,
You made Nanbeng my queen.
But now Fenggai has robbed me of my wife.
I've lost my dear Nanbeng,
And I am upset and distracted and has no desire of
      eating and drinking.
I must take revenge,
And get my queen back.
But I don't have enough power and force.
So I beat the magic drum
To ask for help from heaven.
Oh Awu Ga,
How painful and miserable I am!"
Hearing these words,
Awu Ga shed sympathetic tears.
Holding Haihan's hands,
He let out angry words:
"Damned Fenggai! This is not the first time
He has captured other people's wives and daughters,

当路过勐景罕的时候，	Especially those who are charming and beautiful.
俸改却抢走了全部公猪，	There is hatred for Fenggai everywhere.
还抢走了我那马肚般大的银包。	Once called upon,
东西抢尽还不让我走，	Soldiers from different *mengs* will surely come to your aid.
又把我拉进宫廷前的场院，	Damned Fenggai!
将我的双手勒在脑后捆得紧紧，	In the days before I became an immortal,
我疼痛难忍又骂又叫，	I had been doing some small business for a living.
死去活来受尽煎熬。	One day I bought 300 boars.
可是他还不罢休，	When I passed by Mengjinghan,
又用冷水劈头盖脸全身浇。	Fenggai robbed me of all the boars
然后叫他的妻子也过来，	And a bag of silver as big as a horse belly.
撩起筒裙踩我的肚子踩我的腰。	But still he did not let me go.
此仇此恨我终身不忘，	He dragged me into the yard in front of the palace,
想起往事我怒火中烧。	And bound my hands tightly behind my back.
我一定要为你报仇，	Suffering so much pain and torture,
看俸改这次往哪里逃！"	I screamed and cursed.
说完后阿巫戞回到天上，	But that was not the end.
向布领暖细细报告：	He poured cold water over me,
"你的侄儿海罕，	And even asked his wife
安分守己生活在人间地上，	To stamp on my belly and kick my waist.
从不为非作歹，人人喜欢。	Such enmity I will never forget!
可是俸改却抢走了他的妻子，	Every time when I think of this I just cannot help bursting
他天天痛哭十分悲伤，	into anger.
每天搂着宝刀当嫡崩。	So I will definitely try to help you take revenge.

厘俸 // Li Feng

手中宝刀不离身，
报仇的念头时时在心中。
而今准备进攻勐景罕，
可是他的兵马不够强，
要打败俸改只好求助布领暖。
因此他敲响了仙鼓，
祈求天兵相助。"
布尚勐听了仔细想，
慢慢开口把话讲：
"天兵相助是可以的，
夺取胜利也没问题，
只怕俸改狗急跳墙杀心起，
杀死婻崩来出气，
使我们战斗虽胜而无利，
海罕的悲伤更无期。
为了避免这不幸，
不如首先写信表和意，
请求送还海罕的妻。
黄金一百二十甩①，
作为赔偿同时送还去。
如果俸改他接受，
两勐相安各受益。"
布领暖点头来同意，

① 甩：一甩等于四十四两。

This time Fenggai will find nowhere to flee!"
Having said that, Awu Ga returned to heaven
And reported this to Bulingnuan in detail:
"Your nephew, Haihan,
Lives a peaceful and honest life in the world.
He never commits misdeeds and is loved by all his people.
But for no reason Fenggai went and took away his wife.
His life now is full of tears and grief.
Every day he holds his sword in his arms as if he was
   holding his wife Nanbeng.
With his treasured sword in hand,
He never gives up the idea of taking revenge.
He wants to attack Mengjinghan,
But does not have a powerful army.
To defeat Fenggai he has to ask for help from Bulingnuan.
That is why he beat the magic drum
To plead for heavenly aid."
Hearing this, Bushangmeng pondered for a while,
And slowly gives his suggestions:
"No doubt he will receive heavenly aid.
Without any problem he will win the war.
But what I worry about is that Fenggai may become
   extremely desperate,
And then kill Nanbeng to release his anger.

派遣布尚色、布尚勐下凡到人间。	If so, our victory may benefit us nothing
两天神瞬时已落地，	Because that may make Haihan's sorrow endless.
来到勐景罕，	To avoid such misfortune, instead,
进入俸改居住的八层楼官邸，	Let's write a letter expressing our intention of making peace
屋内金粉涂饰，豪华富丽。	And our request for the return of Nanbeng.
他们不经通报直接进去，	As compensation,
面对俸改既不叩头也不行礼。	Fenggai will have to give Haihan 120 *shuai*① of gold.
俸改见到两位天神，	If Fenggai accepts this condition,
立刻走下龙椅，	It will be mutually beneficial for the two kingdoms."
请他们登堂入座恭敬无比。	Bulinguan nodded his head for approval,
两天神指责俸改：	And sent Bushangse and Bushangmeng to earth,
"你的龙椅如同布领暖的一样豪华，	Where they landed instantly.
	Arriving at Mengjinghan,
你行事从不把人放在眼里，	They went straight into Fenggai's eight-storey mansion,
你为非作歹四处横行。	Which was splendid and magnificent.
现在布领暖传下命令，	Seeing Fenggai,
你应该洗耳恭听不要忘记。	They neither saluted nor kowtowed.
你的妻子已经绰绰有余，	At the sight of the two gods,
为什么还要把婻崩抢劫？	Fenggai quickly got up from his Dragon Throne
你的领土已足够宽广，	And very respectfully invited them into the hall.
为什么还要侵占别人的土地？	The two gods denounced Fenggai:
你应该立即把婻崩送还海罕，	"Your Dragon Throne is as luxurious as Bulingnuan's.
同时赔偿大象二十头，	You behave without having consideration for other people.

① Shuai: One *shuai* is about 44 taels or 50 grams.

厘俸 // Li Feng

还要把金子一百二十甩，银子
　　一线①，放在箱子里，
然后敲锣打鼓连人带物送过去，
外加绸缎、棉布各一百二十匹。
如果你能这样做，
你的生命就能保全，
勐景罕的城池也不会受攻击。
这是布领暖的旨意，
你必须马上考虑，
立即回答这个问题，
布领暖还等待着我们汇报你的
　　想法！"
俸改听后愤怒无比，
双脚跺楼板，暴跳如雷起，
　"你们说海罕是布领暖的侄子，
相助海罕这是天的旨意。
即使用二十把天斧对我劈来，
也无损我一根毫毛。
如今，我决不屈服决不退让，
不仅要继续强占海罕的妻，
还要把他的妻妾、奴仆，
统统归入我的宫里。

———————
①一线：三千三百三十两。

You are doing mischief everywhere.
As messengers, we now convey Bulingnuan's order.
You must listen with respectful attention and never forget.
You have more than enough wives.
Why did you still go to seize Nanbeng?
You have a broad expanse of territory.
Why do you still occupy the land of other people?
You are commanded to send Nanbeng back to Haihan
　　immediately.
To make compensation, you must also send Haihan 20
　　elephants,
A full box of 120 *shuai* of gold and 1 *xian*① of silver,
Plus 120 bolts of silk and satin and cotton fabrics.
You must blow a trumpet to announce
The return of Nanbeng and the indemnity.
Only in this way
Can you save your life
And prevent Mengjinghan from being attacked.
This is the divine order from Bulingnuan.
You must think it over
And tell us your answer now,
For Bulingnuan is waiting for our report!"
Hearing this Fenggai became furious.

———————
① Xian: One *xian* is 3330 taels.

还要到勐景哈耙田撒秧①，	In a frenzy of rage he stamped his feet on the floor.
派我的大将黄达皆去统治！	"You tell me Haihan is the nephew of Bulingnuan,
还要把海罕、桑洛②双双捉拿，	And you regard helping Haihan as a divine command.
当做雉狗，	But I will never give in and make concessions.
关进木笼供人观赏，	I will stay safe and sound
让他们活活气死！	Even if you use 20 heavenly axes to cut me into pieces.
布领暖要叫我回信答复，	I will continue to hold Haihan's wife,
浪费纸张我不愿意。	His concubine, and his slaves and servants.
我的纸张只用来给布天法③写信，	They all belong to me!
你们赶快离开，赶快回去。"	I will also go to plow fields in Mengjingha①
两位天神听罢，	And send General Huangdajie to govern the place!
一怒之下，	I will capture both Haihan and Sangluo②.
拔出宝刀劈向屋柱，	They will be caged like dogs
返回天上禀报。	To amuse the public.
布领暖听后把话说：	I will irritate them to death!
"事态如此不用急，	Now Bulingnuan requires of me a written letter as an answer.
调集天兵下凡去。	It is a waste of paper!
踏平勐景罕。	My letter paper is used only when I write to Butianfa③.
把俸改和他的老窝连根拔！"	So you two, just leave and go!"
两位天神连忙提建议：	The two gods,
"如按天王之意，	In a rage,
踏平勐景罕，	

①管理勐景哈之意。
②桑洛：勐景懂的国王。
③布天法：与布领暖一样的天王。

① It means "rule and govern Mengjingha".
② Sangluo: the King of Mengjingdong.
③ Butianfa: a god like Bulingnuan.

厘俸 // Li Feng

只怕相助无益，
婻崩又遭俸改害。
不如由海罕先出兵，
沿着婻崩被掠走的足迹先行。
我们召集天兵，做好准备，
海罕的兵马一到勐景罕。
各路天兵就可出击。"
布领暖接受建议，
下令天兵齐聚集。

Pulled out their swords and cut the hall columns,
And then went back to heaven.
Hearing their report, Bulingnuan said:
"Don't worry about the situation!
We can rally heavenly troops
And trod down and conquer Mengjinghan,
Eliminate Fenggai and his palace!"
The two gods made a proposal:
"If we follow your Majesty's order
To sweep away Menjinghan,
It may not be very helpful and beneficial,
Because Nanbeng may be killed first in that case.
How about asking Haihan to send out his troops first.
They shall take the road where Nanbeng was taken away.
Meanwhile we will summon our heavenly army and
　　get everything ready.
As soon as Haihan's troops arrive at Mengjinghan,
Our heavenly army will launch the attack."
Bulingnuan accepted their suggestions,
Calling for the heavenly army to gather.

二

海罕按照天意先出兵，
在勐哈坝调遣万马千军。
兵马布满九个坝，
威武的战象结队成群。
象舆①上插着五光十色的孔雀毛，
好像柳条在微风中轻摇身影。
当各路大军整队完毕，
雄赳赳的战士如森林一样。
树枝搭起的营帐布满山间，
星星点点的火堆到处燃起。
营帐像城堡，
火光似星星。
出征的气氛多么热烈又多么神秘！
只等吉日的到来，
一声令下，
千军万马就要出击。
到那时，

---

① 象舆：战象背上载有的供人乘坐的东西。

II

Haihan followed Bulingnuan's order
And began to dispatch his military forces in Mengha Basin.
Soldiers and horses were assembled in nine basins.
Mighty war elephants were gathered.
The howdahs① were decorated with colorful peacock feathers,
Which swung in the wind like willow branches.
Now the army was ready for battle.
The valiant and spirited soldiers looked like trees in a forest.
The tents were set up everywhere on the mountains.
The mountains were also dotted with bonfires.
The tents looked like castles,
And the flames from the fires looked like stars.
What an exciting and mysterious atmosphere for a coming battle!
The only thing to wait for was an auspicious date
When at the word of command
The mighty forces would all rush out.
By then,

---

① Howdah: a carriage which is positioned on the back of an elephant.

厘俸 // Li Feng

犹如蜜蜂出洞，	Like bees going out from their beehives,
万头齐涌。	Thousands of soldiers would charge forward.
前面是武艺高强的刀斧手，	In front of the troops there would be highly skilled soldiers holding knives and axes
风驰电掣疆场打先锋。	To fight like a flash as the vanguard.
紧接着威武的战象结成群，	Following them, herds of mighty elephants
象铃叮当震耳往前冲。	Would rush forward with loud clanging bells.
后面是运送物资的人流，	At the back would be an endless line of people
浩浩荡荡无边无际。	In charge of transporting supplies and provisions.
各路兵将、战象络绎不绝，	In formidable array,
首尾相连倾泻而出似山洪。	Soldiers and elephants would pour out like a torrential flood.
象脚踏出丛林路，	The elephants would blaze a jungle path.
弓弩手刀斧手齐冲锋，	The bowmen and the soldiers holding knives and axes would charge at the same time.
战旗高高飘扬迎风舞。	Our battle flags would wave and flutter in the wind.
吉日已到命令下，	The auspicious date finally came.
冈晓率领全军是先锋。	Gangxiao, as commander in chief, led the vanguard.
战马奔腾动大地，	The war horses were galloping
战象吼声震长空。	And the war elephants were roaring.
夜幕降临白日尽，	When night fell,
露宿山冈和森林。	The troops encamped on the mountains and in the forests.
拂晓太阳又升起，	When dawn broke and the sun rose,

海法起床洗漱毕。	Zhao Haifa got up and finished his breakfast.
吃完早饭到军中，	Then he went to the camp.
成群的婻珍①围身旁，	He was surrounded by groups of *nanzhens*①,
又跳又唱欢声笑语。	With happy laughter and cheerful dance.
海法往北遥遥望，	Zhao Haifa looked into the northern distance,
前锋燃起的火堆未熄灭。	Seeing the fires in the battlefield far away
如同大火烧群山，	Like forest fires
映红半个天空半个地。	Flashing into the sky.
海法起身向前做准备，	Zhao Haifa stood up and put on his glittering armor
金光闪闪的铠甲身上披。	To get himself ready for the battle.
金丝缠绕铠甲上，	His armor was twisted with golden thread.
缀满珍珠的带子在腰际。	His waist belt was studded with pearls.
缀满宝石的统帕②肩上挂，	His *tongpa*② was decorated with gemstones.
这护身的珍品不离他。	These treasures were his amulet and always accompanied him.
镶嵌宝石的战刀腰间挂，	There was a gemstone-inlaid saber hanging on his waist.
头上的王冠闪闪亮，	There was a crown shining brightly on his head.
九颗宝石颗颗大，	The nine big diamonds on the crown were so hard
刀剑不入硬无比，	That neither swords nor spears could pierce them.
海法明亮的脸庞映在王冠下，	Zhao Haifa's bright face and the crown set each other off.
一根金矛手中拿。	

---

① 婻珍：按景谷县藏本，婻珍既是女奴，同时又是宫廷歌女。西双版纳藏本则称为婻宰，音相近，意为妻妾。

② 统帕：挎在肩上的背袋。

① Nanzhen: According to the Jinggu version of this epic, nanzhen refers to both female slaves and sing-song girls of the royal court. According to the Xishuanbanna version, nanzhen is also called nanzai, meaning "wives or concubines".

② Tongpa: a shoulder bag.

厘俸 // Li Feng

侍从牵出占拜舍①，	In his hand he held a gold spear.
海法的坐骑高又大。	His attendant led out Zhanbaishe①.
红色的缰绳绕金丝，	The elephant was tall and huge,
就像阳光下黄色的稻穗。	With red rein twisted with golden thread,
侍从抬出晖罕②架在象背上，	Glittering in the sun like golden grain.
层层紧扣防松塌。	The attendant put a howdah on the back of the elephant,
海法手拿囊皮罗③，	And tightly fastened it so it wouldn't slip.
跃身跨上大象。	With a *nangpiluo*② in his hand,
十万头战象紧跟上，	Zhao Haifa mounted his elephant.
头头大象配金鞍。	Thousands of elephants followed him,
九个铃铛脖上挂，	Each equipped with a golden saddle.
声如洪钟传四方。	Each of the elephants wore nine bells on the neck,
万千虎形彩旗北门出，	Making a great noise that could be heard far away.
锣鼓齐鸣人呐喊。	Thousands of tiger-shaped flags surged out of the North Gate,
海罕的坐骑南门出，	Accompanied by gongs and people's battle cries.
八万护卫军紧跟上。	Haihan's elephant set out from the South Gate,
惊天动地浩浩荡荡，	Followed by eighty thousand guards.
气吞山河不可挡。	What a breathtaking sight!
	What heroic spirit !

---

① 占：大象。拜：一头。舍：有花纹似猛虎般的。
② 晖罕：即象舆。
③ 囊皮罗：用羊皮绘制的地形图。

① Zhanbaishe: Zhan: elephant. Bai: one. She: with a tiger's pattern of stripes.
② Nanpiluo: a map drawn on sheep skin.

冈晓率军渡过江，	Gangxiao's army crossed a river
安营扎寨寨连寨，	And then encamped end to end.
首尾相连似城墙。	All the camps looked like a long wall.
后续部队已来到，	The follow-up forces also arrived.
弓弩手身背箭袋满山冈。	Bowmen could be seen everywhere in the mountains.
八万大军护海罕，	The eighty thousand guards of Haihan
已经到达江对岸。	Also reached the opposite side of the river.
砍倒竹子扎成筏，	Bamboo rafts were made
满载兵将渡大江。	For carrying the soldiers across the river.
战象入水横渡，	Meanwhile the war elephants swam across the river,
鱼龙翻腾卷巨浪。	Making huge splashes and startling the fish in the water.
营帐、彩旗遍江岸，	Both river banks
遥遥相对隔江望。	Were dotted with camps and flags.
海罕命令一声传：	Haihan gave the order:
"发兵两路来作战	"We'll fight in two directions.
一攻勐哈，	One group attacks Mengha,
一取勐老。	And the other conquers Menglao.
如果有人抗拒，	If anyone tries to resist,
把他消灭干净。	Just eliminate him from the world.
如果有人投降，	If anyone wants to surrender,
宽大处理不许杀。	Show your leniency and do not kill him.
百姓的财产，	As for local people's property,
不准何人去抢夺。"	Nobody is allowed to take it."
众兵将听了军令，	At the word of command,

厘俸 // Li Feng

马不停蹄，	The horses galloped on without stop
急速进兵。	And the soldiers marched on in haste.
伙夫忙碌不停。	The cooks were busy preparing food.
海罕大军走出山谷，	Haihan's army marched out of the valley
进入勐老和勐哈。	And entered Menglao and Mengha.
平坝一望无际真壮观	There was a boundless stretch of flatland,
牛马成群悠悠然，	With horses and cattle wandering leisurely on it before
战火一起四逃散。	And fleeing in panic in all directions now.
兵将直逼城堡下，	The soldiers were approaching the city wall,
团团包围桶一般。	And the place was under tight siege.
冈晓率军攻勐老，	Gangxiao was in charge of attacking Menglao.
敌人慌忙关栅栏。	The enemy there quickly closed the gate,
又喊又叫又杂乱，	Shouting, screaming and making everything a mess.
紧闭栅栏想死守，	The gate was closed for better defense,
两军对峙暂观望。	And the battle reached an impasse.

桑洛率军攻勐哈，	Sangluo was in charge of attacking Mengha,
土炮轰击威力大。	Powerful cannons were used.
硝烟弥漫冲天起，	A cloud of smoke floated over the battle field,
骑兵趁势猛冲杀。	Shielding the dashing elephant-mounted soldiers.
敌人死伤多又多，	The enemies were either killed or wounded
急忙收兵败退下。	And had to retreat in haste.
紧闭城门守战壕，	They kept the city gate closed and defended from the trenches.
两军肉搏相格杀。	

勐哈城内象万头,	The two sides were now in hand-to-hand combat.
食禄之地怎能丢。	Mengha had thousands of elephants.
抬过土炮连连发,	A place with such affluence should never be conquered.
重整旗鼓来反扑。	The Mengha side set up their cannons
	To rally their forces for a counteroffensive.
勐老一方的战也打响,	The battle in Menglao also started.
打开城门来迎战。	The Menglao army opened the gate to meet its enemy head-on.
战鼓咚咚,寨门大开,	The war drum was beaten,
兵丁涌出。	And the Menglao soldiers surged out.
双方短兵相接,	Both sides were fighting at close quarters
拼死格杀!	In their last-ditch effort.
桑温、赛伦驰骋疆场,	Sangwen and Sailun dashed about in the battlefield
纵马指挥大军作战。	To direct operations.
激烈的战斗仍在延续。	The fierce combat went on.
海罕的军队越战越勇,	Haihan's army became braver.
勐老、勐哈已危在旦夕,	Menglao and Mengha were on the verge of destruction
敌兵的斗志越来越低。	Due to the lack of fighting spirit of their soldiers.
布冈戈和布冈伴带领援军赶到,	Bugang Ge and Bugang Ban led some back-up troops
猛烈的炮火向对方轰击。	To bombard their enemy fiercely.
勐老、勐哈已溃不成军,	Utterly routed, Menglao and Mengha
继续战斗已没有力量和勇气。	Had no courage or strength to continue the battle.

厘俸 // Li Feng

派出使者向艾召生求和，
愿意献出二十头大象和两个美女，
只要不杀害臣仆和百姓，
他们愿当奴臣和奴婢，
贡赋徭役也心甘乐意。
艾召生拒绝对方的求和，
坚决要进攻到底。
他传出话语：
"俸改抢夺嫡崩，
四面八方人人知悉，
这奇耻大辱怎能忘记？
夺人之爱已是理亏，
本应赔礼道歉知晓正义。
我们忍无可忍远征出战，
本应投降认罪不应抗拒。
你们顽固坚持为敌，
我们宝刀已经出鞘，
不除恨雪耻，
宝刀就将一直高举。
不铲除恶人，
锋利的长矛就要举起。"
艾召生言毕，
使者失望地返回。

A messenger was sent to Ai Zhaosheng to ask for peace.
Menglao and Mengha were willing to pay 20 elephants and 2 beauties
As long as their officials and people would not be killed.
They were willing to be ruled by Haihan as servants and slaves
And pay a tribute to him.
But Ai Zhaosheng rejected their peace-making pleas
And insisted on fighting to the last minute.
This was what he said:
"Everyone knows
That Fenggai grabbed away Nanbeng.
How can I forget such shame and humiliation?
Capturing other people's wives has put Fenggai in the wrong.
What he needs to do is to ask for forgiveness and offer apologies.
We set out on this expedition because things have been beyond enduring.
You should have pleaded guilty and should not have resisted.
Since you stubbornly clung to your wrong position,
We have to pull out our swords
And lift them high

战鼓又鸣,	Until revenge has been taken and hatred has been wiped away.
冈晓的兵丁奋勇冲杀,	The sharp spears also have to be lifted up high
向对方心脏步步进逼。	Until the evils have been eradicated."
敌人魂飞魄散溃不成军,	Hearing these words,
四处逃散各自保命。	The messenger returned disappointedly.
冈晓和桑洛两军捕获大批俘敌,	The battle continued.
他们似绳索捆绑牛羊一般威风尽。	Gangxiao's soldiers marched on bravely,
	Approaching the heart of their enemy' rear area.
	The enemy fled in all directions
	And looked like an army in disarray.
	Gangxiao and Sangluo captured many downcast soldiers
	Who were bound like cattle and sheep.

厘俸 // Li Feng

三

海罕大军随之抵达，
为庆胜利把牲畜宰杀。
宴会盛大官兵举杯，
情绪高涨精神奋发。
海罕起身说话：
"打仗要靠勇猛不怕死，
宰杀牲畜为了犒劳大家。
战火烧到哪里，
哪里就遭受灾难。
为了夺回婻崩，
不得已才进攻勐景罕。
先发制人旗开得胜，
功劳应该归于大家。
战事未完不能松气，
还有勐海和勐我没有攻下。
现在制订下一步的计划。
一千个勐的首领带领兵丁先行，
逼近勐海逼近勐我，
应以象阵在前冲杀，
刀矛、刀斧手齐上阵。
人吼鼓敲造声势，

III

Subsequently Haihan's army arrived.
To celebrate the victory, they killed cattle
And treated the officers and soldiers to a banquet.
Their spirits soared and were refreshed.
Haihan then made a speech:
"Bravery is the key to our victory.
You deserve this food and drink.
Where there is war
There is suffering and pain.
In order to get my Nanbeng back,
I have had no alternative but to attack Mengjinghan.
I fired the first shot and got a quick victory,
Which is attributed to your brave fighting.
The war is not finished yet and we must not relax.
Menghai and Mengwo are still out there unconquered,
And we need to make a plan for the next operation.
A thousand chiefs will lead the army
Heading for Menghai and Mengwo.
We will have the elephants in the front
Followed by soldiers holding knives, spears, and axes.
The roar of soldiers and the sound of drums will be

象冲人奔各奋发。	overwhelming.
千军万马分两路,	The elephants and the soldiers will play their part respectively.
夺取城池第一步。	The army will branch out into two columns.
百官们啊努力吧!"	And our first objective is to seize the cities.
宴会结束情激发,	Let us fight even harder!"
穿林翻山又进发。	When the banquet was over the soldiers were all in high spirits
	And set out again to move across the mountains and the forests.

海罕进兵的消息,	The news about the movement of Haihan's army
传到勐海、勐我两地。	Spread to Menghai and Mengwo.
他们做好准备迎击,	People there were busy getting prepared for the war.
选出勇猛的战士,	They selected valiant warriors
埋伏在密密的树林中,	To create an ambush in the dense forest
埋伏在深深的山谷里。	And in the deep valley.

艾召生来到伏兵前沿,	When Ai Zhaosheng was near the concealed enemy,
一只"蜡达献"鸟怪叫着迎面飞来。	A bird named "Ladaxian" flew towards him, Crying strangely.
他心中感到十分奇怪:	A feeling of weirdness suddenly overwhelmed him:
"我从来未遇到这种现象,	"I have never seen such a strange scene
虽然出征作战已一年。	In a whole year of fighting.
很可能前面有了伏兵,	There is probably an ambush ahead.

厘俸 // Li Feng

望大家警惕敌人突现。
如果情况果然如此，
奋勇冲杀一直向前。"

兵丁小心搜索前进，
转眼到了险峻的滴水崖，
伏兵突然出现，
两军相遇一场混战，
土炮轰鸣山谷震撼。
冈晓率兵拉弓射箭，
骑兵侧身贴马冲锋陷阵。
两翼包抄同时围上，
对方溃退一哄而散。
遍野横尸鲜血流淌，
穷打猛追咬住不放。
直插山谷冲到平坝，
坝子宽阔两军决战。
坝子平坦骑兵如飞，
杀敌如同杀狗一样。
目标指向勐海勐我，
大军压境团团围上。
只见那金幡幢林立，
战旗迎风飞舞飘扬。
战象威武阵前排列，

Let's keep alert in case the enemy shows up suddenly.
If this is the case,
Just keep fighting courageously."

The soldiers then moved forward cautiously,
And got to the steep Waterfall Cliff.
There they encountered the ambush
And were engaged in a tangled fight.
The valley shivered with the roaring of the cannons.
Gangxiao commanded the bowmen to discharge the arrows.
The cavalrymen rushed forward, bending over their horses.
Doubly enveloped,
The enemy dispersed with an uproar.
Dead bodies and blood were seen everywhere.
Gangxiao and his army chased the enemy persistently
And dashed out of the valley and reached a flat land.
There the final fight came.
The flat land was suitable for the cavalrymen to fight,
And made killing the enemy as easy as pie.
Gangxiao's army bore down in force
And moved forward to surround Menghai and Mengwo.
The fields bristled with a forest of golden prayer flags.

雪白的象牙如出土的山笋。	The banners were waving in the wind.
长长的象鼻来回摆动，	The awe-inspiring war elephants lined up in front.
要卷起大风卷起大浪。	Their white tusks looked like newly-sprouted bamboo shoots.
	Their long trunks were swinging back and forth
	As if they were going to stir up a strong wind and big waves.
勐我首领站在庄房，	The chief of Mengwo stood on the roof of the gate tower,
居高临下，	Overlooking the approaching army of Gangxiao.
手摇扇子高声谩骂：	He burst into a string of abusive words while waving a fan in his hand:
"勐景哈的众兵丁啊，	"Soldiers from Mengjingha,
你们听着，	Listen carefully!
得罪你们的事我从未做下。	There is nothing I have ever done to offend you,
就是芝麻大的事也找不出半点，	Not even a matter trivial and small like a grain of sesame,
更不用说像山芋般一样大的事。	Nor a matter significant and big like a taro!
你们来此威胁，	I really cannot figure out why you have come to attack us
为什么调动千军万马？"	With so many hordes of troops and horses?"
冈晓高声回答：	Gangxiao replied loudly:
"你这手拿扇子的老糊涂，	"You silly old man!
眼见千军万马你还嘴硬不怕，	Facing our powerful army you are not frightened
竟在城楼把扇扇，	But wave the fan in your hand on the gate tower instead,
自作镇定卖弄得意。	Trying to calm yourself down complacently.
风吹胡子还在说胡话。	

厘俸 // Li Feng

俸改抢走了海罕的媥崩,
你还瞪着眼睛来装傻。
如今你的头就要落地,
为什么还要为俸改卖命说话?
有胆量你就骑象走出寨门,
你这该死的老东西啊!"
勐我首领恼羞成怒,
挥着扇子连说带骂:
"俸改抢走海罕的媥崩,
并没有从勐我经过,
我怎么知道起因在此?
你毫无道理进攻勐我,
莫非要降就降要杀就杀?
大概是勐我土地肥沃,
坝子美丽又宽又大,
还有大象万头可骑可拉,
这一切使你们心痒毛抓。
但是休想白日做梦,
你们空手而来也同样空手回家。
快快回去耕田种地。
你这个老不中用的人啊!"
话刚落音鸣炮三响。
寨门大开战象蜂拥而出。
战马、刀队紧紧跟上,

You are indeed talking nonsense!
Don't you know that Fenggai captured Haihan's wife
　　　　　Nanbeng?
So don't play dumb and pretend to be innocent!
Very soon you are going to be decapitated.
Why do you still go along with Fenggai in his evil deeds?
Dare you ride your elephant out of the city wall?
You damned old man!"
The chief of Mengwo got so irritated
That he shouted with curses while flapping his fan:
"Fenggai captured Haihan's wife,
But he did not pass by my place.
How can I know this is the fuse of the battle?
You attack Mengwo for no reason.
Why must you conquer and kill us?
Or is it because you covet our fertile fields
And our vast and beautiful land?
Or is it because you covet our ten thousand elephants
Which has long been your concern?
Stop daydreaming!
You come empty-handed and will return empty-handed.
You'd better go back and plough your own land!
You old and useless man!"
Hardly had his words faded away, when, with three

炮手、弓弩手如水出洞，
杀声震天喊声雷动。
象队排阵冲出寨门，
猛士集结冲杀在前。
一声令下，
两军象群相格杀。
你撞我踏横闯直冲，
象吼人叫天翻地覆。
一场混战血肉横飞，
尘土飞扬太阳灰蒙。

桑洛驱象出战，
敌方纷纷从象背滚落。
崩纳宛①率军如出水蛟龙，
如巨浪狂涛。
冈晓不断派兵往前冲，
勐我勐海寡不敌众，
节节败退撤回城中。
城墙残破房屋倒塌，
海罕大军趁胜追杀，

① 崩纳宛：海罕的另一员武将。

cannon shots,
The chief of Mengwo opened the wall gate.
The war elephants surged out, followed by the war horses,
The cannoneers, and the bowmen.
The cries and shouts of battle echoed in the sky.
The elephant array dashed out,
Supporting the soldiers in the fight.
At the command,
The elephants from both sides
Dashed around madly and went on a rampage.
The world was turned upside down
In this tangled fight with so much roaring and bloodshed.
The sun was veiled by clouds of dust.

Sangluo mounted his elephant to fight.
The enemy soldiers fell off the back of their elephants.
The army led by Bengnawan① fought bravely like
    dragons out of water
And powerfully like the great ocean waves and billows.
More troops of Gangxiao were sent to the front.
Being desperately outnumbered, Mengwo and Menghai
Fought against hopeless odds and began to retreat in
    full-scale

① Bengnawan: one of Haihan's officers.

厘俸 // Li Feng

象阵如奔腾的山洪，
兵丁如旋风，
席卷勐海勐我。

勐我大布冈①拼死顽抗，
骑着一只花脸大象，
调转头来冲向冈晓。
冈晓驱赶他的占拜温②，
勇猛向前迎战。
两头大象交锋，
象牙交错力量相当。
殊死格斗"咔咔"有声，
象上的两人也分外紧张。
勐我大布冈用长矛直刺冈晓，
枪枪落空心慌手乱。
冈晓趁势一矛飞刺，
直捣喉头正中大布冈。
他翻身落象像石头一般，
冈晓的武士一拥而上，

To the city with damaged walls and collapsed houses.
Haihan went on to pursue more victories.
Like impetuous flood and whirling wind,
Haihan's elephants and soldiers
Swept across Menghai and Mengwo.

The Grand Bugang① of Mengwo resisted in desperation.
He rode on a painted-face elephant
And suddenly turned around to dash towards Gangxiao,
Who drove his Zhanbaiwen②
Forward to meet the challenge.
Fierce fighting between the two elephants
Was actually a fight of tusks.
The loud sound of crashing bodies and the friction of tusks
Made the masters on their backs very nervous.
The Grand Bugang thrust his spear towards Gangxiao,
But every try failed and he began to panic.
Gangxiao seized this favorable moment
And stabbed him in the neck with his spear.
The Grand Bugang fell off his elephant like a heavy stone.
Gangxiao's soldiers rushed forth

---

① 大布冈：万户以上的首领。
② 占拜温：冈晓所骑战象的名字。

① Grand Bugang: a title for a chief who ruled more than ten thousand households.
② Zhanbaiwen: name of Gangxiao's elephant.

争先恐后砍下大布冈的首级。①	And cut off his head.①
兵将庆祝胜利欢呼高喊，	The soldiers celebrated their victory with cheers and shouts,
攻克勐我捷报飞传！	And news of the defeat of Mengwo spread like wildfire.
勐海首领大布冈，	The Grand Bugang of Menghai
说话喜欢摇头，	Liked to shake his head while speaking,
声音生来抖颤。	And he was born with a trembling voice.
大难临头他拼死抵抗，	Facing the disaster he chose to resist to the last moment.
掉转象头迎着召桑洛。	He turned his elephant toward Zhao Sangluo.
他自恃武艺高强，	Counting on his excellent fighting skills,
长矛直指桑洛连刺数十枪。	He stabbed at Sangluo dozens of times with his long spear.
桑洛右来右拨左来左挡，	Sangluo dodged skillfully
大布冈枪枪落空心发慌。	And the Grand Bugang's stabs came to nothing.
桑洛看准时机找空档，	Sangluo seized the opportunity,
大布冈腋下无铠甲遮挡，	And as there was no armor protection under the Bugang's arms,
一矛刺入腋中央。	His spear pierced into the Bugang's underarm.
只见鲜血飞溅人滚下象，	Blood poured out and the chief rolled down from the elephant.
两旁武士争相把头砍。	The soldiers scrambled to cut the Bugang's head.
兵将庆胜利欢呼高声喊，	The cheering of victory was heard everywhere
攻克勐海捷报飞传。	And the news of victory was spread everywhere.
勐我、勐海二首领遭击毙，	
兵丁失去统帅溃不成军，	

---

① 谁先砍下头来，头有多重，就按其重量赐赏同等重量的银子。　① The man who cut off the Grand Bugang's head would be rewarded with the same weight of silver as the head.

厘俸 // Li Feng

四处奔逃似鸟兽散，
就像一只摔碎在地上的碗。
胜利的海罕向全军发布命令：
"今已攻下勐我、勐海，
不得私藏金银财宝，
应共同分享，
战马战象谁得归谁。"
庆祝胜利摆酒设宴，
全军欢聚举杯痛饮。
战马战象草地放牧，
只可怜妇女遭殃。

Since the Grand Bugangs of Mengwo and Menghai had been killed,

Their troops were completely routed.

Their soldiers fled in all directions,

Like the pieces of a broken bowl on the ground.

Haihan issued an order to his army:

"We have now conquered Mengwo and Menghai.

No one is allowed to have illegal possession of gold, silver and other treasures.

Everything captured must be shared.

The horses and elephants belong to those who capture them."

Feasts and banquets were held

For the whole army to celebrate the victory.

Even the war horses and elephants now found time to graze on the grassland.

Women, unfortunately, suffered the most from the ravages of the war.

四

勐老、勐哈已被攻克，
勐我、勐海也被拿下，
海罕大军又准备向勐谷、勐远
　　进发。
俸改气愤得咬牙说：
"勐谷、勐远如果又丧失，
我也不怕。"
军师布冈很上前说话：
"勐谷、勐远已准备议和，
事到如今，
你也不要难过。"
俸改生气地说：
"你动身到勐谷、勐远，
罚款惩罚他们的错误，
大象二十头、金二十两不算
　　多。"
布冈很骑上快马赶路，
到达勐谷、勐远。
只见田野禾苗碧绿茁壮，
牛马成群结队，
高房林立一排排，

IV

Having conquered Menglao and Mengha,
And having conquered Mengwo and Menghai,
Haihan was now ready to march to Menggu and
　　Mengyuan.
Fenggai was so furious about this and said,
"I won't be frightened
Even if I lose Menggu and Mengyuan."
The military adviser Bugang Hen stepped forward to
　　comfort him:
"Menggu and Mengyuan are now preparing to negotiate
　　peace.
What's done is done.
Please don't be grieved!"
Very annoyed, Fenggai said:
"You now set out for Menggu and Mengyuan
And punish them for their wrong doing.
They must pay me at least 20 elephants and 20 taels of
　　gold."
Hurriedly, Bugang Hen got on a fast horse
And soon arrived at Menggu and Mengyuan.
There was a stunning view of prosperity and abundance:

厘俸 // Li Feng

一派繁荣一派兴旺。	Fields of green vigorous rice shoots,
他走进城楼，	Herds of horses and cattle,
来到混谷远①的楼上说：	And rows of beautiful houses.
"海罕即将进攻你们，	Buganghen went into the city
为什么不做准备迎战？	And met Hun Guyuan① in the city tower, saying:
勐我、勐海危急也不支援，	"Haihan will soon come to attack you.
致使两地落入海罕的手中，	Why don't you prepare well ready for the battle?
听说你们现在又想议和投降，	You didn't help Mengwo and Menghai when they were in trouble,
俸改派我前来传令：	Which resulted in the downfall of the two places.
罚你们一百二十头大象，	It is said that you now want to negotiate peace and surrender.
绸缎一百二十匹，	This is why I have come to pass on the order of Fenggai:
金子一百二十两，	There will be a penalty for you which includes
美女一百二十个，	120 elephants,
还要用铅做出人的形状，	120 bolts of silk and satin,
我如实传达你们如数照办。"	120 taels of gold,
混谷远回答得不急不慢：	120 beautiful women,
"我们没有想过要投降，	And a human figure made of lead.
为什么罚我们这么多的款？	This information I have conveyed to you and you need to obey the order."
还要铅做出人的形状，	Hun Guyuan answered in a slow and calm way:
这样做使我们加重了负担！	"We have never thought about giving up and surrender.
因为这些东西分配下去，	
都出在百姓身上。	
有的可以承担，	

---

① 混谷远：勐谷、谷远的酋长。 ① Hun Guyuan: the chief of Menggu and Guyuan.

有的只能卖儿卖女来抵偿。
你们这种做法，
实在令人痛心不应当！"
话刚说完，
又对兵将们长叹：
"今后不知怎样度过灾难！
我们的心已冷得像雨淋一般，
更像白天的月亮没有亮光。
过去年年给俸改上贡，
还骂我们是吃黄景毛薯①的
　　傈傈。
想起来多么气愤多么悲伤！"
混谷远话刚说完，
拔出宝刀。
布冈很吓得滚下楼房，
不敢停留急忙动身，
浑身发抖骑在马上，
回到勐景罕，
向俸改报告情况。
俸改听了把话讲：
"勐谷与勐景罕路途遥远，
每年的贡品只不过是烧柴，

---

① 黄景：味苦的一种植物。毛薯：味甜，缺粮时以此为主食。

How come you ask for such a huge sum of money as punishment?

And a figure made of lead as well?

In this way you impose too heavy a load on us.

The load will certainly be divided each one of our people.

Some of them may have money to pay for that,

But some of them will have to sell their children to pay the debt.

Your deeds

Are very distressing and very unreasonable!"

Then he turned to the officers and the soldiers

And said with a deep sigh:

"I just don't know how to make it through these tough times!

Our hearts are as cold as the rain

And as pale as the moon in the daytime.

In the past we paid tribute to Fenggai every year, only to be insulted

And called barbarians that eat *huangjing*① and yams.

What an unjust and sorrowful reality it is!"

As soon as he finished his words,

Hun Guyuan pulled out his sword.

---

① Huangjing: a bitter plant.

厘俸 // Li Feng

他不服从也就算了。
有他不多无他不少，
大可不必放心上。"
说完手捋胡须眯眯笑，
似乎事情一小桩。

Bugang Hen was so frightened that he fell down the stairs.

With no hesitation,

He mounted his horse, shivering,

And went back to Mengjinghan

To report all this to Fenggai.

Fenggai said with gross understatement:

"Menggu is far away from Mengjinghan.

Their tribute to Mengjinghan is nothing but some firewood.

Let it be if Menggu does not bow to me.

It is not that important,

And I really don't care!"

He stroked his beard with a smile

As if he was talking about something trivial.

混谷远准备白银一千两，
还有大象二十头，
加上好酒二十坛，
一封书信也带上，
亲自出发送海罕。
见到海罕忙叩头：
"我们地处两勐[1]的交界，
俸改从来不把我们当人看。
现在我愿与你结盟，

Hun Guyuan prepared a gift and sent it to Haihan in person:

A thousand taels of silver,

Twenty elephants,

Twenty jars of good wine,

And a letter to Haihan.

At the sight of Haihan he knelt down and said:

We are located in between the two *mengs*[1]

But I have never been treated as a neighbor and friend

---

[1] 两勐：指勐景哈、勐景罕。

[1] The two *mengs*: Here it refers to Mengjinha and Mengjinghan.

共同进攻勐景罕。	by Fenggai.
我真的希望你找到婻崩,	I now want to make an alliance with you
只希望你的军队不要经过我的领地上。	And fight Mengjinhan hand in hand.
	I do hope that you can find Nanbeng.
我供给你粮草,	My mere request is that your war with Fenggai will not involve Guyuan.
还要派兵马相帮。	
召海法啊,	My promise is provisions for your troops
我知道你是个好心人,	And back-up soldiers and horses as well.
你的心甜得像蜜一样。	Oh, Zhao Haifa,
接受我的请求吧,	I know you are a kind, gentle,
勐谷、勐远的人不会把你忘。"	And warm-hearted man.
海罕点头把话讲:	Please accept my request!
"二位辛苦了,	People in Menggu and Mengyuan will forever remember your favor."
你们的要求我答应,	
这样安排很恰当。	Haihan nodded his head:
同心协力团结起,	"You two have been working very hard.
共同攻打勐景罕!"	I will grant your request
艾召生又接见混谷远说:	Which sounds very reasonable and appropriate.
"勐谷、勐远好地方,	Let's unite and work together
议和结盟是上策,	To defeat Mengjinghan!"
而今安然无恙。	Ai Zhaosheng also had an interview with Hun Guyuan:
好朋好友来相处,	"Menggu and Mengyuan are beautiful and rich places.
我的两位老布冈!"	Alignment is the best choice for all of us.
混谷远此时完全把心放,	Only in this way can we stay safe and peaceful.

厘俸 // Li Feng

高高兴兴转回家。
海罕立即下命令，
停止向勐谷、勐远来进军，
军队安营扎寨半路上。

Let's treat each other like friends,
My two old Bugangs!"
Hun Guyuan finally felt relieved
And returned home with a lightheart.
Haihan gave the word
To stop marching towards Menggu and Mengyuan.
The army then was encamped half way to Mengjingha.

五

海罕坐在营帐中，
艾召生和众将士站立在两旁。
海罕把命令来下达：
"召桑洛啊，
你率领兵丁进攻冈老、冈桑。
混嘿南①也随之前往，
围住冈老、冈桑不放松。"
桑洛大军齐进发，
势如暴风骤雨来得猛。
翻山越岭不停步，
无路之处踏成路。
另一路由艾召生率领打先锋，
目标指向勐帕生和勐帕缓。
十万头大象气势如山，
十万名弓弩手逞威风。
出发的战鼓已敲响，
冈晓奋勇来当先，
桑本紧跟不放松。
大军浩荡上征途，

---

① 混嘿南：海罕的妻子喃崩的弟弟。

V

Haihan was sitting in his tent,
With Ai Zhaosheng and other generals and soldiers standing on the sides.
Haihan issued a new order:
"Zhao Sangluo,
I command you to attack Ganglao and Gangsang.
Hun Heinan① will go with you.
You must besiege the two places."
Sangluo's army then set out
With irresistible force like that of a fierce hurricane.
They climbed mountain after mountain,
Tramping out new paths in the wilderness.
Another group of troops was led by Ai Zhaosheng,
Heading directly for Meng Pasheng and Meng Pahuan.
The troops consisted of thousands of elephants with overwhelming power,
And thousands of bowmen with inspiring spirit.
The departure drum had been struck.
Gangxiao volunteered to be the vanguard,

---

① Hun Heinan: the younger brother of Nanbeng, Haihan's wife.

厘俸 // Li Feng

行程十日真艰苦。	And Sangben followed closely.
勐帕生和勐帕缓映眼帘，	The army set out in formidable array
周围的山头光秃秃。	And marched ten tough days on the way.
高高的山崖为屏障，	Finally Meng Pasheng and Meng Pahuan came into view:
村寨楼房星罗棋布。	The mountains around were barren with steep cliffs,
城池外还有护城河，	Functioning as natural shields.
护城河两岸刺藤多，	The land was dotted with villages and houses.
密密麻麻没有路。	There was a city moat
石崖上凿出路一条，	Thickly sown with thistles and thorns along the banks,
弯弯曲曲多险阻。	Leaving no more place for a road or a path.
城内战象二十栏，	The only road, which was zigzagging and dangerous,
城内宽阔且兵马无数。	Was chiseled on the cliffs.
冈晓一声令下，	There were twenty herds of war elephants in the spacious city.
将其城池重重包围。	There were also innumerable soldiers and horses inside the spacious city.
战象沿阵排列，	At the word of command of Gangxiao,
两耳扇动象鼻上下卷腾。	The city was besieged.
铓锣震天鸣炮三响，	The war elephants were standing in an array,
各路兵马齐准备，	With their ears waving and their trunks rolling up.
冲锋陷阵要攻城。	The thundering gong sound and cannon sound
勐帕生和勐帕缓的两个召布冈①，	Announced that the soldiers and horses were all ready
打开城门来迎战。	To throw themselves into battle and shatter the city.
派遣刀手五百人，	

---

① 召布冈：有时称道布冈或称陶布冈，为一勐之主，既是行政长官，又是军事首领。

悄悄埋伏石崖旁。	The two Zhao Bugangs[①] of Meng Pasheng and Meng Pahuan
接着冲出一队象，	Opened the city gate to fight.
如大雾笼罩一般。	They sent five hundred soldiers holding knives
冈晓兵马被团团围在田坝中，	To wait quietly in ambush alongside the rock cliffs.
他的战象占拜温似猛虎，	And then a team of their elephants rushed out,
如狂飙，	Enveloping everything like a dense fog.
左冲右突不可挡。	Gangxiao's army and horses were surrounded in the fields.
冈晓的卫队挥刀矛，	His war elephant Zhanbaiwen,
左砍右杀来迎战。	Dashed madly in all directions
象牙相交格格响，	Like tigers and hurricanes.
刀光剑影起寒光。	Gangxiao's guards waved their spears and knives
召帕生和召帕缓率军边战边后退，	To kill and defeat the enemy.
高声骂冈晓：	The elephant tusks rubbed together and rattled.
"你一勐之主不像样，	The glittering and flash of the cold swords were seen everywhere.
无理进攻不应当。	Zhao Pasheng and Zhao Pahuan had to lead their soldiers to retreat,
勐帕生、勐帕缓好地方，	Condemning Gangxiao loudly:
土地宽广人口多，	"You are not a real chief!
城池高悬崖石上。	You should not have launched such an unjustified attack.
城中战象十万多，	Meng Pasheng and Meng Pahuan are prosperous places
象牙专指恶人有力量。	
我们犹如成年的猛虎，	

---

① Zhao Bugang: Sometimes called "Dao Bugang" or "Tao Bugang", it refers to the chief of a *meng*, who is in charge of its executive and military affairs.

厘俸 // Li Feng

虎毛长得能拴住牛犊!
我们的武艺素来高强,
但从未想去夺取别人的地方。
如今你带领这班人马,
要夺取勐帕生和勐帕缓。
你还未曾学会怎样骑象,
你的双脚连象耳朵都未碰到。
你是来白白送死,
要活命赶快回转。"

冈晓停住大象,
把崖石两边仔细观望,
要弄清是否有伏兵躲藏。
听了对方的谩骂,
他冷笑一声高声回答:
　"你们的武艺虽然高强,

With a vast land and a large population.
The city is built high above on the cliff.
There are more than a hundred thousand war elephants
　　in the city.
Their powerful tusks are at any time ready to aim at
　　the wicked.
We are like fierce tigers in adulthood
With hair long enough to fasten a calf!
Although we are highly skilled in military operations,
We never want to occupy other people's territory.
Today you come here with your troops
With the purpose of capturing Meng Pasheng and
　　Meng Pahuan.
Don't you know that you are destined to be killed
Because you haven't learned how to ride an elephant yet
And your feet are not long enough to reach elephant ears.
If you want to survive, go back!"

Gangxiao halted his elephant for a while,
Observing both sides of the cliff carefully
To check if there was an ambush or not.
Hearing the above abuse,
He replied loudly with a sneer:
"Your skills may be high.

你们的汗毛虽然长又长,	Your hair may be long.
你们的大象虽然牙齿厉害,	Your elephants may have sharp tusks.
但是还没有和我较量,	But this is only one side of the story.
真有本事就拿出来看看!"	Come to fight with me and show me your talent and skill!"
话刚落音对方就冲过来,	Hardly had his voice faded
双方又是一场恶战。	When the two sides were engaged in a fierce fight again.
冈晓的兵马勇猛向前,	Gangxiao's troops fought so bravely
把对方逼到崖石旁,	That they forced their enemy to withdraw to the cliff
逃进崖洞东躲西藏。	And hide in the cave.
冈晓的兵马冲到城下,	Then the army of Gangxiao rushed down to the city wall.
城中守军丢下铓锣战鼓,	The garrison in the city threw away their gongs and drums,
狂呼乱叫一片慌乱。	Shouting screams in a frantic panic.
冈晓的兵马顺崖石搜索前进,	Gangxiao's troops continued to search along the cliff.
战象猛追突破道道设防。	Their war elephants broke through one fortification after another.
冲到一条夹道时,	When rushing into a tunnel,
对方的伏兵突然跃起,	They suddenly encountered the enemy's ambush.
砍杀冈晓的士卒和战象。	It was really a close combat!
短兵相接难以突围,	Gangxiao had no choice but to fight to death.
冈晓只有决一死战。	The swords were swaying.
只见手起刀落,	The flesh and blood were flying.
血肉横飞,	The corpses were piling up.
尸体堆积层层如山。	Then another twenty herds of elephants were released
崖洞中又放出战象二十栏,	
分两路向冈晓的军队冲来。	

厘俸 // Li Feng

冈晓大惊失色心中慌乱，
伏兵又连连冲出崖洞，
手持帕绕①冲向冈晓，
冈晓的象被砍伤。
占拜温号叫一声连连后退，
冈晓吓得浑身瘫软。
孤军深入吃了大亏，
轻敌冒险上了大当。

from the cave,
Rushing to Gangxiao's army from two directions.
This made Gangxiao very frightened and panicked.
More soldiers in ambush dashed out of the cave
Trying to pierce Gangxiao with their *paraos*①.
Gangxiao's elephant got injured,
And retreated with a mournful howling.
Gangxiao was so frightened that he froze all over his body.
It was progressing deeply alone that led to their great loss.
It was looking down on the enemy that caused his fall.

冈晓的兵将身经数战，
勇猛冲杀突出重围。
帕生、帕缓的兵丁紧紧追上，
城中又放出二十栏大象。
形势危急，
冈晓之弟冈庄的兵马忽然到达。
冈庄脚蹬摆洪②旋风一般，
身后的军队成千上万。
双方又是一场恶战，
尸骨成山血流成河。
帕生和帕缓的军队难以抵挡，

But Gangxiao's officers and soldiers were battle-hardened
And bravely got out of the close siege.
The soldiers of Meng Pasheng and Meng Pahuan
　　chased them closely.
Twenty more herds of war elephants in the city were sent
　　to the battlefield.
At this critical moment,
Gangzhuang, Gangxiao's younger brother, suddenly
　　arrived with his army.
Gangzhuang drove his elephant Baihong② like a gust
　　of wind.

---

① 帕绕：刀。
② 摆洪：冈庄骑的战象。

① Parao: knife.
② Baihong: Gangzhuang's elephant.

退回城中将城门紧关。

冈晓的兵丁退到路旁，
只见占拜温的四足被竹签刺伤，
尾巴也被砍，
身负数伤到处血迹斑斑。
冈晓只能骑马而回，
战旗拖地，
兵丁疲劳不堪，
只好在田坝中安营休整一番。
冈晓安慰众兵将：
"帕生、帕缓防守严密，
地势险峻难以进攻。
但只要把城边的荆棘砍光，
铺平进攻的道路，
然后日夜不停地攻城，
就一定会胜利。"

Tens of thousands of soldiers followed him.
The two sides had another fierce fight.
So many soldiers were killed and so many soldiers were injured!
The army of Meng Pasheng and Meng Pahuan could not resist anymore
And had to retreat to the city and close the gate.

Gangxiao's soldiers retreated to the side of the road.
The four feet of his elephant Zhanbaiwen were wounded by bamboo sticks.
And the tail of the elephant had been cut off.
The elephant was indeed seriously injured.
Gangxiao had no alternative but to ride a horse back instead.
The battle flags trailed on the ground.
The soldiers were so exhausted
That they set up camp in the fields to get some rest and reorganize.
Gangxiao comforted his soldiers:
"Meng Pasheng and Meng Pahuan are defended in a very tight way
And have steep terrain hard to conquer.
But as long as the thorns around the city are cut down

厘俸 // Li Feng

And the way for the attack is paved,
We then can keep attacking the city day and night
And will surely win the battle."

冈晓的战况传到海罕处，
海罕率兵日夜兼程，
两军会合士气高涨，
鼓声锣声山谷震撼。
海罕知道帕生、帕缓坚固难攻，
就请龙王相帮：
"让大水淹没帕生、帕缓，
让这两个地方变成水潭，
啊，我的老龙王！"
龙王听见海罕的呼唤，
就发起大水冲向帕生和帕缓。
顷刻间城墙倒塌，
兵丁有的淹死有的受伤，
剩下的四处逃亡。
海罕的军队趁机冲杀，
但帕生、帕缓两大布冈，
还在坚守应战。
冈晓脚蹬大象奋勇向前，
鼓声雷动，
十万兵丁冲到城边，

Hearing the bad news about Gangxiao's situation,
Haihan and his army set out to back him up.
When the two troops met and were united,
The cheering sound of drums and gongs reverberated
    in the valley.
Haihan knew that Meng Pasheng and Meng Pahuan
    were difficult to conquer
And so asked the Dragon King for help:
"Oh, my old Dragon King!
Let a flood inundate Meng Pasheng and Meng Pahuan!
Let the two places become pools."
The Dragon King heard Haihan's plea
And launched a flood of water in Meng Pasheng and
    Meng Pahuan,
Which destroyed the city walls in just a few seconds.
Some of the soldiers were either drowned or injured.
Some of the soldiers just fled away in all directions.
The army of Haihan took the opportunity to fight at
    one fling.
But the two Bugangs of Meng Pasheng and Meng Pahuan

只见冈晓紧咬牙关，	Kept resisting with all their might.
双脚蹬着象耳，	The thundering sound of drums
双目怒视，手持长枪。	Accompanied Gangxiao marching on his elephant,
土炮齐轰，大火熊熊，	And encouraged thousands of the soldiers to dash to the city wall.
守军像篱笆一样破散。	
两个布冈坚守城池，	Gangxiao clenched his teeth,
又放出二十头大象。	Drove his elephant on, his feet pricking the elephant's ears.
海罕的军队又把象群包围，	Glared at the enemy and held a long spear in his hand.
两个布冈骑着战象，	The fire blazed as the cannons were fired together,
迎着冈晓交战。	Making the defense collapse like a fence breaking into pieces.
只见刀矛飞舞，	
一片眼花缭乱。	The two Bugangs kept at it doggedly,
冈晓看准帕缓的布冈，	And sent out another twenty herds of elephants,
对他的腋下猛刺一枪。	Which were soon surrounded by Haihan's army.
桑本也刺中帕生布冈的肋骨，	The two Bugangs rode their elephants forward
两个布冈滚下大象。	And fought straight against Gangxiao.
士卒一拥而上，砍下首级，	The flash of swords and spears
守军见状乱如蜂拥，	Dazzled everyone in the battlefield.
望风而逃四处奔散。	Suddenly Gangxiao aimed his spear at the Bugang of Meng Pahuan
有的嘴中含草跪在地上，	
战战兢兢举手投降。	And pierced into his armpit with the spear.
冈晓大声发布命令：	Sangben also stabbed the Bugang of Meng Pasheng in his ribs.
"掠到的金银要集中堆放，	The two Bugangs fell off their elephants
象和马谁抢到归谁所有，	And were decapitated by Gangxiao's soldiers flocking around.

厘俸 // Li Feng

不要互相争夺争抢。"

Losing their Bugangs, the defensive side swarmed in disarray,
And fled away in all directions.
Some of the soldiers knelt down on the ground with grass in their mouths,
And raised their hands to surrender, trembling with fear.
Gangxiao loudly issued a new order:
"Everyone must hand in the gold and silver captured to the designated place.
But they can keep the elephants and horses they capture.
Nobody is allowed to loot and rampage."

冈晓大军胜利返回，
来到田坝会晤海罕。
海罕召开庆功大会，
向众官兵赏赐大象。
又把金银奖励全军，
然后杀牛宰马，
举杯欢庆打了胜仗。
海罕起身面对官兵说：
"如今夺取帕生和帕缓，
全军上下人人喜欢。
今后的战斗如何进行，
我们还要仔细商量。
部队的先锋，

Gangxiao's army returned in triumph
And he went to seek an audience with Haihan.
Haihan held a victory celebration
To give the officers and soldiers
Elephants, gold and silver as rewards.
Cattle and horses were killed for a banquet
To toast for the victory.
Haihan rose to his feet and spoke to his officers and soldiers:
"Now we have seized Meng Pasheng and Meng Pahuan.
Everyone is immersed in happiness and cheerfulness.
As for how to fight in the future,
We need further and careful discussions.
The vanguard of the army

仍然是一千个勐的主将。	Is still the core of the military force of the one thousand *mengs*.
你们要继续努力，	You should continue to work hard,
军纪不能放松。	And stick to strict army disciplines.
勇敢要一如既往，	Be brave as always,
每到一处要安营扎寨，	And keep order
秩序井然。"	Wherever you stop to camp."

第二天拂晓，　　　　　　　At dawn the next day,
只听人欢马叫，　　　　　　Along with the bustle of people and the neighing of horses,
战鼓咚咚响，　　　　　　　And the beating of drums,
千军万马又继续前进，　　　Thousands upon thousands of horses and soldiers continued to march forward.
海罕在后慢慢跟着。　　　　Haihan followed slowly at the rear of his troops.
部队到达累莱山脊梁，　　　They stopped to camp
停止前进安营帐。　　　　　At the ridge of the Leilai Mountain.
营帐层层叠叠围，　　　　　Tents were set up in circles
把海罕团团围在最中央。　　To protect Haihan in the middle.
整个营地大又大，　　　　　The camp was so big
营地四周设警戒。　　　　　That close watch was kept all around.
木头做成大栅栏，　　　　　Long wooden fences were built around the camp.
漫山遍野篝火起，　　　　　Campfires were set all over the mountain.
青烟缭起火苗旺。　　　　　Flames were dancing with puff and smoke.
冈晓在前打先锋，　　　　　As the vanguard,
士兵头盔发光亮。

厘俸 // Li Feng

来到原始森林中，	Gangxiao and his soldiers
粗大的藤条一串串。	Encamped in the primeval forest.
兵丁砍下搭营帐，	Thick vines were cut
冈晓的帐篷丝绸做。	To set up tents for soldiers,
烧火做饭炊烟起，	Whereas Gangxiao's tent was made from silk cloth.
人声沸腾多欢畅。	Fires were made for cooking and smoke rose.
另一路大军，	The camping place was full of cheerful conversations.
领头的是桑洛和混嘿南。	More troops
昼夜兼程急行军，	Were led by Sangluo and Hun Heinan.
团团围攻勐冈桑。	They were making a rapid march day and night
派出骑兵用火攻，	To besiege Gangsang.
烧掉城外村和庄。	They sent elephant-riding soldiers
黑烟滚滚冲天起，	To set fire to the villages outside the city.
大火熊熊映天地。	Dark smoke billowed.
俸改站在高楼上，	Raging flames painted the sky red.
放眼四处来眺望。	Fenggai, surrounded by his wife and concubines,
妻妾前呼后拥站身旁，	Stood on a tall building
看到冈老、冈桑坝子烟火起，	And looked into the distance.
转过头来把婻崩问：	He saw the fires and the smoke in Ganglao and Gangsang,
"为什么成这样？"	And turned to Nanbeng and asked:
婻崩轻言细语忙回答：	"What do you think is going on?"
"如果是正月起烟火，	Nanbeng replied in a soft voice:
那是百姓在烧山。	"If you see fire and smoke in January,
如果是二月起烟火，	It must be people burning woods and grass on the mountains.

那是百姓烧火田埂上。	If you see fire and smoke in February,
百姓有吃又有穿，	It must be people burning the straw in the fields.
全靠你治理又有法来又有方。	Our people all have sufficient food and clothing,
年头百姓送牛马，	Because your ruling power is exercised in a very effective way.
年尾还送马和牛，	Your people send you, as tribute, cattle and horses
年中又送酒和肉，	At the beginning and the end of each year.
纳贡的人一年到头不会断。	And in the middle of each year they also send you wine and meat.
祝贺我的生日吉又祥，	Their tribute goes to you all the year round.
这都是因为你啊，	They even send me gifts to make my birthday happy and joyful.
我的召法勐俸罕！"	This is all because of you,
俸改听了心喜欢，	My respectable Zhao Famengfenghan!"
手摸胡须笑哈哈。	Fenggai was so happy to hear that and laughed.
转身面对正妻咪埃汪：	Touching his beard,
"你向我指的地方看，	He turned to his wife Mi'aiwang and asked:
那里起火为哪样？"	"Look where I point at.
咪埃汪急忙来回答：	Why is there a fire there?"
"我的召法勐俸罕，	Mi'aiwang replied quickly:
冈老、冈桑冒火烟，	"My respectable Zhao Famengfenghan!
不是正月百姓在烧田，	I see fire and smoke in Ganglao and Gangsang.
也不是二月山区的百姓在烧地。	It is neither the burning of the woods in January
请你仔细来回想，	Nor the burning of straw in February.
从去年一直到今年，	
桑洛的妻子被你抢，	
桑洛抱着宝刀哭得多悲伤，	

厘俸 // Li Feng

他不会甘心失妻子。
现在烟火已经起，
你的领地可能要遭殃。
过去桑洛率兵来攻打勐景罕，
我们的兵将城楼站，
把他们白眼来相看，
好像燕子看见蚱蜢一个样，
心中的高兴不用说。
他们的兵马实在少，
还不够一个包包来装满。
桑洛扫兴而归白来一趟，
只好天天抱着宝刀徒悲伤。
现在你又跑到贫穷的勐景哈
　　姐报①，
婻崩身为海罕妻，
你为何把她抢？
桑洛和海罕相联合，
已经向你来开战。
你管辖的地方到处战火燃，
我的召法勐俸罕！
海罕是天神的子孙，
他的援军能来自天上。

---

① 姐报：产黄景、毛薯的地方，意为此地贫瘠，而俸改仍去抢掠该地妇女。

Please think about what has been happening.
It is one year
Since you seized Sangluo's wife.
He weeps sadly, sword in hand.
He is sure to revenge.
What you see now are the flames of war!
Your territory will encounter a disaster!
Do you remember when Sangluo once came to attack
　　Mengjinghan,
Our soldiers just stood on the wall tower,
And despised them
The way a swallow despises a grasshopper.
Our soldiers just took it easy
Because at that time Sangluo had a small army,
Which was not even big enough to fill up a bag.
With disappointment Sangluo went back without his wife.
All he could do was to hold his sword, grieving day after day.
The worse is that you continue go to poverty-stricken
　　Jiebao① in Mengjingha.
You know Nanbeng is Haihan's wife.
Why do you still take her away?
Now Sangluo allies himself with Haihan,

---

① Jiebao: a very poor place, but Fenggai still goes there to capture women and take them away.

如果双方来交战，	Declaring war on you.
你管辖的地方一定会丢光。	There are battles everywhere in your territory,
勐景罕就要遭大殃，	My respectable Zhao Famengfenghan!
这一切已经在眼前啊，	Haihan is a descendant of the gods.
我的召法勐俸罕！"	He may ask for back-up troops from heaven.
俸改听后不说话，	If the two sides come to fight you,
闷闷不乐进宫殿，	You will certainly lose all your land and territory.
一头坐在宝椅上，	A disaster is approaching Mengjinghan,
召集百官进宫来。	And the consequences are so obvious to see,
他的宫殿八层高，	My respectable Zhao Famengfenghan!"
金碧辉煌亮又亮。	Fenggai said nothing.
共有房屋三百间，	He walked into his palace sullenly
一间一间不一样。	And sat on his Dragon Throne feeling depressed.
百官进宫忙叩头，	Then officials were called to meet
齐向俸改来问安。	In this eight-story high palace,
俸改手持金杯赐美酒，	Glittering with gold and jade.
百官畅饮心喜欢。	There were three hundred rooms in the palace.
俸改高声问百官：	Each room looked different from another.
"听说海罕、桑洛联合起，	The officials entered the palace,
派出战象数万头。	Bowing and greeting Fenggai in chorus.
为了婻崩和娥宾，	Holding a gold cup, Fenggai invited the officials to have
要和我们来作战。	a drink.
是真是假谁知道，	The officials enjoyed the drinking time very much.
我的忠诚的混俸们！"	Fenggai then asked them loudly:

厘俸 // Li Feng

文武百官坐厅堂,
默默无语不开腔。
只有双线①站出来,
叩头之后把话讲:
"我的召法勐俸罕,
此事我已听百姓在传说,
但不知是真还是假。
听说海罕、桑洛联合来作战,
发动数十万兵马和大象,
为的是夺回婻崩和娥宾。
我们边远的各个勐,
有的陷落有的投降。
千万个村寨已落入敌方,
人被杀死房屋被烧光。
现在桑洛和嘿南,
正在围攻冈老和冈桑。
已经围了一二十天,
已经烧了周围的村庄。
冈老、冈桑即将陷落,
守军正在把援军盼望。
这就是我所知道的,
我的召法勐俸罕!"

"I heard that Haihan and Sangluo are in alliance with each other
And send tens of thousands of war elephants
To fight us
In order to take back Nanbeng and Ebing.
Who knows if this information is true or not?
My loyal officials and officers!"
The officials and officers all sat in the hall
In utter silence
With the exception of Shuangxian①.
Shuangxian bowed to Fenggai and said:
"My respectable Zhao Famengfenghan!
The news has been spreading among the people for a while
But I don't know whether it is true or not.
It is said that Haihan and Sangluo are fighting shoulder to shoulder
With hundreds of thousands of horses and elephants
In order to get back Nanbeng and Ebing.
Some of our remote *mengs* have already been occupied
And some of them have just surrendered to the enemy.
Thousands of villages have fallen into the enemy's hand.
Our people are being killed and their houses are being

---

① 双线:人名,俸改的将官,原是海罕的人,后来投降俸改。

① Shuangxian: the name of one of Fenggai's generals, who used to be Haihan's general but later surrendered to Fenggai.

俸改听了心中阵阵紧张说：	burnt.
"双线啊，	Sangluo and Heinan are now
现在我该怎么办？	Attacking Ganglao and Gangsang.
你骑上我的麻翁潘，	These places have been under siege for more than ten or twenty days.
单独去把实情查看。	The villages have all been burnt and destroyed!
不准带任何人前往，	Ganglao and Gangsang will soon be occupied,
你要快马加鞭，	And is desperately expecting back-up for longer resistance.
尽快弄清楚情况。	This is all I know so far,
麻翁潘是一匹领头马，	"My respectable Zhao Famengfenghan!"
它的长毛像金丝一样黄。	Hearing this, Fenggai became nervous and said:
如果孕妇看见它，	"Shuangxian!
肚中的胎儿就会烟消云散，	What am I supposed to do now?
孕妇还不知道。	You'd better ride my horse Mawengpan,
我的双线啊，	And go to check the real situation on your own.
你要把我说的记在心上！"	Nobody is allowed to go with you
双线向俸改叩头后，	So that you can ride at top speed
走出宫廷来到场院，	And make a clear picture of the situation as soon as possible.
骑上麻翁潘，	Mawengpan is a leading horse with super power
来到一棵大榕树下。	And with long hair as yellow as golden silk.
榕树上附有神灵，	A pregnant woman may lose her baby
神灵们就叽叽喳喳地高声喊叫：	At the sight of the horse
"双线啊，双线！"	Without knowing it.
双线立即抬头看，	My dear Shuangxian,
却不见一个人影，	

厘俸 // Li Feng

领悟到这是神灵的呼唤。
他赶快下马向榕树叩头说：
"神灵啊，
听说海罕和桑洛率领大队人马，
要进犯勐景罕，
现正在围攻冈老和冈桑，
不知道是真还是假？
召法勐命令我去查看，
请神灵保佑我一路平安。"
神灵回话：
"你来到这里已经辛苦了。
应赶快把马头掉转。
千万不能往前再走一步，
再往前走就是死亡。
赶快返回勐景罕去转告俸改，
勐景罕城中有三十九个鲁勒①，
拥有如此广阔而富有的地方，
这是神灵保佑的结果，
可是俸改却把神灵遗忘。
过去每年年头用牛马祭神，
年尾也少不了猪羊，
年中还有茶酒斋饭，
现在把一切都丢光。

Please keep in mind all my words!"
Shuangxian kowtowed to Fenggai
And walked out of the court and went over to the yard
Where he mounted Mawengpan
And rode all the way until he saw a big banyan tree.
The tree was possessed by some gods,
Who chirped and shouted at the sight of Shuangxian:
"Shuangxian! Hi, Shuangxian!"
Shuangxian looked up immediately
But he saw nobody.
He soon realized that it was calls from the gods
And he quickly got off the horse and kowtowed to the tree:
"Dear gods,
It is said that Haihan and Sangluo are leading their troops
To attack Mengjinghan,
And they are now surrounding Ganglao and Gangsang.
Is this true or not?
Zhao Fameng orders me to come to check the truth.
Please bless me with a safe journey!"
The gods replied:
"It is really toilsome for you to come here!
You should turn back at once.
Do not move forward.

---

① 鲁勒：勐景罕城里划分的区域。

如今，	One more step means death!
每月祭祀神灵的只有海罕。	Return to Mengjinghan to convey our words to Fenggai.
他是布领暖的子孙，	Tell him that there are 39 *lules*① in Mengjinghan city.
他为人正直且心地善良。	Possessing such a vast and rich land
不论走到哪里，	Is the result of the blessing of the gods.
神灵和人们都拥护、喜欢他。	But he has forgotten all about this.
他每喝一口酒，	He used to offer cattle and horses as sacrifice at the beginning of each year,
都要请我们碰杯同享。	Pigs and sheep at the end of each year,
谁祭祀我们，	Tea and wine and vegetarian food in the middle of each year.
我们就把他保佑。	But he has forgotten all this.
勐景罕不是我们保佑的地方，	And now,
现在只有等待着灾难。"	Only Haihan pays tribute to the gods every month.
双线听了愤愤不平：	Haihan is the descendent of Bulingnuan
"神灵为何还会偏心！"	And is honest and kind-hearted.
拍马奔驰继续往前。	Wherever he goes,
神灵开口又来阻挡：	He wins the respect and adoration of the gods and the people.
"双线啊，	Whenever he has wine to drink,
我们劝你不听，	He invites us to share it.
你硬往别人的绳索里钻，	We bless those
如同老虎钻扣子，	Who offer sacrifice to us.
不相信你走着试试看！"	
双线日夜兼程把路赶，	
长途跋涉到凉水箐地方。	

---

① Lule: districts of Mengjinghan city.

厘俸 // Li Feng

把马拴在树桩上，	Mengjinghan is not the place we bless.
打开饭盒来吃饭，	What you can wait for is nothing but catastrophe."
只见饭中掺着蛆和血。	Hearing this, Shuangxian felt indignant:
勉强吃一口，	"How come you gods are so unfair!"
又想吐来心又翻，	Shuangxian whipped his horse and decided to ride forward.
丢开饭盒在一旁，	The gods persuaded him again:
用水漱口哗哗响。	"Shuangxian,
抬头一看吃一惊，	Why don't you listen to us
只见海罕、冈晓的士兵割象草，	Instead of insisting on jumping into the trap
四方八面遍山冈。	Like a tiger to be trapped?
割草的兵丁看见他，	Let's wait and see!"
两面包围步步上。	Shuangxian hurried on his journey day and night,
双线逃跑已无路，	And arrived at a place called the Cold Water Valley.
活活擒住被捆绑。	He fastened his horse onto a tree stump.
兵丁押着他见冈晓，	Then he opened his meal box.
他跪拜在冈晓脚下谎言相告。	Inside he saw worms and blood mixed with rice.
冈晓横眉竖眼把他看，	Even a grudging bite
命令士卒送他到花山，	Made his stomach turn and feel nauseous.
交给海罕来审判。	He put the meal box aside
海罕见到双线怒火起：	And washed his mouth with water.
"我日日夜夜都在想，	When he looked up, he was so surprised to see
一有机会就要杀掉你。"	The soldiers of Haihan and Gangxiao mowing grass
双线急得心慌乱，	To feed their elephants roaming all over the mountain.
低声回答叩头响：	The soldiers saw him

"怀①,怀,怀!	And came to surround him from all around.
善良而又尊敬的海罕,	Shuangxian had no way to escape
我投奔勐景罕,	And was captured alive.
并不是真心实意去投降。	He was bound and sent by escort to Gangxiao.
我永远是你的奴臣,	Shuangxian fell on his knees in front of Gangxiao but told him lies.
离开了你我等于死去,	Gangxiao looked him up and down,
请你把我当作死人一样。	And commanded the soldiers to send him to the Mountain of Flowers and Fruits
现在你要讨伐傣改,	And hand him over to Haihan for trial.
但全勐的人都还不知道。	Haihan was in a fury at the sight of Shuangxian:
俗话说得好:	"Day and night I have been thinking about
葫芦从肚里开始烂。	Killing you as soon as I have the opportunity."
勐景罕防守坚又固,	On hearing this, Shuangxian could no longer keep clam.
没有内应来帮助,	He made deep kowtows and replied in a low voice:
只靠外攻太困难。	"*Huai*①! *Huai*! *Huai*!
今天如能放我走,	Kind and respectful Haihan!
到时你驱赶战象万头,	I left you and went to Menjinghan
我做内应放把火,	Not because I really betrayed you.
在城中烧毁勐景罕。	I remain to be your follower and servant as always.
立功赎罪重做人,	Without you I am just an empty body without life.
回头还做你的臣。	So please treat me as a dead man.
海罕啊,	
你贤明又善良,	

---

① 怀:主人呼喊奴隶时,奴隶的应声,即"奴隶在"的意思。

① Huai: Huai is a slave's answer to his master's call, meaning "Your slave is here at your service."

厘俸 // Li Feng

给予恩赐我永不忘！"
海罕相信他的话，
赐给他一顶慕专罕①，
还有一件舍王爹仿妥②，
然后杀鸡摆酒来招待。

You are now planning to oppress Fenggai
But the people of Mengjinghan are not aware of that yet.
As the saying goes,
The rot of a gourd starts from inside.
Mengjinghan has a strong and powerful defense network.
Depending solely on the outside attack is not enough.
A plant inside Mengjinghan is really needed.
If today you let me go,
When you and your war elephants go to attack Mengjinghan,
I will act as a plant from inside
And burn the city of Mengjinghan.
By doing that, I will redeem my guilt
And be your servant again.
Oh Haihan!
You are so wise and kind!
Bestow on me an opportunity and I will forever remember it!"
Haihan then believed what he said.
He gave Shuangxian a *muzhuanhan*①
And a *shewangdiefangtuo*②.

---

① 慕专罕：雕饰有花纹，涂有金粉的帽子。
② 舍王爹仿妥：四川出产的战袍。

① Muzhuanhan: a hat with decorative designs and a thin layer of golden powder.
② Shewangdiefangtuo: a war robe made in Sichuan province of China.

	He then treated Shuangxian with wine and chicken.
冈晓看到怒火起，	Gangxiao was so angry to see all this
竹棍痛打双线背。	That he beat Shuangxian on the back with a bamboo stick.
边打边斥责：	He denounced him as he beat him:
"该死的畜生应知罪，	"You damn beast should admit your guilt.
你挑拨离间搬是非。	You made mischief and sowed discord.
婻崩被抢你有责，	You should take responsibility for the capture of Nanbeng,
她落虎口，	Which led to
导致战争成灾难。"	The disaster of war."
冈晓怒火止不住，	Blazing anger burnt in Gangxiao's heart.
双线已经被打翻。	Shuangxian was knocked down on the ground.
冈晓踏上一只脚，	Gangxiao trampled Shuangxian,
双线闭眼把死装。	Who closed his eyes and pretended to be dead.
海罕看了心生气，	Haihan was not happy with this.
连连跺脚把话讲：	Stamping his feet in anger Haihan said:
"我已同意把他放，	"I have decided to release him.
你又把他拉来打。	Why do you still beat him this way?
如此无理真该死，	If you keep losing your sense of reason,
不想活命那就算！"	You may lose your life as well."
手持长矛刺冈晓，	Haihan threw a spear towards Gangxiao
冈晓眼快忙躲开，	But Gangxiao's keen eyes helped him avoid the spear,
长矛刺在屋柱上。	Which pierced into a wooden column.
冈晓无奈往外跑，	Gangxiao had no choice but to run out of the tent,

厘俸 // Li Feng

急忙在众头领中躲藏，	Trying to hide himself in the crowd of officials.
众头领团团围住来保护。	The surrounding officials provided him with protection.
冈晓面如土色把话讲：	Gangxiao's face became pale and he said:
"我们出征一百二十天，	"We have been on expedition for 120 days.
衣服鞋子都已烂，	Our clothes and shoes are all worn out,
海罕却不发新装，	But we cannot get new ones from Haihan.
双线该死却释放，	Shuangxian should be killed but is set free.
又是同情又怜悯，	He has won Haihan's sympathy and mercy
又送衣来又吃饭。	And got new clothes and good food from him.
我担心送的战袍要作靶，	I am afraid the robe given to Shuangxian will be used as a target,
象征海罕被捉拿，	Symbolizing that Haihan is seized,
矛又刺来刀又砍。"	And stabbed by spears and cut by swords."
冈晓边说边走盯双线，	While Gangxiao was speaking he kept staring at Shuangxian.
双线地上爬起向海罕，	Shuangxian felt scared and hastily stood up
慌忙叩头急出帐。	And quickly kowtowed and walked out of the tent.
冈晓暗中发信号，	Gangxiao gave a nod to one of his soldiers
士兵尾随双线紧跟上。	To follow Shuangxian secretly.
走出一段路，	After walking some distance,
抓住双线不再放。	The soldier caught Shuangxian,
剥下海罕送给的衣裳，	Took off the robe given by Haihan and
又把颈枷套在脖子上。	Fastened chains around his neck.
拉到河边刚要杀，	He then dragged Shuangxian to the riverside to be killed
山神暗中来阻挡。	
士兵突然眼发黑，	

双线乘机跳入河，	When the gods stepped in.
潜水而逃到对岸。	They made the soldier blind
不怕野兽来伤害，	And helped Shuangxian escape by jumping into the river
跑进山林中躲藏。	And swimming to the opposite river bank.
日夜不停向前走，	Shuangxian then ran into a forest
双脚血泡起成团。	Regardless of the danger of being attacked by the beasts.
茅草划背背出血，	He walked on and on, day and night.
伤痕道道多又长。	Blisters came out on his feet.
眼看来到勐景罕，	He had long and bloody thatch scratches
坝子空旷河水淌。	On his back as well.
渡口附近行人多，	Finally he was back in Mengjinghan,
双线藏身丛林招手喊：	Where the land was spacious and the river was flowing as usual.
"我有急事要见混俸，	Seeing that there were many people waiting for the ferry,
请送给我一件衣服穿。"	Shuangxian shouted from his hiding place in the bush:
行人脱下衣服送给他，	"I have an urgent message to report to Hunfeng.
他胡乱穿起忙进城。	Please give me something to wear."
这时双线的妻子站在凉台把丝线晒，	A passer-by took off his clothes and gave them to him.
抬手遮阳往远处看。	Shuangxian then quickly put on the clothes and walked towards the city.
忽见远方来一人，	At that time Shuangxian's wife was drying her silk threads on the balcony.
好像是儿子他爹啊！	When she looked into the distance, using her hand as a sun-shade,
不知究竟为什么，	
他穿的是百姓的衣裳，	
跟跟跄跄把路赶。	

厘俸 // Li Feng

他为什么一人独行？
为什么不见坐骑麻翁潘？
双线刚回到家中，
妻子儿女问长又问短。
双线坐下安安心，
把全家人员都召集。
流着眼泪把话讲：
"你们赶快把家中财物来收藏，
提防勐景哈的小伙子来抢。
然后把桂冠给我戴上，
装宝物的背袋也取出，
铠甲也快给我来穿上。
过了今日不穿戴，
今后是否还能穿？
穿好我就要出门，
事急要去见俸改。
离勐多日不回头，
有去有回才像样，
否则俸改起疑心，
我一去无音讯，
就像乌鸦一般，
飞到空中不知去向。"

She saw someone walking towards her.
The man looked so much like the father of her children!
But the man was somehow
Dressed like a civilian
And was staggering and stumbling along.
Why was he walking alone?
Where was his horse Mawengpan?
Shuangxian finally got back to his home.
His wife and children all came to ask him various questions.
Shuangxian sat down to calm himself for a while
And then called all his family together.
He told them in tears:
"You must quickly hide all our valuables and belongings
In case the people of Mengjingha come to rob us.
Now give me my laurel,
My treasure bag amulet
And my armor as well.
If I do not wear them today,
I wonder if tomorrow I will be still alive and wearing them.
I am ready now to leave again,
For I have something important and urgent to report to Fenggai.
I have been away for some days.
A mission is not a mission when there is no return report!
Fenggai may be suspicious

	If there is no news heard from me,
	Who, like a raven, flies into the sky
	With no trace to be found."

双线穿戴完毕，	Shuangxian dressed up
赶到宫廷里。	And went to the palace in a hurry.
俸改斜倚宝座上，	Fenggai was leaning on his Dragon Throne
双线叩头下拜来行礼，	When Shuangxian came to kowtow,
嘴唇贴在地板上说：	His lips kissing the floor:
"尊敬的召法勐俸罕啊，	"My respectable Zhao Famengfenghan!
我从海罕的刀尖逃出来，	Thanks to Haihan's kindness,
亏得海罕心地善良，	I just had a narrow escape!
如果他像你召法勐俸罕一样，	I could have lost my life
我的性命早已完。	If Haihan had the same character as you.
我已经见到了海罕，	I saw Haihan
花言巧语把他骗，	And cheated him with lies.
他才把我放。	Otherwise I could not have been released.
他的军队驻扎在深山里，	His army is stationed in a deep forest
他的营地庞大无比。	And his camp is vast.
他的帐篷搭在花果山，	His tent is set up on the Mountain of Flowers and Fruits.
他的士兵多得像蚂蚁一样，	The number of his soldiers is as countless as ants.
漫山遍野火光明亮。	Torches can be seen all over the mountain.
海罕的坐骑很凶猛，	With tusks as thick and tough as salt mortar,
象牙粗如盐白大又长，	Haihan's elephant is quite ferocious

厘俸 // Li Feng

不惧水火不怕刀枪。
海罕的象群身高体壮,
每二十头象为一栏,
平时精心饲养。
海罕的军队源源不断,
箐沟踏成大道,
营帐布满山冈。
现在桑洛和嘿南的人马,
正在围攻冈老和冈桑。
他们用鸡毛火炭写成信,①
和海罕取得联系报告情况。
这就是我所了解的情况,
我的召法勐俸罕!"
俸改听完后抒起手袖说:
"海罕、桑洛即使扭成绳一般,
我也并不害怕。
驾驭万头战象来进犯,
也不能攻破我的城池。
他们是一口袋米,
怎能与一粮仓米对抗。
战斗一千年,
也不能把我的一根毫毛扯断。

And fears no water, no fire, no swords, and no guns.
His war elephants are all tall and strong.
Every twenty elephants is organized into one herd,
Which have been raised with careful breeding in peace time.
Haihan has a very steady and sufficient supply of troops.
The valleys have been trodden and turned into the broad roads.
The mountains are covered by tents and camps.
Now the troops of Sangluo and Heinan
Are attacking Ganglao and Gangsang.
They sent Haihan "a letter of chicken feathers and charcoal"①
To keep in touch with each other and report the situation.
This is all the information I got,
"My respectable Zhao Famengfenghan!"
Having heard this, Fenggai rolled up his sleeves and said:
"I am not frightened
Even if Haihan and Sangluo are united and allied like a twisted rope.
My city won't be conquered,
Even though they invade us with ten thousand elephants.
They are a sack of rice but we are a barn.

---

① 用鸡毛和火炭粘在信中表示事急。

① Chicken feather and charcoal are stuck on a letter to indicate "urgency".

他们费尽精力而来,	How can they be comparable to us?
只能空手而返,	Fighting for a thousand years
含羞而归!"	May not tear and break even one of my hairs.
俸改不把海罕放在心上,	They will definitely come with all their might
依然饮酒寻欢,	But return empty-handed
在轻歌曼舞中度过时光。	And disgraced."
	Fenggai did not take Haihan's attack seriously.
	He continued his binge as usual
	And spent his time in sweet music and graceful dance.
第二天拂晓,	At dawn the next day,
俸改召集百官说:	Fenggai summoned his officials:
"海罕正在围攻冈老和冈桑,	"Haihan is now besieging Ganglao and Gangsang.
如不支援就要失守,	Without reinforcements, these two places will be conquered.
应马上行动派出援兵,	We should send out reinforcements at once.
人马要出几十干①,	The soldiers and horses must be assembled from dozens of *gans*①.
还要战象数千头,	Thousands of elephants are also needed.
请大家仔细来商量。"	Let's talk over this issue."
文武百官不出声,	The officials and officers remained silent
默默无言互相看。	And looked at each other in silence.
俸改面对双线又开口:	Fenggai then turned to Shuangxian and asked:
"双线啊,双线,	

---

① 干:一个首领所统率的区域,相当于一个勐或数个勐。

① Gan: the area a chief rules. It includes one or several *mengs*.

厘俸 // Li Feng

你怎样来实现我的愿望？
你骑着大象代我出征，
援助冈老和冈桑。
兵马武器我为你准备，
战象我会为你挑选，
象舆的一切装饰也会为你置办，
一日之内你应把路赶。"
双线不敢拒绝俸改，
强打精神起身站起说：
"只怕途中遇伏兵，
不能到达冈老和冈桑。
为了俸改我不怕死，
只求给我勇猛善战的大象，
我的召法勐俸罕！"
俸改点头同意了，
下令牵出战象英着节，
它的四足又粗又大如蜂盘。
双线看了看大象说：
"这头象走路走得慢，
冈老、冈桑那么远，
耽误时间不划算，
请重新挑选重新换。"
俸改又令牵出占艾滇，
象牙歪斜在左边。

"Shuangxian, oh, Shuangxian!

How are you going to make my wish come true?

You should ride an elephant

And go to assist Ganglao and Gangsang on my behalf.

I will prepare the army and the weapons for you.

I will select war elephants for you.

I will equip the elephants with howdahs for you.

You are required to set out in one day."

Shuangxian did not dare reject the order.

He gathered his energy and rose to his feet:

"The only thing I worry about is the ambush we may encounter midway

That may prevent us from arriving at Ganglao and Gangsang.

I am not afraid of fighting to the death for you

If you give me valiant and powerful war elephants,

My respectable Zhao Famengfenghan!"

Fenggai nodded to show his approval

And ordered the war elephant Yingzhejie to be led forward,

Whose four feet were strong and big.

Shuangxian looked at the elephant and said:

"This elephant walks quite slowly.

Ganglao and Gangsang are very remote places.

双线见了把话讲：	Too much time would be wasted on the way.
"这头大象最怕火，	Let's choose another one instead."
又怕杀声又怕喊。	Then Fenggai ordered Zhan'aidian to be led forward,
听见喊杀声就逃离战场，	Whose tusks were deflected and crooked on the left side.
请重新挑选重新换。"	Shuangxian said:
俸改又牵出占拜黄，	"This elephant is afraid of fire
象背上一条红线长又长。	As well as cries and shouts.
双线见了又开口：	It may flee when it hears the battle sounds.
"这头大象怕战马，	Let's choose another one instead."
还怕途中遇路障。	Then Fenggai asked Zhanbaihuang to be led out
看见路障就回头，	With a red and long scar on its back.
请重新挑选重新换。"	Shuangxian was still not satisfied:
俸改又牵出占拜翁，	"This elephant is afraid of war horses
一条紫色项圈套在象脖上。	And obstructions on the road.
双线见了又摇头说：	It may turn back at the sight of road obstructions.
"这头大象怕土炮，	Let's choose another one instead."
听见炮声就转头，	Fenggai then asked Zhanbaiweng to be led out
踩踏自己的兵和将，	With a purple leash on its neck.
军队纷纷乱一团，	Shuangxian shook his head and said:
不听指挥不听令。	"This elephant is afraid of cannon sound.
即使用钩镰挖象头，	It may turn back on hearing the sound of cannon shot.
也只是歪歪脖子不动弹，	And it may tread on our own soldiers and generals.
请重新挑选重新换。"	This may cause stampede in the troops
俸改又牵出占艾赖，	And make the commands and the orders totally ineffective.

厘俸 // Li Feng

象牙粗大如盐臼，
脑门宽宽五尺长，
眼角也有五寸多，
尾巴又粗又壮，
不怕炮也不怕枪。
双线见了又犹豫说：
"这是俸改的坐象，
部下怎能随便骑。
俸改要给我不敢要，
请重新挑选重新换。"
俸改又牵出占拜中，
它也是俸改的坐象。
这头大象跨大步，
走出象栏气势如山。
四只脚上有花纹，
花纹也在背脊上，
尾毛雪白如丝线。
它见到火光往前扑，
听到枪炮声往前闯。
双线见了点点头，
抬出晖罕架在象身上，
紫色缰索牢牢绑。
双线宝刀身上挎，
闪亮的铠甲也披上。

Even if I use a reaping hook to hit its head,
It may just swing its head a little bit.
Let's choose another one instead."
Fenggai then asked Zhan'ailai to be led out,
Whose tusks were as thick and big as salt mortar.
It had a broad forehead,
Long eyes,
And a strong thick tail.
The elephant was afraid of neither cannon sound nor gun shot.
Shuangxian still hesitated and said:
"This is your elephant.
As your subordinate I do not have the right to ride it.
I dare not accept this elephant.
Let's choose another one instead."
Fenggai then required Zhanbaizhong to be dragged out.
This was Fenggai's elephant as well.
The elephant strode out of the shed
In a vigorous and imposing manner.
There were patterns on its four feet
And on its back.
The hairs on its tail looked like snow-white silk thread.
At the sight of fire, it would rush forward.
On hearing the sound of guns, it would dash forward.

铠甲金光四射如鱼鳞，
背上还背着一个通香①。
千军万马已齐备，
双线率领上征程。
马不停蹄象不卸鞍，
日夜兼程把路赶。
到达凉水箐地方，
只见冈晓的兵马在对岸，
营寨星罗棋布遍山冈。
双线隔岸来安营，
众兵将又摩拳来又擦掌，
要求立即进兵来开战。
双线劝说性莫急，
待机行动不为慢。
养精蓄锐是上策，
安营扎寨理应当。

Shuangxian finally nodded his head with satisfaction.

He put the howdah on the back of the elephant

Fastening it tightly with a purple rein.

Shuagnxian wore his sword

And put on his shining armor.

The armor shone like fish scales.

There was even a *tongxiang*① on the back of the armor.

The mighty military force was ready

And Shuangxian then set out on his expedition.

They marched day and night

With no stop for rest.

At last they got to a place called Cold Water Valley.

They saw Gangxiao's army on the opposite side.

Their camps and tents were scattered all over the mountain.

Shuangxian's troop stopped to camp.

His soldiers and generals could not wait any longer,

And came to ask for an immediate battle.

Shuangxian persuaded them not to be hasty.

Biding their time did not mean wasting time.

Reserving and conserving strength was the best strategy.

Pitching camps was natural and reasonable.

Gangxiao saw the arrival of Shuangxian

---

① 通香：装宝石的袋子，为一种护身符。

① Tongxiang: a gem bag used as an amulet.

厘俸 // Li Feng

冈晓虽见双线到，
若无其事不慌乱。
不急不慢喝闲酒，
只令鼓声不要断。
佳肴美酒传不停，
冈晓边喝酒边把话讲：
"双线曾经被捉到，
没有杀死真可叹。
送给海罕去审讯，
海罕心地太善良。
相信双线的假话一串串，
还指望双线为内应，
放火烧毁勐景罕。
海罕、双线倒友好，
我等反要被除斩。"
冈晓越说越气愤，
酒杯砸地纷纷碎。

第二天拂晓炮声响，
双线大军穿过花果山，
目标指向冈老和冈桑。

But he acted as if nothing had happened.
He drank his wine at ease as usual.
The only order from him was to keep making the drum sound non-stop.
While enjoying exquisite wine and delicious food,
Gangxiao said:
"When Shuangxian was caught last time,
It was a mistake that I sent him to Haihan for a trial
Instead of killing him myself.
But Haihan was so kind-hearted
That he believed all Shuangxian's lies.
He even expected Shuangxian to become a plant
Who might set fire to destroy Mengjinghan in the coming battle.
Haihan and Shuangxian became friends
And we became people to be destroyed."
The more Gangxiao said the angrier he became.
He threw a wine glass on the ground and it broke into pieces.

The next day at dawn, cannon sound was heard.
Shuangxian's troops had passed the Mountain of Flowers and Fruits,

双线的坐骑占拜中,
摆头甩鼻大步走,
双线稳坐金幢①下。
冈晓见状急发令,
又敲锣来又打鼓,
鼓声响彻云霄上,
人声沸腾刀矛叮当响。
手持高早②的兵丁打先锋,
后续部队紧跟上,
手中的武器是黄贺罕③。
鼓声咚咚催人心,
千军万马已出发。

冈晓骑上占拜温,
要和双线的占拜中决战。
双线看见冈晓来阻击,
急驱坐骑来迎战。

---

① 金幢:一种用绸缎精制的,系有飘带,色彩斑斓的伞形装饰物,插于象舆后面。
② 高早:一种锐利兵器。
③ 黄贺罕:涂有金粉的长矛。

And were heading for Ganglao and Gangsang.

Shuangxian's elephant Baizhanzhong

Swung its head and tusks and strode forward.

Shuangxian was sitting steadily under the golden prayer flag① fixed to the howdah.

Seeing this, Gangxiao also quickly issued an order to battle.

The beat of gongs and drums

Echoed to the sky.

There was a riot of sound of people and weapons everywhere.

The soldiers holding *gaozao*② in their hands were the vanguard.

Other soldiers followed closely behind

And held *huanghehan*③ as their weapons.

The drum beats inspired

Tens of thousands of soldiers and horses to set out promptly.

Gangxiao mounted Zhanbaiwen,

Ready for the decisive battle with Shuangxian's Zhanbaizhong.

Seeing Gangxiao coming to block his army,

Shuangxian rode his elephant to meet the challenge.

---

① Golden prayer flag: a colorful umbrella-like decoration with ribbons, which is made of fine silk and fixed on the howdah.
② Gaozao: a sharp weapon.
③ Huanghehan: a long spear with a coating of golden powder.

厘俸 // Li Feng

两军相对杀声起，	The two sides fought face to face.
人喊马叫乱成团。	The shouts of soldiers and the weighing of horses covered the whole battlefield in disarray.
双线的兵丁，	Shuangxian's soldiers
个个武艺高强，	Were all highly skilled
两侧围击冈晓的兵，	And surrounded Gangxiao's troops from both sides.
专砍马脚和象脚。	They cut the feet of the enemies' horses and elephants.
占拜中卷鼻飞奔冲又闯，	Zhanbaizhong dashed and bumped
迎着冈晓来格斗。	To attack Gangxiao.
冈晓痛骂双线高声喊：	Gangxiao condemned Shuangxian severely and loudly:
"卡腊艾巴话①双线，	"Shuangxian, you *kala'aibahua*①.
数日前曾把你捉拿。	Several days ago you were caught by us
只因海罕太善良，	And would have been killed
否则你早已把命丧。	If it not for Haihan's kindness.
你靠谎言骗海罕，	You told lies and cheated Haihan
回去多吃了几天热饭。	And got the chance to go back and live a few days longer.
现在你又杀心起，	Now you go so far as
胆敢再次来挑战。	Venturing to challenge us again.
天理人情不容忍，	This is intolerable in terms of both heavenly principles and human feelings.
你要遭雷公惩罚。"	You will definitely be punished by the God of Thunder!"
双线嘴硬把话讲：	Shuangxian ignored this accusation and said:
"卡腊艾巴话冈晓，	
你虽曾把我抓住，	

① 卡腊艾巴话：说话口吃的下贱人。

① Kala'aibahua: a stammer of low status.

想不到我今天又骑着战象，	"Gangxiao, you *kala'aibahua*!
要和你交战。	You did capture me for a while.
我用甜言蜜语欺骗了海罕，	But you never expected that I could once again
他因此才放我归山。	Ride my elephant and fight you!
其实我怎么能归顺海罕？	I deceived Haihan with sugary words
想当年，	To make him let me go.
海罕为了与婻崩成婚，	How could it be possible for me to yield to Haihan?
命令我把鸡卦看。	Back in the old days
多次卜卦，	When he was going to marry Nanbeng,
都不吉祥，	He asked me to tell his fortune by looking at some chicken bones.
使海罕失望。	But none of the divinations
海罕发怒，	Was propitious and auspicious.
他用鸡卦在裤裆里一摸，	This made Haihan quite disappointed
就戳在我的眼睛上。	And even furious.
当我走出宫廷时，	He took out a chicken bone from his trouser pocket
你安然而坐态度傲慢，	And stabbed it straight into my eye.
高高在我之上。	When I walked out of the palace,
我受了侮辱不能忍受，	You were still sitting there peacefully and arrogantly,
投奔俸改为了报仇。	Showing superiority over me.
在俸改那里我完全两样，	I could not put up with such humiliation
自由自在地出入宫廷。	So I went to serve Fenggai and waited for later revenge.
俸改对我从不傲慢，	In Mengjinhan I was treated in a totally different way.
将领敬我把我高抬，	I could go to the palace freely.
人人称我大哥使我喜欢。	

厘俸 // Li Feng

前后对比我怒火中烧,
我今天要和你决一死战!"
冈晓冷笑一声把话讲:
"双线啊,双线,
你过河来到对岸,
怎能随便把大话讲?
即使龙王不把你吞掉,
苍天也不能容忍你的猖狂!"
话刚说完一声令下,
士兵奋勇向前冲杀。
冈晓与双线也开始交战,
双线把护身宝石一摇,
顿时,
风驰电掣雷声震撼,
山摇地动天昏地暗。
两头战象势均力敌,
象牙交错格格发响。
冈晓的长矛飞舞直刺双线,
双线的铠甲坚固难穿。
占拜中吼声连天,
猛冲、猛撞占拜温。
占拜温倒退几步,
扑倒在地上。
天神在旁看了大吃一惊,

Fenggai was never insolent and rude to me.
His officials and generals also treated me in a respectful way
And they called me "elder brother" in an intimate way.
The more I compare these two, the more I am burning with anger.
Today I will fight you to the end!"
Gangxiao sneered and said:
"Shuangxian, oh Shuangxian!
You are now on our side of the river.
How can you brag like that?
Even if the Dragon King does not swallow you,
Heaven will not be able to tolerate your insaneness and madness!"
Hardly had his words faded away
When his troops dashed out to fight.
Gangxiao and Shuangxian began to combat each other.
Shuangxian shook his treasure bag amulet to pray for protection.
Suddenly
Wind galloped and thunder roared,
Earth quaked and the sky dimmed.
The two elephants fought head to head.
Their tusks collided with each other, making a squeaky sound.

双线趁机挥矛直刺,	Gangxiao aimed spear straight towards Shuangxian
冈晓的铠甲被刺穿,	But the spear could not pierce into his hard armor.
只见鲜血喷涌,	Zhanbaizhong shouted out with roaring cries
染红了占拜温的皮毛。	And dashed forward to strike Zhanbaiwen,
冈晓面色苍白身负重伤。	Who was forced to take several steps back
正在危急关头援兵来到,	And then fell down on the ground.
冈晓的结拜兄弟艾包和尼崩,①	The gods were surprised to see this happen.
桑混伦和赛道,②	Shuangxian seized the chance and stabbed Gangxiao.
还有波道坚混缅③,	His spear pierced into Gangxiao's armor.
曾饮鸡血酒,	Blood gushed out
共发誓言,	And colored the hair of Zhanbaiwen red.
愿同生共死。	Gangxiao was seriously injured and looked pale.
他们一齐蹬着战象,	At this critical moment his back-up troops arrived.
举矛直刺占拜中。	Gangxiao's sworn brothers, Ai Bao, Ni Beng,①
双线驱赶战象后退,	Sang Hunlun, Sai Dao,②
占拜中也身负重伤难熬。	And Bodaojianhunmian③ all came to rescue him.
双方士卒仍在混战,	They once drank wine with drops of chicken blood
只见刀矛寒光闪闪,	As a token of their oath
杀声刺耳,刀剑叮当响!	To live and die together.
鲜血四溅染满脸膛儿,	Now they rode on their war elephants
如小河流淌。	And aimed their spears together at Zhanbaizhong.

① 艾:老大。尼:老二。
② 桑:老三。赛:老四。
③ 波道坚混缅:勐缅(今普洱或临沧)的长官。

① Ai: the first brother. Ni: the second brother.
② Sang: the third brother. Sai: the fourth brother.
③ Bodaojianhunmian: the magistrate of Mengmian (in today's Pu'er or Lincang).

厘俸 // Li Feng

放眼望去，
令人心惊胆战。
冈晓掉转战象高声斥责：
"双线啊，双线，
你的阴谋一时得逞，
但你决坐不稳大象。
今天我虽然受了伤，
但勐景罕的主人一定要换，
我冈晓将占有勐景罕！
今日收兵回营，
待来日，
再见分晓。"
两军各自鸣鼓收兵，
战场上尸横遍野，
犹如乌云遮月亮，
暗淡无光。

Shuangxian had to withdraw
Because Zhanbaizhong was also seriousry injured.
The soldiers from both sides continued to fight.
The cold flash of sword and spear could be seen.
Battle cries and the clattering of swords could be heard.
Blood gushed out and stained the faces of the soldiers,
Flowing like a river.
Whoever looked about
Would be shocked by such a terrible sight.
Gangxiao turned back and cursed loudly:
"Shuangxian, oh Shuangxian!
Your dirty tricks have worked for the time being.
But you will never continue to sit still on the back of
　　　your elephant.
Although I am wounded today,
I still have the determination to change the master of
　　　Mengjinghan.
I will occupy and take Mengjinghan!
I will withdraw my troops today
And wait for another battle in the days to come.
Let's wait and see!"
The two sides then beat gongs and withdrew their armies
　　　respectively.
The battlefield was a scene of great carnage,

	Like a gloomy moon
	Covered by dark clouds.
消息传到花果山，	The news reached the Mountain of Flowers and Fruits.
海罕拔出宝刀怒声呵斥：	Haihan pulled out his treasured sword and reproached himself angrily:
"平时你们吹嘘如何勇敢，	"Quite often you boast of your bravery,
所向无敌以一当百，	Your invincibility and your powerfulness,
破一勐之地只需一头战象。	Saying you need only one elephant to conquer a *meng*.
现在和双线交战，	Now when you encountered Shuagnxian and his troops,
却损兵折将。	You suffered such heavy casualties.
我恨不得挥刀将冈晓斩！	I really itch to kill and decapitate Gangxiao!
我要杀一儆百让众人看。"	I want to make his death a big warning to others."
布冈伴和布冈戈急忙跪拜说：	Bugang Ban and Bugang Ge both knelt down to plead:
"亲爱的召海法海罕，	"Dear respectable Zhao Haifa Haihan!
斩了冈晓犹如丢了十个冈①，	Killing Gangxiao is just like losing ten *gangs*①.
犹如丢了万头战象。	Or losing ten thousand elephants!
不再有人愿意佩带宝刀，	If you kill Gangxiao,
为你冲锋陷阵去打仗。	No one else will be willing to put on their swords and fight for you.
自古只有猛将战死沙场，	Ever since ancient times brave generals have fought to death in the battlefield
没有死于主帅的刀枪。	Rather than be killed by their commander-in-chief.
请你考虑吧，	
尊敬的召海法海罕！	
我们可以写信给冈晓，	

---

① 冈：勐。　　　　　　　　　　① Gang: *meng*.

厘俸 // Li Feng

叫他重整旗鼓与双线再战，
如果还不能战胜双线，
那就叫他自己把头割下，
那时无人再说情，
我们的召海法啊！"
海罕听了把头点，
命令冈庄走过来，
满脸怒气把话讲：
"你是冈晓的亲弟弟，
去把我的书信交，
再把我的命令传。
明日出战要取胜，
否则撤职斩首不留情，
还要满门全家来抄斩。
事情紧急快备马，
日夜兼程把路赶！"
冈庄叩头接军令，
转身起程奔路上。
急行一日见冈晓，
交出书信传命令。
冈晓伤势已好转，
冈庄叩头说道：
"我亲爱的兄长，
你如同一只笼中鸡，

Think it over,
Our respectable Zhao Haifa Haihan!
We can write a letter to Gangxiao,
Commanding him to rally his army and fight again with Shuangxian.
If he fails once again,
You can have his head cut off.
No one will intercede for him at that time.
Our respectable Zhao Haifa Haihan!"
Haihan nodded his head
And asked Gangzhuang to come over.
He said in an angry voice:
"You are the younger brother of Gangxiao.
You go and give him
My letter and pass him my order.
Tomorrow he must fight again and win the battle,
Otherwise he will be decapitated without mercy.
His entire family will also be killed or slaughtered.
The situation is urgent.
Get your horse ready and hurry on your journey day and night."
Gangzhuang kowtowed to receive the order
And quickly left.
After one day's ride at full speed he met Gangxiao

只等别人把酒下。	And passed the letter to him.
你如同砧板上的一块肉,	Gangxiao's wound was getting better.
只等葱姜蒜来锅里炒。	Gangzhuang kowtowed to him and said:
想当初,	"My dear elder brother,
你挑选的战象力大又勇敢,	You are now like a rooster in a cage
象牙粗壮亮汪汪,	Waiting to become other people's dish to go with their wine.
凶猛异常!	You are now like a piece of meat on the cutting board
可是现在反被别人来刺伤。	Waiting to be fried in a pot with onion, ginger and garlic.
你调转象头败下阵,	I can still remember the time
暴跳如雷是海罕。	When your elephant was strong and brave,
他一怒之下要把你斩,	Fighting fiercely
二位军师忙求情,	With his shining and thick tusks!
才免你一死保性命。	But now instead you have been injured.
海罕叫我把命令传,	On hearing that you were defeated,
下次再战必取胜,	Haihan became furious.
否则性命就要丧!	In a rage he decided to kill you.
管辖的十冈也收回。	His two counselors pleaded for you
请你想一想,	And thus saved your neck.
我亲爱的兄长!"	Haihan asked me to pass on his order,
冈晓听了怒火燃,	Requiring you to win the next battle.
又吐唾沫又跺脚,	If not, you will surely lose your life
震得帐篷摇晃晃。	And also the ten *gangs* under your administration.
他又急又气开了口:	Please think it over
"兄长我虽身中枪刺,	My dear elder brother!"

厘俸 // Li Feng

但有牙窝莱和牙黄，①	On hearing these words Gangxiao simmered with rage.
很快可以治好伤。	He spat and he stamped his feet,
亲爱的弟弟啊，	Quaking and shivering his tent.
海罕的头领多又多，	He started to talk in an impatient and angry way:
但无人敢把先锋当。	"I, your elder brother, received several wounds.
海罕的饭人人吃，	But I have *yawolai* and *yahuang*.①
但无人拔出宝刀当先锋。	That may quickly heal my wounds.
只有我冈晓一人打头阵，	My dear younger brother,
忠心卖命为海罕。	Haihan has so many generals
可是到头来还要把首斩，	But few dare to fight in the vanguard.
真叫我有口难言说不出。	Many people rely on Haihan for a living
战斗失利不怪我，	But few would pull out their swords and march in the front.
只因坐骑受了伤。	Only I, Gangxiao, take the lead
此仇不报我不瞑目，	And fight for Haihan with great loyalty.
我和双线的事也不会完！"	But eventually I was almost decapitated
说完怒目举长矛，	And this really embarrasses me.
长矛对准占拜温就刺，	The failure of the battle was not due to me
占拜温号叫着乱蹦跳。	Because my elephant was injured.
冈晓转身亲手敲战鼓，	I won't close my eyes and die before I take revenge.
将士耳听鼓声震天响，	I will continue to fight Shuangxian!"
急忙蹬象上战场。	Gangxiao raised his spear

---

① 牙窝莱：牙，一种草药；窝莱，叶呈花色，即花仙草。牙黄：能医治枪伤，百步之后伤势即愈合。

① Yawolai: Ya means "herbal medicine". Wolai refers to a kind of grass with colorful flower-like leaves. Yahuang: herbal medicine that can cure gunshot wounds and sword cuts within minutes.

冈晓紧扣九层甲,
宝石背袋肩上挎,
缀有金丝带的宝刀挂胸前,
头盔闪闪发光亮。
披戴完毕大步走,
边走边把命令下:
"这次务必打胜仗,
要把双线的首级来割下。
祈求众神来保佑,
活捉俸改和战象。
只要我的幢崩舍①迎风展,
临阵逃兵首级落。
全军战象齐列阵,
列列队行紧相连,
冲锋齐向前!"
冈晓左手举旗指向前,
右手握宝刀插云霄,
左右将士杀声起,
势如破竹不可挡。
冈晓在怒吼,
战象斗志昂。
将士如卷风,

And stabbed at Zhanbaiwen in an angry way.
Zhanbaiwen howled and bounced about.
Gangxiao then turned to beat a drum.
Hearing the thundering sound of drum beats, all the officers and soldiers
Mounted their elephants and marched to the battlefield.
Gangxiao fastened his nine-layer armor,
Carried over his shoulder the treasure bag amulet,
Hung in front of his chest his sword decorated with golden ribbons,
And put on his shining and sparkling helmet.
He then strode out
And gave his order:
"We must win the battle this time,
And cut off Shuangxian's head!
I earnestly pray for support from the gods
So that I can catch Shuangxian and his elephant alive.
As long as my *zhuangbengshe*① is fluttering in the wind,
Anyone who shirks from the battle will be killed.
The war elephants now all stand in array
One after another.

---

① 幢崩舍:绣有虎形图案的幡幢。

① Zhuangbengshe: prayer flags with embroidery of tiger images.

厘俸 // Li Feng

摧枯拉朽!　　　　　　　　　　Let's begin to march forward."
　　　　　　　　　　　　　　　Gangxiao pointed the flag in his left hand forward
　　　　　　　　　　　　　　　And held his treasured sword in his right hand.
　　　　　　　　　　　　　　　The officers and the soldiers fought along both sides
　　　　　　　　　　　　　　　With irresistible force.
　　　　　　　　　　　　　　　Gangxiao roared
　　　　　　　　　　　　　　　And his elephant was highly-spirited .
　　　　　　　　　　　　　　　The officers and the soldiers swept over the battlefield
　　　　　　　　　　　　　　　Like a tornado.

双线见冈晓又出战,　　　　　　Shuangxian met Gangxiao's new charge head-on
敲鼓鸣炮急相迎。　　　　　　　With rapid drum beats and cannon sounds.
两强相遇如斗鸡,　　　　　　　Both sides fought like red-eyed gamecocks
分外眼红不相让。　　　　　　　With no intention of letting up.
双线驱赶占拜中,　　　　　　　Shuangxian rode his Zhanbaizhong
迎着冈晓直冲上。　　　　　　　And dashed towards Gangxiao.
身后兵丁紧紧跟,　　　　　　　Some soldiers followed Shuangxian closely
吼声如雷震大地。　　　　　　　With thunder-like shouts and roars.
冈晓的占拜温稳如山,　　　　　Gangxiao's elephant Zhanbaiwen, however,
四脚扣地有力量。　　　　　　　Stood steadily and firmly on the ground.
两象交锋,　　　　　　　　　　The two elephant's tusks struck each other
牙响如疾风吹树干,　　　　　　With a sound like tree trunks
咔咔嚓嚓响。　　　　　　　　　Snapped off by a strong wind.
两军交锋用刀矛,　　　　　　　The soldiers fought with swords and spears,

刀矛交错叮当响。	Making sound of clanging metal.
双方伤亡数不清，	The injured and the dead were countless.
拼死相杀不退让。	But neither side had any intention of giving up.
冈晓紧紧咬牙关，	Gangxiao clenched his teeth,
胡须在飞扬！	With his beard swinging in the wind.
怒视双线眼喷火，	Gangxiao glowered at Shuangxian
伺机把双线打落。	And watched for his chance to defeat him.
双线见状怒火起，	Shuangxian was burning with fiery wrath
指着冈晓就大骂：	And could not help cursing Gangxiao:
"冈晓啊，冈晓，	"Gangxiao, oh Gangxiao!
听说你已死亡，	They say that you are dead already.
为何今日又来捣乱？	How come you come to make trouble again?
前次交锋中我一矛，	You were stabbed by my spear last time.
已把你送往阴间。	You should have been on your way to the underworld.
今天又要来寻死，	Today you come to seek death again
看你左右拼命胡乱闯。	By dashing about desperately.
现在你我来交锋，	Let's now fight face to face,
不知老天留谁在世上！"	And let our fate be decided by heaven!"
冈晓从容来回答：	Gangxiao replied in a calm way:
"天意必留我和海罕，	"Heaven definitely will leave Haihan and me alive in this world.
你口吐狂言脸不红，	You are talking sheer nonsense with no sense of shame.
不到死时话不完，	You won't stop talking nonsense till you die.
今日我决不把你放！"	I will surely not let you go today!"
说完举矛直刺占拜中。	

厘俸 // Li Feng

占拜温甩鼻腾空翻，	Gangxiao then raised his spear and threw it towards Zhanbaizhong.
两象拼死来格斗，	Zhanbaiwen swung his trunk in the air
烟尘蔽天日，	And fought with Zhanbaizhong with the greatest force.
不见人马战象。	The dust veiled the sky
双线舞矛似闪电，	And the soldiers, the horses, the elephants just could not see each other.
令人眼花又缭乱。	Shuangxian waved his spear as quickly as a flash
冈晓沉着来应战，	In an eye-dazzling and bewildering way.
寻找机会来下手。	Gangxiao met the attack steadily and calmly,
忽见双线护耳落地上，	Seeking for the appropriate opportunity to fight back.
冈晓手疾眼快，	Suddenly Shuangxian's ear-protector dropped to the ground.
一矛刺中双线耳腮帮。	With his keen eyes and agile hands
双线翻身滚落象，	Gangxiao seized the chance and stabbed Shuangxian on the cheek.
一只脚还倒跨在象身上。	Shuangxian fell off his elephant,
脖上的红绸把头盖，	But one of his feet still hung on the back of his elephant.
占拜中拖着双线东奔西闯。	His head was covered by the red silk from his neck.
冈晓兵丁见状，	Zhanbaizhong ran about madly, dragging Shuangxian along.
发出一片胜利的狂叫，	Seeing this, the soldiers on Gangxiao's side
驱赶战象紧追上，	Cried out cheerful shouts of victory
将占拜中团团围在正中央。	And chased Shuangxian's elephant closely.
只见手起刀落一声响，	
金幢已经落地下。	
又听一片呐喊声，	
双线的首级已被砍。	
双线的兵丁军心散，	

冈晓俘敌一万又四千。	Zhanbaizhong was surrounded by a tight ring.
铓鼓齐鸣全军欢呼,	With a quick raise of a hand and a quick fall of a sword,
占拜中被俘,众围观,	The golden prayer flag broke and fell to the ground.
只见鲜血滴滴淌。	There was another cheerful shout of victory
冈晓命令拿篾笼,	Announcing that Shuangxian has been decapitated.
双线的首级往里装,	Shuangxian's soldiers lost all their courage
又将占拜中这头被俘的花象,	And fourteen thousand of them became Gangxiao's captives.
一同送去给海罕。	Gongs and drums were beat at the same time and the whole army cheered.
海罕见了心喜欢,	
连忙把兵丁来询问:	A bloody Zhanbaizhong was also captured
"为何冈晓不前来?	And draw a large crowd to look.
一同庆祝打胜仗。	Gangxiao asked his men
快快派人去请他,	To put Shuangxian's head into a cage,
我要用金杯盛酒来嘉奖。	And sent it, together with the captured elephant Zhanbaizhong,
还要送给他帅罕①,	To Haihan.
祝他长寿又健康。"	
侍从官接令忙动身,	Haihan was happy with all this
快马加鞭来到冈晓前。	And asked:
只见遍地是营帐,	"Why doesn't Gangxiao come along
欢声笑语四处传。	To celebrate the victory together?
侍从官叩头见冈晓,	I will soon send somebody to invite him.
忙把来意细细讲:	I will reward him with gold cups filled with wine.

---

① 帅罕:金项链。

厘俸 // Li Feng

混勐①请召生黑②去欢庆，
其余头领也前往。
剩下的坚守营寨要站岗，
战马、战象要喂饱。
请你动身吧，
我们的召生黑冈晓。"
冈晓手持酒杯摸胡须，
听完之后心里想：
"前战失利遭训斥，
令我痛心又难堪，
为人手下真困难。
听营中鼓声不停，
酒杯叮当响。
我不知如何是好，
心里乱！
为海罕两战双线，
为海罕出征勐景罕，
受苦担险从不怨，
他是我的混勐理应当。
现在传令把我请，
一片好意难推辞，
往事如烟算了吧，

I will give him a *shuaihan*① as a gift,
And wish him longevity and good health."
His attendant set out
And rode a horse at top speed to meet Gangxiao.
Tents were seen everywhere
And joyful sounds were spreading far and wide.
The attendant kowtowed to Gangxiao
And explained his purpose in coming:
Hunmeng② invites Zhao Shenghei③ for a celebration.
Your generals and officers may also go with you.
Those who stay should keep alert
And feed the war horses and elephants well.
Let's now set out,
Our Zhao Shenghei Gangxiao."
Hearing this, Gangxiao held a wine cup in his hand
And touched his beard thoughtfully:
"Haihan's rebuke on my failure in the last battle
Still makes me feel distressed and embarrassed.
To go or not to go: that is the question.
I really don't know what to do
When I hear the constant drum beats
And the unceasing sound of wine glass tinkling.

---

① 混勐：对海罕的尊称。
② 召：官。生：高级官员。黑：勇猛。

① Shuaihan: gold necklace.
② Hunmeng: here a respectful way to address Haihan.
③ Zhao: official. Sheng: high-ranking official. Hei: brave.

把它放在脚底板！"	I feel very confused!
想到这里把令下，	It is for Haihan that I fought Shuangxian twice.
牵出占拜温罩上象舆。	It is for Haihan that I went on an expedition to Mengjinghan.
召集众将集合起，	I take all the sufferings and hardship for granted
鸣鼓开道向花果山。	Just because he is my respectable Hunmeng Haihan.
来到花果山见海罕，	Now he sends his attendant to invite me for a victory celebration.
海罕设宴摆酒已妥当。	It is impossible to reject such a well-intentioned invitation.
冈晓骑上占拜温一马当先，	Past events should have faded like puffs of smoke.
脖系铃铛响叮当！	Let them be and never take them seriously!"
众将齐拥后，	Gangxiao then decided to go
冈晓一行抵营寨，	And asked his men to put the howdah on the back of Zhanbaiwen.
齐下象。	He summoned his generals and officers to go with him
混勐相迎见冈晓，	To the Mountain of Flowers and Fruits.
面带笑容把手招。	They arrived there and met Haihan.
冈晓略一迟疑把头叩，	The banquet was ready.
海罕弯腰来相扶，	Gangxiao rode his mount Zhanbaiwen in the front,
又把帅罕挂在他的脖子上，	The bell tinkling on the elephant's neck.
祝冈晓长寿又健康。	Gangxiao, followed by his generals,
海罕开口面带笑：	Arrived at the king's camp.
"你辛苦了，	They got off their elephants together.
我的冈晓！	Hunmeng Haihan came out to meet Gangxiao,
为讨伐勐景罕，	Waving his hand and smiling.
风餐露宿不顾寒和暖。	
你有功劳啊，	

厘俸 // Li Feng

我的冈晓弟！"
海罕手捧金杯斟满酒，
递给冈晓心意表。
又把金杯传众将，
连声慰问辛苦了。
宴席盛大酒菜香，
摆满桌子一盘盘。
席间互相来碰杯，
只听一片杯盘响。
吃又吃来喝又喝，
吃饱喝足心欢畅。
宴会结束海罕起，
又和冈晓把战事来商量。

Gangxiao hesitated for a second but finally kowtowed
　　　to Haihan.
Haihan stooped to raise him,
And then hung the *shuaihan* on his neck,
Blessing Gangxiao with longevity and good health.
Haihan said, still smiling:
"You've fought so hard,
My dear Gangxiao!
In order to defeat Mengjinghan,
You've gone through various trials in the wilderness and
　　　awful weather.
You have made great contributions,
My dear younger brother Gangxiao!"
Haihan filled the gold wine cup in his hand
And passed it to Gangxiao to show his sincerity.
The wine cup was passed to all the generals and officers
To show Haihan's commendation.
It was a big banquet
With so many dishes and lots of wine on the tables.
People proposed toasts to each other
With the clinking of wine glasses.
People ate and drank
Till they were greatly contented.
Haihan rose to his feet at the end of the banquet

	And began to discuss the war situation with Gangxiao.
召桑洛和嘿南在另一战场，	Zhao Sangluo and Heinan were fighting in another battlefield,
围攻勐冈老和勐冈桑，	Besieging Meng Ganglao and Meng Gangsang.
双方正在激战。	Both sides were fighting fiercely.
阿巫戛见到这种情况，	When Awu Ga noticed such a situation,
就劝告两位主将：	He persuaded the two generals:
"召桑洛啊，召桑洛，	"Zhao Sangluo, oh, Zhao Sangluo!
刀不快莫把竹节砍，	Do not cut bamboo joints if your knife is not sharp enough,
刀刃卷曲无人修。	For nobody can repair the broken blade for you.
人不勇猛将不多，	Do not attack a city
就不要把城来攻。	If you do not have enough brave generals.
听我阿巫戛的劝告吧，	Listen to my advice.
不要再打没有希望的仗。	Do not fight a hopeless war.
今夜赶快撤离，	Abandon your positions tonight
迅速靠近海罕。"	And move to be close to Haihan."
桑洛听了来回答：	Sangluo replied:
"攻不下冈老和冈桑，	"I fail to take Ganglao and Gangsang
并不是由于我无能，	Not because I am incompetent
而是没有听从你指教。	But because I did not follow your instruction.
前次出征勐景罕，	Last time when I went on an expedition to Mengjinghan,
不但未得手，	I not only failed
反被讥笑出丑相，	

厘俸 // Li Feng

巴札哇①奚落说：

'你是哪里来的小毛孩，

赶着水牛②来找麻烦。'

我十分生气把话讲：

'我的妻子被俸改抢，

所以来攻打勐景罕。'

巴札哇听了哈哈笑道：

'来者为贵客，

欢迎你到勐景罕玩耍、嬉闹！

喜欢打哪里，

随便你去打。

不过你小心别把路走错，

否则回不了家。'

说完他掉转马头回城了，

我只好垂头丧气往家返。

这次教训我永难忘！

现在我听你的指教吧，

夺不回娥宾我心不甘。

我的阿巫戛啊，

请求你来帮助我！"

桑洛退兵后，

阿巫戛就把石头变大象，

But was also jeered and sneered at.

Bazhawa① laughed at me and said:

'Where are you from little lad?

You are driving your buffalos② to make trouble.'

I said angrily:

'My wife was captured by Fenggai.

That's why I came to attack Mengjinghan.'

Bazhawa replied with laughter:

'All the visitors are our respected guests.

We welcome you to play and have fun in Mengjinghan!

You can go and attack

Wherever you want to attack.

But be careful not to take the wrong way.

Otherwise you won't be able to go home.'

He finished his words and went back to the city.

I had no choice but to go back home downheartedly.

That was really an unforgettable lesson for me!

Now I would like to follow your advice.

I won't give up until I can take back my wife Ebing.

Oh, my Awu Ga!

Please come to help me!"

When Sangluo had withdrawn his army,

---

① 巴札哇：俸改的将领。
② 把象比作水牛。

① Bazhawa: one of Fenggai's generals.
② Buffalos: Figuratively, it refers to "war elephants".

芭蕉变成人，	Awu Ga transformed rocks into elephants,
森林变帐篷，	Banana trees into soldiers,
到处安营寨，	And forests into tents.
团团围住冈老和冈桑。	Then it looked like there were tents and camps everywhere,
阿巫夏又将桑洛的情况告海罕，	Tightly surrounding Ganglao and Gangsang.
同时为桑洛来求情，	Awu Ga then went to report to Haihan about Sangluo's situation
海罕听了心中不欢畅。	And begged for leniency.
	Haihan was not happy about that.
第二天天刚亮，	The next day at dawn,
布冈老、布冈桑吃过早饭，	When the chiefs of Ganglao and Gangsang had just finished their breakfast,
只见深山密林树枝摇，	They saw wobbling tree branches
里面有数不清的大象。	And countless elephants in the dense forest.
两人先是惊奇后悲伤，	They were at first surprised and soon became sorrowful.
大声哭来大声喊：	They shouted and cried loudly:
"桑洛的军队已经伤亡一大半，	"Half of Sangluo's troops are either injured or dead.
怎么还有这么多的兵马和大象？	How come there are still so many soldiers, horses and elephants?
就像洞中蚂蚁一团团，	They are like colonies of ants in an underground hole.
越打越多不会完。	The more you attack, the more they appear.
又像田中的稻穗密密麻，	They are like bunches of grain,
满田满坝一串串。"	Thickly dotting in the fields."

厘俸 // Li Feng

阿巫戛对海罕说：	Awu Ga said to Haihan:
"我的侄儿召海法啊，	"My nephew, respectable Zhao Haifa!
桑洛围攻冈老和冈桑，	Sangluo has not conquered Ganglao and Gangsang
久攻不破已撤兵，	And has now withdrawn his army
现在退到林中把营扎。	And pitched a camp in the forest.
望尘莫及心有气，	He is far behind his originally planned objective
如大病一场。	And is in a bad mood like someone who is ill.
你应出兵支援他，	You should go to support him.
否则难取冈老和冈桑。	Otherwise it will be difficult to take Ganglao and Gangsang.
冈老、冈桑不攻破，	Before Ganglao and Gangsang are conquered,
怎能直捣勐景罕？"	Attacking Mengjinghan directly is impossible."
海罕开口把话讲：	Haihan then said:
"杀鸡占卜看鸡卦，	"We need to kill a chicken first and tell fortune by looking at its bones.
选择吉日来占卜，	We need to choose an auspicious day for the divination.
命令召莫①捉鸡来，	Call Zhaomo① to catch a chicken
给鸡洗脸洗脚图吉祥。"	And wash its face and its feet for good luck."
边洗边来做祈祷：	The Zhaomo prayed while cleaning the chicken:
"神灵啊，	"Oh, gods,
请保佑我们的召②，	Please bless our Zhao② Haihan!
保佑召永远穿戴美丽，	Bless him to be always dressed in beautiful clothes!
保佑召幢③人人平安。	

① 召莫：巫师。
② 召：指海罕，即主子、主人的意思。
③ 召幢：赏赐有金幡幢的勐的首领。

① Zhaomo: wizard.
② Zhao: It refers to Haihan, meaning "master".

邪恶不沾身，	Bless all the Zhaozhuangs① to be safe and sound.
鸡卦显神灵。"	Bless them to be far away from evil spirits.
边说边把头来叩，	The divination now please reveal."
刀起血溅鸡蹬脚，	He kowtowed while saying these words.
手持曼该细端详。	Then he killed the chicken
喜见曼该两头相对称，	And examined the bones carefully.
如似他人送金杯。	He was happy to see the two ends of the selected bone were symmetrical
冈晓弹舌把话讲：	Like a gift gold cup.
"何必再把鸡卦看，	Gangxiao said impatiently:
双线的兵马我已俘，	"There is no need to check the chicken divination.
何不用计夺取冈老和冈桑？	Shuangxian's troops have been defeated.
请海罕给我俘获的双线坐骑占拜中，	Why don't we just use strategy to take Ganglao and Gangsang?
再给我双线戴过的莫央拍①。	Give me the elephant Zhanbaizhong that Shuangxian once rode,
我装扮成双线的模样，	And give me the *moyangpai*② that Shuangxian once put on.
前往冈老和冈桑。	I will dress up as Shuangxian
只要对方城门开，	And go to Ganglao and Gangsang.
我的兵丁就冲进城，	As soon as the city gate opens,
就能活捉布冈老和布冈桑。	My soldiers will dash into the city
如果此战不胜利，	And capture the chiefs of Ganglao and Gangsang alive.
从此不叫艾召生。"	
海罕听了连点头，	

① 莫央拍：头盔。

① Zhaozhuang: *meng* chiefs who are awarded golden prayer flags.
② Moyangpai: helmet.

厘俸 // Li Feng

命令牵出占拜中，
只见它一对象牙锐利又粗壮。
冈晓叩头回营寨，
身后跟随众将官。

If this tactic does not work and I do not win the battle,
I should no longer be called Ai Zhaosheng."
Haihan agreed with a nod
And give the order to lead out Zhanbaizhong by a pair
  of sharp and strong tusks.
Gangxiao kowtowed goodbye and returned to his tent,
Followed by his officers.

次日清晨天刚亮，
冈晓戴上双线的帽，
又把双线的衣服穿。
敲起双线的战鼓，
照双线的军队来装扮。
将士整装待出发，
冈晓又把命令下：
"派人通知桑洛和嘿南，
只等夜幕降，
一旦耳闻鼓声响，
伴装败退往回返。
化装的我军骗敌人，
诱使敌人开城门。
听到城门嘎嘎响，
我军冲进冈老城。
耳闻炮轰鸣，

The next day at the crack of dawn,
Gangxiao put on Shuangxian's helmet
And put on Shuangxian's clothes.
The soldiers beat Shuangxian's drums
And were dressed the way Shuangxian's soldiers dressed.
Everything was ready
When Gangxiao gave the order:
"Send someone to inform Sangluo and Heinan,
Tell them when the night falls
And when they hear the drum beat,
Pretend to be the retreating troops of Shuangxian.
The disguise will help us
To lure the enemy to open the city gate.
When we hear the squeaking sound of the gate opening,
We will dash into Ganglao city.
When you hear the gunshots and cannon sound,

急速把城围,	Come to the city quickly
千万莫进城。	To surround it instead of entering it.
碰到敌人来逃窜,	When you find the fleeing enemy,
迎头堵住歼灭光。"	Stop them and kill them all."
使者动身去送信,	The messenger quickly set out to send the message.
冈晓一切安排妥。	When everything was ready,
下令大军来出发,	Gangxiao gave orders to set forth.
马不停蹄人不歇。	The horses and the soldiers walked on and on without rest,
山谷密林成大道,	Making a trodden path in the forest.
走出山谷抬头看,	When they walked out of the forest,
冈老、冈桑现眼前。	Ganglao and Gangsang were in sight.
冈晓又把命令下:	Gangxiao gave another order:
"人人口中含树枝,	"Everyone must hold a small branch in his mouth
不准讲话出声响。"	To make sure that he does not speak or make a noise."
大军到达城墙下,	Finally the disguised army reached the city wall.
冈晓轻声细语喊:	Gangxiao shouted in a soft voice:
"尊敬的布冈老和布冈桑,	"Respectable chiefs of Ganglao and Gangsang!
听说海罕、桑洛万头大象来攻城,	It is said that Haihan and Sangluo are attacking your city with ten thousand of elephants.
混俸心里又焦急来又不安。	This made Hunfeng Fenggai anxious and uneasy.
指派侄儿我双线来援助,	He has appointed me, his nephew Shuangxian, to come to back you up.
请把城门快快开,	Please open the city gate
援兵进城同作战。	And let us enter the city and fight shoulder to shoulder.
尊敬的冈桑父母官!"	

厘俸 // Li Feng

两老布冈在城楼开了腔：
"海罕派桑洛来攻城，
我们奋起来抵抗，
城池未破安如山。
我们从未去求援，
你们究竟是何人？
是否海罕、桑洛人马来伪装？
为什么白天不到来，
天黑才来把门喊？"
冈晓稳坐象骑把话说：
"海罕的军队、千马和万象，
已攻克勐老、勐哈、帕生和帕缓。
由于互相不支援，
勐我、勐海又被占，
你们消息闭塞不知道。
还有勐谷、勐远已投降，
只因孤军守孤城，
没有援军才这般，
这些教训多么深！
我是混俸手下的将官，
按照命令带兵来支援。
共同守城来抵抗，
事紧急来莫迟疑，

Respectable magistrates of Ganglao and Gangsang!"
The two Bugangs replied from the wall:
"Haihan sends Sangluo to attack us.
We have made great efforts to resist their attacks
And made our city impregnable like a mountain.
This is why we never send for back-up.
So who on earth are you?
Are you the troops of Haihan and Sangluo in disguise?
Why don't you come in the daytime
Rather than at night?"
Gangxiao answered in a clam way:
"Menglao, Mengha, Meng Pasheng and Meng Pahuan have all been conquered
By Haihan's mighty force and invincible war horses and elephants.
Mengwo and Menghai are also occupied
Due to the lack of back-up.
You are too ill-informed to know all about this.
Moreover, Menggu and Mengyuan have surrendered to Haihan
Just because they fought on their own
And did not have reinforcements.
What costly lessons!
I am a general of Hunfeng Fenggai.

城门紧闭不应当。	I am commanded to come to support you.
如果敌军来突袭,	So let's guard the city hand in hand.
我们怎么能抵挡?	There is no time for hesitation in such a critical situation.
一切后果你们负,	You should have opened the city gate and welcomed us.
人员伤亡百倍还,	If there is a sudden attack from the enemy,
占拜中如遭劫难,	How can we resist it?
万倍来赔偿,	You must be responsible for all the consequences in that case.
还要金银千百两。	You will have to pay compensation for a hundred times of the actual injuries.
事情一旦像这样,	You will have to pay compensation, along with a large sum of gold and silver,
只能落得臭名扬。	Ten thousand times of the cost
想想吧,	If Zhanbaizhong gets wounded or killed.
亲爱的布冈老和布冈桑!"	If things turn out to be like this,
二位大布冈互相做暗示,	You will surely become infamous.
点燃火把仔细看,	Think it over,
只见四脚花象占拜中,	Dear chiefs of Ganglao and Gangsang!"
双线的头盔金光闪。	The two chiefs helped each other to see more.
大象尾上的毛如雪白的丝线,	By the light of torches,
确实是混俸的好坐骑,	They saw Zhanbaizhong's feet with patterns.
这是混俸信任双线让他骑。	They saw Shuangxian's helmet glittering.
头盔也确系双线戴,	They saw the snow-white silky hair on the tail of Zhanbaizhong.
兵丁的衣领和袖口,	
缀有金线果是双线的军队。	
两大布冈看了高声喊:	
"原以为海罕的军队来骗我们,	

厘俸 // Li Feng

因而迟疑不开门。
现在知道你们是混俸的真猛将，
双线也是混俸的侄儿，
我们马上来开门。"
只听咚咚嘎嘎连声响，
紧闭的城门已打开。
冈晓心中暗欢喜，
不动声色咬牙关，
双脚紧紧蹬大象，
只等城中的妇女哭叫找丈夫①。

It was indeed the elephant of Hunfeng Fenggai.
He trusted Shuangxian so much that he let Shuangxian ride the elephant.
The helmet was definitely Shuangxian's.
The collars and cuffs of the soldiers were embroidered with golden thread.
They were surely Shuangxian's soldiers.
The two chiefs then shouted loudly:
"We thought that you were the disguised army of Haihan.
That is why we hesitated and did not open the city gate.
Now we believe you are Hunfeng Fenggai's soldiers and generals.
We also know that Shuangxian is his nephew.
We will soon open the gate."
With creaking sounds
The city gate opened.
Gangxiao's heart leaped with joy
But he stayed calm and collected.
His feet clamped his elephant tightly,
Waiting for the women in the city to cry for their husbands.①

---

① 意为冈晓的军队入城后，将对方兵丁格杀，而妇女在战乱中纷纷哭叫寻找丈夫下落。在战争中对妇女是不加屠杀的，而将其俘掠为妻奴。

① When Gangxiao's troops enter the city, they will kill the enemy soldiers. Their wives, in such chaos caused by war, will search for their husbands' whereabouts. Women are usually not killed in wars. They are captured and made wives and slaves by the winning side.

冈晓的八万大军进了城,	Gangxiao's mighty force then entered the city.
占拜温紧跟占拜中之后。	Zhanbaiwen followed Zhanbaizhong.
两布冈捧出金杯酒,	The two chiefs held gold wine glasses,
兵丁列队欢迎站两旁。	Standing along the roadside with their lined soldiers in welcome.
东方拂晓天刚亮,	When dawn broke
冈晓的军队鸣炮击鼓又敲铓。	Drums were beaten and gongs struck in Gangxiao's army.
信号一发突开战,	The signal of war was released
刀砍矛戳杀声起,	And the two sides began to fight with their swords and spears.
就像春碓声一样。	There was a pourding clash of weapons everywhere.
尸横遍地如柴堆,	The dead bodies piled up like firewood.
小孩惊吓到处窜。	Children were so scared, rushing here and there.
敌人前仆又后继,	However, the enemy fought bravely and courageously,
拼死拼活来抵抗。	Resisting with every ounce of their strength.
占拜温、占拜中冲何处,	Wherever Zhanbaiwen and Zhanbaizhong charged,
何处似山倒塌, 敌丧胆。	There was an avalanche of terror.
布冈老牙齿打战,	The chief of Ganglao,
喊叫声发抖,	With his teeth chattering and his trembling shouts,
骑着大象冲向冈晓。	Rode his elephant towards Gangxiao.
冈晓沉着应战稳如山,	Gangxiao remained calm and collected like a mountain.
占拜中昂着卷鼻又怒吼,	Zhanbaizhong rolled up its trunk and roared angrily.
两象相遇不退让,	The two elephants did not give way to each other,
两将相见怒火上。	
布冈老手持长矛指冈晓,	

厘俸 // Li Feng

风驰电掣矛飞翻。
冈晓技高来躲闪,
布冈老矛落空而心发慌,
脸变青色怒火旺。
冈晓武艺精又精,
长矛猛一晃,
布冈老眼花缭乱,
身中一矛肋骨穿!
鲜血喷涌染人象。
扑通一声滚下来,
兵丁齐欢呼,
吼声传远方,
争先把头砍。
冈晓战象也有功,
象牙挑敌未间断,
鲜血滴滴往下淌。

布冈桑坚持顽抗不投降,
骑着大象又出战。
敲起战鼓咚咚响,
兵丁排队列阵一层层,

And the two generals on their backs simmered with rage.
The chief of Ganglao aimed his spear at Gangxiao
And threw it like lightning.
Gangxiao dodged the spear skillfully,
Making the chief of Ganglao panic, furious,
And blue in the face.
But unlike him, Gangxiao was a skillful warrior.
He used a make-believe thrust
To distract the chief of Ganglao, who was dazzled.
The spear finally pierced the chief's ribs!
Blood gushed from the wound and stained the chief
  and his elephant red.
The soldiers all hailed
When they saw the old chief fall off his elephant.
The soldiers wrestled to decapitate the old chief.
Their roars spread into the distance.
Gangxiao's elephant made great contributions in the battle.
It fought with its tusks without a break.
Blood dripped from a wounded tusk.

The chief of Gangsang showed no sign of giving up.
He rode his elephant to the battlefield again.
When the war drums beat,
The soldiers lined up in arrays,

把占拜中围在正中央。	Surrounding Zhanbaizhong in the center.
冈晓的军队如山立，	Gangxiao's army was as strong as a mountain,
严阵以待来应战。	Ready to fight against them.
两军杀得天昏地又暗，	The two armies fought fiercely and violently,
一场肉搏如旋风转，	And wrestled at close quarters like a whirlwind,
似剁生①搅拌，	Like mixing *duosheng*①
又如伐木刀砍树，	And chopping wood.
遍地横尸，	The battlefield was full of dead bodies
成堆成摞，	Piling up in a mound.
血流如小河！	Blood flowed like a stream!
布冈桑见势心惊胆战，	The chief of Gangsang was terrified by this scene,
掉转象头，	And turned his elephant away,
退入城中城②。	And retreated into the inner city②.
兵败如山倒，	The rout was like a landslide.
布冈桑的将士们互相践踏夺路逃。	The soldiers of Gangsang tried to escape.
冈晓紧跟不肯放，	Gangxiao did not give up
穷追猛打不停步。	And chased them immediately.
血战一场又一场，	There was battle after battle.
只见布冈桑的兵丁两边倒，	Gangsang's soldiers fell down on the ground
死的死伤的伤。	Either wounded or dead.
	The chief of Gangsang was trapped in a desperate situation.

---

① 剁生：生猪肉配上作料后剁细搅拌，即可食用。
② 城中城：即内城，多为上层人物居住。

① Duosheng: seasoned raw ground pork, a local delicacy.
② The inner city was where the upper classes lived.

厘俸 // Li Feng

布冈桑陷入绝境,	He had no choice but to fight his way out.
他只有背水一战。	He drove his elephant straight toward Gangxiao.
他蹬着大象迎冈晓,	The two elephants collided headlong with each other.
两头大象猛顶撞,	Their tusks crashed and rattled.
象牙交错格格响。	The chief of Gangsang waved his long spear like a flash.
布冈桑的长矛如闪电,	Gangxiao dodged and looked for opportunities to attack.
冈晓左挑右挡找机会。	And very soon he grabbed a chance
手疾眼快挺长矛,	To stab his spear into the chief of Gangsang,
一矛刺中布冈桑。	Who fell off his elephant.
布冈桑翻身落下象,	Gangxiao's *maozai*[①] scrambled to cut off his head.
冒宰[①]争相把头砍。	The roar of victory shook the inner city!
吼声震天内城撼!	The rest of Gangsang's soldiers fled in all directions.
残敌四散逃,	Gangxiao's soldiers chased after them closely,
冈晓的兵丁紧紧追。	Using their hooked spears
拿出钩镰枪,	To hook the enemy soldiers and their elephants.
钩人又钩象。	Fighting in the battle excited Zhanbaiwen,
占拜温东奔西突战得欢,	Making everyone terror-stricken by its mighty force.
敌人一见就丧胆。	Each *hong*[②] was caught in chaos.
各洪[②]乱哄哄,	The soldiers all put down their swords and spears,
大刀长矛纷纷放,	

[①] 冒宰:贴身卫士。西双版纳称为侍卫军,只有官员之子才能充当。
[②] 洪:小城子内的各个村落。

[①] Maozai: bodyguard. In Xishuangbanna, they are called "imperial bodyguard". Only the sons of government officials can be a *maozai*.
[②] Hong: hamlets within a small town.

口衔呀热草地下跪。①	Kneeling down with *yare* grass① in their mouths.
祈求召生黑把命饶：	They all begged Zhao Shenghei to spare their lives:
"已经杀了布冈老和布冈桑，	"You have already killed the chiefs of Ganglao and Gangsang.
砍树要留根，	When you cut trees, you leave the tree stumps.
不要把我们杀光。	So similarly please do not kill us all!
留下普囡宾海②，	Leave us to be your *punanbinhai*②
日后为你们砍柴割草，	To cut firewood and grass for you in the future.
召生黑冈晓啊。"	Oh! Zhao Shenghei Gangxiao."
战斗已经近尾声，	The war was coming to an end.
桑洛、嘿南也从南面冲入城。	Sangluo and Heinan dashed into the city from the south.
两军会师，	When the two forces joined triumphantly,
兵丁满城烟消散。	The city was full of their soldiers and the smoke of battle had dissipated.
战斗结束冈晓军令下：	Gangxiao gave a command after the war:
"两布冈的住宅谁也不能进，	"No one is allowed to enter the houses of the two chiefs.
要把门封闭，	Close the doors,
等待海罕前来看。"	And wait for Haihan to come and make an inspection."
兵丁有的安营寨，	Some of the soldiers then went to encamp,
有的清理战场。	While others cleaned up the battlefield.
众头领来来回回在奔忙，	
把战果向冈晓来报告。	

---

① 战败投降时，放下武器，跪在地上，把杂草、树枝或其他东西含在口中，表示投降。

② 普囡宾海：下对上的自称，即小人、奴隶之意。

① Yare grass: a kind of grass. When the soldiers are defeated, they put down their weapons and put grass or small tree branches in their mouth as a surrender gesture.

② Punanbinhai: a humble way to refer to oneself, meaning "servants, slaves".

厘俸 // Li Feng

桑洛、嘿南俘敌一千多，
回到城外守营帐。

Officers walked in and out of Gangxiao's tent
To report to him about their combat achievements.
Sangluo and Heinan captured more than one thousand enemy soldiers.
They now went back to guard their camps outside the city.

第二天拂晓天刚亮，
桑混①见面把事商。
三头战象真威风，
三把金幢金光闪。
冈晓手捻胡须眯眯笑，
接着把话讲：
"召桑洛啊，召桑洛，
你来攻打勐景罕，
要把妻子来讨还。
为什么久战不胜城不克？
为什么海罕的军队打胜仗？
而你打起仗来无气又无力，
就像病人一个样。
妻子怎能夺回到你身旁？
若不是我们来支援，
怎能攻下冈老和冈桑？

The next day at dawn,
The Sanghun① came to meet and discuss the war affairs.
The three owe-inspiring elephants were equipped with
Three glittering golden prayer flags on their backs.
Gangxiao touched his beard,
And said with a smile:
"Zhao Sangluo, oh Zhao Sangluo.
You came to attack Mengjinhan
To get your wife back.
Why after a long time of combat could not you still conquer the city?
Why does Haihan's army win battles all the time?
You fight in a feeble and weak way
Like a sick man.
How, in this case, could you take back your wife
If we did not come to help you?

---

① 桑：三。混：头领。桑混即三个头领。

① Sang: three. Hun: chief, head. Sanghun means "three chiefs".

我冈晓为了杀敌人，	How could you defeat Ganglao and Gangsang?
宝刀已经磨损直到把，	I, Gangxiao, in order to kill the enemy,
为的是把两混①的爱妻来讨还。	Have worn out my sword.
如今已取冈老和冈桑，	My only objective is to take back the wives of two *huns*①.
他们的住宅不准抢，	Now we have defeated Ganglao and Gangsang,
要让海罕前来看。	But we cannot take anything from the houses of the two chiefs.
报告的信件已送出，	We should wait for Haihan to come and check.
你们要执行命令严看管，	My report has been sent,
两布冈的住宅禁止受侵犯。"	And you should closely put a watch on the houses and carry out my command.
	Neither of their houses are allowed to be invaded."
海罕接信笑颜开，	After reading the letter,
对着信使把话讲：	Haihan's face lit up with pleasure:
"攻占冈老和冈桑，	"All our soldiers and generals have made contributions
兵丁有劳将有功。	In the process of defeating Ganglao and Gangsang.
城中的财富尽可抢，	As for the wealth in the city,
谁抢归谁理应当。	Those who grab it will become the owners.
两布冈的住宅也同样，	The same is true for the houses of the two chiefs.
住宅无须我来看。	I don't need to check their houses at all.
金银财宝我不稀罕，	Gold and silver and treasure are not what I care about.
夺回婻崩才是我所想。	Taking back my Nanbeng is what I want.

---

① 两混：指海罕、桑洛。

① The two *huns*: Here it refers to Haihan and Sangluo.

厘俸 // Li Feng

亲爱的艾召生弟弟啊，
我的心愿记心上！"
信使接令往回返，
冈晓又把军令传：
"所俘战象赶出来，
合理分配人人享。
滚勒汉显①要杀尽，
普勒该尼②留活命，
二者对待不一样。"
一切占伙③分配完，
冈晓转身回营帐。
大队人马相跟随，
人欢马叫战鼓响。
俘虏的俸少④随军到，
沦为冈晓滚赖⑤的妻。
俸少日晒如火烤，
脸发烫，汗流淌，
脚上血泡步难行，
身欲倒。
只因俸改太作恶，

Dear younger brother Ai Zhaosheng,
Please keep my wishes in mind!"
The messenger then returned with the order.
Gangxiao made a new command:
The captured elephants should be gathered
And distributed in a reasonable way.
*Gunlehanxian*① should all be killed,
While *pulegaini*② should survive.
The two groups should be treated differently."
When all the *zhanhuo*③ was divided up,
Gangxiao went back to his camp.
His army followed him,
With soldiers cheering and horses whinnying.
The captured *fengshaos*④
Became the wives of Gangxiao's *gunlai*⑤.
Burned by the scorching sunlight,
Their faces turned red and their sweat streamed.
With blisters on their feet,
They could hardly walk.
Just because of Fenggai's evil deeds,

---

① 滚勒汉显：有武艺的恶人。
② 普勒该尼：善良的驯服者。
③ 占伙：财产，包括人、畜、财物。
④ 俸少：成群的未婚少女。
⑤ 冈晓滚赖：指冈晓的兵将。

① Gunleihanxian: fighters who are skillful and evil.
② Pulegaini: kind persons who surrender.
③ Zhanhuo: property, including persons, cattle, money and goods.
④ Fengshao: a host of unmarried young maids.
⑤ Gangxiao gunlai: Gangxiao's officers and soldiers.

百姓遭殃受煎熬。	People suffered so much.
兵丁赶路日夜行，	Then the soldiers marched day and night
已到海罕驻扎的大本营。	To get to the base camp where Haihan stayed.
见遍地营帐相连接，	Everywhere tent after tent was seen.
大象悠闲把食觅。	The war elephants foraged leisurely.
冈晓坐骑停蹄，	Gangxiao's elephant stopped.
卸舆放装，	The howdah was removed and the equipment unfastened.
安扎营寨！	It was time to put up tents for rest!
桑洛、嘿南也来到，	Sangluo and Heinan also arrived.
脸上无光愧疚无语。	They felt too ashamed to say anything.
太阳初升天大亮，	When the sun rose and day broke,
众将领前来叩拜海罕。	The officers paid a formal visit to Haihan.
战冈老、冈桑获大胜，	After winning a convincing victory over Ganglao and Gangsang,
奉献成群的马和象，	Herds of horses and elephants were offered as tribute
金子银子驮马上。	As well as gold and silver carried on the horses' back.
海罕下令奖全军，	Haihan gave the command to reward the whole army
战象是奖品，	With elephants,
还有美丽的色披罕①。	And beautiful *sepihan*①.
再把板汉阿明②来举行，	After that the ritual of *banhan* and *aming* was held.②
全军兵将心欢畅。	All the soldiers and officers were in a cheerful mood.
布冈桑的女儿也被俘，	

---

① 色披罕：缀有精致图案的战袍、衣服。
② 板汉：叫魂。阿明：祝福，祝贺。

① Sepihan: war robes or clothes with exquisite and fine patterns and designs.
② Banhan: soul-calling. Aming: blessing, congratulation.

厘俸 // Li Feng

一个赐给弟弟召桑洛作奖赏。
一个赐给混嘿南，
为他铺床睡觉把身暖。
布冈老的小女儿也被抓，
赐给弟弟冈晓作财产。
金银奖给有功者，
鼓励他们打胜仗。
混勐又把命令传：
"两布冈的首级绸缎包，
莫①举杯来祭神灵。
让他俩的灵魂留在地，
等俸改死后一同把天上。
双混陶勐②啊！"
一切安排妥当，
摆酒设宴庆功忙。

The daughters of the chief of Gangsang were also
　　　captured.
One was presented to Zhao Sangluo as a gift,
The other was given to Hun Heinan,
To make his bed and warm him while he slept.
The youngest daughter of the chief of Ganglao was also
　　　captured.
She was presented to Gangxiao as his property.
Gold and silver were awarded to everyone who contributed
　　　to the battles
And encourage them to win more victories.
Hunmeng Haihan gave another command:
"The silk cloth used to wrap the two Bugang's heads
Should be offered as sacrifice to the gods by the *mo*①.
The soul of the two chiefs should remain
And wait for the soul of Fenggai to leave the world
　　　together.
Dear Shuanghun Taomeng②！"
Everything was ready.
Everyone took part in the celebration and feasts.

---

① 莫：占卜师。
② 双混：二位官员。陶勐：掌管勐的头人。

① Mo: fortune teller.
② Shuang: two. Hun: official. Taomeng: chiefs of *mengs*.

六

庆功活动刚刚完,
海罕又把命令传:
"全军备战无松懈,
下一仗攻打勐景罕。
虽然我军连取胜,
不少地方已攻占,
但是讨伐俸改为时已三载,
还未见到我的妻婻崩。
这次出战意义大,
要详细记录在纸上,
留给后人永不忘。
各路大军要记住,
坚决占领勐景罕!
先把城池来围困,
冈晓打先锋,
桑本紧跟上,
召桑洛跟在桑本后,
桑温、赛伦的铁骑来压阵。
布冈戈和布冈伴负责搭营帐,
安排我的大本营,
迎接我到来。

VI

When the celebration activities had just finished,
Haihan gave another order:
"The whole army should prepare for the subsequent battles and remain vigilant,
The next target is Mengjinhan.
We have won a series of battles
And have conquered many places.
But it has been three years since we started to fight against Fenggai.
I haven't seen my wife Nanbeng yet.
This battle will be the most significant one,
And should be recorded in detail in writing words
So that it can be passed down to our descendants.
All of you should keep in mind that
You must be determined to capture Mengjinhan with determination!
First we need to besiege the city.
Gangxiao will play a vanguard role in the front,
And should be closely followed by Sangben.
Then comes Zhao Sangluo.
Finally there will be the cavalry of Sangwen and Sailun

厘俸 // Li Feng

号令一响就开战,
汉高波滚哇①攻城打头阵,
杀进城后把火放!"
海罕说完下命令,
千军万马齐出发,
如龙出海虎下山。
鼓声震天旌旗摇,
烟尘滚滚莱累②晃。
冈晓的军队如潮水涌,
召桑温的骑兵林中穿。
人如海,似雾满布,
宜将勐俸翻江倒海。
三日路途一日行,
急行五六日。
涉过水来又翻山,
九个坝子脚下过。
出了山垭口,
已经俯瞰勐景罕。
用石垒城堡,
统帅大营住海罕。
只听凿石声声响,
响声传到勐景罕。

at the rear.
Bugang Ge and Bugang Ban are responsible for putting up tents,
Arranging my headquarters at my base camp
To await my arrival.
The battle will be launched at the words of my command.
Han Gaobo Gunwa① will begin the fight,
Then set a fire after you rush into the city!"
At the words of Haihan's command,
Tens of thousands of soldiers and horses started off,
Like dragons jumping out of the sea and tigers dashing down the mountains.
The drums beat with deafening sound and the flags waved in the wind.
The smoke rolled and Lailei② Mountain trembled.
Gangxiao's army surged out like a tide,
And the cavalry of Zhao Sangwen went through the jungle.
There was a sea of people, like an interminable fog,
Ready to overturn the city of Mengjinghan.
A three-day journey was completed in one day.
The troops marched speedily for five to six days.
They climbed mountains and crossed rivers.

---

① 汉:敢死队。高波:人名。滚哇:勇猛。
② 莱累:山名,靠近勐景罕。

① Han Gaobo Gunwa: Han means "suicide squad". Gaobo is the name of a person. Gunwa means "brave".
② Lailei: a mountain near the city of Mengjinghan.

冈晓立在山垭口,	They went through nine stretches of flat land.
只见俸改的高楼金光闪。	Finally they walked out of the mountain pass
往北看,	And could see Mengjinghan from the mountain.
景罕城一眼难望穿。	The troops stopped to build a temporary castle
往西看,	With stones for Haihan to live in.
无边无际白茫茫。	The sound of chiseling stones
一发鲁非①射进城,	Spread to Mengjinhan.
如火龙在飞舞。	Gangxiao stood at the mountain pass,
土炮轰隆又一响,	Seeing the glittering buildings of Fenggai.
烟雾弥漫勐景罕。	Looking to the north,
城外百姓纷纷逃,	He found the city of Mengjinghan too large to see its end.
妇女牵着儿女喊。	Looking to the west,
男子腰带满地丢,	He saw a stretch of endless city.
各色帕拉②迎风响。	A *lufei*① was fired into the city
冈晓、桑洛、桑本齐下令,	Like a dancing fire dragon.
放出铁骑去追杀。	A cannon shot was fired,
满田满坝死无数,	Covering the city of Mengjinghan with smoke and fog.
人似牛群乱如麻。	Outside the city people were seen quickly fleeing.
活着的举手来投降,	Women with children were screaming and shouting.
群群俘虏一串串。	Men's waist belts fell on the ground everywhere.
桑本再令把房烧,	*Palas*② in different colors were blown away by the wind.
烈火熊熊烟万丈。	Gangxiao, Sangluo and Sangben gave orders at the

---

① 鲁非:一种燃烧的火药筒。
② 帕拉:背巾。

---

① Lufei: gunpowder cartridge.
② Pala: a piece of cloth for carrying babies.

厘俸 // Li Feng

俸改站在高楼上，
扶着好贺①放眼看。
皇后、公主成群齐拥出，
手扶栏杆也来望。
俸改转头问妻妾：
"城外何以烟雾漫？
是否百姓烧地忙？"
妻妾抢着来回答：
"曾经劝你你不听，
反把我们骂一场。
不是百姓在烧地，
海罕大军已临城。
百姓死成堆，
他们又把火来放，
只为你把海罕的妻子抢。
你的妻妾多又多，
终日在你身边团团转。
心不满足又把嫡崩占，
今天大家同遭殃。
我们将要沦为海罕的妻，
待来日心欢畅，
我们的混俸罕！"
俸改听了把话传：

same time,
Requiring their troops to chase after the fleeing people.
There were countless injuries and deaths in the fields.
People were all in chaos like herds of cattle.
The surviving ones raised their hands to surrender,
And became captives in great numbers.
Sangben gave the order to burn all the houses.
The smoke rose up in billows.
Standing in a tall building,
Fenggai looked into the distance, his hands holding the *haohe*①.
The queen and the princesses crowded around him,
Leaning on the rails to see what was happening.
Fenggai turned to ask his wife and concubines:
"Why is there smoke outside of the city?
Is it because my people are busy burning straws in their fields?"
His wife and concubines answered eagerly:
"We have told you before
Only to be scolded by you.
It is not people burning straw in the fields.
It is Haihan's troops coming nearer and nearer.
Numerous people have lost their lives.

---

① 好：栏杆。贺：大楼房。

① Hao: rails. He: big buildings.

"来人是为来讨妻,
快把酒席摆出来。"
婻崩手扶栏杆远远望,
一心盼着混海罕。
娥宾用手指远方,
小声来把婻崩问:
"亲爱的姐姐呀,
群群马队和大象,
无数金矛闪闪亮。
是谁的军队来到了?
一匹白马红笼头,
绣有孔雀的旗帜迎风展。
人群如蜂一般,
是谁率领大军来?"
婻崩笑着来回答:
"大队人马的统帅是桑洛,
为把你娥宾讨回到身旁。"
婻崩说话声响亮,
声声回荡在宫廷。
娥宾又开口把话讲:
"白色金幢迎风展,
金色的战鼓敲得响。
一队骑兵弓弩手,
风驰电掣向前闯。

Now they have set fires and will try to burn the city,
Only because you have seized Haihan's wife.
You already have so many wives and concubines,
Serving you every day.
But you are so greedy that you took Nanbeng by force.
Today we all have to suffer with you
And are going to become Haihan's wives
To please him in the coming days.
Our respectable Hun Fenghan, Haihan!"
Hearing this Fenggai made a command:
"Haihan is coming here to take his wife back.
Let's prepare a feast to welcome him."
Nanbeng leaned on the rail to look into the distance,
Expecting Hun Haihan to come.
Ebing pointed to the horizon,
Asking Nanbeng in a low voice:
"Dear sister!
Do you see those herds of horses and elephants
And the large number of shining spears?
Whose army is coming?
There is a white horse with a red harness.
There are flags embroidered with peacock designs
　　waving in the wind.
There are countless people coming like swarms of bees.

厘俸 // Li Feng

后面的兵丁带宝剑,
挥刀骑在象身上。
姐姐啊,
这是谁的兵马在前方?"
婻崩笑着又回答:
"这是海罕的二弟桑本的兵马,
带有战马数万匹,
还有数万个弓弩手。"
娥宾手指远方又来问:
"绸子做的金幢迎风展,
群群战马满山冈,
就像野花开满坝。
前锋是刀矛,
象鼻上下甩,
统率这队人马的又是谁?"
婻崩笑着来回答:
"那是海罕的弟弟桑温。"
娥宾又再问:
"马队二十群,
直奔勐景罕,
急驰如鬼影,
林中皆大象。
淡绿色的金幢,
如金线在阳光下,

Who is their commander?"
Nanbeng answered with a smile:
"Sangluo is the commander of the troops.
He comes here to take you Ebing back."
The powerful voice of Nanbeng
Echoed in the palace.
Ebing then spoke again:
"The golden prayer flags are fluttering in the wind.
The beat of war drums is loud and deafening.
Arrays of cavalrymen and bowmen
Are rushing forward at top speed like lightning flashes.
Behind them are the soldiers carrying swords
And riding on the back of elephants.
Oh, my sister,
Whose army is this?"
Nanbeng smiled and answered:
"These are the troops led by the second younger brother
    of Haihan, Sangben.
He has tens of thousands of horses under his command,
And tens of thousands of bowmen."
Ebing then pointed into the distance and asked:
"Golden prayer flags made of silk are waving in the wind.
Herds of horses are all over the mountains
Just like wild flowers blooming in the fields.

发出点点亮光。	Soldiers with swords and spears are in the vanguard.
大队人马浩浩荡荡在行进，	The war elephants are swinging their tusks in high spirits.
如大雨哗哗响，	Then who is the leader of these troops?"
它又是谁来统率？"	Nanbeng answered with a smile:
嫡崩开口又回答：	"That is Haihan's younger brother, Sangwen."
"它的统帅是桑温。"	Ebing asked again:
娥宾又指远方把话讲：	"I see twenty herds of horses
"幡幢迎风团团转，	Coming directly to Mengjinghan
大队人马在田坝，	As quickly as the shadows of ghosts move.
旗帜似孔雀尾巴齐飞扬。	Everywhere in the forest there are elephants.
长矛加上弯钩刀，	The golden prayer flags in light green
还有大象数不完。	Are shining in the sunlight
端坐幡幢下的又是谁？"	Like golden threads.
嫡崩开口又回答：	The soldiers and horses in great numbers march on
"那是海罕最小的弟弟，	With a sound like that of heavy rain.
赛伦做统帅。"	Then who is the commander of these troops?"
娥宾问话不停顿：	Nanbeng said:
"一群马队坡下冲，	"The general is Sangwen."
大象滚滚来，	Pointing to a distant place, Ebing said again:
士卒如排山倒海。	"The prayer flags are swirling in the wind,
幡幢的杆有花纹，	Indicating that there are many troops in the fields.
象鼻在摆动，	The flags are flying upward like peacock tails.
端坐在幡幢下的又是谁？"	There are spears as well as sickles with hooks,
嫡崩开口又回答：	And countless elephants.

厘俸 // Li Feng

"那是勇敢的罕高波,
他专门把敌人首级砍。"
娥宾又指一处问:
"耳闻战鼓咚咚响,
金盔明亮映阳光。
战马战象满田坝,
大象的獠牙似星星,
齐把金幢团团围,
这位统帅又是谁?"
婻崩开口又回答:
"他是军师布冈伴,
专为海罕设营帐,
只等海罕的到来。"
娥宾手又指远方:
"你看东方又一队,
坝中扎寨把营安,
犹如巨星一颗明又亮。
声音四起很杂乱,
那是放牧的马和象,
金幢高高迎风转,
这队人马又是谁统率?"
婻崩开口又回答:
"这队人马的军师是布冈戈,
他们也专为海罕设营帐。"

Who is that man sitting under the prayer flag?"
Nanbeng replied:
"That is Sailun, the youngest brother of Haihan.
Sailun is the commander."
Ebing kept asking questions without a break:
"A herd of horses is racing downhill.
Elephants are moving forward like rolling stones.
Soldiers come in overwhelming numbers.
The post of a prayer flag has decorative patterns on it.
The elephant trunk is swinging.
Who is that man sitting under the prayer flag?"
Nanbeng answered:
"That is brave Hangaobo
Who is skilled in beheading enemy soldiers."
Ebing pointed somewhere else and asked:
"I hear loud war drum beats
And I see shiny helmets in the sunlight.
I find war horses and elephants everywhere in the fields.
The tusks of elephants are as numerous as stars in the
　　　　night sky,
Surrounding the golden prayer flag.
Who is this general then?"
Nanbeng replied:
"He is the counselor Bugang Ban

娥宾又指一处问：	Who is responsible for setting up camp
"前方象队排着来，	And awaiting the arrival of Haihan."
人和马队紧跟后。	Ebing then pointed again at another place:
马队后面是鼓手，	"Look, there are more troops to the east.
绸缎做旗随风翻。	They are setting up camp in the fields,
华丽的象舆罩象身，	Like a star big and bright.
戴着红帽的人骑着象，	There is noise coming from all sides,
拿矛的兵丁一排排。	Made by pasturing horses and elephants.
有一架象舆最出众，	The golden prayer flag is fluttering high in the wind.
黄色的虎旗插在上，	Who is the general of these troops?"
帽顶是红色的兵丁把它团团围，	Nanbeng answered again:
抬高早的兵丁走在大象前。	"The counselor of these troops is Bugang Ge,
一队人马持红矛，	Who is in charge of putting up tents as well."
左右两边骑兵雄又壮。	Ebing pointed at another place:
亲爱的姐姐啊，	"There are elephants in array in the front,
这队人马的将领是否是召海法海罕？"	Followed closely by soldiers and horses.
	There are drummers behind the cavalrymen.
她俩的对话犹如吹奏比景牙①。	Their silk flags are waving in the wind.
又听娴崩来回答：	On the back of the elephants there are gorgeous howdahs.
"他们的将领不是召海法海罕，	Men in red hats ride on the elephants,
海罕在最后面。	Followed by lines of soldiers holding spears.
这队的将领是冈晓，	There is one howdah quite different from the others.
海罕之下就是他。	A yellow flag with a tiger stands on it.

---

① 比景牙：用象牙制作的箫。

厘俸 // Li Feng

他足智多谋最勇敢，
是海罕的心腹人。
专为海罕铺垫金丝绸缎床，①
打仗历来是先锋。
行军路上建远负②，
远负先后建九次，
海罕对他最信服。"
娥宾又指远方问：
"象牙密如天上星，
条条象腿似森林。
兵丁多如蜜蜂群，
幡幢如雪白皑皑，
这队的统帅又是谁？"
婻崩开口又回答：
"他是召尼的小舅子，
名字叫作混嘿南，
他边建远负边攻城。"
娥宾手指远方又发问：
"那边又来一大群，
犹如滚滚黑云般，
密密麻麻似蜂团。
只见象牙白花花，

① 意为冈晓是海罕的得力助手。
② 远负：在行军途中的临时城池。

The soldiers in red hats surround the elephant from all sides.
And there are soldiers holding *gaozao* walking in front
    of the elephant.
A team of soldiers carrying red spears
Protect the elephant on both sides.
Dear sister,
Is this commander the respectable Zhao Haifa Haihan?"
The dialogue between them continued like playing the
    *bijingya*①.
Nanbeng answered:
"This is not the respectable Zhao Haifa Haihan.
Haihan will come in the rear.
The commander of these troops is Gangxiao,
Who has the second highest rank below Haihan.
He is very clever, resourceful, and very brave,
And thus is Haihan's most reliable and trusted confidant.
He is the man who makes the gorgeous bed for Haihan.②
All the time he acts as the vanguard in battle,
Building *yuanfus*③ on the way to the war front.
He has built nine such *yuanfus*.
Haihan trusts him the most."
Ebing pointed to another distant place and asked:

① Bijingya: a flute made of ivory.
② It means that Gangxiao is Haihan's right-hand man.
③ Yuanfu: temporary quarters for the troops.

大象奔跑快如飞。	"There are elephant tusks as countless as stars in the sky.
彩旗飘飘迎风展,	There are soldiers as numerous as bees.
长矛全都用铜铸。	There are elephant legs as numerous as trees in a forest.
幡幢插在一头象身上,	There are forests of prayer flags as white as snow.
直指勐景罕。	Then who is leading these troops?"
这是谁的兵马又来到？"	Nanbeng answered:
婻崩看看来回答：	"He is Zhao Ni's brother-in-law.
"那是冈晓的弟弟为统帅,	His name is Hun Heinan.
他的名字叫冈庄。"	He builds the *yuanfu* and attacks at the same time."
娥宾手指一转又开口：	Ebing pointed to another distant place and asked:
"一队人马远方来,	"There is a big crowd of elephants over there,
正在匆忙建远负。	Just like rolling black clouds
帐篷都是绿颜色,	And thickly swarming bees.
再用木桩当栅栏。	I can see the elephants with white tusks
战象多又多,	Run as quickly as a flash.
战马吃草遍山冈。	The colorful flags are fluttering in the wind.
紫色的幡幢飘带飞,	All the spears are made of copper.
带兵的统帅又是谁？"	The prayer flags stand on the back of the elephants.
婻崩马上来回答：	The troops go straight to Mengjinghan.
"他是崩南宛多发,	Whose troops are these?"
他的表哥是海罕。"	Nanbeng looked ahead and responded:
娥宾睁大眼睛看远方,	"That is Gangxiao's younger brother.
拉着婻崩把话讲：	His name is Gangzhuang."
"那边人马黑压压,	Ebing's finger turned to another place and asked:

厘俸 // Li Feng

九个洼地全布满，
如同大雨洒落一般。
兵丁双手抬景罕①，
他们的帽顶插着孔雀尾，
战象头尾相连不间断。
另一队兵丁头戴金色帽，
金色的旗帜如林一排排。
战马成群在奔跑，
马龙头配着彩色绒线团。
锋利的战刀挎肩上，
战刀上缀有老虎尾。
队伍后面战鼓擂，
象队在后紧跟上。
矛手随象后，
千军万马浩浩荡荡。
战旗像森林，
贯发晕②震天响。
金幡幢下端坐一员将，
手摇虎头扇，
周围战马团团转。
先头部队进坝子，

"An army is coming from far away,
And is busy in constructing camps.
The tents are all green.
They are using piles of timber to build fences.
There are numerous elephants.
The horses are eating grass all over the mountains.
Purple prayer flags are flying in the wind.
Who is the commander in charge of these troops?"
Nanbeng replied:
"He is Bengnanwanduofa,
A cousin of Haihan."
Ebing opened her eyes wide and looked into the distance.
She kept on asking Nanbeng questions:
"Over there are thickly dotted with people
Filling nine vales,
Like a heavy rain pouring into them.
The soldiers are carrying *jinghans*① in their hands.
Their hats are decorated with peacock tail feathers.
There is a long array of elephants.
Another team of soldiers wear golden hats.
Their golden flags stand like rows of trees.

---

① 景罕：一种武器，如斧状，杆用金粉涂饰。
② 贯发晕：一种火药炮，爆炸后不会伤人，是用来助威的。

---

① Jinghan: a weapon that looks like an axe, its handle painted with a coating of golden powder.

后面的人马还在绕山腰。
军容整齐毫不乱，
人马大象热闹不寻常。
口弦、三弦齐鸣奏，
悦耳动听不一般。
亲爱的姐姐呀，
是谁如此有气派？"
婻崩高兴地回答：
"这就是召海法海罕，
我俩的哥哥就是他。
历尽艰辛越岭又翻山，
为的是找到我婻崩回身旁。"
娥宾又指另一方：
"那边骑马渡河的，
划船渡河的，
大象渡河的，
争先恐后多么忙。
象牙白如野白花，
遍布江中和江岸。
红色的幡幢映水中，
巨龙看见也躲藏。
那是谁的兵马又来到？"

The war horses are running in herds.
Their heads are decorated with colorful balls of string.
The soldiers all carry swords
With tiger tails painted on them.
Drums are beaten behind the team.
The elephants follow closely behind.
The spearmen follow the elephants
In a powerful and formidable array.
There is a forest of flags.
The sound of a *guanfayun*① quakes the sky.
A general sits under the golden prayer flag,
Waving his fan that has a tiger head pattern.
The horses crowd around him, galloping.
The front of the army is down in the city
While the rear is still on the mountainside.
The soldiers are well-dressed and follow a strict discipline.
The soldiers, the horses and the elephants are exordinarily active.
Buccal reeds and three-stringed fiddles are played melodiously,
Which gives an atmosphere of excitement.
My dear elder sister,

---

① Guanfayun: a kind of cannon, the explosion of which does not harm people. It is usually used to cheer the soldiers on.

厘俸 // Li Feng

娴崩看了把话说：
"那是召勐帕相冈①。"
娥宾手指又一转：
"黄牛、水牛和马群，
山中吃赶。
彩旗哗哗在飞舞，
抬矛背弓的人连绵不断。
金幡幢随风扬，
那是谁的兵马在赶路？"
娴崩开口又回答：
"那是桑混伦和赛道。"
娥宾手又指远方：
"冈晓左侧又一队，
战马战象相混杂。
紫色象舆映阳光，
兵丁手中持金矛。
红色幡幢金晃晃，
还有众多的兵丁抬着亥短②，
骑马的弓手斗志昂。
这队人马似赶集，
它又是谁来统率？"
娴崩看看又回答：

Who is the man surrounded with such an air of greatness
    and powerfulness?"
Nanbeng responded happily:
"This is Zhao Haifa Haihan,
Our elder brother.
Having gone through a lot of hardships and climbing
    so many mountains,
He comes to bring me, Nanbeng, back to him."
Ebing pointed to the other side:
"Over there people are crossing the river by
Riding horses,
Paddling boats,
And riding elephants.
The elephant tusks are as white as wild white blossoms,
Covering the middle of the river and the banks of the river.
The red prayer flags are reflected in the water,
Making even huge dragons afraid and flee.
Whose troops are these?"
Nanbeng took a look and said,
"That is Zhao Mengpa Xianggang①."
Ebing turned her finger to another direction:
"There are cattle, baffalos and horses

---

① 召勐帕相冈：勐帕的首长。
② 亥短：一种护身的兵器，似盾。

① Zhao Mengpa Xianggang: the chief of Mengpa.

"那是勐缅的波道坚大官。"	Driven in the mountain.
娥宾开口又来问：	Colorful flags are flying
"前方又来一队象，	Soldiers holding spears and bows are countless in number.
人骑象上缓缓行，	Golden prayer flags are waving in the wind.
互相挑逗在游玩。	Whose troops are on the way?"
士卒众多在急行，	Nanbeng responded:
骑兵手持红色的亥短。	"They belong to respectable Sang Hunlun and Sai Dao".
幡幢的颜色蓝又蓝，	Ebing pointed into the distance again:
幡幢之下不见人。	"There is another group of troops to the left of Gangxiao.
它的首领又是谁？"	The horses are mixed with the elephants.
媥崩开口又回答：	The purple howdah shines in the sun.
"它的首领是冈罕，	Some of the soldiers hold golden spears in their hands.
他的父亲就是召生黑。"	A red prayer flag is glaring in the sunlight.
娥宾遥望远方问：	Some of the soldiers carry *haiduan*①.
"又见马队成群来，	The bowmen on horseback are highly spirited.
已经来到湖水边，	Like they are going to the fair.
准备渡水忙又忙。	Who is leading these troops?"
士卒持长矛，	Nanbeng took a look and answered:
湖埂也踏翻。	"That is the great officer Bodaojian from Mengmian."
营帐是白色，	Ebing asked again:
阳光下闪亮。	"There is a group of elephants in front.
战象有的在吃草，	People are riding the elephants slowly
有的如石滚下湖去，	As if they are having fun.

---

① Haiduan: a kind of weapon for protection, like a shield.

厘俸 // Li Feng

有的在水中嬉戏玩。	The rest of them are proceeding quickly.
伙夫收炊忙，	The cavalrymen are holding red *haiduan*.
有的在灭火，	People under blue prayer flags
烟往天上窜。	Are invisible.
有的还未吃完饭，	Who is the commander of this legion?"
有的正在套马上鞍。	Nanbeng answered:
黄色幡幢缓缓来，	"The commander is Ganghan,
迎风哗哗响，	Whose father is General Gangxiao."
这是谁的军队又来到？"	Ebing looked into the distance and asked again:
婻崩看后又回答：	"There are herds of horses coming
"这是召勐洪①的军队来参战。"	To the lake side.
娥宾指着远方又发问：	They are busy preparing to cross the lake.
"前面又来人和马，	The soldiers hold long spears,
彩色斑斓如虎皮，	And their stamping has damaged the lake embankment.
布满勐景坝。	Their tents are white,
兵丁手舞刀矛画圆圈，	Glittering in the sun.
有的拿着钩镰枪。	The war elephants either graze on the grassland,
一群大象在甩鼻，	Or roll down into the lake water
战马成群又结队。	To play and have fun.
兵丁头盔亮闪闪，	And the cooks are busy preparing food.
孔雀尾巴缀战刀。	Some are extinguishing fires
骑兵跃马在奔跑，	And the smoke rises into the air.
象舆高插金幡幢。	Some have not finished their meal yet.

① 召勐洪：勐洪地方的酋长。

这是谁的军队呀？"	Some are putting saddles on their horses.
婻崩看看又回答：	The yellow prayer flags are moving slowly
"它的首领叫艾包，	And make the sound of a gust of wind.
作战历来很勇敢，	Whose troops are coming then?"
召尼令他做后卫。"	Nanbeng took a look and replied:
娥宾手又指远方问：	"This is the army of Zhao Menghong[①] joining in the battle.
"骑兵遍野跑，	Ebing pointed into the distance, asking:
人群满坝站。	"More soldiers and horses are coming,
战象甩长鼻，	Covering the whole Mengjing Basin
炮手背长刀。	Like bright-colored tiger skin.
战马一百群，	Some of the soldiers are waving their swords and spears in circles.
群群头高昂，	
准备把城攻。	Others are holding hooked spears.
战象又一队，	The elephants are swinging their trunks.
目标勐景罕。	The horses are gathering by herds and groups.
一头战象的舆上，	The soldiers' helmets are shining.
插着紫色金幡幢。	Feathers from peacock tails are used as ornaments on the swords.
这队人马的首领又是谁？"	
婻崩来回答：	The cavalrymen are riding their horses at a gallop.
"他是召尼崩，	The howdahs are decorated with golden prayer flags.
他的人马很勇敢。"	Whose troops are these?"
娥宾手又指一方问道：	Nanbeng looked and answered:
"田坝中士卒在打桩，	

---

① Zhao Menghong: the chief of Menghong.

厘俸 // Li Feng

准备围成大栅栏。
兵丁割草又挑柴，
战马成群跑得欢。
幡幢一顶色金黄，
一员大将坐中央。
这个首领又是谁？"
婻崩开口把话讲：
"这是陶桑海，
统率预备队。
亲爱的妹妹啊，
海罕的全部人马已到战场！"

"Their leader is Ai Bao,

Who has always been brave in fighting.

Zhao Ni① made him a rear guard."

Ebing pointed into the distance, asking again:

"The cavalrymen are seen everywhere in the fields.

The flat land is filled with crowds of people.

The elephants are swinging their trunks,

The gunners wear long swords.

One hundred herds of horses

All hold their heads high,

Ready to attack the city.

Another team of elephants has been sent out

To go straight to Mengjinghan.

On a howdah on the back of one elephant

Stands a purple and golden prayer flag.

Who is the leader of these troops?"

Nanbeng answered:

"He is Zhao Nibeng.

His soldiers are brave."

Ebing turned to another place and asked:

"Some soldiers in the field are driving piles into the earth

To bulid big fences.

Others are busy cutting grass and collecting firewood.

---

① Zhao Ni: Here refers to Haihan.

The horses are running around happily in herds.

There is a golden umbrella

Under which a general is sitting.

Who is this general?"

Nanbeng answered:

"This is Tao sanghai

Leading the reserve force.

My dear younger sister,

All the troops of Haihan have already come to the battlefield!"

围攻勐景罕，	The attack of Mengjinhan
战斗已打响。	Had begun.
冈晓的军队猛冲锋，	The army of Gangxiao charged fiercely.
桑洛的军队北面攻。	The army of Sangluo marched from the north.
桑本的军队南面上，	The army of Sangben attacked from the south.
桑温正面出击凶又猛。	Sangwen launched the attack straight from the front.
杀声震动勐景罕，	The sound of killing and fighting shook Mengjinghan.
千军万马冲城池。	Thousands of horses and soldiers dashed into the city.
用火来攻，	Fire tactics were used,
烟雾腾腾直往云霄升。	And the clouds of smoke rose into the sky.
勐景罕城池宽又长，	The city of Mengjinghan was long and wide,
海罕的兵马虽很多，	Making it difficult for Haihan's troops
围城仍然有漏空。	To tightly surround the city.

厘俸 // Li Feng

赶集的百姓往城里逃，
你冲我撞死伤重。
兵丁点燃火把烧村庄，
村庄攻占六十个。
冈晓在原地把营安，
他眼望城池把话说：
"打仗不但要靠气势猛，
也还要把鬼神祭，
人马作战才更勇敢。
攻进城去有奖赏，
俸改有几头雪白的大象，
女儿美丽又漂亮。"
桑本急忙开了口：
"我打头阵攻入城，
俸改的小女儿就归我。"
桑洛也开口紧接上：
"我打头阵先入城，
俸改的小女儿应归我。"
冈晓摆手来阻挡：
"你们二人莫争吵，
一切事由阿巫戛来定，
说千道万听他讲。"

People in the market outside of the city now fled into the city,
Bumping into one another, causing many injuries and deaths.
The soldiers took sixty villages
By setting them on fire and burning them down.
Gangxiao then stopped and put up tents.
He looked in the direction of the city and said:
"Winning a battle depends not only on an upsurge of momentum
But also prayers to the spirits and gods,
So that the soldiers will fight more bravely.
Rewards will be given for breaking through the city wall.
Fenggai has a few snow-white elephants.
His daughters are charming and beautiful."
Sangben spoke quickly:
"If I attack the city first,
Fenggai's youngest daughter will be mine."
Sangluo also spoke:
"If I attack the city first
Fenggai's youngest daughter will be mine."
Gangxiao waved them to stop:
"You two please do not quarrel with each other.
Awu Ga will make every decision.

Please listen to him later."

城内守军见人来冲杀，	The soldiers in the city found Haihan's troops had come to attack,
慌忙又击鼓来又敲铓。	And hurried to beat the drums and gongs.
城中兵丁奔又跑，	They ran in a rash
手持武器来应战。	And picked up their weapons to get ready for the fight.
站在城头齐把弓弩发，	Standing at the top of the city wall,
飞箭射满象身上，	They shot arrows at the elephants.
如同豪猪身上刺一般。	With arrows all over their bodies, the elephants appeared to be hedgehogs.
城门忽然大大开，	Suddenly the city gate opened.
俸改的兵马滚滚冲出来。	Fenggai's army rushed out like a great sea wave.
象脖上的铃铛震天响，	The bells on the elephant necks rang loudly
如雨急来似风狂，	Like the sound of heavy rain and strong wind.
瞬时冲到海罕军队前。	Instantly they rushed to the front of Haihan's army.
冈晓一时难抵挡，	For a moment Gangxiao could not resist
往后急急退，	And had to withdraw in haste.
二十布冈①把命丧。	The soldiers of twenty Bugangs① had lost their lives in this battle.
冈晓见状传令把兵退，	Gangxiao gave the order to retreat
拉开距离稳住阵。	And regained their footing after withdrawing to a safe
之后，	
一杆旗帜插地上，	
一声军令传出来：	

---

① 布冈：为一个村寨的头人，二十布冈指二十布冈率领的士卒。

① Bugang: head of a village. Here "twenty Bugangs" refers to the soldiers led by twenty Bugangs.

厘俸 // Li Feng

"不准再后退,
否则把头砍!"
对方趁势往前追,
帕达汉①骑着大象猛冲来,
冯达望和雪达荒②紧跟随,
雪达亥③举着长矛也冲来。
达黄皆④的兵马有十万,
莫英法⑤的每头大象系着九个铃铛。
皆闷⑥的坐骑有九个金铃脖上挂,
其手下的兵丁帽顶是红的,
几员大将出城来作战。
达黄皆和皆闷战桑本,
桑本沉着应战稳如山。
两人又冲杀布冈戈和布冈伴,
杀声喊声震天响,
胜负难分难解。
俸改的兵源源出城来增援,
只见帕达汉和莫英法围攻桑本。

① 帕达汉:俸改的一员大将。
② 冯达望和雪达荒:两人均为俸改的大将。
③ 雪达亥:俸改的大将。
④ 达黄皆:俸改的大将。
⑤ 莫英法:俸改的大将。
⑥ 皆闷:俸改的弟弟。

distance.
Then,
A flag was set up on the ground
And an order was passed:
"No retreat beyond this flag is allowed.
Otherwise you will be killed!"
The enemy took the opportunity to chase them.
Padahan① rushed forward on his elephant,
With Fengdawang and Xuedahuang② following him closely,
Xuedahai③ also gave chase with his spear.
Dahuangjie④ had one hundred thousand soldiers.
Moyingfa's⑤ elephants each had nine bells on their necks.
Jiemen's⑥ elephant had nine gold bells on its neck.
His soldiers wore red hats.
These generals dashed out of the city and fought hard.
Dahuangjie and Jiemen fought together against Sangben,
Who met them calmly like a mountain.
Then the two turned to attack Bugang Ge and Bugang Ban.

① Padahan: one of Fenggai's generals.
② Fengdawang and Xuedahuang: two of Fenggai's generals.
③ Xuedahai: one of Fenggai's generals.
④ Dahuangjie: one of Fenggai's generals.
⑤ Moyingfa: one of Fenggai's generals.
⑥ Jiemen: Fenggai's younger brother.

帕达汉骑着的大象，	There were shouts of killing and fighting.
人血顺着它的牙滴滴淌。	The battle was at a stalemate.
桑本边战边退靠近冈晓，	More and more of Fenggai's troops came out of the city
兵退如潮冲坝倒。	as reinforcements.
冈晓见状怒火上，	Padahan and Moyingfa fought against Sangben.
命令战鼓猛敲响。	Human blood was dripping from
冈晓骑象冲敌阵，	The tusks of the elephant Padahan rode.
战象横冲又直撞。	Sangben moved close to Gangxiao while retreating.
冲到哪里哪里让，	The soldiers retreated like a landslide.
敌兵死的死来伤的伤。	Gangxiao was so angry to see this happen.
雪达亥、雪达荒自吹是大官，	He ordered the drum to be beaten
蹬着大象往前冲，	And dashed forward to fight in person.
手持金矛战冈晓，	His elephant dashed and rampaged
士兵如潮紧跟上。	While the soldiers dodged and made way for it.
达黄皆也骑象战冈晓，	The enemy soldiers were either wounded or killed.
冈晓驱象来迎战。	Xuedahai and Xuedahuang paraded themselves as great
只听达黄皆的大象一声惨叫，	officers
扑通一下倒在地。	And drove their elephants to the fight.
冈晓趁势用矛刺，	They attacked Gangxiao with their gold spears.
达黄皆一命呜呼倒在田坝中。	Their soldiers followed them closely.
冈晓再把象头钩，	Dahuangjie also urged his elephant on and joined the fight.
达黄皆的头已被士卒砍。	Gangxiao drove his elephant to meet their attack.
欢呼之声响又亮：	With a scream,
"我们勐景哈的冒宰本事强！"	Dahuangjie's elephant fell on the ground with a thump.

厘俸 // Li Feng

对方大惊失色心发慌,	Gangxiao took advantage of this and stabbed
退入城中城门关。	Dahuangjie with his spear.
第二天拂晓天刚亮,	Dahuangjie then fell down and died in the field.
冈晓开口把话讲:	Gangxiao used a hook to drag the elephant's head
"各路将官,	While his soldiers cut off Dahuangjie's head.
你们人人有金幡幢,	There were loud cheers of joy:
应服从布冈戈和布冈伴。	"How strong the *maozais* of Mengjingha are!"
战壕营寨应筑牢,	The enemy was greatly frightened
众士卒动手一齐干,	And retired their city and closed the gate.
做好准备重开战。"	The next day at dawn,
转眼又过了一天,	Gangxiao began to issue his new order:
海罕率军下了山,	"Generals and officers of all the troops!
来到勐景罕大坝。	All of you have been awarded with golden prayer flags,
骑兵八万,	So you must listen to our counselors Bugang Ge and
矛手三十万,	Bugang Ban.
头戴铁甲的士卒五十万,	You should consolidate your camps and trenches.
七十万兵丁挥大斧,	Every soldier and officer must work together
钩镰枪手八十万,	And get well ready for the next battle."
长刀队有九十万,	Another day had passed
头戴金帽亮闪闪。	When Haihan moved down from the mountain
海罕骑着占拜舍,	And came to Mengjinghan Basin.
来到坝子浩浩荡荡。	His army included eighty thousand calvarymen,
占拜舍好似一蜂王,	Three hundred thousand spearmen,
脖系金铃九个响叮当。	Five hundred thousand soldiers in armor and helmets,

十万头大象相跟随，	Seven hundred thousand soldiers holding axes,
贯发晕沿路阵阵响。	Eight hundred thousand soldiers holding hooked spears,
海罕心急如火烧，	And nine hundred thousand soldiers holding long swords.
因为还未攻下勐景罕。	The soldiers all wore shining golden hats.
冈晓看见海罕到，	Haihan rode his Zhanbaishe
急得淌大汗，	And came to the basin with these arrays of troops.
慌忙下象骑上马，	Zhanbaishe was like a queen bee.
手拿金壶金杯见海罕。	On its neck were tied nine gold bells jinging and tinking.
见到海罕就开口：	A hundred thousand elephants followed him.
"我的召海法呀，	*Guanfayun* was fired all the way to cheer on the soldiers.
你何以这么急来这么忙？	Haihan was anxious
你只要稍作安排就可以，	Because Mengjinghan had not been captured yet.
就像宝刀在鞘中，	At the sight of Haihan,
只要拔出一点露亮光，	Gangxiao sweated with worry.
不必操心费神太劳累。	He quickly got off his elephant and then rode on the horse.
你应该了解勐景罕，	He met Haihan with a gold pot and a gold cup in his hands.
土地宽阔没有边。	As soon as he saw Haihan, he said:
老鹰离巢往外飞，	"My respectable Zhao Haifa!
飞回来时找巢难。	Why do you come to the front in such a hurry?
喜鹊、八哥高高飞，	Actually you can just give orders from the rear,
飞来飞去飞不过界。	Like a sword in a scabbard
同是勐景坝，	
由于土地太广大，	
十里气候不一样。	

厘俸 // Li Feng

此处天晴那里阴,	To be pulled out just a little and the light will be shown.
东边下雨西边出太阳。	You don't have to be so tired and overworked.
远远望去地连天,	You must know that Mengjinghan
并非一朝一夕能够到尽头。	Is a vast land without a boundary.
勐景罕城中大又大,	If an eagle flies away,
二十多处赶集场。	It will be difficult for it to find the way back.
练兵场宽一百排,	As for magpies and starlings, they fly high above but
弩箭装满一千仓。	never fly outside of Mengjing Basin.
城中鲁勒三十九,	In this flat land,
每个鲁勒的大门饲养大象二十头。	The weather differs every ten miles.
	It may be sunny here and cloudy there.
大象每天出又进,	It may be rainy in the east but fine in the west.
路面踏出深坑一串串。	When looking into the distance, you will find the earth
我的召海法呀,	attached to the sky.
我担心夜间敌人来偷袭。	You can not walk to the end of its territory one day.
三十万支标枪一齐发,	Mengjinghan is a big city
俸改还有猛士三千人,	With more than twenty fairs and markets.
刀枪不入的就有一百五十双,	Their drill ground is wide enough to hold hundreds of
如果他们发现你,	rows of soldiers.
把你围住杀翻了,	Their provision of bows and arrows are stored in a
那时军心动摇人心散,	thousand warehouses.
很多人马就会去投降,	The city is divided into thirty nine *lules*
如同丝线被拉断,	And each *lule* raises twenty elephants.
再也接不上。	The elephants come out every day

我的召海法呀，	And their stamping makes the road bumpy with puddles.
请你仔细想一想！"	My respectable Zhao Haifa!
海罕听了把头点，	I am so worried about the enemy's possible sneak attacks at night.
骑着占拜舍往回走。	They may fling their three hundred thousand spears at you at the same time.
群象跟着回远负，	In addition, Fenggai has three thousand warriors.
海罕安居营寨等待捷报传。	Three hundred of them are invulnerable.
	If they come and find you here,
	They will surround you and kill you.
	In that case the morale of our army will be shaken
	And many of our soldiers will surrender,
	Like a broken thread
	Which will never be connected again.
	My respectable Zhao Haifa!"
	Think it over!
	Haihan agreed
	And rode his Zhanbaishe back to the mountain.
	His elephants followed him back to the *yuanfu*.
	There Haihan stayed and waited for the news of victory.
第二次战斗又打响，	The second battle began.
铓鼓声声炮火乱。	There was the sound of drums and gongs and gunshots everywhere.
十万战象齐出战，	

厘俸 // Li Feng

硝烟弥漫火烧山。
海罕的各路兵马猛冲杀，
一冲冲到城池边。
土炮火炮声不断，
只见城中大火燃。
冈晓奋力往前奔，
士卒紧紧齐跟上。
城头大石哗哗往下滚，
檑木齐下如狂浪。
土炮火炮又齐发，
冈晓士卒成肉浆，
大象倒在城墙旁。
士卒高举发巴梯①，
要把大石檑木挡，
可力量太大挡不住，
许多士卒震昏迷。
帕达汉趁机出城战，
打开栅栏放象群。
帕达汉头盔金光亮，
指挥象队的是雪达荒，
雪达亥也率兵来出战，
莫英法手指冈晓大声骂：

One hundred thousand elephants went out to fight.
Clouds of smoke floated over the battlefield.
Haihan's troops dashed forward
To the foot of the city wall.
There were constant cannon shots,
And big fires in the city.
Gangxiao fought hard,
With his soldiers behind him.
Fenggai's soldiers pushed down wave after wave
Of rocks and logs from the city wall.
Their cannons were fired as well.
Some of Gangxiao's soldiers were ground into mince meat
And their elephants fell down at the foot of the city wall.
Other soldiers held their *fabatis*①
To stop the falling stones and logs,
But failed.
Hit by the stones and logs, many of them fainted.
Padahan, with a shiny helmet on his head,
Seized the opportunity and dashed out of the city.
He let out his elephants to join the fight.
Xuedahuang was the commander of the elephant teams.
Xuedahai came out as well.

---

① 发巴梯：一种专门用来抵挡檑木、滚石的防御物。

① Fabati: a defensive weapon to hold back falling rocks and logs.

"艾冈晓啊，艾冈晓！	Moyingfa pointed at Gangxiao and condemned him loudly:
一望无际的勐景罕，	"Ai Gangxiao, oh, Ai Gangxiao!
好似一座铁铸的城。	Mengjinghan is vast in area.
二十道铁索桥放寒光，	It is like a city made of iron.
你们休想来攻占。	There are twenty cable bridges
你们的大象如猪一般，	That are hard to take over.
怎能爬过护城河。	Your elephants are just like pigs
你们来打勐景罕，	And will never swim across our moat.
就像野鸡扑野猫，	You come to attack Mengjinghan
来多少就死多少。	The way a pheasant snaps at a wild cat.
就像小鱼千万条，	You will all die,
进入龙嘴落肚肠。	Like tens of thousands of small fish
又像狗咬老虎自投网，	Swallowed by a dragon,
二十条也喂不饱。	Or a dog biting a tiger,
你以为勐景罕的狗无牙，	Putting itself right into the trap.
才把肉送到门上？	Do you think that the dogs in Mengjinghan have no teeth,
你们别来送死了，	So that you came here, not afraid of being torn into pieces?
快快回家去栽秧！"	Do not seek your doom!
冈晓大声来回答：	Go back quickly to transplant rice seedlings."
"你们的棒改太霸道，	Gangxiao answered in a loud voice:
到处把别人的妻子抢。	"Your master Fenggai is so imperious and despotic.
人人恨他紧握拳，	He goes everywhere to capture other people's wives.
心中怒火高万丈。	People all hate him,
你们真是太骄狂，	

厘俸 // Li Feng

大象未死就拔牙，	Clenching their fists in rage.
反被象牙戳肋巴。	You are really very arrogant.
老虎未死拔虎牙，	You want to pull an elephant's tusks even before it dies
虎牙爆炸变火花。	And will surely be stabbed by the tusks in the chest.
烈火烧到勐景罕，	You want to pull a tiger's teeth even before it dies
海罕是天神的侄儿威力大，	And will certainly be hurt by an explosion of the tiger teeth.
俸改却把他来污辱，	Now the fire of war is ignited in Mengjinghan.
把他的爱妻婻崩抢。	Haihan is the powerful nephew of gods,
海罕骑着占拜舍，	But Fenggai still controls his wife Nanbeng.
要把俸改亲手斩。	This insults and humiliates Haihan so much.
召尼本为婻崩来，	This is why Haihan comes on his elephant
可恨俸改不回头，	To kill Fenggai with his own hands.
只可怜勐景罕的人死如山。	Zhao Ni came for Nanbeng
你们几个小奴才，	But unfortunately Fenggai will not admit defeat.
胆敢来和我胡缠，	The poor people in Mengjinghan will die in great numbers.
眨眼你们就要死，	How do you insignificant ones
二十头大象瞬间毙。"	Dare to compete with me?
雪达亥听了怒火冒，	You and your twenty elephants
骑着大象出来战。	Will all die in a blink of the eye."
冈晓驱赶占拜中，	Hearing these words, Xuedahai became furious.
毫不畏惧迎头上。	He rode his elephant to fight.
两头大象长鼻扭，	Gangxiao rode his Zhanbaizhong
象牙交错咯吱响。	To meet him without fear.
景罕的兵丁滚滚来，	

两军交锋天昏暗。	The two elephant's trunks twisted together
战马铁蹄急，	And their tusks clashed and clattered.
战场尘土扬，	The soldiers of Mengjinghan came in torrents.
喊声杀声如雷声一般。	The sky over the battlefield became dim and gloomy.
雪达亥手持长矛连连戳，	The hasty sound of horse hoofs were heard,
冈晓沉着冷静左右挡。	Dust rising into the air.
趁势刺矛雪达亥铠甲穿，	The shouts of killing were deafening.
雪达荒急忙来援助，	Xuedahai thrust his spear again and again
双方士卒争抢雪达亥。	But Gangxiao dodged it calmly.
战马对阵相残杀，	Gangxiao then got a chance and thrust his spear into Xuedahai's armor.
土炮如洒沙。	
冈晓左飞奔来右驰骋，	Xuedahuang promptly came to the rescue.
敌阵纷纷两边倒。	The two sides were struggling to take Xuedahai.
雪达荒拼死来迎战，	Their war horses fought against each other.
两象交锋互不让。	The cannons were fired and a rain of sand fell down.
雪达荒长矛左发右射上下挑，	Gangxiao dashed to the left and to the right,
冈晓怒火心头燃，	Killing the enemy soldiers on his side.
狠狠一矛刺过去，	Xuedahuang fought desperately.
正中雪达荒肋下。	The two elephants charged at each other.
一声惨叫还未出，	Xuedahuang waved his spear up and down
翻身滚下象。	And made Gangxiao angry.
葬身矛下刚闭眼，	He threw his spear forcefully
兵丁争相把头砍。	And stabbed Xuedahuang under his rib.
雪达荒的士卒见此状，	Without even a shout of pain,

厘俸 // Li Feng

人人心发慌。
往后败退如山倒，
冈晓紧追不放松。
战斗层层来推进，
边打边把黑横①来围上。
敌军战败军心动，
桑稳②更是火直冒，
严厉斥责众兵将：
"昨日一战输得惨，
俸改得知则头难保。
只有把冈晓的首级斩，
把他剁成肉酱，
给召法勐俸罕献上，
才会将功补过有奖赏。
今天我们齐出战，
活捉冈晓放在砧板上，
让我们的妻子把刀拿，
放上葱和姜，
合在一起剁肉酱，
然后分给父老共同享。
还要将此事记下来，
留给后人代代传！"

Xuedahuang fell off his elephant.
Just when he breathed his last breath
His head was cut off.
Seeing this,
Xuedahuang's soldiers began to panic
And withdrew like hill sliding.
Gangxiao chased after them relentlessly.
Gangxiao's troops advanced steadily
And built *heiheng*① while fighting.
The enemy was defeated and became discouraged.
Sangwen② was extremely furious about this.
He reprimanded his soldiers and officers:
"We lost the battle yesterday.
If Fenggai was informed of that, he would kill us all.
Only by cutting off the head of Gangxiao,
Chopping him into pieces,
And presenting it to our Zhao Famengfenghan,
Can we atone for our defeat and be rewarded.
Today let us fight together.
Let us catch Gangxiao and put him on a chopping block.
Then let our wives use their knives
To mince his meat

---

① 黑横：栽下木桩，用横木围成坚固的栅栏，作为防御工事。
② 桑稳：俸改的一员大将。

① Heiheng: logs used to build strong fences, for defense in a war.
② Sangwen: one of Fenggai's senior generals.

话刚说完就下令，	Hardly had he finished these words
骑着大象重开战。	When he ordered his troops to resume the battle.
身后兵将千千万，	He was followed by thousands of soldiers,
就像乌云遮太阳。	Like dark clouds covering the sun.
战象獠牙白花花，	Their war elephants with white tusks
脖上金铃响叮当。	Wore golden bells on their necks, ringing and jingling.
桑稳冲杀在北边，	Sangwen dashed to fight in the north,
桑洛勇敢来迎战。	And Sangluo came to meet him head-on bravely.
俸改又一路兵马杀南方，	Another wave of Fenggai's troops attacked in the south,
在城脚遇上布冈戈和布冈伴。	And encountered Bugang Ge and Bugang Ban at the foot of the city wall.
双方一场混战，	The two sides began to fight in a melee.
喊杀声如瀑布哗哗响。	The sound of yelling and killing was like that of a waterfall.
士卒有的死在矛下，	Some soldiers died under the spear,
有的中土炮。	Others were shot by the cannon.
两军谁也不相让，	Neither side gave up.
象阵对象阵，	The elephants of the two sides fought hard,
只听大象粗气喘。	Breathing heavily.

桑稳杀向冈晓的阵营，　　Sangwen dashed to the camp of Gangxiao,

厘俸 // Li Feng

指着冈晓放声骂：
"冈晓啊，冈晓！
上数天大把地盖，
下数召法温管辖下的地最广。
你们来此为哪样？
一头象怎能战胜百头象？
你冈晓任凭武艺多高强，
来此只不过自取灭亡。
你的百头象对勐俸的万头象，
虽然力大似猛虎，
竹篮打水也枉然。
既然你已来挑战，
就不要心惊胆战。
冈晓啊，
我要把你的象牙来绞断！"
冈晓听了也大骂：
"你手拿金把羽毛扇，
模样像个老憨官。
我俩相交战，
不知谁先亡？
你口口声声说大话，
勐景罕的大象虽多如草，
有哪头大象能善战？
勐景罕的战象虽多如崖石，

Pointing at Gangxiao and cursing loudly:
"Gangxiao, oh Gangxiao!
Above in heaven, it is the sky that is big enough to cover the world.
Down on the earth, it is Zhao Fawen who has the most extensive territory.
What did you come here for?
How can one elephant defeat one hundred?
However strong and skillful you Gangxiao are,
You came here for inevitable failure.
Your one hundred elephants are facing one hundred thousand in Menjinghan.
Although your elephants are as powerful as tigers,
All will be in vain just like drawing water with a sieve.
Since you have come for the challenge,
Then don't be frightened.
Oh Gangxiao!
I'll break your elephant's tusks!"
Hearing these words, Gangxiao also cursed:
"You take a feather fan with a gold handle in your hand,
Looking like a stupid old man.
When we fight against each other,
I really do not know which one of us is going to be killed first?

又有哪一头能把我们的象牙绞断？	You are always bragging.
既然你已来挑战，	You say the elephants of Mengjinghan are as numerous as grass,
也不要心慌发抖腿发软！"	But can you tell me which elephant is good at fighting?
说完，脚蹬大象冲过去，	You say the elephants of Mengjinghan are as countless as stones.
桑稳的士卒两边让，	But can you tell me which one can break our elephants' tusks?
桑稳出阵来迎战。	Since you have come to challenge me,
两象相遇吼声起，	Then don't be scared and weak in the knees!"
你来我往，	Then Gangxiao drove his elephant forward.
一场生死激战，	Sangwen's soldiers had to move aside.
令人眼花缭乱。	Sangwen came out to fight Gangxiao.
冈晓手疾眼快刺桑稳，	The two elephants roared at each other
一矛正中咽喉上。	And engaged in
桑稳扑通滚下象，	Fierce fighting,
士卒拥上把头砍。	Dazzling the soldiers that stood by.
呜呜……吼声传四方，	Gangxiao grabbed an opportunity and thrust his spear
人又欢来马又狂。	Right at Sangwen's throat.
勐俸人马慌忙退，	Sangwen flopped down from the elephant
损兵折将斗志丧。	And Gangxiao's soldiers swarmed to slice off his head.
争相入城忙躲藏，	The sound of a hurrah spread in all directions.
来把魂魄安。	Gangxiao's soldiers were happy and their horses excited.
其余各路也败退，	The troops of Fenggai withdrew in a hurry,
拖着战旗城里窜。	

厘俸 // Li Feng

At the cost of losing both soldiers and courage.
The troops scrambled to flee into the city
Where their shock finally wore off.
And the rest of Mengjinghan's troops also lost their battles,
Escaping back to the city with their flags dragging on
　　　the ground.

桑洛收兵回远负，	Sangluo returned to the *yuanfu* with his soldiers.
布冈戈和布冈伴，	Bugang Ge and Bugang Ban came back as well,
抬着孔雀尾战旗数千杆也退回。	Carrying thousands of ther flags decorated with peacock tail feathers.
冈晓的军中最热闹，	Gangxiao's army became the most bustling, with the sound
锣鼓喧天战旗飘。	Of gongs and drums echoing in the sky and flags fluttering in the wind.
八万大军回营帐，	The eighty thousand soldiers were now back to their camps
洗脸休息又吃饭。	To wash away the dust and have their meals.
冈晓夜间睡不宁，	Gangxiao could not sleep well at night.
朦胧间，	In a mysterious state,
梦见自己变成一只大鹞鹰，	He dreamed of himself, like a big hawk,
腾空飞起在云端。	Flying high in the clouds.
梦中惊醒心急跳，	He was awakened and his heart beat fast.
不能入睡到天亮。	Then he could not fall asleep again till dawn broke.
一早起来吃过饭，	He quickly got up and finished his breakfast,
骑上快马见海罕。	And rode his horse at top speed to see Haihan.
海罕见了很奇怪：	
"往次你来很热闹，	

何以这次单身独马进营帐？	Haihan was surprised to see him come:
满面愁容心不安？"	"You used to come to me with an entourage of guards.
冈晓边哭边回答：	Why do you come all alone this time,
"我的召海法呀，	Looking sad and worried?"
只怕象倒不吃草，	Gangxiao answered in tears:
我离人世留下你，	"My respectable Zhao Haifa!
放心不下愁断肠。	An elephant will die if it refuses to eat.
不知老天降下什么灾和难，	I am sad and worried
昨夜迷迷糊糊做个梦，	Because I may die and leave you in the world.
梦见我变成一只花蝴蝶，	I don't know what disasters and troubles I may encounter.
飞进棒改大鼓中，	Last night I dreamed a strange dream,
后又变成乌鸦，	In which I turned into a colorful butterfly
飞在棒改的剎生上。	And flew straight into Fenggai's drum.
又梦见骑着天马在空中，	Then I turned into a crow,
天神赐给我衣服，	Hovering over Fenggai's *duosheng*.
可左穿右穿套不上。	I dreamed of myself riding a heavenly horse in the sky.
又梦见妻子和女儿，	The gods gave me some clothes as a gift
在家欢喜地吃剎生。	But I just could not put them on.
还梦见宝石挎包散落地，	I dreamed about my wife and daughter.
一群商人来抢光。	They were eating *duosheng* at home with great pleasure.
梦见蜜蜂来叮头，	I dreamed about my treasure bag amulet falling on the ground,
形勇①咬我全身痒。	And a group of businessmen came to grab it.

---

① 形勇：生活在江边的一种极细小的蚊虫。

厘俸 // Li Feng

梦见南哈①遍身淋，
浑身乌黑不发光。
梦见宝剑出刀鞘，
如同铅巴一样软。
梦见长矛脱了杆，
只剩一只空杆把人戳。
梦见你的坐骑占拜舍，
右边象牙已折断，
呆呆站立不吃草。
梦见我的占拜中，
左边象牙也折断。
梦见你的宝刀缺了口，
缺口如同芝麻一般大。
梦见我的宝刀弯，
如同象牙一个样。
我的混勐啊！
只怕我冈晓死了，
婻崩不能回到你身旁。
如果我真的离开你，
婻崩就不能和你同桌来吃饭。
没有我冈晓，
谁来为你冲锋又陷阵？

① 南哈：生锈的水。

I dreamed about bees coming to sting my head,
And *xingyongs*① coming to bite me and make me itch
    all over.
I dreamed about *nanha*② poured over me,
And painting me dark all over my body.
I dreamed about my sword being pulled out of the
    scabbard,
And it was as soft as lead.
I dreamed about my long spear losing its head,
Leaving only a pole to poke at the enemy.
I dreamed about your elephant Zhanbaishe,
With its right tusk broken,
Standing rock still without eating grass.
I dreamed about my elephant Zhanbaizhong,
With its left tusk broken off.
I dreamed that your sword was no longer sharp
And had bad nicks in it.
I dreamed about my own sword,
Curved like an elephant tusk.
My respectable Hunmeng!
I'm afraid I am dying
And cannot help you take back your Nanbeng.

① Xingyong: small mosquitos living by rivers.
② Nanha: rusted water.

只要我不变成鬼，	If that happens,
你就尽管把心放。	Nanbeng will not return to eat with you at the same table.
我的混勐啊，	Without me,
我的心中很悲伤！"	Who else do you have to charge forward for you?
海罕听了忙安慰：	But as long as I remain alive,
"你清早来向我说梦，	You don't have to worry about that.
祝你寿命万年长。	My respectable Hunmeng!
你详细给我讲了梦中事，	I feel sad deep in my heart!"
愿你的灵魂永远和我相伴。	Haihan hurried to comfort him:
亲爱的冈晓啊，	"You come to tell me about your dreams early in the morning.
不要难过又悲伤。"	I wish you longevity!
说完拿出金项链，	You tell me in detail about what happened in your dreams.
挂在冈晓脖子上，	May your soul be with mine forever!
作为阿敏①来护身。	Dear Gangxiao!
项链金光射衣服，	Do not be sad and feel sorrow."
衣服发出道道光。	Then he took out a gold necklace,
海罕又为他来把魂招：	And put it on Gangxiao's neck
"愿你同海罕同过好日子，	To protect him like *amin*①.
白发到老不分散。	The golden light of the necklace was reflected
我的冈晓弟啊，	On Gangxiao's clothes.
如果梦吉祥，	Haihan then helped him to call back his spirit:
神灵会给我们金银财宝。	"May you have a good life with Haihan.
如果是凶梦，	

---

① 阿敏：护身符。　　① Amin: amulet.

厘俸 // Li Feng

死亡来临不要慌,
自古人人都如此。
相信我们会长寿,
白发到老升上天。
我们二月和俸改来作战。
参战兵马多又多,
你不用发愁。
只等布领暖的天兵到,
共同配合打胜仗。
你的梦不祥,
莫忙上战场,
把酒摆上桌,
和众官共畅饮,
并和我同住绸缎帐。
亲爱的艾召生弟弟啊,
听我的安排不要慌。"
冈晓听了又回答:
"我亲爱的召海法哥哥啊,
俗话说得好,
富人怕儿子无才华,
整天围着自己转。
勇士怕儿子衣服破烂, ①

We will spend the rest of our lives together.
My younger brother Gangxiao!
If your dream is auspicious,
We will get treasures from the gods.
If your dream is not auspicious,
Let's welcome death in a calm way.
It has been so since ancient times.
Please believe we are going to live long
Until our hair turns grey and before we go to heaven.
We have been here fighting against Fenggai since Feburuary.
Our soldiers and horses are numerous.
You don't have to be anxious.
When Bulingnuan's heavenly soldiers come,
We will coordinate and win the war.
If you think your dreams are ominous,
Then don't go back to fight in a hurry.
Put some wine on your table
And have a drink with my officers.
You can stay here and stay in my tent of silk and satin.
My dear younger brother Ai Zhaosheng,
Do as I arrange and don't panic."

---

① 指怕儿子不成才。

到处坐门槛。①	Gangxiao replied:
谁又会让孤儿来当官，	"My dear brother, Zhao Haifa!
只有咬着衣服扣子在悲伤。	As the saying goes,
将死但战旗不能倒，	Rich people are afraid that their sons are not talented
士卒不能散。	And just stay with them all the time.
如果我冈晓战死了，	Warriors are afraid that their sons wear worn out clothes①
你要扶持我的儿子艾冈罕。	And sit on door steps everywhere.②
请求你啊，召海法，	Who will let orphans come to be officials?
不要让我的儿子判②。	They can only bite their clothes' buttons sorrowfully and alone.
请给他官做，	When a general dies, his flag should not fall,
食禄一个勐。	And his soldiers should not be dispersed.
我的混勐啊，	If one day I die in a battle,
我的心愿请你记心上！"	Please support and assist my son Ai Ganghan.
	I beg you, my respectable Zhao Haifa,
	Do not let my son be *pan*③.
	Please give him an official position
	And let him receive pay from a *meng*.
	My respectable Hunmeng,
	Please keep in mind my wishes."

---

① 无所作为。
② 判：贫困、无知、困难，无吃无穿。

---

① Meaning that they are afraid that their sons will not grow to be useful and excellent people.
② Meaning they are idling their days away.
③ Pan: poor, ignorant, living a hard life and having nothing to eat or wear.

厘俸 // Li Feng

冈晓话刚完，	At the time when Gangxiao just finished these words,
俸改的兵将又开战，	Fenggai's soldiers launched another attack.
放火烧远负，	They burnt Gangxiao's camp.
各路大军只退不抵挡。	The soldiers retreated without any resistance.
退兵似牛群，	The soldiers were routed
你挤我拥纷纷乱。	Like herds of cattle pushing each other.
眼看靠近海罕的大营盘，	The enemy was approaching Haihan's camp,
俸改的兵将仍源源不断出城来。	And still more of them were surging out from the city.
形势危急人心慌，	In a situation so critical,
冈晓大声把话讲：	Gangxiao spoke loudly:
"我离开战场只片刻，	"It was just a moment ago I left my camping place.
战局就成这个样。	How can the situation turn out to be like this so quickly?
我不出战怎么行，	What if I do not go out and fight?
俸改攻破我军怎么办？	What if Fenggai breaks through our defences?
我宁可战死在象上，	I'd rather die riding on my elephant
让绸缎衣服挂在象身上！	And leave my silk clothes to be hung on its back!
我的召海法呀，	My respectable Zhao Haifa,
话说多了口会干，	I have said too much and I have become thirsty.
快把烈酒拿过来，	Get me some liquor.
烈度不高的给阿巫戛。	Get Awu Ga some which is not that strong.
你要亲手拿酒给我喝，	Pass me the liquor with your own hand,
让酒的热气满胸膛！"	And let the liquor burn in my chest."
阿巫戛连忙来劝说：	Awu Ga hurriedly came and persuaded him:
"烈酒不能过多喝，	"Don't drink too much liquor,

我的侄儿冈晓啊！"	My nephew Gangxiao!"
边说边大碗大碗的酒往肚里灌。	He then quickly drank bowl after bowl of liquor.
冈晓看了就发问：	Gangxiao asked:
"你叫我烈酒不要喝，	"You told me not to drink liquor
可是你却喝了那么多，	But you yourself have drunk so much.
一罐接一罐，	Liquor from one jar after another
酒往嗓管过，	Is poured into your mouth,
好像箐水在流淌。"	Like a flowing stream."
阿巫戛听了就回答：	Awu Ga replied:
"我可以喝一千条江河的水，	"I can drink all the water from a thousand rivers.
喝二十坛的酒也不会醉。"	I will not be drunk even when I have drunk twenty jars of liquor."
冈晓听了把话讲：	Gangxiao then said:
"你已经老了不中用，	"You are old and useless,
什么大话都乱放。	And dare to brag and boast.
你阿巫戛聪明就去指挥作战吧！"	Now that you are so smart, why don't you go to command our troops?"
说完，放下杯子，	Then he put down the glass,
转身策鞭上马。	And turned round to mount his horse.
回到营帐里，	He went back to his camp,
穿上衣甲，	Put on his armor
戴上金盔，	And golden helmet,
拉过占拜中，	Led out Zhanbaizhong,
换上新象舆，	Put a new howdah on him,
左转右转仔细看。	
冈晓一声令下，	

厘俸 // Li Feng

战鼓擂起来，
占拜中昂首大声吼叫，
士卒离营奔战场，
势如翻江倒海卷巨浪。
鲁非横空似红霞，
土炮轰鸣齐开花。
只见人群纷纷倒地上，
战袍已被鲜血染。
冈晓脚蹬占拜中如流星闪，
俸改的兵丁两边哗哗倒，
急急忙忙退入城。
俸改站在高楼举目望，
见冈晓攻城来势猛，
兵丁如大雾弥漫白茫茫。
到处只听喊杀声。
炮声隆隆震天响。
俸改见了怒火烧，
下令抬出大酒坛，
放在宫廷正中央。
他手中拿起瓜戛占①，
捋起双袖跺脚骂：
　"海罕养的象能作战，

And checked all his equipment carefully.
At his command,
The drum was beaten.
Zhanbaizhong strode forward with a loud roar.
All the soldiers left their camps and dashed to the battlefield
Like overwhelming billows.
The *lufei*s were fired and rose-coloured smoke rose in the sky.
The cannons were fired, like flower blossoms.
The soldiers fell down dead and injured.
Their blood stained their war robes.
Gangxiao drove Zhanbaizhong like a meteor,
Forcing Fenggai's soldiers in front of him to dash away in fear
And flee to the city.
Fenggai stood on a high building and looked into the distance,
And saw Gangxiao attacking in a ferocious way.
Gangxiao's soldiers covered the battlefield like dense fog.
There were shouts of killing and fighting everywhere.
There were deafening rumbles of cannon fires everywhere.
Fenggai was very angry to see this

---

① 瓜戛占：傣族首领特有的一种盛酒的金制器皿，状如缸钵。

养的人勇猛又善战。	And asked his men to carry out a big jar of wine
只听说，	And put it in the center of the court.
这边的人马是冈晓的，	With a guagazhan① in his hand,
那边的人马还是冈晓的。	He rolled up his sleeves, stamped his feet and shouted:
我们的儿孙死了不知有多少，	"Haihan's elephants have high combat effectiveness.
我养的大象不能战，	Haihan's soldiers fight bravely and skillfully.
象牙虽粗大，	I am told
牙根不长包。①	That the soldiers and horses here are Gangxiao's,
我养的士卒不像样，	And the soldiers and horses there are also Gangxiao's.
贪生又怕死，	How many of our sons and grandsons have been killed
不论令哪个召冈②去作战，	in the battle?
都推说象牙已受伤。	My elephants are not good at fighting.
派出将领上战场，	Their tusks are thick and strong,
回来象尾被砍伤。	But at the end of their tusks there are no bulges.②
召幢已经死了七员将，	My soldiers are all cowards.
你们都白吃我的饭，	They are mortally afraid of death.
勐景罕将要陷落变水塘。	No matter which Zhaogang③ is ordered to go for a fight,
是否冈晓以铁当饭？	He will shirk his responsibility by saying that his elephant
刀枪不能伤他。	is wounded.
是否他的妻子用铁当菜让他吃？	I have sent some officers to the battlefield

---

① 牙根长包的象凶猛。
② 召冈：小头领，勐的首长。

---

① Guagazhan: a wine vessel used only by the chiefs of the Dai people.
② Elephants with bulges growing on the end of their tusks are considered to be fierce and brave.
③ Zhaogang: the chief of a *meng*.

厘俸 // Li Feng

谁和他战谁灭亡。
我的众官啊！
谁有胆量不怕死，
饮下我手中这杯酒，
砍下冈晓的头给我看，
我就将最美丽而宽广的地方赏给他，
将最漂亮的姑娘送他做妻子，
还要再把黄金赏，
冈晓的首级有多重，
所赏的黄金就重头三倍。
如果黄金不足赤，
再加上银两。"
一千个勐的首领端坐金椅上，
召冈、召伴①列位坐后排，
垂头静听不讲话，
宫廷悄悄无声响。
俸改的弟弟皆温和皆伴，
身子歪靠椅背上。
一员大将站起来，
他的名字叫卫大罕。
他认为自己艺高人胆大，
日夜想着要与冈晓决一死战。

---

① 召伴：千夫长。

And they all come back with their elephant tails cut off.
I have already lost seven officers.
I provide for you in vain.
Mengjinghan is going to fall and become a pool.
I wonder if Gangxiao eats iron as rice,
Because he is so invulnerable.
I wonder if his wife let him eat iron as vegetables?
Whoever fought against him died.
My dear officers!
If you are bold enough and not afraid of death,
Come and drink this glass of wine in my hand
And cut off Gangxiao's head and present it to me.
Then you will get a beautiful and vast land as a reward,
The most beautiful girl as your wife,
And also gold.
You will get gold three times
The weight of Gangxiao's head.
If the gold is not pure enough,
I can give you some silver."
The chiefs of one thousand *mengs* sat up in their golden chairs,
With Zhaogangs and Zhaobans① sitting behind them.
They all listened to Fenggai quietly but did not speak.

---

① Zhaoban: the chief who rules a thousand households.

他抒起手袖骂众官，	No sound was heard in the whole court.
唾沫横飞气焰狂。	Fenggai's younger brothers Jiewen and Jieban
皆温、皆伴叩头向俸改问：	Were leaning on the backs of their chairs.
"我俩为何不能出战？	A senior general rose to his feet.
冈晓即使有虎熊般百倍之威，	His name was Weidahan.
也要把他头来斩。	He thought he was skillful and brave,
亲爱的召法温俸罕，	Always wanting to wage a life-and-death fight against Gangxiao.
我们要想出好计谋。	He rolled up his sleeves and pressed his officers,
不要只把冈晓攻，	Blustering with overwhelming arrogance.
否则援兵会助战。	Jiewen and Jieban kowtowed to Fenggai and asked:
应首先攻打东方，	"Why can't we two go to fight?
那里的首领是桑洛。	We would like to cut off Gangxiao's head
再派矛手攻桑本，	Even if he has power hundreds of times that of tigers and bears.
又派骑兵紧跟上，	Dear respectable Zhao Fawenfenghan!
手持弓弩去偷袭。	We need to figure out a good plot and scheme.
我俩再驱赶百头象，	We should not just attack Gangxiao,
中路径直取冈晓。	For that will only lead to the arrival of reinforcements.
即使他是铁一块，	We should attack the east side first.
也要把他化成汤。	The commander there is Sangluo.
敬爱的召法温俸罕啊，	We should send spearmen to fight against Sangben.
我们的主意怎么样？"	Let the cavalry men follow closely
俸改听了连点头，	And launch a sneak attack with bows.
接着就把命令下：	

厘俸 // Li Feng

"三千哈火塔①做准备，
长刀日夜不离身，
刀鞘亮闪闪。
三百哈火吞②，
把刀当妻抱着睡。
入山不怕虎，
声如熊虎嗥。
棍棒戳眼眼不眨，
矛戳脸面如抓痒。
弩射肋骨多舒服③，
边练武功边吃饭。
用刀互砍闹着玩，
不是这样手痒痒。
三千冒暖冈④，
五十万冒暖转⑤，
三百万召暮烈⑥，

We two will drive hundreds of elephants
To go straight for Gangxiao.
Even if he is a piece of iron,
We will melt him into water.
Dear respectable Zhao Fawenfenghan,
How do you like our idea?"
Fenggai nodded his head again and again.
Then he gave an order:
"Three thousand *hahuotas*① should get ready,
Always carrying their long swords with them.
The sheath of their swords must be polished.
Three hundred *hahuotuns*②
Should hold their swords like their wives when they sleep.
You should go to the mountains without fear of tigers.
You should shout like a bear roars.
You must not blink your eyes when the sticks stab at you.
You should consider the poke of spears as scratching an intch,

---

① 哈火塔：指俸改的猛士，十分凶悍的人。
② 哈火吞：指俸改的猛士，十分凶悍的人。
③ 弓弩射不穿，反而有舒服之感。
④ 冒：未婚男青年。暖冈：守卫俸改正官的卫士。
⑤ 冒暖转：守卫官廷的卫队。
⑥ 暮烈：戴铁盔的士卒。

---

① Hahuota: warriors of Fenggai, who are very fierce and tough.
② Hahuotun: warriors of Fenggai, who are very fierce and tough.

七百万召海短①,
这些猛士全出征,
我一个也不留身旁。
随同战象倾城出,
密密麻麻把大地铺盖,
一点空隙也不留,
直捣对方象鼻上!
众官们啊,
这次必须打胜仗!"
皆温、皆伴得命令,
请求俸改赐战象。
俸改又把话来传:
"我的两位将领啊,
需要什么自己看!"
俸改下令牵出英着节,
手拿瓜戛占,
盛酒入金杯,
洒在地面上。
开口把话说:
"八百头战象,

---

① 召海短:穿着前胸后背由铜片做成的形如圆状的护身衣甲的士卒。

And the pierce of an arrow into your ribs as being comfortable.
You should keep drilling even while having meals,
Then you will feel comfortable
If you are not busy fiddling with your guns and swords.
Three thousand *Mao Nuangang*①,
Five hundred thousand *Mao Nuanzhuan*②,
Three million *Zhao Mulie*③,
Seven million *Zhao Haiduan*④,
Will all be sent to the battlefield.
I won't keep any one of these warriors with me.
They are going with all the elephants in this city,
To cover the land completely
Without any holes or cracks.
We are aiming right at the elephant trunks of the enemy.
My dear officers!
We must win the battle this time!"
Jiewen and Jieban took the order
And asked Fenggai to reward them with war elephants.
Fenggai then said:

---

① Mao Nuangang: Mao: unmarried young men. Nuangang: soldiers guarding Fenggai's central palace.
② Mao Nuanzhan: the soldiers guarding Fenggai's court.
③ Mulie: the soldiers wearing iron helmets.
④ Zhao Haiduan: the soldiers wearing armor made of round copper pieces in the front and at the back.

厘俸 // Li Feng

任凭你们来挑选。
英着节脚粗如蜂窝盘，
送给皆温弟弟去作战。"
又牵出占艾兰①，
送给卫大罕。
这头象的牙粗如盐臼般，
不怕炮也不怕枪，
几条花纹背上长。
将领们啊！"
俸改一声把令下，
鸣炮三声震天响。
千军万马如流石，
呐喊奔跑赴战场。
北方城门大大开，
涌出骑兵和战象。
南方城门大大开，
万马如缅卯②，
出洞遮天来。

"My dear generals,
Just take the ones you are satisfied with!"
Fenggai ordered a soldier to bring out Yingzhejie.
He took a guagazhan in his hand,
Poured some wine in the gold cup,
And sprinkled the wine on the ground.
He then spoke:
"Eight hundred war elephants
Are here for your selection.
The legs of Yingzhejie are as thick as a huge beehive.
This elephant is suitable for my younger brother Jiewen."
Then he led out Zhan'ailan①
And gave it to Weidahan.
The tusks of this elephant were as thick as a mortar.
It is afraid of neither cannons nor guns.
On its back there are some stripes.
My generals!"
At the words of Fenggai's command,
Cannons were fired with a deafening sound.
Tens of thousands of soldiers and horses
Rushed to the battlefield like rolling stones.
The northern city gate opened.

① 占艾兰：大象名。
② 缅卯：雨季时经常出没的一种会飞的蚂蚁。

① Zhan'ailan: name of an elephant.

	The cavalrymen and the war elephants surged out.
	The southern city gate opened.
	Thousands of horses dashed out like *mianmaos*[①].
	Coming out as if they would block out the sky.
冈晓抬头看北门，	Gangxiao looked up at the north gate,
象头、长矛密密麻。	Where he saw numerous elephant heads and spears.
转头再往南门看，	Then he turned to the south gate,
大象的脚步声震云端。	Where he heard sound of elephant footsteps giving the sky tremors .
东门只见人流涌，	At the east gate he saw streams of people,
炮声震耳聋。	And heard deafening sound of cannon shots.
又见桑洛蹬着大象，	He also saw Sangluo drive his elephant
雄踞壕沟来迎战。	Across the ditch to meet the charge.
刀砍矛戳，	There were cold flashes of
道道寒光冷飕飕，	The waving swords and thrusting spears,
双方人马死无数。	Leading to countless deaths and injuries on both sides.
战象互拼杀，	The war elephants fought against each other,
相持不退让。	Refusing to retreat.
又见敌军围桑本，	He then saw the enemy soldiers surrounding Sangben
砍杀之声比雷响。	With shouts of fighting louder than thunders.

---

① Mianmao: flying ants that appear in the rainy season.

厘俸 // Li Feng

俸改又把命令下：	Fenggai gave another order:
"直取冈晓，	"Go and kill Gangxiao!
以一当百要血战，	Fight to the last drop of your blood!
冈晓再勇也难逃。"	However brave he is, Gangxiao will have no way to flee."
三千哈伙塔把他围，	Three thousand *hahuota* warriors surrounded Gangxiao,
皆温的象队左边上。	With Jiewen's elephant herds to their left.
象牙的尖端铜来包，	The tips of the elephant's tusks were wrapped with copper
又坚又硬难抵挡。	To make them impenetrably hard and tough.
右边又来卫大罕，	On the right side, there were Weidahan's soldiers
士卒手持钩矛齐呐喊。	Yelling with hooked spears in their hands.
左右齐向前，	The troops on the left and on the right moved forward at the same time,
冈晓已被紧包围。	And surrounded Gangxiao tightly.
两军相战，	The two sides fought
人如海，象如潮。	With a sea of soldiers and a wave of elephants.
俸改的兵马源源不断又出城，	Fenggai's soldiers and horses continued
千军万马黑压压，	To surge out of the city like black clouds
如洪水暴发江河涨，	And like a flood from an overflowing river.
海罕的大军难抵挡。	Haihan's army could hardly resist such a powerful attack.
冈庄想去救冈晓，	Gangzhuang wanted to go to rescue Gangxiao
蹬象象不往前走，	But his elephant refused to move forward
反而怒吼往回转。	And turned back with a roar instead.
俸改的士卒又放土炮又发箭，	Fenggai's soldiers fired
犹如雨点般。	A rain of cannon shots and arrows
弓箭射在象身上，	

头头大象插满箭。	At the enemy elephants,
满坝只听象吼叫，	Who, with arrows sticking into their hides,
海罕各路兵丁退田坝。	Howled with pain all over the land.
冈晓仍然被围困，	All the troops of Haihan had to pull back to the fields.
就像乌云遮太阳。	Gangxiao was still trapped
海罕在远负高台站，	Like the sun covered by dark clouds.
目睹冈晓形势急，	Haihan stood on a high platform of the camp
心中不安又慌乱。	And witnessed Gangxiao's critical situation.
向天跪拜连叩首说：	Upset and in panic,
"神灵啊，	He knelt down and kowtowed to heaven:
千棵万棵树死了，	"Oh, gods,
请留下中间的那棵。	If thousands of trees have to die,
千人万人死了，	Leave the one in the middle alive please.
请把弟弟艾召生留在世上。"	If thousands of people have to be killed,
天神拨开云雾，	Leave my younger brother Ai Zhaosheng alive please."
对着海罕把话讲：	The gods pushed aside the clouds
"海罕啊，海罕，	And spoke:
前几天冈晓把鸡卦吃了，	"Haihan, oh, Haihan!
这是对天神的冒犯，	A few days ago Gangxiao ate the chicken bones meant for divination.
我们不再保护他。	This offended us,
你的象如石崖般多，	So we won't protect him anymore.
为什么不给冈晓骑一头？	You've got elephants as numerous as rocks.
现在冈晓的坐骑是双线的，	Why didn't you give him one?
原是俸改的战象。	

厘俸 // Li Feng

等一会就会有人叫喊：	Gangxiao is riding Shuangxian's elephant.
旧刀不要把主子砍，	It was originally Fenggai's.
旧锄头不要去把根挖！	Soon you will hear somebody shout:
天要他死了，	An old knife should not cut its master
你不要怕孤单。	And an old hoe should not dig up its own root!
攻城怎么不齐心合力？	Gangxiao is destined to die!
天神的子孙啊，	Please do not be afraid to be alone.
是善良的人！"	Moreover, why didn't you attack the city with all your troops?
海罕听了心悲伤，	Descendant of the gods,
不知如何是好，	You are so kind-hearted!"
像热锅上的蚂蚁团团转。	Hearing these words, Haihan became sorrowful
他定下心来想了想，	And really didn't know what to do,
急忙下令把话传：	And got anxious like a cat on hot bricks.
"赶快把占拜舍牵出来，	He calmed down and thought for a while,
我要去攻勐景罕，	And ordered:
我要去救冈晓，	"Lead out Zhanbaishe quickly.
今天就同他一起战死吧！"	I'm going to attack Mengjinghan.
阿巫戛圆睁两眼对海罕说：	I'm going to save Gangxiao.
"求求你呀召海法，	I'm going to fight to the death with him today!"
明知自己刀不快，	Awu Ga was shocked to hear that and said to him:
偏要去把竹节砍，	"Please don't! My respectable Zhao Haifa!
刀口缺了无人再复样。	Obviously you know your knife is not that sharp,
你不要心急啊！	But you insist on cutting bamboo joints.
俸改的城池这么大，	

里面的鲁勒不知有多少。	Nobody can repair it if the knife blade gets some nicks.
心莫急，	Don't be so impatient!
否则要把事弄坏。	Fenggai's city is so big
我的召海法呀，	And we don't know how many districts it has.
冷静下来作打算。"	Don't be so impatient!
海罕叫来陶桑海说：	Otherwise things may be ruined.
"快快骑上我的占拜舍，	My respectable Zhao Haifa!
支援冈晓莫迟缓。	Please calm down and make a careful plan."
我身边的兵和将，	Haihan then called Tao Sanghai and said to him:
你身边的那些大象，	"Ride my Zhanbaishe
一个不留全部上战场，	To support Gangxiao without delay.
让冈晓安全往回转。"	The soldiers and the officers at my side
陶桑海立即率兵出发，	And the elephants at your side
如流星般直杀勐景坝。	Should all go the battlefield
他见冈晓重重被包围，	To help Gangxiao return safely."
金幡幢在中间团团转。	Taosanghai set off at once with the troops,
陶桑海不敢再拖延，	And hurried to Mengjing Basin like a shooting star.
蹬着占拜舍冲上前。	He found Gangxiao heavily surrounded by the enemy,
弓弩炮一齐发，	With his golden prayer flag fluttering around in the middle.
对着占拜舍射过来。	Tao Sanghai could not delay any more
占拜舍一边吼叫一边闯，	And drove Zhanbaishe forward.
冈晓看见火气上说：	The enemy's bows and the cannons
"你这下贱的陶桑海，	Were all aimed at Zhanbaishe.
海罕的战象千万头，	Zhanbaishe roared and dashed about.

厘俸 // Li Feng

你为何专骑占拜舍?
让人家又炮轰来又刀砍,
海罕怎能离开占拜舍?
你打仗实在太无能,
只会骑着占拜舍来游玩。"
陶桑海听后怒火起,
回口大骂不相让:
　"下贱的冈晓你懂啥,
死神已降临你身上。
海法才令我骑上占拜舍,
急急忙忙来救你。
兄弟之间要同心,
合在一起有力量。
今天即使战死了,
也要死在象身上。
现在俸改的兵马到处是,
我们为什么还要互相骂?
你说话就像疯子一般。
冈晓啊,
既然如此你就等着看。"
陶桑海一怒之下往回转,
冈晓又被紧包围。
俸改的大象如石滚滚来,
援兵一眼看不断。

Seeing this, Gangxiao said angrily:
"You shameless Tao Sanghai!
Haihan has so many elephants,
But why do you especially choose Zhanbaishe to ride?
Now the elephant is at risk of being shot and cut.
What if Haihan loses his Zhanbaishe?
You are incompetent in fighting
And can only ride Zhanbaishe here for sightseeing."
Tao Sanghai was so angry to hear that
And could not help condemning Gangxiao:
"You shameless Gangxiao!
The god of death has come to you!
This is why Zhao Haifa asked me to ride his Zhanbaishe
To come to rescue you.
As brothers we should fight as one man
To make us more powerful.
If we have to die today,
We must die on the back of our elephants.
Now Fenggai's soldiers and horses are everywhere
　　around us.
Why do we still waste our time cursing each other?
You spoke like a maniac.
Oh Gangxiao!
In that case, let us wait and see."

冈晓被围千百层，	Tao Sanghai turned back to his camp in a rage.
阵脚却没有乱。	Gangxiao then was under siege again.
士卒久战沙场心不慌，	Fenggai's elephants came like rolling stones.
背靠背来四面战。	His einforcements kept coming out as well.
占拜中往左猛一冲，	Gangxiao was surrounded circle by circle,
对方刹那倒下一大片，	But he was not thrown into confusion yet.
再往右一闯，	His soldiers were battle-hardened and never panicked.
哗哗又倒一大堆，	They began to fight back to back.
俸改兵丁难抵挡。	Zhanbaizhong dashed to the left,
一场血战，	And the enemy soldiers fell down in crowds.
双方的人马战象，	Then Zhanbaizhong dashed to the right,
疲劳不堪难再战。	And the enemy soldies lay down in piles.
冈晓下令射火炮，	Fenggai's soldiers could hardly resist.
火炮的红光映天空，	In this bloody battle,
只见城墙轰隆倒。	The soldiers, horses and the elephants of both sides
冈晓紧蹬大象往前冲，	Were all fatigued to the extreme and could fight no more.
兵将在后齐声喊。	Gangxiao ordered his men to fire the cannons
龙腾虎跃越战壕，	And destroy the city wall.
俘获大象二十栏。	The red light of the cannon illuminated the sky.
俸改兵败退回城，	Gangxiao drove his elephant forward,
冈晓乘胜追击不肯放。	With his soldiers and officers cheering behind.
转眼来到一悬崖，	Gangxiao's troops crossed the trenches
到处巨石林立，	And captured twenty herds of enemy elephants.
崖石陡峭。	Fenggai's troops had to retreat into the city.

厘俸 // Li Feng

突然间，流石滚滚如天降！	Gangxiao chased after the retreating enemy
冈晓兵将遭伏击，	And finally came to a cliff
死伤无数。	Where there was a forest of huge rocks
战象欲退却不能，	And steep cliffs.
往前更艰难。	Suddenly rolling rocks came down.
俸改的兵丁手持大刀和长矛，	Gangxiao's army fell into an ambush
如旋风卷杀而来。	And many of the soldiers were killed or injured.
冈晓退一步，	Their elephants wanted to pull out but failed.
戴头盔的士卒遭伤亡。	It was even more difficult for them to move forward.
冈晓退三步，	Fenggai's soldiers held their swords and long spears
二十乃干①又落下马。	And came as a whirling and sweeping wind.
城楼上，	Gangxiao took one step back,
助威呐喊声响云端。	And the soldiers wearing helmets suffered heavy casualties.
冈晓抬头看前方，	Gangxiao took three steps back,
二十头大象甩着长鼻冲过来。	And another twenty *naigans*① fell off their horses.
左路也来围，	On the city wall,
右路也来堵。	The cheer of Fenggai's side echoed in the sky.
冈晓仰头把天看，	Gangxiao looked ahead
愁云笼罩黑茫茫。	And saw twenty elephants swing their trunks and dash towards him.
冈晓心中也悲愁，	He was surrounded from the left,
不知老天让谁亡。	And blocked from the right.
他蹬着大象往右冲，	Gangxiao looked up at the sky.
俸改的兵将纷纷落下象。	

---

① 乃干：村寨的头领。

① Naigan: head of a village.

他蹬着大象往左冲，	The sky was enveloped in gloomy clouds.
到处是土坎，	Gangxiao became sad and low-spirited
俸改的兵将冲得跌跌撞撞。	And did not know who was destined to die first.
冈晓的矛在飞舞，	He commanded his elephant to dash to the right
只听鬼哭狼嚎一片乱，	And struck Fenggai's soldiers off their elephant's backs.
俸改的兵马四处散。	He ordered his elephant to dash to the left
	Where there were bumps everywhere,
	And drove Fenggai's soldiers to stagger along.
	Gangxiao's spear was waving
	And the enemy soldiers cried and screamed like ghosts
	And ran away in all directions in confusion.
俸改骑着飞马，	Fenggai, on his flying horse,
在天空中来回往下看，	Observed the situation from high above.
看见形势太危急，	He found the situation so critical
声如炸雷高声喊：	And shouted in a voice like a clap of thunder:
"占拜中啊，我的象，	"Oh Zhanbaizhong, my elephant!
旧锄莫挖根，	An old hoe should not dig up its own root.
旧刀莫把主人砍！"	An old knife should not cut its master!"
占拜中听到叫吼声，	Zhanbaizhong stopped
站立倾听一动不动。	And listened to the shouting motionlessly.
不管冈晓怎么蹬，	No matter how hard Gangxiao drove it,
占拜中把象牙插地高声吼。	Zhanbaizhong just poked its tusks into the ground and yelled loudly.
冈晓怒气上心头，	

厘俸 // Li Feng

用矛戳大象。	Gangxiao got irritated
占拜中疼痛忽狂奔,	And pricked the elephant with his spear.
如醉又似疯。	Zhanbaizhong could not bear the pain
冈晓直往城里冲,	And dashed around madly like a drunk and crazy man.
越过九条沟,	Gangxiao rushed straight into the city.
冲杀到安望①。	He crossed nine ditches
占拜中满身是刀伤,	And reached Anwang①.
冈晓士卒紧跟上。	Zhanbaizhong was wounded all over its body.
俸改放出大象二十栏,	Gangxiao's soldiers followed it closely.
又把冈晓来包围。	Fenggai then sent out twenty herds of elephants
俸改的弟弟皆温来出战,	To surround Gangxiao again.
各路兵将也出动,	Fenggai's younger brother Jiewen came out to fight.
锐利长矛肩上扛。	Soldiers and generals of other troops also set out
冈晓的兵将背靠背,	With sharp spears carried on their shoulders.
拼尽全力来抵抗。	Gangxiao's soldiers fought back to back
无奈俸改兵将多,	And resisted with all their strength.
死了一个十个上。	However, Fenggai's soldiers outnumbered Gangxiao's too many.
冈晓的兵马在减少,	When one got killed ten more would come to fight in his place.
如同河中沙石慢慢被水淹,	Gangxiao's soldiers were decreasing in number,
如同碗中米饭一口一口被吃掉。	Like sand eroded by river water,
俸改的三千名武士拿大刀,	Like rice in a bowl eaten bit by bit.
七千名钩矛手往前闯,	
直指冈晓大象占拜中。	

---

① 安望：城中一地名，地势宽阔。　① Anwang: the name of a flat place in the city.

皆温骑在大象上,	Fenggai's three thousand warriors carrying knifes and swords
金舆高插孔雀尾,	And seven thousand spearmen holding hooked spears rushed
指挥兵马来作战。	Towards Gangxiao's elephant Zhanbaizhong.
兵丁和大象蜂拥而出,	Jiewen rode an elephant,
就像地裂和天崩,	With peacock's feathers plugged into the golden howdah,
刀矛发出动人心魄的声响!	To command his troops in the battle.
	His soldiers and elephants swarmed out.
	The swords and spears clashed with a sound
	Like that of earthquakes and landslides.
另一支人马是卫大罕的,	Another group of troops, led by Weidahan,
迎着冈晓来追赶。	Came to attack Gangxiao.
冈晓象队摆开阵,	The elephants of Gangxiao met them head-on.
一场恶战又开始。	Another fierce battle began.
冈晓的战象战死一头,少一头,	When one of Gangxiao's elephants got killed, he lost it.
对方的战象战死一头,十头上。	When one of Fenggai's elephants got killed, he put in ten more.
冈晓的兵丁阵亡一个,少一个,	When one of Gangxiao's soldiers died, he lost him.
俸改的兵丁战死一个,十个上。	When one of Fenggai's soldiers died, he added ten more.
占拜中精疲力又尽,	Zhanbaizhong was exhausted,
其余大象也无力再冲闯,	And so were the rest of the elephants.
慢慢靠拢相保护。	They slowly drew close to protect each other.
俸改的铁甲猛士逼上来,	Fenggai's warriors wearing armor approached
长矛大刀挥起又落下,	And slashed them with swords and knives.
刀断矛弯血四溅,	

厘俸 // Li Feng

声声惨叫传四方。
天摇地动鬼神嚎,
人仰马翻一片乱。
五色头盔遍地是,
无数尸体堆成山。
惨淡红光映天空,
地上血流如溪淌。
一场混战终停歇,
冈晓的士卒全阵亡,
只有冈晓活下来。
只见他,
胡须飞飘,
紧咬牙关。
俸改的兵将不敢近,
后边冲来卫大罕,
蹬着大象高声喊:
"艾冈晓啊,艾冈晓,
最凶恶的人也要死于刀枪,
你坏事做尽不得好报,
必将成为别人的刀下肉,
剁生就是你的下场。
最顽强的人也要成为刀下鬼,
到时妻儿收尸不见头,
只能用葫芦来充当,

The swords were broken, spears bent, and blood spattered everywhere.
The screams of pain spread all over the battlefield,
As if the earth and the sky were spinning violently.
There was complete chaos in the battlefield.
Colorful helmets were scattered all over the ground.
Dead bodies piled up into mounds.
The sky was reflected with light red.
Blood flowed on the ground like streams.
At last the fierce battle ceased.
All of Gangxiao's soldiers died in the battle.
Gangxiao was the only one left alive.
With his beard fluttering in the wind,
Gangxiao
Clenched his teeth.
Fenggai's soldiers and officers dared not approach him.
Weidahan rushed forward from behind
And shouted on the back of his elephant:
"Gangxiao, oh Gangxiao!
Even the most ferocious person like you will die by a gun or a sword.
You have done no good deeds and surely will not be well rewarded.
Becoming *duosheng* is your destiny.

死后灵魂不归身。	Even the most tenacious person like you
死神已到你身旁,	Will become a ghost under a sword.
你别发抖别害怕!"	Your wife and children will not be able to find your head
冈晓开口便大骂:	When they come to bury you and will have to bury a gourd instead.
"你这下贱的小人,	Your soul thus cannot return to your body.
残忍的豹子!	The god of death now comes.
我蹬大象来此地,	Don't be scared and frightened!"
是要砍倒大树连根拔。	Gangxiao cursed:
俸改横行霸道太猖狂,	"You despicable villain!
把海罕妻子活活抢。	Cruel leopard!
召尼率领千军万马来讨伐,	I rode my elephant here
欲从虎口救妻回家里。	To cut the big tree and uproot it.
可怜俸改的兵将空卖命,	Fenggai is so arrogant
白白死在我刀下。	That he captured the wife of Haihan.
可怜无辜的勐景罕,	Zhao Ni, the respectable Haihan, led his great army
臭气熏天遭大殃。	To rescue his wife from the mouth of a tiger.
俸改到处把别人的妻子抢,	It is a pity that Fenggai's soldiers and officers
人人怒火填胸膛。	Died in vain under my sword.
如果不把俸改杀,	It is a pity that the innocent city of Mengjinghan
我冈晓决不停止作战。	Suffers disaster and becomes a disgusting place.
天不容俸改作恶,	Fenggai goes everywhere to capture the wives of other people,
也不容你们横行又猖狂!	And fills everyone's heart with anger.
假若我冈晓战死在象身上,	
灵魂不上天,	

厘俸 // Li Feng

变鬼也要坐大象，	I will never ever stop fighting
帮助海罕来攻打勐景罕。	Until Fenggai is killed.
现在我俩比高低，	Fenggai's devilry and atrocity are intolerable!
不知天要谁先亡。	His tyrannous manners and ferociousness are intolerable!
即使我先死，	If I die on the back of my war elephant,
天神也要保海罕。	My soul won't ascend to heaven.
说了半天你是谁？	I'll remain on my elephant even if I turn into a ghost,
有胆量就来同我较量！"	And help Haihan attack Mengjinghan.
卫大罕傲然把话讲：	Now you and I am competing with each other,
"我是卫大罕大官，	And who knows who is destined to die first.
心中早已发了誓，	Even if I die first,
日夜盼望把你斩。	The gods will still protect Haihan.
今日良机终来到，	Who in hell are you, anyway?
乘坐我的占艾兰，	If you are courageous enough, just come and fight!"
与你决斗见刀枪。	Weidahan said arrogantly:
即使我死了，	"I am officer Weidahan.
也要留名传四方。	I have anticipated for this opportunity day and night
艾冈晓啊，	And made up my mind to kill you.
你的末日来到了。"	Now the good chance comes.
卫大罕抽出长梭镖，	I will ride my Zhan'ailan
梭镖搭在象头上，	And fight against you.
道道绿色寒光闪。	Even if I die,
两象怒吼来交锋，	My name will be cherished and spread all around.
占艾兰在占拜中鼻下团团转，	Oh Gangxiao,

灰尘蔽天鼓炮鸣。	You are doomed to die today."
冈晓取出通香来摇晃，	Weidahan pulled out his long spear
可它在黑暗中不发光，	And placed it on the head of his elephant.
神灵已不护冈晓！	The spear emitted a cold greenish light.
冈晓见状心不慌，	The two elephants howled and fought.
他久战沙场不一般。	Zhan'ailan turned around and around under
左来左挡，	Zhanbaizhong's tusks.
右来右挡。	The drums beat and the sky was veiled by dust.
矛杆咔嚓一声被折断，	Gangxiao took out his amulet bag and shook it.
占拜中受伤跟跟跄跄，	But it did not shine in the darkness.
金幡幢东摇西又晃。	The gods did not protect Gangxiao any more!
俸改的士兵挥长刀，	But Gangxiao, as an experienced fighter,
想把占拜中的脚来砍。	Did not panic at all.
占拜中晕头迷方向，	He withstood an attack from his left
三千个武士冲上来，	And resisted the fight from his right.
三百把钩刀挥起来，	A spear broke with a cracking sound.
占拜中的脚被砍。	Zhanbaizhong was injured and staggered.
大吼一声倒地下，	The golden prayer flag on its back swayed.
象牙插进泥土中。	Fenggai's soldiers waved their swords
冈晓端坐象舆上，	To cut the feet of Zhanbaizhong.
拔出宝刀猛挥舞。	Zhanbaizhong was confused and disoriented.
俸改的兵将眼花缭乱，	Three thousand warriors dashed forward
卫大罕拿起梭镖飞向冈晓，	And waved their three hundred hook knives
冲上十个大汉挥铁棒，	And cut off Zhanbaizhong's feet.

厘俸 // Li Feng

冈晓连人带舆倒在象身上。
众兵将争相举刀来乱砍，
可是冈晓皮肉毫不伤。
卫大罕跳下大象来，
抽出宝刀砍下冈晓的头，
冈晓死在象身上。
俸改的士卒争先恐后去拾头，
冈晓的两耳还坠着闪亮的金耳环。
俸改的兵将高兴地把舌头弹，
七嘴八舌开了腔：
"火旺能降水，
九层地狱都烧尽。
水大能降火，
我们人多胜冈晓。
人死首级离僵尸，
冈晓死了还把牙关紧紧咬，
脸不变色怒气还未消。
冈晓首级放在象舆，
胡须还在迎风飘。"

The elephant roared loudly and fell down,
Its tusks poking into the ground.
Gangxiao sat on the howdah on the elephant,
And pulled out his sword to chop and hack,
Dazzling Fenggai's soldiers.
Weidahan threw his spear at Gangxiao.
Ten burly chaps rushed forward and beat Gangxiao
    with fists.
Gangxiao and his howdah fell from the elephant's back.
Then the soldiers cut him with their knives,
Only to find that they could not hurt Gangxiao.
Weidahan jumped down from his elephant
And pulled out his sword and cut off Gangxiao's head.
Gangxiao died on the back of his elephant.
Fenggai's soldiers picked up the head.
Gangxiao's ears still wore shiny gold ear rings.
Fenggai's soldiers were so happy that they made faces,
And all tried to say something:
"Water yields to a big fire,
Which can burn out the nine layers of hell.
Fire also yields to water.
Likewise, we defeated Gangxiao by outnumbering him.
Gangxiao's head is separated from his body,
But he still clenches his teeth tightly

And his rage is still not allayed.

His head is put on the howdah on the back of his elephant.

His beard is still dancing in the wind."

俸改的军队打胜仗，	Fenggai's army won the battle
锣响鼓敲闹嚷嚷。	And there were gongs and drum beats everywhere.
手摇金把羽毛扇，	People waved fans with golden handles,
又唱歌来又跳舞。	Singing and dancing, welcoming
欢声雷动迎凯旋，	The triumphant return of the army with cheers and laughter.
战马整齐来列队。	The war horses stood in arrays.
战象十头为一排，	The war elephants lined up in groups of ten.
战旗迎风齐招展，	The war flags fluttered in the wind.
浩浩荡荡穿城过，	They walked across the city with great strength and vigor.
百姓倾城齐欢迎。	People in the city all came out to welcome them.
有的站在转颂①上，	Some of them crowded on a *zhuansong*①,
熙熙攘攘高处看。	Watching from high above.
崩珍②争相来迎接，	The *bengzhens*② scrambled to welcome the army as well.
姑娘倾心英雄汉，	They admired heroes
眉目传情把手招。	And winked at them with amorous glances.
俸改站在转颂上观望，	Fenggai stood on a *zhuansong* and watched the triumphant return,
几百妻妾相跟随。	Followed by hundreds of wives and concubines.
美酒佳肴已摆上，	

---

① 转颂：八层高楼的凉台。

② 崩：一群。珍：宫廷中的女奴。

① Zhuansong: balcony of an eight-storey building.

② Beng: a group. Zhen: female slaves in the royal court.

厘俸 // Li Feng

设宴慰劳兵和将。
胜利战鼓齐声鸣,
俸改只等冈晓的首级到。
俸改事先把话传:
"人人要说海罕死,
海罕的首级已被砍。
首级如今已送上,
哄骗婻崩死了心,
跟随俸改不思返。"
婻崩听到大吃惊,
跑到转颂探实情。
俸改开口把话讲:
"你说海罕是天神的子孙,
别人杀他杀不死。
你说尼苏①是烂皮②的子孙,
任凭你戮不会亡。
现在我已打胜仗,
你的哭声最动听,
让我听听细欣赏。
婻崩啊,
你也不要太伤心!"
婻勐③以为是真话,

① 尼苏: 对海罕的贬称。
② 烂皮: 神灵。
③ 婻勐: 婻崩。

Good wine and delicious food were served
To reward the soldiers and the generals.
The drums were beaten to celebrate the victory.
Fenggai was waiting for Gangxiao's chopped-off head.
He passed on a message in advance:
"Everyone must say that Haihan is dead,
His head has been cut off
And presented to us.
In this way Nanbeng will live with me
Without thinking of returning to Haihan."
Nanbeng was shocked to hear that
And went to the *zhuansong* to find out the truth.
Fenggai spoke to her:
"You say Haihan is a descendent of the gods
And will never be killed.
You say Nisu① is a descendent of Lanpi②,
And will never die.
But now you see that I've won the battle.
To me your cries are the most melodious,
So let me enjoy and appreciate them.
Oh Nanbeng,
Please don't be too grieved!"

① Nisu: a disparaging term for Haihan.
② Lanpi: divinities.

撩起筒裙往外跑，	Nanmeng① believed his words to be true
如醉如疯如断肠。	And lifted up her straight skirt and ran out
跑到宫中找首级，	Like a drunken, crazy and heart-broken person.
拿起威罕①把人头洗。	She ran to the palace, found the chopped-off head,
只见眉毛有三横，	And washed it in a *weihan*②.
嘴上胡须长。	She found that there were three eyebrows
婻崩大声来呼喊：	And a long beard.
"这不是我的海罕哥，	She shouted loudly:
这是我的弟弟艾召生冈晓。	"This is not my husband Haihan,
他的性格太刚强，	But my younger brother Ai Zhaosheng Gangxiao.
历来做事不依劝。	He had a strong personality
他生前管辖着十个干，	And never listened to the advice of others.
地位仅次于海罕。	He commanded ten *gans* before he died
他是海罕的贴心人，	And was second only to Haihan in position.
终身为海罕来打仗。	He was Haihan's intimate brother,
召尼让他为先锋，	Fighting for Haihan all his life.
谁也同他比不上。	Zhao Ni, our respectable Haihan, asked him to lead the vanguard
他有大象十万头，	And nobody was as qualified as he was.
海罕的兵将有几万个干，	He has ten hundred thousand elephants,
他怎么会亲自来交战？	But Haihan has soldiers and generals from tens of thousands of *gans*.
海罕又有大象千千万，	
他怎么会亲自骑象来攻城？	

---

① 威罕：金制的盛水器皿。

① Nanmeng: Nanbeng.
② Weihan: a gold water vessel.

厘俸 // Li Feng

冒冒失失把命亡。"
婻崩端出撒帕永尖亥①，
放在边罕②上，
又拿一只黑公鸡，
公鸡的尾巴长又弯。
她举起金杯祭冈晓，
哀哀呜呜很悲伤。
"为了我使你遭劫难，
我亲爱的冈晓弟啊！
听说你死时还未吃早饭，
我把饭和水亲自献给你，
让俸改的灵魂同你一起吃，
让他死在海罕的刀口上！
以此了我心头恨。
你要升天请神灵，
邀约天神桑浪、桑良下凡来，
共把俸改烧成灰。
你要到水中去告诉龙王，
让大水淹没勐景罕。

① 撒：剁生。帕永：酸菜、姜、葱、盐巴等食物。尖：和、与、同。亥：鸡蛋。
② 边罕：竹篾编制的桌。直径三十厘米，涂漆并涂金粉。

How is it possible for Haihan to come to the battlefield in person?
Haihan has tens of thousands of elephants.
How is it possible for him to ride on his elephant to the front in person
And recklessly lose his life?"
Nanbeng took out *sapayongjianhai*①
And put it on the *bianhan*②.
She then caught a black rooster
With a long and curving tail feathers.
She raised a gold cup for a memorial ceremony
To express her sadness and grief:
"You died for me
My dear younger brother Gangxiao!
I heard that you had not had your breakfast yet when you died
So I bring some rice and water to you.
Let Fenggai's spirit share the food with you!
Let him die under the sword of Haihan!
Only in this way can I vent my hate.

① Sapayongjianhai: Sa: *duosheng*, meaning raw meat mince. Payong: pickled cabbage, ginger, green onion and salt, etc. Jian: with; Hai: egg.
② Bianhan: a bamboo table with a diameter of 30cm, painted with golden powder.

再祈求尼戛干好宰①,	You must ascend to heaven and ask
用角把勐景罕挑陷落,	God Sanglang and God Sangliang to descend to the earth
让它变成海洋白茫茫,	To burn Fenggai into ash.
再用尾巴把俸改紧紧缠。	You must go under water to tell the Dragon King
我亲爱的冈晓弟啊,	And ask him to drown Mengjinghan with a flood.
有人为你报仇莫悲伤!"	You must beg Nigaganhaozai①
俸改听后怒火起,	To destroy Mengjinghan with his horns
抽出宝刀骂婻崩:	And turn it into a vast sea.
"你的话痛心又刺人,	Beg him to entwine Fenggai with his tail.
我要亲手把你斩。	Don't be sad, my dear brother Gangxiao!
留着你是祸害我不放心!"	Because someone will avenge your death!"
婻崩拿起牙万冷②往俸改脸 　　上喷,	When Fenggai heard this, anger rose in his heart. He pulled out his sword and rebuked Nanbeng:
俸改宝刀落在地,	"Your words hurt me and make me feel heart-broken.
手肘搭在婻崩小肚上,	I will kill you with my own hands.
抱着婻崩又是亲来又是吻。	If I leave you alive you will surely cause disasters."
婻崩含泪强作笑,	Nanbeng took out *yawanleng*② and sprayed it on
心中的怒火熊熊燃。	Fenggai's face.
俸改高声下命令:	Fenggai then dropped his sword
"把冈晓的头颅挂在大鼓旁,	And put his hands on Nanbeng's stomach.
鲁冒③杀鸡来祭奠。"	He embraced Nanbeng and kissed her again and again.

---

① 尼戛干好宰:一条有九种花纹的龙,传说这条龙十分凶恶。
② 牙万冷:一种迷魂药。
③ 鲁冒:冒宰,宫廷侍卫。

① Nigaganhaozai: a dragon with nine different skin patterns, said to be very ferocious.
② Yawanleng: a kind of magic potion.

厘俸 // Li Feng

鼓响酒杯碰，
嫡少^①斟酒到处忙，
满城齐欢腾！
俸改开口又传令：
"用绸缎往冈晓脸上盖。"
他手持酒杯把话讲：
"你上天不要一人单独走，
要叫海罕的灵魂同你一起行，
同到天堂把福享。
艾冈晓啊，你去吧！"
话刚说完又擂鼓，
与众将领开怀畅饮，
举杯欢庆！

Nanbeng, with rage and anger inside her heart,
Forced a smile.
Fenggai gave his order loudly:
"Hang Gangxiao's head by the big drum.
Let the *lumao*① kill chickens to be a sacrifice."
The drum was beaten and wine glasses raised for a toast.
*Dishaos*② were busy filling wine glasses.
The whole city was full of rejoicing and jubilation!
Fenggai gave another order:
"Cover Gangxiao's face with a piece of silk and satin."
He held a wine glass in his hand and said:
"Don't go to heaven on your own.
Invite Haihan's spirit to go with you
And enjoy life in heaven together.
Go, Gangxiao! Go!"
Then the drum was beaten again.
Fenggai had a hearty drink with his generals
And toasted their victory.

---

① 嫡少：被选入宫的未婚少女，既是歌女、奴婢，又是王子的妻妾。

① Lumao: royal guards, also called "*maozai*".
② Dishao: an unmarried young maid who is selected to serve in the palace as a singer, a servant, and wife or concubine of a prince.

七

海罕举目远望，
眼前已不见冈晓的兵和将，
就像大海退潮一个样。
他心急如焚无所措，
稍作镇定发军令：
让各贺摆①次日来商量。
第二天转眼已来到，
只见象牙到处闪。
海罕端坐把话讲：
"俸混②啊，俸混！
记得刚刚出征勐景罕，
大家都喝了鸡血酒，
人人开口发了誓，
不论谁战死，
都要夺回尸首来安葬。
现在冈晓已经死，
他的火勐③谁也不能抢，
火浪④也要照原样。

---

① 贺摆：乘坐大象的官员。
② 俸：一群、大家。混：官。
③ 火：一切、全部。勐：地方。
④ 火浪：兵马。

VII

Haihan looked into the distance
And could not see any of Gangxiao's soldiers and generals.
They just disappeared like an ebbing tide.
He was anxious and nervous with worry
But still pretended to be calm and ordered all the *Hebais*①
To come to discuss the situation with him the next day.
Soon the next day came.
Shiny elephant tusks could be seen everywhere.
Haihan sat up and spoke:
"Fenghuns②! Oh, Fenghuns!
I remember when we just set out for Mengjinghan,
All of us drank wine with chicken blood drops in it.
All of us swore that
No matter who dies in a battle
We should take back his body and bury him.
Now Gangxiao is dead.
Nobody is allowed to take his *huomeng*③.
His *huolang*④ should be kept as usual.

---

① Hebai: an officer who rides an elephant.
② Feng: a group. Hun: officials.
③ Huo: all, Meng: land.
④ Huolang: soldiers and horses.

厘俸 // Li Feng

他的金幡幢，	His golden prayer flag
传给他的儿子艾冈罕。	Should be passed over to his son Ganghan.
冈罕啊，冈罕，	Ganghan, oh, Ganghan!
树修枝为的是发蓬，	People prune and trim trees for better growth.
父死儿继位。	A son succeeds when his father dies.
你父亲战死在勐景罕，	Your father fought to the death in Mengjinghan,
死前还没有吃早饭。	And had not even had breakfast before he died.
你要坐着大象抢回尸体，	You should ride your elephant and go to take back his body.
我要隆重来安葬。	I will bury your father in a glorious and solemn way.
他管辖的火勐和火浪，	All of his *huomeng* and *huolang*
一切交给你来管。	Will be passed over to your hands.
我还要把最富饶的地方赐给你，	I will also give you the most fertile land as a reward.
我还要让你挑选最猛的大象。"	I will let you choose the most fierce elephant."
冈罕挥泪又叩头说：	Ganghan burst into tears and said:
"去年我刚刚十岁满，	"Last year when I was just ten years old,
还在母亲腋下睡。	I still rested under my mother's arms.
只怕我年轻无力量，	I am afraid that I am too young and powerless
管不好火勐和火浪。	To rule huomeng and huolang.
但你的命令我要听，	However I will listen to you
不报父仇我心不甘。	And take revenge for my father.
尊敬的召海法啊，	Respectful Zhao Haifa,
请把命令向各勐传，	Please pass your command to each *meng*.
集合各路兵和将，	Assemble our soldiers and generals
按照计划快出发。	And we will set out as planned.

我要顺着父亲走过的路，	I will follow the way my father went,
夺回他的尸体来安葬。	And take back his body for burial.
目的不达到，	I will never give up
永远不回返！	Until my goal is reached!
目的达到了，	If I finally succeed
你将肥沃的土地赐给我，	And you give me the fertile land,
我一定接受不推让。"	I will accept it and won't decline."
海罕听了点点头，	Haihan nodded his head
就叫冈罕挑大象。	And asked Ganghan to select his elephant.
牵出花象占拜扁，	Zhanbaibian was led out.
冈罕见了忙摇头：	Ganghan shook his head at the sight of the elephant:
"占拜扁怕马，又走得慢，	"Zhanbaibian is afraid of horses and walks slowly.
蹬它它不往前走，	When you drive it, it never moves forward,
还要回头朝后看，	But turns back instead.
这头懒象我不要。"	I don't want this lazy elephant."
混勐又叫人牵出占拜散，	Zhanbaisan was led out.
一条红线在其背上。	There was a red thread fastened on his back.
冈罕见了把话讲：	Ganghan said when he saw it:
"这头大象也不行，	"This one won't do, either.
象牙实在太一般，	The tusks are so ordinary
好似用模子倒出来。	As if they were shaped in a mould.
它听到枪炮就吼叫，	It roars on hearing gunshots
并掉过头来往回闯，	And then turns around
把自己人马来踏伤。"	And even stomps on our soldiers."

厘俸 // Li Feng

混勐又叫人牵出占拜崩，	Zhanbaibeng was led out.
它的脑门有七寸宽。	It had a forehead seven inches wide.
冈罕见了又摇头说：	Ganghan still shook his head:
"这头大象最怕火，	"This elephant is particularly afraid of fire.
蹬它它不上战场。	It would not march forward
镰钩挖它也不走，	Even if you drive it with a hook.
反而弯着脖子往后看。	It would look back instead.
这头大象我不要，	I don't want this elephant.
我想要的是白象。	I need a white elephant
象牙洁白似月亮，	With tusks as white as a bright moon.
又凶猛来又顽强。	It must be strong and fierce.
驯服的大象我不要，	Such a tamed elephant I do not need.
我专要这头占拜汉。	In fact I like Zhanbaihan.
海罕啊，	Oh Haihan,
请你把它送给我，	Please give it to me.
我一定为你拼死来作战，	I will certainly fight to the death for you
就像我的父亲一个样，	As my father did.
誓死为混勐来效力！"	I swear I will pledge my life to you, my Hunmeng!"
海罕心中不愿意，	Haihan was reluctant
但还是答应给冈罕。	But finally agreed to give the elephant to Ganghan.
占拜汉本属天神布领暖，	Zhanbaihan was originally the elephant of God Bulingnuan.
现在把它赐给了冈罕。	Now it belonged to Ganghan.
这头大象看见火光就冲上去，	The elephant would dash forward at the sight of fire
一见弩炮就往前闯。	And rush ahead at the sight of bows and guns.

侍从牵出占拜汉，	The servants led out Zhanbaihan.
它大步走向石阶来，	It strode towards the stone steps
闪闪金舆罩身上。	With a golden howdah covering its back.
舆上饰有金丝线，	The howdah was decorated with golden threads.
长汉①上点缀有飘带，	Its *changhan*① was embellished with ribbons.
长行②上朵朵金星亮又亮，	Its *changxing*② was embroidered with little shiny golden stars.
长永③上颗颗宝石华光闪，	Its *changyong*③ was inlaid with bright and shiny diamonds
两边飘带坠着金银链，	With two ribbons hung on both sides.
晖罕上插着孔雀尾，	There were colorful peacock feathers on the howdah,
五彩缤纷迎风展。	Swinging in the wind.
多么威武的占拜汉，	What a mighty and powerful elephant!
犹如混勐骑的象。	It looked quite like the elephant of Hunmeng Haihan.
冈罕见了心喜欢，	Ganghan liked it so much
当着海罕把衣甲穿。	And began to put on his armor in front of Haihan.
左转右看金光闪，	His armor shone brightly
节节衣甲用金丝紧扣连。	With each piece of it connected with golden threads.
宝石包脖上挎，	The jeweled bag hung from his neck.
宝刀一把明晃晃，	His shining sword was decorated with gold threads
刀上系有金丝线，	And its sheath and handle
宝石缀满刀鞘和刀把。	

---

① 长汉：遮盖在大象屁股上的装饰物。
② 长行：象舆左右两旁各有一块遮盖到大象肚子的装饰物。
③ 长永：从脑门到鼻子的一块装饰物，两边有飘带。

① Changhan: a piece of cloth with decorations to cover an elephant's rear.
② Changxing: a piece of cloth with decorations to cover the two sides of an elephant's middle.
③ Changyong: a piece of cloth with decorations and ribbons to cover the forehead of an elephant.

厘俸 // Li Feng

又把金盔戴头上，	Were inlaid with jewels on.
金色飘带两边摆。	Ganghan put on his golden helmet
脖上又系金绳带，	With golden ribbons at both sides.
再把金矛手中拿。	He tied a golden tie on his neck
他大步走向占拜汉，	And held a golden spear in his hand.
手拿金杯祭神灵：	He strode up to Zhanbaihan
"神灵啊，	And prayed to the gods with a golden cup in his hand:
请喝一盅金杯酒。	"Oh, gods!
因得不到神灵的相助，	Please drink the wine in this golden cup.
我父亲战死在勐景罕，	My father fought to death in Mengjinghan
占拜中也遭了难。	And his Zhanbaizhong got killed
他战死不是为自己，	Due to the lack of aid from you.
为的是嫡崩和海罕。	He fought not for himself
现在海罕下命令，	But for Nanbeng and Haihan.
要我夺回父亲的尸体来安葬。	Now Haihan orders me
祈求天神保佑我，	To get back my father's body so as to bury him honorably.
让我免灾又避难。	Bless me please!
天啊，神啊，	Keep me from disasters and catastrophes.
请求你们来相帮！"	Gods, oh gods,
冈罕说完准备坐上大象，	Please come to help me!"
占拜汉四腿跪下冈罕上。	Finishing his words Ganghan was ready to get on his elephant.
冈罕唤来众侍从，	Zhanbaihan knelt down and Ganghan mounted.
发布命令各召传。	Ganghan called his bodyguards
转身又对桑洛和嘿南说：	To send his messages to all his officers.

"我们这次攻勐景罕，
决不退缩要勇敢。
接连不断来冲杀，
不让艾俸温①喘口气。
如果你俩不勇猛，
就不算作男子汉。
你们赶快穿戴好，
分兵几路把勐俸围，
不让俸改有躲藏。"

桑洛接令热血涌，
按捺不住要作战。
他亲手来把大鼓敲，
鼓声急促震天响。
军队出征浩浩荡，
武艺高强的猛士打前锋，
身穿红衣火一样。
只见红顶绿身的幡幢，
桑洛坐在大象上，
率领全军去作战，
象头长矛指前方。

He then turned to Sangluo and Heinan:

"This time when we attack Mengjinghan,

We should be brave and never give up.

We will launch attacks one after another

So that Ai Fengwen① can find no breathing spell.

If you are not brave

You will not be called a man.

Put on your armor quickly

And go to surround Mengfeng.

Let Fenggai have no place to hide."

Sangluo received the order with righteous ardor

And could wait to go to the battle.

He beat the drum himself

And the sound of drum beats shook the world.

His army set out in great arrays.

The most skillful warriors, in red uniforms,

Went in the front.

Sangluo sat on the back of his elephant,

With colorful prayer flags on its head,

And led his army to fight.

All the spears pointed forward.

---

①艾俸温：对俸改的贬称。

① Ai Fengwen: a derogatory term used to address Fenggai.

厘俸 // Li Feng

桑本接令穿戎装，	Sangben got the order and put on his armor.
作为战时预备队，	As a reserved force,
随时准备援冈罕。	He was ready at any time to back up Ganghan.
他也亲手敲战鼓，	He also hit the drum himself
翻身骑在象身上。	And then got on his elephant
坐骑的铃响叮当，	With the rings jingling and clinking on its neck
头上是白色绸缎金幡幢，	And white silk prayer flags on its head.
士卒手持金钩枪。	All his soldiers held golden hooked spears.
混嘿南的象阵整整齐，	The orderly elephants of Hun Heinan stood
列成纵队二十行。	In twenty columns.
战鼓声声不停息，	The drum was beaten constantly.
目标直指勐景罕，	Mengjinghan was the target.
兵将直捣城墙下。	Soon the troops reached the foot of the city wall.
军中准备了发巴梯，	Fabatis were prepared as defences.
万名弓弩手强又壮。	Ten thousand strong bowmen took their places.
召冈、召伴冲在前，	Small chiefs like Zhaogangs and Zhaobans dashed in the front,
率领弩手打先锋。	Leading the bowmen to fight as the vanguard.
大象求战不耐烦，	The elephants could not wait any longer for the battle
象鼻甩动如浪翻，	And waved their trunks like rolling waves.
只等命令一声下！	The only thing to wait for was the "order"!
还有崩南宛多法，	Bengnanwanduofa also

也把戎装穿,	Put on his military uniform.
他的兵丁如出窝的蜂,	His soldiers were just like the bees flying out of a beehive
如大雾弥漫的江河。	Or a river hidden in the mist.
士卒的长矛锋又利,	The long spears of the soldiers were sharp.
象牙洁白如星星。	The tusks of the elephants were as white as stars.
象舆高插孔雀尾,	The howdahs were decorated
迎着轻风齐招展。	With peacock feathers flying in the wind.
战鼓声声把人催,	The drum beats were motivating the soldiers
只等进攻勐景罕。	To launch the attack at the word of command!
还有汉戛召勐央①,	And there was Hanga, Zhao Mengyang,①
亲擂大鼓把令传。	Who hit the big drum in person
鼓声响遍村和寨,	And spread the order to fight to all the villages.
兵将集合斗志昂。	The soldiers and the generals assembled in high spirit.
象牙用铜紧紧箍,	The elephant tusks were wrapped with copper.
士卒着金衣②,	The soldiers were dressed in golden clothes②
佩带金矛③和长刀。	And carried golden spears③ and long knives.
召麻④如潮涌出来,	Zhaoma④ surged out like waves
战象脚踏鼻又甩,	And war elephants stood impatiently, waving their trunks.
只等出发往前闯。	All they waited for was to set out and marching forward.

---

① 汉戛:人名。召:官。勐央:较大的地方。
② 金衣:涂有金粉的衣甲。
③ 金矛:涂有金粉的长矛。
④ 召麻:马官。

① Hanga: name of a person. zhao: official. mengyang: a big place.
② Golden clothes: armor painted with a coat of gold powder.
③ Golden spear: a spear painted with gold powder.
④ Zhaoma: horsemen.

厘俸 // Li Feng

还有桑温和赛伦,　　　　There were also Sangwen and Sailun,
两将兵马也出阵,　　　　Whose soldiers, horses and twenty herds of elephants,
还有大象二十群。　　　　Were sent out to join the battle.
鼓声咚咚震人心,　　　　Accompanied by inspiring drum beats,
土枪土炮已上膛。　　　　The guns and the cannons were all loaded,
长矛搭在象头上,　　　　And the spears were placed on the heads of the elephants.
势如风暴席卷来,　　　　Everything was ready for a sweeping battle.
只等令下把敌穿。　　　　The only thing to wait for was the command of fighting.

还有冈晓的弟弟冈庄,　　Gangzhuang, Gangxiao's younger brother,
也亲手把大鼓来擂响。　　Also beat his big drum.
鸣炮声声催出发,　　　　The rumble of cannons called for an immediate departure.
漫山遍野是大象,　　　　Elephants all over the mountain
多如缅卯一般。　　　　　Were just like swarms of flying ants.
冈庄坐在象身上,　　　　Gangzhuang sat on the back of his elephant
面对各勐首领把话讲:　　And spoke to the chiefs of the *mengs*:
"我哥冈晓虽战死,　　　"Though my elder brother Gangxiao has fought to the death,
但帅旗不倒兵将在。　　　His general flag did not fall and his troops are still there.
今日来此重开战,　　　　Today we come to resume the fight
不报血仇不回返。　　　　And will never return if we don't take revenge on our
　　　　　　　　　　　　　　enemies.
奋力拼杀不后退,　　　　Let's fight with all our might
誓死攻下勐景罕!"　　　And pledge to occupy Mengjinghan."

还有向冈和向戛①，	There are Xianggang and Xiangga①, too,
手中鼓槌不停挥，	Waving drum sticks in their hands.
鼓声咚咚全勐响。	The sound of drum beats spread all over the *meng*.
向冈率领万头象，	Xianggang led an army consisting of ten thousand elephants,
还有大队兵和将．	And a great number of soldiers and officers
将士袖口缀金线，	Whose cuffs were embroidered with golden threads.
马队奔腾如冒短②。	Their horses galloped like *maoduan*②.
海螺一声齐出发，	When the conch horn blew they were all ready to set out.
长矛搭在象头上。	The long spears were placed on the heads of elephants.
象身着金舆，	Golden howdahs decorated with peacock tail feathers
孔雀尾高插金舆上。	Were fixed on elephant backs.
众士卒怒视前方，	Streams of soldiers stared ahead
人流滚滚进入田坝！	And marched into the plain!
还有艾包、尼崩和桑混伦，	There were also Ai Bao, Ni Beng,
赛道和波道坚混缅，	Sang Hunlun, Sai Dao and Bodaojianhunmian.
当年和冈晓同结拜，	Who, in those years,
兄一般来弟一样。	Had become the dearest sworn brothers of Gangxiao.
曾和冈晓同发誓：	They swore to each other:
不论谁阵亡，	Whoever dies in battle,

---

① 向冈、向戛为兄弟两人，是勐的头领。
② 冒短：一种三月开花的荆棘，花为艳红色。

① Xianggang and Xiangga are brothers, and both of them are *meng* chiefs.
② Maoduan: a kind of thistle and thorn that blossoms with bright red flowers in March.

厘俸 // Li Feng

都要夺回尸体来安葬。	His body must be taken back and burried.
如今冈晓已战死,	Now Gangxiao was dead.
如果誓言不实现,	If the pledge was not fulfilled,
冈晓九泉不合眼。	He would die with everlasting regret.
他们求战心急坐不安,	They were anxious to combat Fenggai,
只怕战象不勇敢,	But were afraid of suffering defeats like Gangxiao
只怕力量不足难破城,	And failing to attain their goals
与冈晓一样遭了殃,	Because of their elephants' lack of courage
未能如愿以偿。	And the inadequacy of their forces.
他们杀鸡来奠祭,	So they killed a chicken to hold a ritual to
请求冈晓的魂灵来相帮:	Invoke Gangxiao's soul for help:
"亲爱的冈晓哥啊,	"Dear brother Gangxiao!
请你暂不忙升天,	Please do not go to heaven right now.
请你站在象头上,	Please stand on the heads of our elephants
共同杀敌齐作战,	And fight with us.
夺取胜利报大仇,	We are determined to win the battle and take revenge,
把你的尸体来安葬。	And then give you a proper burial.
冈晓大哥啊,	Brother Gangxiao!
我们的心愿请你记心上!"	Please keep our wishes in mind!"
祭祀完毕下命令,	After that, the order was given
金鼓齐鸣海螺响,	And the drums were beaten and the conch horns blown.
千军万马齐出发,	Thousands of soldiers and horses set out,
十万大象跑得欢,	Accompanied by ten thousand elephants
象鼻直指勐景罕。	Hopping happily with their trunks all pointing to

Mengjinghan.

海罕大军已出动，	Now all of Haihan's troops set out
浩浩荡荡越山冈。	And passed over mountains in an endless procession.
人马如雾没有边，	The soldiers and horses were boundless like a fog,
人马相挤又相撞。	Colliding and bumping into each other.
厩中还有大象未放出，	The elephants that were still shut in the stables
踢腿扬鼻吼得慌。	Stomped their feet and raised their trunks impatiently.
海罕坐镇大本营，	Haihan commanded from his base camp,
他从容镇定稳如山。	Steady and calm as a mountain.
战象关在栅栏里，	The war elephants were kept fenced up.
二百万兵丁，	Two million soldiers
好贺罕孙帅①来武装，	Were equipped with *haohehansunshuai*①.
还有配备好贺罕的大军九百万，	Nine million more soldiers, armed with powerful spears,
都把占拜舍团团围，	Stood around Zhanbaishe
忠心耿耿保海罕。	And protected Haihan with loyalty and devotion.
海罕开口下命令：	Haihan gave his order:
"金扁和召跟冈代替我督战，	"Jinbian and Zhao Gengang will supervise the battles on my behalf,
率领我的战象援冈罕。	And lead my elephants to support Ganghan.
只能前进不能退，	You will march forward and never retreat.
谁要退却把头砍！"	Whoever retreats will be killed."
出征的鼓声震撼勐景罕，	

---

① 好：长矛。贺罕：带有钩的矛。孙帅：矛上缀有金丝链条。

① Haohehansunshuai: a hooked spear decorated with golden chains.

厘俸 // Li Feng

轰然一声炮三响，	The drums of expedition shook Mengjinghan.
金扁、召跟冈拔营出战。	With three shots from cannons,
占拜舍昂头又卷鼻，	Jinbian and Zhao Gengang decamped and set out.
不吃草料连吼叫，	Zhanbaishe raised up its head and rolled its trunk,
栅栏中战象更慌乱，	Howling constantly and refusing to eat more.
乱蹦又乱跳，	The elephants in the stables were even more uneasy,
心急似火燎。	Kicking and leaping
海罕又把命令下：	Impatiently and restlessly.
"一队兵将用鲁非，	Haihan gave another order:
火攻勐景罕。	"One array of our soldiers will use *lufeis*
一队战象运土炮，	To attack Mengjinghan with fire.
炮轰城和墙。"	Another will transport cannons
出征兵丁似野火烧山，	To bombard the city and the city wall."
滚滚卷向勐景罕！	The soldiers dashed in overwhelming numbers to Mengjinghan
	As quickly as wild fire burning on the mountains!
冈罕坐在大象上，	Sitting on the back of his elephant,
左手一挥一声喊，	Ganghan waved his left hand with a shout
士卒分开成两行。	And ordering his soldiers to divide into two columns.
右手一挥又开口：	He then waved his right hand and spoke:
"众神灵啊，	"Oh, gods!
我天天给你们献饭，	I offer you rice every day.
今天要请你们保佑。	Today I need your blessing in return.

我将攻打勐景罕，	I am going to attack Mengjinghan.
幢崩舍帅旗已插在象舆上。	My prayer flag embroidered with a tiger has been put on the howdah.
我要夺回父亲的尸体报大仇，	I want to take revenge,
并把遗体运回家安葬！"	Get back my father's body and bury him in our hometown."
开口又对士卒讲：	Then he spoke to his soldiers:
"今日出战不一般，	"This is an unusual battle.
贪生怕死必遭殃。	Those who act in a cowardly way will surely be punished.
三千花矛手成纵队，	Three thousand spearmen will be organized in columns
稳扎稳打不要乱。	And fight firmly and steadily.
五百召牙背①紧跟占拜汉，	Five hundred *zhaoyabeis*① will follow Zhanbaihan closely
等待把敌酋首级砍。	And decapitate the enemy chiefs in battle.
手持高召的紧接上，	Then the soldiers holding the weapon *gaozhaos* will join the battle.
其余兵丁再跟上。"	Finally will come the rest of the troops."
冈罕指挥兵丁向前进，	Ganghan led his army to march forward
父亲的足迹在脚下。	Along the road his father once walked.
想到父亲遭劫难，	Thinking of his father's tragedy,
眼中流泪心悲伤：	He burst into tears of great sadness:
"我的父亲啊，	"Oh father!
你虽然已经离人间，	Though you have died and left us,
海罕没有把你忘。	Haihan didn't forget you.
你的领地归我管，	Your territory is now under my rule.
海罕又赐给大象。	
你的帅旗没有倒，	

---

① 召牙背：率领长刀队的头领。   ① Zhaoyabei: the leader of soldiers holding long knives.

厘俸 // Li Feng

还有兵马还有将。
你虽死不要有怨言,
不要变心把自己人来伤。
你的灵魂要回来,
战时附在象身上,
帮助攻打勐景罕。
攻下勐俸城,
了却心头恨。
亲爱的父亲啊,
儿的心愿你要记心上!"
占拜汉甩鼻又踢脚,
迫不及待想冲锋。
金鼓咚咚敲得急,
鼓声传到勐景罕。
沿着冈晓走的路,
占拜汉步履很轻快,
如攀枝花在飞扬。
兵丁已经到安望①,
冈罕驻足细察看。
各路兵丁已来到,
重兵齐集在城下,
如旋涡塘中的浪花,
守城士卒心惊胆又战。

---

① 安望:冈晓战死之处。

Haihan has rewarded me with an elephant.
Your general banner has not fallen
And your soldiers and generals are still there.
You are dead but do not complain and grumble,
And never change your mind or harm your own people.
Your soul should come back,
Give magic power to our elephants during the war
And help us attack Mengjinghan.
We are going to conquer the city
And thus release the load of hatred in our hearts.
My dear father,
Please keep in mind the words of your son!"
Zhanbaihan swung its trunk and stomped its feet,
Eager to charge forward.
The fast beats of a golden drum
Spread to Mengjinghan.
Along the road Gangxiao took before,
Zhanbaihan walked briskly
Like the bombax flowers waving in the air.
When all his soldiers arrived at Anwang①,
Ganghan stopped to observe the situation more carefully.
Haihan's troops had all arrived
And assembled under the city wall

---

① Anwang: the place where Gangxiao was killed.

	Like spindrifts in a whirlpool.
	Fenggai's soldiers on the city wall were frightened.
勐景罕南面地势险,	The south of Mengjinghan was difficult of access.
一道铁索桥架河上,	There was a cable bridge over the river,
一条独路通两方,	Which was the only access to the city.
一夫当关,万夫挡。	If one man guarded the bridge, ten thousand couldn't get through.
俸改明知海罕大军到,	Fenggai knew clearly that Haihan's troops had arrived,
照旧摆酒设宴把客待。	But still gave a banquet to treat his guests.
开怀畅饮不慌张,	They drank freely with great joviality,
一点没把海罕放在心头上。	And did not take Haihan's attack seriously at all.
俸改手下的召曼①多又多,	Fenggai had many Zhaomans①,
带领兵丁城头看。	Who watched from the gate tower with their soldiers.
吹罢海螺吹牛角,	They blew conch and horn,
各就各位在备战。	Urging everyone to be prepared for the war.
战象多如山上石,	The elephants were as numerous as mountain rocks
栅栏一开放出来。	And were wating to be sent into the battlefield.
兵将手中拿武器,	The soldiers all held a weapon in their hands
个个严阵以待,	In battle array
准备决一死战。	To fight once and for all.
冈罕的大军鼓在响,	In Ganghan's army, the drums were beaten,
各路兵马齐向前。	And all the armies and horses moved forward together.
桑洛抵达北城门,	

---

① 召曼:村寨的头人。　　① Zhaoman: head of a village.

厘俸 // Li Feng

守军出城来迎战。	When Sangluo arrived at the north gate,
枪声炮声震天地,	The garrison came out to meet their attack.
狂奔而来是群象。	The sound of gunfire shook the world.
战马两翼来包抄,	Herds of elephants rushed forward.
兵分多路齐围上。	The war horses outflanked from two sides.
两军相接杀声起,	Enemy soldiers from different legions closed in.
刀光剑影闪闪亮,	The two sides now fought at close quarter.
麻香①砍得乱飞扬。	With the glint and flash of swords and knives,
一场血战动心魄,	*Maxiang*① bushes were slashed and flew in the air.
鬼神哭号天昏暗。	In such a bloody battle,
俸改一方布象阵,	The sky became dark with crying ghosts.
桑洛从容来应战。	Fenggai lined up his elephants to start a charge,
势均力敌难分解,	And Sangluo met it calmly.
双方各有死和伤。	Well-matched in strength,
	Both sides suffered deaths and injuries.
崩南宛多法、汉戛召勐惹,	Bengnanwanduofa and Hangazhaomengre,
还有那赛道和嘿南,	Toghether with Saidao and Heinan,
合力围攻城南方。	Joined forces to besiege the south of the city.
俸改命令兵马出城来,	Fenggai ordered his troops to go out
迎战汉戛召勐惹。	And fight against Hangazhaomengre.
长矛明亮映阳光,	The spears shone in the sun.
栅栏一开放大象。	The stables were opened and the elephants rushed out.

---

① 麻香:一种荆棘,结有红色果实。

① Maxiang: a kind of thistle and thorns bearing red fruits.

两军交锋声如雷，	The two sides fought with thundering shouts
杀声震撼勐俸城。	That shook and quaked the city of Mengjinghan.
汉戛召勐惹被围困，	Hangazhaomengre was besieged,
心中着急拼死战，	And was anxious to break through
突出重围往后退，	And retreat from the encirclement.
退回营地仰天叹：	Back in his camp he looked up and sighed deeply:
"天上勇敢数布领暖，	"Up in heaven the bravest man is Bulingnuan.
天下数我最好强。	Down in the world the strongest man is me.
二十头大象来围我，	Even though there were twenty elephants coming to attack me,
我也不应败退见海罕。	
战死沙场不回头，	I should not have retreated.
才能算作英雄汉！"	I should die fighting on the battlefield
哥哥崩南宛多法，	And be a real hero!"
看到此情此景，	When seeing this,
担心他性命难保，	His brother Bengnanwanduofa
急蹬大象来相帮。	Worried that he might lose his life
战象奔腾狂风起，	And drove his elephant to offer help.
一鼓作气往前冲。	The elephant rushed forward at top speed
刀矛横飞眼花缭乱，	And raised a gust of wind.
如同伐木一般咚咚响。	The swords and spears flew in a dazzling way,
汉戛得到哥哥的支援，	Like the sound of timber being felled.
士气大振越战越猛。	With the assistance and support of his brother
只见战壕到处血流淌，	Hangazhaomengre's soldiers fought more valiantly.
俸改兵将慌忙退入城，	Blood flowed everywhere in the trenches.

厘俸 // Li Feng

如同潮水回海洋。	Fenggai's troops had to retreat into the city
	Like ebbing tides of the sea.

嘿南的兵将临城下， Heinan's troops reached the city gate.
俸改急忙调兵又遣将。 Fenggai ordered his army to meet the attack.
如同飞蚂蚁般齐出动， They rushed out in great numbers like flying ants
把嘿南紧紧包围桶一般。 And covered Heinan tightly like a bucket.
黑云压顶形势急， The situation was critical, like black clouds hanging over the sky.
嘿南沉着不慌忙。
他施展计策巧安排， Heinan, however, calmly carried out his tactics
分兵两路装败退， By dividing his troops into two groups,
退到一片开阔地， Pretending to be defeated
两路合围又开战。 And withdrawing to an open area.
　　　　　　　　　There the two groups united to continue the fight.

桑温、赛伦攻城东， Sangwen and Sailun were attacking the east of the city
长矛无数林一般。 With a forest of long spears.
勐俸城池坚又固， The city of Mengjinghan had strong defences,
道道封锁严设防。 Tightly protected by barriers and blockades.
木石垒起层层大栅栏， Big fences were built of logs and stones
保护战壕和城门。 To protect the trenches and the city gate.
桑温、赛伦调兵将， Sangwen and Sailun
三千土炮黄铜铸， Ordered their soldiers
连续不断来轰击。 To constantly fire three thousand copper cannons,

只见勐景罕城中烟雾弥漫。	Engulfing the city of Mengjinghan in smoke.
四万门土炮紫铜铸,	Then forty thousand red copper cannons
不断发炮震天响。	Fired constantly with a deafening noise.
城内烟雾腾腾大火起,	Smoke rose high and the city was on fire.
城门倒塌敌慌乱。	The collapse of the city gate caused panic among the enemy.

向冈、向戛兄弟俩,	The two brothers, Xianggang and Xiangga,
也在进攻城西边。	Were attacking the west of the city.
东南西北已围困,	Mengfeng was encircled from the east, south, west and north,
勐俸将要临大难。	And was in deadly danger now.

俸改一方大鼓响不停,	Fenggai's soldiers kept beating drums.
各路兵马听鼓响,	Hearing the drum beats, all the troops
纷纷出城来迎战,	Came out of the city to meet the attack.
几面包抄围冈罕。	They surrounded Ganghan from all sides.
冈罕从容来对阵,	Ganghan met the challenge calmly,
弯刀手紧跟占拜汉。	Ordering soldiers holding machetes to follow Zhanbaihan closely.
俸改的大象滚滚来,	Fenggai's elephants came in great numbers,
如同乱石齐下山。	Like stones rolling down the hills
如蒙蒙大雾把天地粘。	Or a dense fog veiling the earth.
冈罕的大军形势急,	Ganghan's army was facing an urgent situation.
众将坐在大象上,	The officers passed orders
大声呼喊把令传:	

厘俸 // Li Feng

"佯装败退引敌人，
把象阵引入陷阱内。
两边乘机来包围，
夹攻敌人打胜仗。
勇士们啊，
执行命令不要乱！"

From the back of their elephants:
"Pretend to be defeated
So as to lure the enemy's elephants into our trap.
Then encircle them from both sides
And win the battle.
Warriors,
Excecute these orders and do not panic!"

守军蹬象围冈罕，
千名弩手齐发射，
射中坐骑占拜汉，
它身上的箭如豪猪身上刺。
双方战马在厮杀，
刀矛交错声杂乱。
篱笆旁，战壕边，
一场一场混战，
血肉横飞尘土扬。
俸改的士卒抵不住，
纷纷后退又回城。
冈罕的大军紧追上，
城头檑木滚石如山崩，
士卒忙用发巴梯来挡。
城中再用土炮轰，
冈罕的军队死上万。

The troops of Mengjinghan surrounded Ganghan with elephants.
A thousand crossbows
Shot at Ganghan's Zhanbaihan,
Making the elephant look like a porcupine.
The war horses of the two sides kept fighting.
Soldiers fought with swords and spears, making a lot of noise.
By the fences and by the trenches,
The two sides were locked in a tangled fight.
Blood and flesh flew in the dusty air.
Fenggai's soldiers could not hold on,
And had to retreat into the city.
Ganghan's army chased after them closely.
Suddenly, logs and rocks rolled down the wall like a landslide.

他下令三千炮手齐还击，	Ganghan's soldiers had to defend themselves with the defense weapon *fabati*.
四万门土炮也轰响。	Cannons were fired from within the city,
烟尘大起遮太阳，	Killing ten thousands of Ganghan's soldiers.
天空暗淡无光芒。	He ordered his men to fire his three thousand copper cannons
鲁非飕飕又发射，	And forty thousand red copper cannons, as a counterattack.
城内烈火熊熊燃，	The rising dust blocked the sun,
房屋倒塌人逃散。	Darkening the sky.
大象乱跑又乱跳，	*Lufeis* were fired as well,
有的围困在栅栏。	Causing big fires inside the city.
冈罕下令捉大象，	Houses collapsed and people fled.
大象身大力又大，	Elephants ran around madly and jumped wildly,
有的无法捉得住。	Some of them trapped in the stables.
士卒着急怪自己，	Ganghan ordered his soldiers to catch the elephants,
力小无能自责骂。	But some of the elephants
冈罕攻进勐景罕，	Were too big and powerful to be caught.
二十层①防线开了端。	Ganghan's soldiers blamed themselves
兵不休息马不停，	For being too weak and feeble.
允龙还在城中央。	Ganghan's troops broke into the city of Mengjinghan.
只见城中尸遍地，	The first of the twenty layers① of defenses were torn down.
血流如水臭气扬，	The soldiers and horses progressed without stopping to
满目疮痍一片凄凉。	
冈罕的大军源源不断急行进，	

---

① 勐景罕城内有大小城池（即城中城）二十层，俸改住中间一层，称允龙，也称王城。

① There were twenty cirles of cities in Mengjinghan. Fenggai live in the innermost circle, called Yunlong, or "The City of the King".

厘俸 // Li Feng

来到四周都是绝壁处。	rest
地势险要路艰难，	Towards Yunlong in the center of the city.
仅有独路一条通前方。	Everywhere there were dead bodies lying on the ground;
冈罕坐骑占拜汉，	Everywhere there was blood flowing like foul water.
坎坎坷坷过难关。	It was indeed a scene of devastation.
第二道城池已来到，	Ganghan's army marched forward quickly
守军跳出战壕来迎战。	And came to a place with cliffs all around.
双方又砍又杀又吼叫，	This was a place difficult to gain access
一场恶战又进行。	And there was only one road leading to the south of the city.
鲜血飞溅满衣裳，	Ganghan rode his Zhanbaihan
不知血从何方来。	And managed to go through the hindering pass,
冈罕的马队突奔袭，	Arriving at the second circle of the city
杀得俸改的兵丁人仰马也翻。	And encountering the enemies' resistance from the trenches.
尸体成堆填战壕，	The two sides cut, killed, and howled,
城中百姓也遭殃，	And another fierce battle started.
小孩哭叫找爹娘。	Blood splashed on the clothes of the soldiers
百姓咒骂俸改太作恶，	From out of nowhere.
使百姓惨遭难。	Ganghan's war horses launched a sudden attack
遍地烽火无处躲，	And killed many of Fenggai's soldiers and horses.
到处都是冈罕的兵和将。	Dead bodies filled up the trenches.
百姓纷纷逃内城，	The civilians in the city suffered a lot as well.
火烧眉毛跑得忙，	Children were crying for their parents.
到处都是哭泣和呼叫。	People all cursed Fenggai for his wickedness
俸改来到高楼上，	

指指点点看远方。
得知兵丁伤亡大,
他对巴扎哇①说:
"你骑上快马去打听,
问明是谁来攻城。"
巴扎哇快马又加鞭,
奔出内城到前沿,
勒住马头问:
"坐在绿色幡幢里,
面目不清一小将,
你从什么地方来?
你像一只还不会啼鸣的公鸡,
一朵未开的花,
快快把你名字传,
攻打我们为哪样?
你人虽小却凶猛,
攻城势如砍甘蔗。
可惜你到此白送死,
冈晓虽勇猛,
可头也落地。
你的脚杆短又短,
要蹬象耳还够不上。
你的脖子短如毛虫样,

---

① 巴扎哇:倮改的一员将领。

That had brought about such disasters.
There were fires everywhere and people had no place to hide,
As Ganghan's soldiers and generals were everywhere.
People all fled to the inner city
Hurriedly as if their eyebrows had caught fire.
There was weeping and shouting everywhere.
Fenggai climbed to a high tower
And looked into the distance.
When he was informed of the great loss of his army,
He said to Bazhawa①
"Get on your fast horse. Go and find out
Who is attacking the city."
Bazhawa rode his horse at lightning speed
And went out of the inner city and arrived at the front.
He drew back the reins and asked:
"Young general sitting under the green prayer flag!
I cannot see your face clearly.
Where are you from?
You're like a rooster that can't crow yet,
And a flower not in full blossom.
Tell me your name!
Tell me why you have come to attack us!

---

① Bazhawa: one of Fenggai's generals.

厘俸 // Li Feng

满身乳气还未干。"
冈罕把话来回答：
"我没有名也没有姓，
我是个神志不清的人。
我从石缝钻出来，
姑娘不和我玩。
我心中有气无处发，
才来攻打勐景罕。
你说攻打勐景罕难上难，
我说如同耍弄一根棍或棒。
我像一条无毛的虫，
鸡见了也会咯咯叫。
我像无牙的老虎一个样，
吃肉也要慢慢嚼，
就像老牛吃草慢又慢。
我身材矮小没有力，
就像一只小狮子。
如果冈晓没有死，
侄儿我也不会来到勐景罕，
也见不到你们大爷叔伯们。
因为艾召生已阵亡，
我才骑着占拜汉，
到这个地方来游玩。
你们哪头大象最凶猛，

You are young but fierce,
Attacking us like cutting sugarcane.
But I am afraid you have come to die in vain.
Gangxiao was brave,
But still had his head cut off.
Your legs are too short
To reach the ears of an elephant and drive it.
Your neck is as short as a caterpillar.
You are still wet behind the ears."
Ganghan replied:
"I don't have a name,
And I am in a confused state of mind.
I was born out of a stone crack.
Young girls never play with me.
My anger has no outlet,
So I came to attack Mengjinghan.
You say that it is extremely difficulty to attack Mengjinghan,
But I say attacking it is as easy as playing with a stick.
I'm just like a hairless worm.
Cocks will cackle in fear when they see me.
I'm just like a toothless tiger,
Chewing meat slowly at meals,
Or an old cow eating grass very slowly.
I'm short and weak,

就请你们放出来，	Like a lion cub.
和我冈罕决一战！"	If Gangxiao were not dead,
巴扎哇掉转马头急回返，	I, your nephew, will never come to Mengjinghan
急忙报告俸改说：	And meet you, my uncles.
"亲爱的召法温俸罕，	It is because
这次打仗不像前一仗，	Ai Zhaosheng was killed in the battle
我们可能要失败。	That I ride my Zhanbaihan here.
冈晓虽死，	Whichever elephant is the fiercest here,
可他还有兵和将。	Send it out
海罕决不会心甘，	And fight me!"
他又派兵来抢夺尸。	Bazhawa turned his horse and hurried back.
冈晓的帅旗迎风飘，	He reported to Fenggai hastily:
掌旗的统帅是冈罕。	"Dear respectable Zhao Fawenfenghan!
大队人马浩浩荡荡，	We are facing a battle like none of the previous ones.
战象被捉村寨陷，	We may lose.
我们的兵丁死又伤。	Though Gangxiao is dead,
我已亲眼见冈罕，	His soldiers and generals are still there.
身材矮小娃娃样，	Haihan will never give up.
脚短不够蹬象耳，	He now has sent his army to take back Gangxiao's corpse.
脖如毛虫一般短。	Gangxiao's general flag still flutters in the wind.
他骑的大象不一般，	The one holding the flag is Ganghan.
象牙粗粗如盐臼，	Their troops march forward with great strength and vigour.
把土挑起朝天上。	Our war elephants have been caught and our villages occupied.
尾巴粗长拖到地，	

厘俸 // Li Feng

不怕炮也不怕枪。
冈罕开口很不凡，
估计武艺很高强。
如果谁和他对阵，
必死无疑不能回，
死后也要变魔鬼。
我们应该怎么办？
召法温俸罕！"

俸改冷笑一声下命令，
招来卫大罕大官，
充当先锋战冈罕。
卫大罕弹舌嗒嗒响，
捋起手袖高声说：
"冈晓都死在我刀下，

Our soldiers are either injured or dead.
I have seen Ganghan myself.
He is short, like a child.
His legs are too short to reach the elephant's ears.
His neck is as short as a caterpillar.
But his elephant is an unusual one,
With tusks that are as thick as salt mortars
And that can dig the earth.
Its tail is thick and long enough to drag on the ground.
It fears neither cannons nor guns.
Ganghan speaks eloquently.
I guess he is also a highly-skilled general.
Whoever fights him will surely die,
Never come back alive,
And become a devil after death.
What shall we do?
My respectable Zhao Fawenfenghan!"

Fenggai sneered and gave the word.
He summoned his senior general Weidahan
To lead his army as the vanguard to fight Ganghan.
Weidahan clicked his tongue,
Rolled up his sleeves and said loudly:
"Even Gangxiao died under my sabre,

何况一个毛孩来挑战。	Let alone an inexperienced little lad.
我要把他活擒拿，	I can easily catch him alive,
捉来暂时不宰他。	But will not kill him at once.
听说他聪明又漂亮，	I heard he was smart and handsome,
我要把他养起来。"	So I would like to raise him as my own."
达黄浓大罕又献计：	Dahuangnongdahan offered advice again:
"既然是个小毛孩，	"Since he is a mere lad,
就不必费力动刀枪。	We do not have to get the army involved.
先用好话来相劝，	We can first talk to him as friends
选送一群小姑娘。	And then give him some girls,
姑娘的皮肤要白如玉，	Who have fair complexions and shiny black hair.
头发乌黑又发亮。	The girls should be the same age
年龄身材像冈罕，	And the same size as Ganghan,
冈罕见了定喜欢，	So that Ganghan will fall in love with them,
无心拼杀再打仗。"	And have no desire for further fighting and battles."
俸改听了把头点，	Fenggai noddingly agreed.
选送几个小姑娘，	Hence a few girls were selected,
前往军营见冈罕。	And sent to Ganghan's camp.
到了军营又害怕，	When arriving there,
人人提心又吊胆。	The girls all were haunted with fear.
有的转身要想往回跑，	Some of them even wanted to run away.
有的壮了壮胆，	Some of them, however, summoned up their courage
见到冈罕开了口：	To meet Ganghan and say:

厘俸 // Li Feng

"我们的召法冒勐哈①，	"Our Zhaofamaomengha①!
你是一位好长官，	You are an excellent officer,
长得英俊又漂亮。	Handsome and beautiful.
你不应该来攻城，	You should not attack Mengjinghan,
你应当归附勐景罕。	But pledge allegiance to it.
将来成为俸改的附马，	You can be Fenggai's son-in-law in the future,
在宫廷里把官做。	And have an official position in the court.
整天有好酒和好肉，	Every day you will enjoy good wine and delicious meat.
早晚有姑娘来同床。	Every night you will sleep with beautiful girls.
你还是一个少年，	You are still young,
你不应该来打仗，	And should not be involved in a war.
你应该和姑娘在一起。	You should stay with girls.
你想与谁共餐？	Who do you want to dine with?
你想与谁饮酒？	Who do you want to drink with?
凭你来挑选，	It's all up to you.
我们愿意陪伴你，	We would like to accompany you.
绫罗绸缎任你穿。"	You can wear any silk and satin you like."
姑娘话说完，	With that,
捋起筒裙露身体。	The girls pulled up their skirts and showed their bodies.
大腿雪白赛白鹭，	Their legs were as white as egrets,
乳房圆圆似月亮。	And their busty breasts were as round as full moons,
冈罕既不动心也不看，	But Ganghan was not attracted and showed no interest.

① 召法：大官、首领、酋长。冒：未婚青年。勐哈：海罕管辖下的地方。

① Zhaofamaomengha: Zhaofa: officer, chief, leader. Mao: unmarried young man. Mengha: a place ruled by Haihan.

蹬着大象往前冲。	He mounted his elephant and dashed forward.
占拜汉猛奔如发狂，	His elephant rushed madly,
后边的士卒紧紧跟，	With some soldiers following behind,
势如卷席风吹浪。	Like sweeping storms and waves.
姑娘吓得惊又怕，	The girls were so frightened
逃回城里跌跌撞。	That they staggered back into the city.
俸改调兵又遣将，	Fenggai was busy deploying his forces.
挑选三千哈火塔，	He selected three thousand *hahuotas*,
身背宝刀宽又长。	Who carried long and sharp sabres.
又挑选三百哈火吞和三千冒暖冈，	Three hundred *hahuotuns*, three thousand *maonuangangs* of the inner city,
还有九十万冒暖转，	And ninety thousand *maonuanzhuans*,
命令他们决死战。	Were ordered to fight to the death as well.
俸改又指派食禄地方的坐象官，	Fenggai also appointed the local chiefs
备好戎装同出战。	To get ready for the war.
加上召冈和召伴，	And Zhaogangs and Zhaobans,
以及大大小小的将和官，	Along with generals and officers at all levels,
随军出发战冈罕。	Must also set out to fight Ganghan.
俸改厉声下命令：	Fenggai shouted out an order harshly:
"谁往后退我要斩。"	"Anyone who retreats will be killed!"
话刚落音鸣炮三响，	With that, three cannon shots were fired
锣响鼓鸣奔战场。	Drums and gongs were beaten to signal the start of the charge.
象队成群齐出发，	
脚步咚咚震大地，	

厘俸 // Li Feng

天塌地陷尘土扬。

The elephants set out in arrays,
Tramping on the ground with a loud noise
And raising clouds of dust in the air.

俸改的弟弟叫皆温，
绿色的贺罕戛扎①身上穿。
带领兵将也出动，
大象成群又结队，
红漆涂在象舆上。
还有都恨②巴扎哇，
此人专会讲大话，
小时俸改就把他栽培当了官，
让他管辖一百二十干。
他是俸改的贴心人，
谁也不敢同他比高低，
此人也带兵参了战。
撒马姓③也兵分两路出了城，
还有如鹞鹰般凶猛的牛仰罕④，
又率人马又驱象。

Jiewen, the younger brother of Fenggai,
Dressed in *hehangazha*①,
Also led an array of soldiers.
His elephants are marching in herds,
With red howdahs on their backs.
There was also Bazhawa from Duhen②,
Who was always boasting and bragging.
Fenggai trained him to be an official at an early age,
Governing a hundred and twenty *gans*.
Knowing he was a confidant of Fenggai,
No one dared to compete with him.
He was now leading his troops to join the battle.
There was Samaxing③, whose troops marched out of the city in two columns.
And there was Niuyanghan④, fierce as a hawk,

---

① 贺罕戛扎：衣甲名，颜色如同会飞的昆虫的翅膀外壳发出油绿色的光亮。
② 都恨：夜不闭户。
③ 撒马姓：人名，力大无比，能用脚把石头跺得粉碎。
④ 牛仰罕：人名，俸改的将领。

① Hehangazha: the name of armor, the color of which is like the greenish luster of flying insect wings.
② Duhen: a place which is safe at night. People do not even close the doors.
③ Samaxing: the name of a person with super power, who can break stones into pieces with his foot.
④ Niuyanghan: the name of an officer of Fenggai.

俸改的忠臣伴龙法,	Who commanded both soldiers and elephants.
赶着象队齐出脖铃响。	The loyal minister Banlongfa
还有那马门罗虎当①,	Drove the elephant herds with jingling bells on their necks.
全身皮肤红似火,	And there was Mamenluohudang①,
官名叫召麻哈,	Who had a complexion as red as fire.
他专管马队是马官,	His official title was Zhao Maha.
马队的马鞍全部涂红,	He was in charge of war horses.
火焰一般红又亮。	All the horse saddles were painted red,
	Shining like fire flames.
俸改一声命令下,	Fenggai ordered Weidahan
先锋还是卫大罕。	To lead the vanguard.
卫大罕坐在大象上,	Weidahan sat on his elephant,
歪着身子偏着头,	Leaning his body and tilting his head.
金幡幢下的他很傲慢。	Under the golden prayer flags he appeared to be very arrogant.
军队出发上了路,	The troops were on the way to the battlefield.
二十员将领带白盔,	Twenty generals and officers wore white helmets
金龙绘在白盔上。	Painted with golden dragons.
弓弩手数万走在前,	Hundreds of thousands of bowmen walked at the front.
五千士卒随大象,	Five thousand soldiers holding sabres
他们手中持大刀,	Wore leather armor.
牛皮衣甲身上穿。	

---

① 马门罗虎当：人名。　　① Mamenluohudang: the name of a person.

厘俸 // Li Feng

各路兵马涌出城，	The troops surged out of the city,
翻江倒海卷巨浪。	With an overwhelming power
俸改的大军围冈罕，	Like that of huge billows.
两军立刻交了战。	Fenggai's army surrounded Ganghan,
占拜汉一见人马来，	Thus the battle began.
扬鼻挺牙往前闯。	Facing the enemy, the elephant Zhanbaihan,
俸改的战将巴罗法，	Swung his trunk, raised his tusks and dashed forward.
蹬着大象猛冲锋，	Fenggai's general Baluofa
眼明手快迎冈罕。	Drove his elephant forward,
冈罕的人马难抵挡，	And was quick to meet Ganghan's attack with swift action.
他大声呐喊鼓士气，	Ganghan's army could not resist at all.
士卒返身又死战。	He shouted loudly to encourage his soldiers
千军万马格斗急，	To continue the fight.
天崩地陷日光暗。	Thousands of soldiers and horses were engaged in the battle,
双方死伤惨又重，	Shaking the world and dimming the sun.
占拜汉发怒乱冲撞，	Both sides took heavy casualties.
象牙上人血滴滴淌。	The fierce Zhanbaihan made wild charges and attacks.
巴扎哇带领马队蹬着象，	Human blood dripped along his tusks.
直向冈罕奔杀来，	Bazhawa led his horses and elephants
撒马姓也跟着上。	To dash straight toward Ganghan.
冈罕人少力量弱，	Samaxing followed him.
背靠着背奋力战。	Ganghan's army, smaller and less powerful,
巴扎哇挺矛迎冈罕，	Fought back-to-back.
两头战象牙交错，	Bazhawa lifted his spear to fight Ganghan.

如风吹树干嘎吱响，	The two elephants' tusks interlocked and clanged,
士卒互相砍杀如舂碓。	Like tree trunks whipped by a strong wind.
巴扎哇左手挥矛，	The soldiers killed each other with the sound of crunching and slashing.
右手舞着钩镰枪，	
风驰电掣向冈罕。	Bazhawa, with a spear in his left hand,
冈罕不慌也不忙，	And a hooked spear in his right hand,
乘机一矛刺出去。	Ran at Ganghan with lightning speed.
巴扎哇腿上中一枪，	Ganghan, in no hurry,
鲜血喷出染大象。	Seized a chance and thrust with his spear
大象慌忙往后退，	And wounded Bazhawa on his leg,
巴扎哇靠在象舆上。	Where blood gushed out.
冈罕乘胜又追击，	The elephant turned back in a hurry.
再补一矛肋骨上。	The injured Bazhawa leaned on the howdah on his elephant.
痛叫一声落大象，	Ganghan chased after him,
众冒宰争相把头砍。	And stabbed Bazhawa in the ribs.
呜，呜……	Bazhawa gave out a cry of pain and fell off his elephant.
胜利的吼声，	Ganghan's *maozais* rushed to cut off Bazhawa's head.
震动勐景罕。	Hurrah! Hurrah!
伴龙法见势大不妙，	The roar of victory
掉转象头往回跑，	Shook the city of Mengjinghan.
冈庄蹬象紧跟上。	Seeing the hopeless situation,
伴龙法转身又迎击，	Banlongfa made a turn and fled.
两象交锋互不让，	Gangzhuang chased after him.
象牙斗得喀喀响。	Banlongfa had to turn back and fight.

厘俸 // Li Feng

两员大将相较量，	The two elephants showed no signs of concession.
势均力敌艺相当。	Their tusks clinked and clanged.
伴龙法拼力刺一矛，	This was a fight between two senior generals
冈庄衣甲被穿通，	And a battle of neck-and-neck competition.
鲜血喷涌流地上。	Banlongfa, exerting all his energy,
冈庄忍痛蹬大象，	Pierced through Gangzhuang's armor.
拔出宝刀猛力砍。	Blood gushed out and flowed on the ground.
伴龙法一只手受了伤，	Putting up with the great pain,
靠着象舆死一般。	Gangzhuang pulled out his sword and cut violently.
冈庄乘势往前冲，	Banlongfa's hand was injured,
敌兵溃退如坝倒。	He was leaning on the howdah, dying.
	Grasping the opportunity, Gangzhuang dashed forward,
	Forcing the enemy to retreat like a dam collapsing.

冈罕把象脖用力按，	Ganghan forcefully pressed the neck of his elephant,
占拜汉猛冲似发狂，	Zhanbaihan, who charged forward wildly,
后面群象紧紧跟，	Followed closely by a crowd of elephants,
数来共有四百头，	Four hundred in all.
卷起狂风尘土扬，	They created a gale and sent dust into the air,
象牙尖上滴人血。	Human blood dripping from their tusks.
俸改的士卒心胆寒，	Fenggai's warriors were scared,
畏缩不前向后退，	And retreated like cowards.
损兵又折将。	Many lost their lives.

撒马姓见状怒火起,	Samaxing was so furious
胡子几乎翘天上。	That his beard stood up and almost touched the sky.
众将也把舌头弹得嗒嗒响,	The generals clicked their tongues and made a loud noise,
驱赶士卒又冲锋,	Driving their soldiers forward,
乌云一般压冈罕。	Who overwhelmed Ganghan like a dark cloud.
冈罕沉着无所惧,	But Ganghan stayed calm and fearless,
占拜汉奔腾如飞不可挡。	As his Zhanbaihan galloped swiftly and powerfully.
撒马姓自认为他骑的大象了不起,	Thinking that his elephant was great,
蹬着它奔向占拜汉。	Samaxing urged it to charge at Zhanbaihan.
两只大象只战了一回合,	After only one round of fighting,
撒马姓的公象惊又慌,	Samaxing's elephant was so frightened
往后退缩不向前,	That it retreated, refusing to fight no matter
再蹬也不敢再战。	How hard it was spurred.
冈罕步步紧逼不放松,	Ganghan did not let go.
撒马姓挥矛乱刺杀,	Samaxing brandished his spear in all directions,
矛矛落空不见伤。	But missed each and every hit.
冈罕看准机会挺长矛,	Ganghan seized an opportunity
一矛正中对方咽喉上。	And hit right at his foe's neck.
撒马姓长矛宝刀齐落地,	Samaxing's spear and sword dropped
翻身倒下离大象。	And he fell off his elephant.
众冒宰争先涌上来,	All the *maozais* rushed up
手起刀落把头砍。	And cut off his head.
只听呜、呜……	Roaring cries and sounds of clicking tongue
	Were heard!

厘俸 // Li Feng

吼声阵阵弹舌响！	Having lost two generals,
俸改的大军连损两员将，	Fenggai's army fled the battlefield
纷纷逃窜败下阵，	And hastened back the city.
各路兵马急回城。	Ganghan's army cleared the battlefield
冈罕的军队乘胜追击扫战场，	And captured many enemy soldiers, elephants
俘虏、大象成栏成圈，	And countless knives and spears.
还有无数刀和枪。	Sangluo's troops also joined in the battle.
桑洛率兵也参战，	His opponent was Weidahuang, Weidahan's younger brother,
对手是卫大罕的弟弟卫大荒，	
还有贺哇仁占邦①，	And Hewarenzhanbang①,
他们声如虎熊猛如狼，	Who roared like tigers and fought like wolves.
蹬着大象离贺勐②，	They mounted their elephants and left Hemeng②,
气势汹汹扑桑洛。	And charged at Sangluo fiercely.
两军象阵齐交锋，	The elephants of the two armies engaged
一场恶战，	In a terrible battle,
人仰马翻。	Killing many on both sides.
吼声震动天和地，	Battle cries shook the earth.
势均力敌，	The two armies were equally strong,
难分难解。	And it seemed that neither side could win.
城东杀声也不断，	At the east of the city, there were continuous war cries, too.
守军是俸改部将牛仰罕，	The general who defended there was Niuyanghan,

---

① 贺哇仁占邦：俸改的另一员将领。
② 贺勐：地名，在勐景罕城的北边。

① Hewarenzhanbang: one of Fenggai's generals.
② Hemeng: the name of a place near the city of Mengjinghan.

对手是海罕的两员将，	Fenggai's subordinate.
一个是崩南宛多法，	His opponents were two of Haihan's generals.
一个是嘿南。	One was Bengnanwanduofa,
战壕一条中间隔，	And the other was Heinan.
里里外外杀声起，	A trench lay in between.
如山倒崖塌乱石滚，	Thundering battle cries rose on both sides,
血飞溅，	As if mountains fell and huge stones rolled down.
死伤成千上万。	Blood splashed.
双方力量差不多，	Thousands died.
胜负难分持久战。	As the two sides were equivalent in strength,
	The battle dragged on with no victory in sight.
还有战场另一方，	In another battlefield,
红红一团是火焰，	There was a red flame.
原来是马门罗虎当。	It turned out to be Mamenluohudang,
他肉皮红红蹬着象，	Who had red skin and urged his elephant on,
来势汹汹如洪水泛滥，	Rushing at Xiangga and Xianggang
就像木渣杂草水上漂，	Like a violent flood
滚滚冲往向戛和向冈。	Carrying logs and grass forward.
弟兄二人怒火起，	The two brothers were irritated
互相依靠齐混战。	And met the enemy head-on.
指挥士卒成两行，	They ordered their soldiers to form two lines
一左一右来包抄。	And surrounded the enemy from two sides.
弟兄二人两头象，	The two brothers, each riding an elephant,

厘俸 // Li Feng

冲杀马门罗虎当。	Rushed at Mamenluohudang.
你来我往矛飞舞，	As they fought,
道道光圈绕头上。	Their spears flashed in the air.
马门罗虎当手疾眼又快，	Mamenluohudang was very quick.
一矛划破向戛皮。	He cut a wound in Xiangga's skin.
向戛猛力蹬大象，	Xiangga spurred his elephant violently
咬紧牙关刺长矛。	And pierced the enemy with his spear despite his pain.
马门罗虎当一声叫，	Mamenluohudang let out a cry.
肋骨已经被刺中。	He was hit in his ribs.
他掉转大象就要逃，	He turned his elephant around and tried to flee.
弟兄二人紧追赶。	But the two brothers followed closely behind.
向冈长矛又飞出，	Xianggang thrust out his long spear
一矛刺在象肚上。	And hit the elephant in the belly.
手中斧头又抡起，	He then swung his axe
一斧砍在象头上。	And cut the elephant's head.
大象一声惨叫倒地死，	The elephant fell dead, groaning
象身压着马门罗虎当。	And crushed Mamenluohudang under it.
兄弟二人乘胜追，	The two brothers drove the enemy soldiers away
风卷残云敌丧胆。	Like wind sweeping scattered clouds.
俸改的弟弟皆温和皆伴，	Jiewen and Jieban, Fenggai's younger brothers,
还有那凶猛的卫大罕，	And fierce Weidahan,
三把金幡幢迎风展，	Were three major commanders in the army.
他们是军中三员主将。	Their three golden prayer flags fluttered in the wind.

率领象队浩浩荡荡，	Their elephant troops were mighty,
只见孔雀尾摇摇晃晃。	With peacock feathers waving on the howdahs.
三员大将已汇集，	The three commanders gathered together
如八月洪水两岸漫，	Like an August flood overflowing the banks
如夏天江水翻巨浪，	And river billows rising high in summer.
三军合力围冈罕。	They attacked Ganghan from three sides with joint forces.
冈罕稳坐象舆上，	Ganghan sat safely on his elephant's howdah,
面对全军大声喊：	Shouting to his soldiers:
"谁能战胜卫大罕，	"Whoever defeats Weidahan
我将赏给黄金许许多，	Will be rewarded with gold
比卫大罕的脑袋三倍重。"	Three times the weight of his head."
卫大罕一听怒火上，	Hearing this, Weidahan became furious
分兵两路杀将来。	And charged at Ganghan with two columns of troops.
冈罕人马齐迎战，	Ganghan's troops met the enemy with a counterattack,
好似水闸大开洪水放，	Like an overwhelming and irresistible flood
一泻千里不可挡。	Rushing out of a sluice gate.
对方大象密密麻，	But the enemy's elephants were numerous,
如田野稻穗望不断。	Endless like ears of rice in a vast field.
冈罕心中已清楚，	Ganghan knew that
卫大罕的队伍力量强，	Weidahan's army was very strong,
父亲死在他们手中。	And that his father died in their hands.
原班人马在眼前，	These were the same people that had killed his father.
旧恨新仇如火燃。	His anger was fueled with hatred like a fire.
冈罕无所畏惧添力量，	Fearless and stronger than ever,

厘俸 // Li Feng

蹬着大象一马当先，	He urged his elephant on
目标向着卫大罕。	And rushed towards Weidahan,
卫大罕忽然高声喊，	Who suddenly yelled
声音如雷震耳响。	In a thundering voice,
"冈罕啊，冈罕！	"Ganghan, oh Ganghan!
你父冈晓不够我宰杀，	Even your father Gangxiao was not my match.
我甩着空刀往回返。	I went back with dissatisfaction.
你是一个小毛孩，	You are a little baby,
刚生下地没几天，	Born just a few days ago.
就胆大包天骑着象，	How dare you get on an elephant
要来进攻勐景罕。	And attack Mengjinghan!
莫非你父死了还不够，	Is it not enough that your father died
你还要随父来死亡？	And that you must follow him?
父子二人双双亡，	It will be shameful
让人记录下来，	If both you and your father's death
留给后人知晓太丢脸，	Are recorded for future generations to read.
只可怜你年纪还太轻，	You are so young.
何必跟着父同亡！	You don't have to die with your father.
冈罕啊，	Oh Ganghan,
今天你有来无回，	If you fight, you will never go back and
再也不能见海罕！"	See your brother Haihan again!"
冈罕怒目来回答：	Ganghan stared at him and answered:
"卫大罕啊，卫大罕！	"Weidahan, oh Weidahan!
你说冈晓不够杀，	You said that Gangxiao was not your match.

天下是否你最大？	Are you the strongest in the world?
前次如果是我来，	Last time, if I had come instead of my father,
你的性命就已完。	You would have been killed.
钩住你的肩胛骨，	I would have hooked your shoulder
耍狗一般院中转。	And played with you like a dog in the yard.
可惜召生死了才派我来，	It is a pity that I was sent here only after Zhaosheng, my father, had died.
今天我决不轻饶你。	Today I won't let you go so easily.
只要占拜汉的牙不折断，	I will never stop fighting you
我誓不罢休与你战。	As long as Zhanbaihan's tusks do not break.
卫大罕啊，	Oh, Weidahan,
是好是坏刀矛见，	We will see who is stronger by fighting, not talking.
今天你是来送死，	You've come to seek your doom
再也不能回家去，	And will never go back
与你妻儿相见！"	To see your wife and children!"
卫大罕心头冒火蹬大象，	Weidahan was angered and spurred his elephant on.
两头大象牙绞牙，	The tusks of the two elephants locked together,
响声如石滚下坡，	Making a crashing sound like boulders rolling down a slope,
吱吱嘎嘎似要断。	As if they would break.
冈罕稳坐象舆上，	Ganghan sat firmly on his elephant.
卫大罕上下来巡视，	Weidahan looked at him from head to foot,
待机要把冈罕算。	Waiting for an opportunity to capture him.
双方小心又谨慎，	Both were very cautious,
谁也不是个憨人，	
撩开衣甲让人来戳杀。	

厘俸 // Li Feng

冈罕衣甲坚又固，	As neither was foolish enough
卫大罕挥矛如电闪。	To expose his own vulnerability to the enemy.
冈罕武艺很高强，	Ganghan's armor was strong
手中长矛左右挡。	And Weidahan's spear flashed like lightning.
然后取出一宝袋，	Ganghan was a skilled fighter
对着天空轻摇晃。	And defended himself with his long spear.
天空忽然电光闪，	Then he took out a treasure bag amulet
冈罕匍匐象身上，	And shook it lightly up toward the sky.
两眼紧盯卫大罕。	Suddenly, there was a flash in the sky
卫大罕矛矛落了空，	And Ganghan bent down on his elephant back,
心急如火露破绽。	Staring hard at Weidahan,
冈罕看准机会猛一刺，	Who missed every one of his hits
正中卫大罕咽喉上。	And carelessly exposed his vulnerable spot.
只听咚的一声响，	Ganghan seized the chance to give him a fatal strike,
卫大罕倒在象身上，	Hitting him in the throat.
紧抱象头死一般。	There was a thump
冈罕上下仔细看，	And Weidahan fell on the elephant's back,
卫大罕脖上的铁甲已松塌，	Holding its head with his arms as if he was dead.
咽喉被刺穿，	Ganghan looked carefully and found that
血正在流淌！	The iron armor on Weidahan's neck was loosened
勐景罕的士卒，	And his throat was pierced through,
为了保护他们的妻室和儿女，	Bleeding!
挣扎着反扑过来。	Mengjinghan's soldiers
勐景罕的男儿，	Started another attack

人人也是英雄汉，	To protect their wives and children.
个个奋勇当先，	These men of Mengjinghan
又砍象脚又把人来砍。	Were all indeed heroes.
一场混战，	They charged fiercely,
血流成河死上万。	Chopping elephants' feet and cutting people.
卫大罕身中一矛无力再战，	There was a chaotic fight.
又气又怒如醉汉，	Blood flowed like a river and thousands died.
抱着象头往后转。	Due to the spear wound, Weidahan could no longer fight.
冈罕怎肯善罢休，	Angry like a drunken man,
紧紧追赶其后。	He ran away on his elephant back.
占拜汉长牙连连挑，	But Ganghan was not willing to let him go,
挑在卫大罕坐骑屁股上。	Attacking him from behind.
两头大象在格斗，	His elephant Zhanbaihan poked repeatedly
声如闷雷一般响。	At the hip of Weidahan's elephant.
卫大罕从象背滚下来，	The two elephants got into a fight,
占拜汉怒目挥长鼻，	Roaring like muffled thunder.
长牙猛戳卫大罕。	Weidahan fell off the back of his elephant.
两边士卒围上来，	Zhanbaihan waved its trunk and
争先恐后把头砍。	Pierced him violently with its tusks.
首级手中捧，	The soldiers rushed forward
弹舌嗒嗒响。	And cut off his head.
"嗨、嗨……"之声传四方！	They held his head in their hands
冈罕复仇心欢畅，	And clicking his tongue loudly.
勐景罕人人听后毛骨悚然。	The sounds of "cheers" echoed in the universe!

厘俸 // Li Feng

    Ganghan was happy with his revenge.
    But the people of Mengjinghan all shivered with fear.

卫大罕的妻子站在转颂上，	Weidahan's wife stood on the *zhuansong*,
边晒丝线边叫喊：	And shouted while drying her silk threads:
"求召法冒勐哈，	"Please listen to me, Zhaofamaomengha!
杀死你父亲的人多又多，	Many people took part in killing your father.
不仅仅是卫大罕。	Weidahan was just one of them.
如果他死了，	When he dies,
你不要像南瓜一样把他砍。	Please do not cut his head up like cutting a pumpkin.
求你赐给红绸一小块，	Please use a piece of red silk
裹着他的头回来，	To wrap up his head
我要把他来安葬。	So that I can bring it back and bury it.
你不要像砍黄瓜一样把他砍，	Please do not cut his body up like cutting a cucumber.
求你赐给绫罗绸缎一大块，	Please use a large piece of silk and satin
裹着他的尸体，	To wrap up his body
我要运回村中埋！"	So that I can move it back and bury it in our village."

冈罕的军中锣鼓响，	There were drum beats of celebration in Ganghan's army.
士卒齐声欢腾涌进城，	The soldiers all went into the city with great joy
抢夺财产和大象。	And began to take valuables and elephants.
妇女胆战心又惊，	The women inside the city were all thrown into panic.
放下织机丢下布，	They put away their looms and cloth
四散奔逃四处藏。	And fled in all directions.

母亲紧紧牵孩儿，	The mothers held their children's hands tightly,
脸变颜色手脚颤。	Trembling with fear and turning pale.
老妇把孙儿紧紧抱，	The old women held their grandchildren tightly
如同猴子把儿护，	Like monkeys protecting their babies
坐在窗前向外看。	And observed the situation from the windows.
俸改的弟弟皆温和皆伴，	Jiewen and Jieban, Fenggai's younger brothers,
蹬着大象堵冈罕。	Spurred their elephants on to stop Ganghan.
占拜汉横冲又直撞，	Zhanbaihan dashed and struck
一场恶战又开始，	And another fierce battle began.
杀声震山冈。	There were shouts of fighting all over the hills.
勐景罕弩手三千人，	Three thousand bowmen of Mengjinghan
弓箭齐发嗖嗖响。	Released their arrows at the same time.
鲁卡、鲁汪[①]被射中，	*Lukas* and *luwangs*[①] were all shot.
冒宰举起盾来挡。	The *maozais* raised their shields
边挡利箭边前进，	And marched forward while fending off the arrows.
越过荆棘跨过沟。	They jumped over the thorns and crossed the trenches
势如八月涨大水，	Like a river flood in August
洪水上岸冲沙滩。	Washing away sand on river banks.
向冈从左来增援，	Xianggang came from the left side
到处都是象斗象。	To aid with the elephants.
向戛从右来增援，	Xiangga came from the right side

[①] 鲁：儿；卡：奴隶；汪：山区。鲁卡、鲁汪指冈罕的士卒，社会地位处于最底层的人。

[①] Lu: son. Ka: slave. Wang: mountainous areas. Here it refers to Ganghan's soldiers, who came from the lower social class.

厘俸 // Li Feng

大队人马呼又喊，	To reinforce with soldiers and horses
象队列阵冲杀来。	And herds of elephants as well.
艾包、尼崩、桑温和赛伦，	Ai Bao, Ni Beng, Sangwen and Sailun,
还有波道坚混缅，	Together with the Bodaojianhunmian,
蹬着大象也来支援冈罕。	Also drove their elephants to back up Ganghan.
响声如雷惊天地，	The shouts of fighting shook the sky and the earth.
人马纷纷死又伤。	The soldiers and horses were either injured or killed.
俸改的弟弟皆伴，	Jiewen, Fenggai's younger brother,
骑在象上大声喊：	Rode on his elephant and shouted loudly:
"冈罕啊，冈罕，	"Ganghan, oh Ganghan!
你年纪那么小，	You are still so young
不应来送命。	And should not have come here to be killed.
可怜你一个嫩娃娃，	You poor little lad
死了实在不应该。	You should not lose your life.
你一无本事二无力，	You have neither talents nor strength.
有什么能力攻打勐景罕，	How dare you come to attack Mengjinghan?
只能空来此地走一转。	You will leave empty-handed.
冈罕啊，冈罕，	Ganghan oh Ganghan!
你年纪那么小，	You are still so young
为什么来此攻城不怕死？	Why did you come to attack us without any fear?
低下头来想一想，	Think it over carefully!
今天你是来送死，	You come to seek your doom today
再也不能回到尼混渤	And will never go back to Nihunle
——见海罕！"	And see Haihan again!"

冈罕开口来回答：	Ganghan replied:
"俸改的陶姐冈①啊，	"Fenggai's Taojie Gang①!
神灵拳头早握紧，	The gods have long clenched their fists,
因为俸改不信鬼神，	Because Fenggai does not believe in them
早已不把神灵祭，	And has not offered them a sacrifice for a long time.
神灵对他有怨恨，	They thus have a grudge against him
灾难已降临他身上。	And a disaster is to befall him.
如果你们不相信，	If you don't believe my words,
今日你我来较量，	Then come to fight with me
看看天要谁死亡。	And see who is destined to die.
你的大话莫要讲，	You should stop boasting.
前次如果我出征，	Last time if I came to attack you instead of my father,
你们的城池早已变灰烬！	Your city should have been utterly destroyed!
现在我来讨伐你，	Now I come to fight you
即使城墙比悬崖更坚，	And will sweep over the city
我也要把它踏平。	Even though the city wall is stronger than a cliff.
我这次来勐景罕，	This time I come
一是要夺回父亲尸体来安葬，	Firstly to take back my father's body for burial
二是顺便来游玩。	And secondly to travel around.
如果天神布领暖的兵将到，	When the troops of God Bulingnuan arrive,
勐景罕就要彻底垮，	Mengjinghan will break down completely

---

① 陶姐冈：古代傣族民主选举的有威望的老人，这里指俸改的弟弟皆伴。

① Taojie Gang: In ancient times, the old people selected by local people as the most prestigious ones were called taojiegang. Here it refers to Fenggai's younger brother Jieban.

厘俸 // Li Feng

就像砸碎在地上的一只碗。	Like a bowl dropped on the ground.
不管你们有多硬，	No matter how tough you are,
即使是从小吃石头长大，	Even if you grew up eating stones,
也是枉然！	All your fighting will be in vain.
死神已降你身上，	The god of death is approaching you,
竟不醒悟还自夸。"	So wake up and stop boasting."
皆伴听了怒火起，	Jieban was irritated by these words
骑着大象冲过来，	And dashed forward on the back of his elephant,
铜箍的象牙尖利粗又长。	Who had thick and sharp tusks wrapped with copper.
冈罕蹬着占拜汉，	Ganghan spurred his Zhanbaihan
从容不迫来迎战。	And met the charge unhurriedly.
两象交锋牙相错，	The two elephants' tusks clashed
只听咚咚震耳响。	With a deafening sound.
皆伴目不转睛紧盯冈罕，	Jieban stared at Ganghan
突然一矛飞出去，	And suddenly thrust out his spear
矛尖落在象舆上。	At Ganghan's howdah.
矛如雨点连连下，	A rain of spears fell down
冈罕左晃右来挡。	And Ganghan had to dodge quickly.
他心不惊手不慌，	He stayed calm
双目牢牢盯对方。	And kept glaring at his opponent.
突然一矛如迅雷，	He thrust his spear all of a sudden
矛尖刺进皆伴的胸膛。	And pierced it into Jieban's chest.
皆伴往后身一仰，	Jieban leaned backwards
斜身靠着金幡幢，	On the golden prayer flag,

一脚挂在大象胸带上，	With one of his feet hung on the chest rein of the elephant.
鲜血如水在流淌。	His blood gushed out like water.
他的卫士护左右，	His soldiers protected him
齐把冈罕来抵挡。	From Ganghan's attack.
俸改援兵不断来，	Then more of Fenggai's reinforcement arrived,
一场混战卷地起，	And another battle started,
搅得天昏地又暗。	Darkening the whole world.
大象久战力已竭，	All the elephants fought to their exhaustion.
人马昏沉不辨向。	All the soldiers and horses lost their way.
皆伴负伤趁机逃，	Jieban fled wounded
后边追来占拜汉。	But Zhanbaihan followed him closely behind.
皆温远远已看见，	Jiewen saw the situation from far away
带领象队冲过来。	And rushed forward with his team of elephants.
他自认勇猛不可挡，	He thought he was fierce and invincible,
坐在象上大声骂：	And sat on his elephant spoke abusive words:
"冈罕啊，冈罕，	"Ganghan, oh Ganghan!
勐景罕站得稳又稳，	Mengjinghan stands on the ground
好像三脚大鼎立地上。	Firmly and steadily like a cooking vessel with three legs.
勐景罕土地宽又广，	Mengjinghan has a vast extension of land
喜鹊、鸽子飞不到边，	Which magpies and pigeons cannot fly across
老鹰飞过迷方向。	And where hawks get lost in the sky.
勐景罕城池多又多，	There are many cities in Mengjinghan
各城的大象排成栏。	Where elephants line up in herds.
勐景罕兵强马又壮，	Mengjinghan has a powerful army.

厘俸 // Li Feng

进城容易出城难。	It is easy to enter the city but difficult to get out of it.
你冈罕小小年纪嫩又嫩，	You are young and weak.
为何胆敢来侵犯？	How dare you come to invade us?
如今你还不成人，	You have not grown up yet
未到死期却来找麻烦。	But come here to make trouble.
你有来无回死已定，	You are destined to die
不能回到妈身边，	And cannot go back to your mother
再把奶水饮！"	And suck her breast!"
冈罕大声回答说：	Ganghan answered loudly:
"皆温啊，皆温，	"Jiewen, oh Jiewen!
你这俸改的弟弟也太狂。	As Fenggai's younger brother, you are too arrogant.
勐景罕宽广算什么？	Mengjinghan is broad and vast, but so what?
还比不过召法尼的大象一只脚印，	It is not even larger than a footprint of the elephant of our Zhao Fani, Haihan.
何必对我把口夸！	So you don't have to brag before me!
你自诩战象成栏，	You boast that you have herds of elephants.
何不数数我来听？	Why don't you just tell me how many you have?
你的战象算什么，	Your elephants are nothing.
哪一头胜过占拜汉？	Which one of them is superior to Zhanbaihan?
哪一头能把它的牙挑断？	Which one of them can break its tusks?
你们自称是英雄，	You call yourself a hero
似乎天下第一强。	As if you were number one in the world.
死到临头还不知，	You are not aware that you are going to die soon
还要嘴硬叫嚷嚷。	And still talk big.

如果你有真本事，	If you are a true fighter,
你我蹬象来较量。"	Just come forward and fight me."
皆温蹬象冲过来，	Jiewen dashed up on the back of his elephant,
象牙粗大如臼棒。	Whose tusks were thick like a mortar.
两象交锋吼声响，	The two elephants were engaged in a battle, roaring,
你来我往不相让。	And did not compromise at all.
占拜汉长牙猛一挑，	Zhanbaihan attacked violently with its long tusks
皆温的大象往后退。	And forced Jiewen's elephant to retreat.
二十头大象又冲上，	Twenty more elephants dashed out in two columns
分成两路迎冈罕。	To fight Ganghan.
双方士卒相残杀，	Soldiers from both sides were killing each other.
双方大象互冲撞。	And elephants from both sides were bumping each other.
俸改的马队又出动，	Then Fenggai's cavalry set out
左右两边围上来。	And closed in from the left and the right side.
士卒下马挥长矛，	The cavalry got off their horses and fought with their spears.
兵马相搏血飞溅，	Blood and flesh flew all around as the fight went on,
如同婚嫁喜事般，	Like meat chopped on the cutting board
一一砍肉剁砧板。	For a marriage feast.
只见刀光闪闪人倒下，	Soldiers fell under the flash of swords.
双方人死象又伤。	Both sides suffered heavy casualties.
艾包、尼崩率兵援冈罕，	The arrival of Ai Bao and Ni Beng
冈罕一见心欢喜，	Made Ganghan very happy.
越战越猛不可挡。	He fought more valiantly.
皆温双手紧握矛，	Jiewen held his spear tightly

厘俸 // Li Feng

对着冈罕连连刺，	And hit at Ganghan again and again
矛矛都被冈罕闪。	But missed him every time.
冈罕趁机刺一矛，	Ganghan caught a chance and
皆温中矛鲜血淌。	Stabbed Jiewen,
皆温负伤忙逃命，	Who got wounded and had to retreat in haste,
众兵众将全败退，	So did his soldiers and generals.
百头大象阵脚乱。	His elephants were thrown into confusion.
冈罕蹬象急追赶，	Ganghan chased after them closely
追到一地叫安望，	Till they reached a place called Anwang,
冈晓战死在这里，	Where Gangxiao had fought to the death.
昔日尸骨堆如山，	The remains of the dead soldiers have been piled up like mounds
冈晓的尸体也还在，	And Gangxiao's body was found there,
紧紧扑在象身上。	Lying prone on his elephant
象舆一半压在身，	And underneath his howdah.
左手搭象脖，	His left hand was on the elephant's neck
右手拖在草地上，	And his right hand touched the grass.
战袍还在闪金光。	His war robe was still shiny.
二十位将领默默看，	The twenty generals all looked in silence
人人流泪心悲怆。	And shed tears of sorrow.
大家弯腰齐动手，	They bent to lift the body
抬起尸体放象上。	And put it on the back of an elephant.
冈罕双手捂住脸，	Ganghan covered his face with his hand
边哭边说声打颤：	And said in trembling voice:
"我的父亲啊，	

你为什么死在勐景罕，	"Oh my father,
听说你死时饿着肚，	How can it be that you died in Mengjinghan!
忙着冲锋未吃饭。	I heard that you died hungry
混勐命我亲率兵，	Because you fought so hard
夺回尸体去安葬。	That you forgot to eat your meals.
请你坐着占拜温，	Hunmeng ordered me
和我一同往家返。	To come to bring you back home
亲爱的父亲啊，	On the back of Zhanbaiwen.
你不要责怪你的儿，	My dear father,
请你保佑我攻下勐景罕。	Please do not put blame on your son.
你死了莫要变心肠，	Please bless me to conquer Mengjinghan.
请你坐着大象，	You should not change your mind after death
和我一道把俸改杀。"	But sit on my elephant
冈罕说完下命令：	And kill Fenggai with me."
各路兵马转方向，	Ganghan then ordered his troops
如蜂子出窝退出城。	To turn around
来到城外齐列队，	And withdrew from the city like bees flying out of a honeycomb.
把冈晓的尸体棺中装。	They lined up outside the city
忽然空中传声音，	And put Gangxiao's body in a coffin.
原来是神灵城头喊：	Suddenly there were voices of the gods
"冈罕啊，冈罕，	In the direction of the city wall:
人死为何抬回去，	"Ganghan, oh Ganghan!
是否要把肉来分？"	Why do you bring a dead person back?
冈罕听了不回头，	

厘俸 // Li Feng

率领兵马回远负，
尘土遍地旗飞扬。
桑本、桑洛还在攻城，
见到冈罕已退兵，
也纷纷撤离战场往回返。

千军万马回远负，
冈罕开口对兵将说：
　"要像冈晓未死时那样，
热热闹闹下河洗澡去游玩。"
然后走进远负营寨内，
众将出来迎冈罕。
可怜战象占拜汉，
浑身到处都是伤。
冈罕清点兵马查人数，
阵亡召冈、布冈六十个。
冈晓灵柩回远负，
尸体洗净衣服换。
灵柩抬到海罕处，
海罕大哭心悲伤，
手拿金杯悼冈晓：
　"艾冈晓弟啊，

Do you want to distribute his flesh?"
Ganghan did not listen to them
And returned to the *yuanfu* with his troops,
Dust rising and banners fluttering.
Sangben and Sangluo were still attacking the city.
When they saw Ganghan withdraw,
They returned to their camps as well.

When his troops were back in the *yuanfu*,
Ganghan spoke to his soldiers and generals:
"Go and swim in the river and have fun
As you did before Gangxiao died."
Then he went into the *yuanfu*
And was welcomed by the generals and officers.
Poor Zhanbaihan
Had wounds all over its body.
Ganghan counted the number of his soldiers and horses
And found that he had lost sixty Zhaogangs and Bugangs.
Now Gangxiao's coffin was carried back,
His body cleaned and clothes changed.
When the coffin was carried to Haihan's camp,
He wept and cried in sorrow.
He held a gold cup up to mourn Gangxiao:
"Gangxiao, my younger brother!

你要像活着时候一个样,	You are still alive in my heart!
我用金杯敬你酒,	I drink a toast to you with this gold cup
愿你灵魂得平安。	And wish you find peace of soul!
你虽然已经战死了,	Though you have fought to the death,
请不要急忙上天堂。	Do not go to heaven so quickly
要帮助我们攻勐俸,	But wait for Fenggai's soul.
等着俸改灵魂一同上。	We need you to help us attack Mengjinghan.
你生前为我管辖的勐,	The places you governed for me
五谷丰登人畜旺,	Produce good harvests and prosper.
人人都把你赞扬。	You are highly praised by the people.
我要派出阿巫戛,	I will send Awu Ga
上天告诉布领暖,	To tell Bulingnuan all about this,
向他讨要仙丹来,	And ask for an elixir
让你重新又复活。	To bring you back to life.
艾召生弟弟啊,	My younger brother Ai Zhaosheng,
我的心中太悲伤！"	I feel so grieved and heart-broken!"

厘俸 // Li Feng

八

第二天早晨天刚亮，
海罕起床洗脸吃早饭。
然后召集众将官，
又把战事来商量。
海罕开口说了话：
"阿巫戛啊，阿巫戛，
俸改的弟弟皆伴，
如今已经战死了，
消息震动勐景罕。
卫大罕也把命丧，
俸改士气大大降。
我怕俸改红了眼，
要把婻崩来杀害。
你要急忙去察看，
保护婻崩不被伤，
我的阿巫戛啊！"
阿巫戛取出万倮诺①，
身上一抹变飞鸽，
展翅飞向勐景罕。
他从空中往下降，

① 万倮诺：仙丹。

VIII

At dawn the next day,
Haihan got up, washed his face and finished his breakfast.
Then he summoned his officials and generals to come
To discuss the war affairs.
He said:
"Awu Ga, oh, Awu Ga!
Jieban, Fenggai's younger brother,
Died in the war.
The news has shocked all Mengjinghan.
Weidahan has also lost his life,
Discouraging Fenggai's army so much.
I am afraid that Fenggai may be driven
By crazed blood-lust to kill Nanbeng.
You'd better go and check the situation,
And protect Nanbeng from any possible harm,
My dear Awu Ga!"
Awu Ga took out his *wanluonuo*① and smears it on his body.
He then transformed himself into a pigeon,
Flying swiftly towards Mengjinghan.

① Wanluonuo: elixir.

飞进婻崩的窗户，	He descended from above in the air
只见婻崩卧床睡，	And slipped into Nanbeng's room through the window.
蒙则①侍候在一旁。	He saw Nanbeng lying on her bed,
等到蒙则走出门，	With a *mengze*① serving by her side.
阿巫戛对婻崩把话讲：	Awu Ga did not speak to Nanbeng
"海罕叫我告诉你，	Until the *mengze* went out of the room:
勐景舍②的婻崩啊，	"I am here to deliver Haihan's message to you.
海罕虽是天神的子孙，	Oh, Nanbeng from Mengjingshe②!
可是还被俸改欺，	Haihan is a descendant of the gods,
使得你俩双离散，	Yet Fenggai still bullies him,
不能同桌来吃饭。	Causing you and Haihan to be separated from each other,
海罕带军队来复仇，	And no longer able to eat at the same table as usual.
皆伴已经被杀死，	Haihan is now leading his army to take revenge.
卫大罕也已把命丧。	Jieban has been killed
勐景罕元气已大损，	And Weidahan has lost his life.
俸改心急会红眼。	The power of Mengjinghan has been greatly undermined
海罕怕你被暗算，	So Fenggai may become exasperated and may plot against you.
要你小心又注意，	
白天黑夜细提防。	Haihan sent me to remind you
海罕虽包围了勐景罕，	To be more cautious both day and night.
不幸冈晓已阵亡。	Haihan has surrounded Mengjinghan
海罕的人马虽然多，	But has unfortunately lost his general Gangxiao.

---

① 蒙则：宫中的女仆。
② 勐景舍：婻崩的家乡。

① Mengze: maid.
② Mengjingshe: name of Nanbeng's hometown.

厘俸 // Li Feng

但不能把景罕团团围。	Haihan has a strong army,
不知道俸改还有几个召幢，	But can not surround Mengjinghan tightly.
不知道他还有多少兵将。	He doesn't know how many Zhaozhuangs Fenggai still has And how many soldiers and generals Fenggai still has.
婻崩啊，	
海罕心中很着急，	Oh Nanbeng,
如果攻不下勐景罕，	Haihan is now so anxious!
他就要蹬着占拜舍回家乡！"	If he can not occupy Mengjinghan,
婻崩听完哭着说：	He will have to ride Zhanbaishe
"叔叔啊，叔叔，	And return in vain to his hometown!"
请你告诉海罕，	On hearing these words Nanbeng cried and said:
俸改的弟弟虽已死，	"Uncle, oh, Uncle!
但他的帅旗没有倒。	Please tell Haihan what I know.
卫大罕虽然已身亡，	Though Fenggai's younger brother has died,
他的帅旗仍在扬。	His general banner has not fallen.
父死儿把兵马接，	Though Weidahan has lost his life,
俸改一声命令下，	His general banner still flies high in the air.
他们的儿子做了官。	Their troops have been handed over to their sons
城中大象仍然多，	By command of Fenggai.
多得像风雨来临般。	Their sons have succeeded to their titles and become officers.
城里赶集闹如常，	There are still a large number of war elephants in the city,
召幢不知有多少，	As many as rain drops in a storm.
又像云来又像雾，	The market in the city is as busy and lively as usual.
左数右数数不完。	
虽然俸改势力大，	

可海罕的力量比他强。	The number of Zhaozhuangs is actually unknown
请他不要半途废，	Because they are mysterious like clouds and mists
我嫡崩日夜把他盼。	And it is not easy to count the number.
还有情况告诉他：	Fenggai is powerful,
俸改有矛手三十万，	But Haihan has overwhelming superiority.
还有四万镖枪手。	Tell Haihan not to give up halfway.
要小心作战别急躁，	Tell him Nanbeng is expecting him every day and night.
攻城不要亲自往前冲。	Here is more information to tell him:
要保护自己不被伤，	Fenggai still has three hundred thousand spearmen
如果他被伤害了，	And forty thousand dart men.
留下我一人怎么办？	So tell Haihan not to be hasty and impatient while fighting
就如丝线中间断，	And not to dash in the front while attacking.
他我分离接不上，	Ask him to protect himself well.
千年万年空悲伤。	If he gets killed
阿巫戛啊，	I really do not know what to do!
请你把这些转告海罕！"	He and I then will be just like a silk thread
阿巫戛点头后又变鸽，	Broken in the middle and never able to be connected,
飞回远负见海罕。	Grief-stricken for ten thousand years!
见到海罕开了口：	Awu Ga, oh, Awu Ga!
"嫡崩叫我把话传，	Please tell Haihan what I said!"
请你攻城别急躁，	Awu Ga nodded his head and once again turned into a pigeon
不要冲锋打头阵。	And flew away to report to Haihan at his *yuanfu*.
勐俸地方宽又广，	Awu Ga said:
城中壕沟密密麻，	

厘俸 // Li Feng

弓弩存千仓。	"Nanbeng asks me to tell you
俸改内城防守严，	Not to be hasty and impatient while attacking
栅栏围着二十层。	And not to be the first to dash to the front.
每道栅栏大象守，	Mengjinghan is a vast land.
每栏大象二十头。	Trenches are built everywhere in the city.
俸改还有一头象，	Bows and crossbows are stored in thousands of warehouses.
名叫恩着节丁法，	The inner city is heavily-defended.
脚大如蜂盘。	There are twenty-layers of fences,
还有一头叫占艾兰，	Each guarded by a herd
凶猛无比难抵挡。	Of twenty elephants.
海罕啊，	One of Fenggai's elephants,
嫡崩的口信多又多，	Whose name is Enzhejiedingfa,
我全部把它向你转。"	Has feet as large as a beehives.
海罕听了低头想，	Another elephant, called Zhan'ailan,
然后抬头把口开：	Is invincible in terms of its ferocity and fierceness.
"这次攻打勐景罕，	Oh Haihan,
没有俘虏一头象，	These are the messages
嫡崩未能夺回来，	That Nanbeng has for you."
还失去冈晓一员将。	Haihan thought for a while
眼看勐俸攻不下，	And then said:
嫡崩不能归。	"In this battle between Mengjinghan and us,
我心中着急无奈何，	We've lost Gangxiao,
只好骑着大象回家乡。"	But have not captured even one single elephant,
阿巫戛听了圆睁眼说：	Let alone took Nanbeng back.

"既然勐俸攻不下，	I am so anxious and distressed because
也俘虏不了一头象，	Mengfeng remains unoccupied
为什么又要往回返？	And Nanbeng is still in Fenggai's hand.
要夺妻子夺不回，	I have no alternative but to go home."
要想报仇仇未报，	Awu Ga was surprised and said:
为什么空手返家乡？	"Now that you can not capture Mengfeng,
我的召海法啊，	And have seized no elephant,
各勐供应酒和肉，	Why do you want to retreat?
粮草源源没有断，	You haven't taken your wife back yet,
还把儿孙送前方。	Nor have you taken your revenge.
现在你中途又收兵，	How can you return to your hometown empty-handed?
岂不丢脸在家乡？	My respectful Zhao Haifa
现在要把神灵祭，	You have continuous provisions of food and fodder
把俸改的灵魂招过来，	And a steady supply of army recruits
杀了他才能心欢畅。	From each of your *mengs*.
冈晓战死有原因，	But now you want to withdraw halfway.
因为他不把神灵祭。	Isn't it a big disgrace?
他像一只公鸡咯咯叫，	What you need to do now is to offer sacrifices to the gods,
一见伙伴就乱斗，	Pleading with them to call Fenggai's soul here
不听劝和说。	And kill him to vent our hate.
当时我们祭神灵，	The reason why Gangxiao died in the war
他不但不把鸡卦看，	Was that he never offered sacrifices to the gods.
反把鸡卦来吃掉。	He was like a cackling cock,
神灵见了怒火上，	Always fighting aimlessly

厘俸 // Li Feng

因此身亡在战场。	And seldom listening to others.
海罕啊，	When we sacrificed a chicken to the gods,
你的心中不用急，	He did not look at the chicken bone divination
你有大象几万头，	But ate the chicken bone instead.
召幢多多如森林，	The gods were irritated
何必急躁把气丧。	And this is why he died on the battlefield.
攻城要靠意志坚，	Oh Haihan!
齐心合力就不难。	You don't have to be so worried yet.
无论时间有多长，	You still have tens of thousands of war elephants.
千万不要丧斗志，	You still have as many Zhaozhuangs as the trees in a forest.
更不要背着宝刀空手返！"	Why should you be so impatient and discouraged?
海罕听了又回答：	Willpower and persistence, and united efforts
"阿巫戛啊，阿巫戛，	Are the key to capturing the city of Mengjinghan.
费心费力来攻城，	No matter how much time the battle will take,
夺不回婻崩，	Remain in high spirits.
获不得大象，	Never return empty-handed!"
我怎么会空手回家乡？	Haihan replied:
刚才我说丧气话，	"Awu Ga, oh, Awu Ga!
为的是试试你的心。	With a great effort I came to fight.
为了夺回婻崩我的妻，	If I can't take back my Nanbeng
我毫不动摇决心战到底。	And fail to capture any elephants,
即使占拜舍倒在地，	How can I go home empty-handed?
把我压在象舆下，	I said those depressing words just now
为婻崩战死也心甘。	

让我们共同来商量，	In order to test your faithfulness.
如何攻下勐景罕？	I have made up my mind to fight to the last minute
假话请不要当真言，	And get my wife Nanbeng back.
阿巫戛啊，阿巫戛！"	Even if Zhanbaishe falls down and
阿巫戛点头对海罕说：	I am pressed beneath the howdah,
"当日出征要打仗，	I will be most willing to accept death.
我祭神灵卜鸡卦。	Let's discuss together
那次鸡卦告诉我，	How to conquer Mengjinghan.
此次出征必胜利，	Please do not take my depressing words seriously,
因为天上神灵在保佑，	Awu Ga, oh, Awu Ga."
派出神兵和神将。	Awu Ga nodded his head and said:
有只红公鸡的鸡卦上，	"The day when you headed for the battle field,
看出这次战争要夺万头象，	I offered sacrifices to the gods and I did a divination.
还有一万个姑娘。	The chicken bone divination indicated that
另一只鸡卦可看出，	You would win this war
天神用手轻一画，	Due to the blessing from the gods,
一万个村寨将归顺你管辖。	Who will send you heavenly soldiers and generals.
又一只鸡卦可看出，	One red chicken bone divination showed that
媥崩正在忙梳妆，	You would capture ten thousand elephants
等你接她回家去。	And ten thousand young girls in the war.
我的海罕侄儿啊，	Another chicken bone divination suggested that
你应当收集所有花牛和怪兽，	The gods would give you
用来祭祀神灵做供品。	Ten thousand villages.
我已跑遍四面和八方，	A third chicken bone divination said that

厘俸 // Li Feng

潜入水底进龙宫，	Nanbeng was busy dressing and making up,
绿色海水洗身上，	Waiting for you to take her back home.
干干净净祭神灵。	Haihan, my nephew!
我又上天见混宛①，	You should find all the black-and-white cows and other strange beasts
看到一只花母牛，	And offer them to the gods.
头上长有五只角，	I have been to so many places recently.
牛是混宛儿媳的，	First I dove into the water and went to the Dragon Palace,
外祖父送她作嫁妆。	Cleaning my body with blue sea water,
牛栏围了二十层，	So that I could worship neat and tidy.
早晚混宛喂草忙。	Then I went to heaven to meet Hunwan①
每当太阳落下山，	Where I saw a black-and-white cow
牵牛河边去饮水。	With five horns on its head.
三十根绳索前面牵，	The cow belonged to his daughter-in-law
天神羡慕个个看。	As dowry from her grandfather.
五十根绳索后面拉，	The cattle pen was made up of twenty circles of fences.
神灵个个都想要。	The cow was fed by Hunwan himself.
如果我们要去买，	At sunset, he led the cow,
天神一定会答应。	With thirty reins in front
如果我们去乞讨，	And fifty at the back,
可能也会把它送。	To the river side to drink water.
我们写书信一封，	The gods looked at the cow enviouly
盖上我们的大印，	And wanted to have it very much.
付上价值一头象的白银，	

---

① 混宛：管太阳的神灵。　　① Hunwan: the Sun God.

再加黄金一兰①。	If we go to buy the cow,
混宛一定心欢喜，	The Sun God will surely agree.
会把花牛牵给你。	If we go to ask for the cow without compensation,
再做一条筒裙漂漂亮，	He may also give it to us.
用金丝绣上花鸟和图案，	We'd better write a letter
送给混宛的儿媳。	Stamped with our seal.
还要发誓对她讲：	We should also send some silver worthy of one elephant,
如果攻下勐俸，	Plus one *lan*① of gold.
定要送她一小勐，	He must be happy to receive these
千户人家归她管。"	And agree to give you the cow.
于是海罕下命令：	We should also make a beautiful straight skirt
阿巫戛立即出发去牵牛，	Embroidered with patterns of birds and flowers
桑温、赛伦齐同行。	And give it to his daughter-in-law as a gift.
三人日夜兼程不停步，	We should promise to her that
来到神灵洞口旁。	If we finally capture Mengfeng,
进入洞门一片黑，	We will additionally send her a small *meng*.
走出洞门仔细看，	With a thousand households."
已经来到勐混宛，	Haihan then delivered his order:
只见到处是村寨。	Together with Sangwen and Sailun,
阿巫戛告诉桑温和赛伦，	Awu Ga would set out immediately to get the cow.
放马休息卸下鞍，	The three of them hurried along with their trip day and night
他先进村去打听，	
如果同意给花牛，	And finally came to the entrance of the Sun God's cave.

① 一兰：等于三千三百三十两。

① Lan: unit of weight, equaling 3300 taels.

- 251 -

厘俸 // Li Feng

再叫他俩进村寨。	It was dark inside.
阿巫戛一人进了村，	When they came out of it,
急急忙忙进宫廷。	They found themselves at Meng Hunwan.
看见混宛端坐殿中央，	Where there were villages all around.
金幡幢下面，	Awu Ga told Sangwen and Sailun
脚蹬在象牙雕刻的平台上。	To rest the horses and take off the saddles.
宫廷富丽又堂皇，	He himself went to a village first for more information.
花虫鸟兽到处都刻满。	If Hunwan agreed to give them the cow,
阿巫戛开口问混宛：	He would come to ask them to enter the village.
"我的侄儿啊，	Awu Ga went into the village alone
你不挖战壕不筑城，	And in a hurry he entered the court.
太平日子过得欢。	Hunwan was sitting in the middle of a hall,
海罕、桑洛下凡到人间，	Under a golden prayer flag,
他们那里到处战火燃。	His feet resting on an ivory-carved platform.
每日只听喊杀声，	The palace looked so splendid and gorgeous,
因为围攻勐景罕。	With flowers, insects, birds and animals carved every where.
侄儿啊，	Awu Ga asked him:
请你伸手帮一帮！"	"My nephew,
混宛点头忙回答：	You don't have to dig trenches and build the city
"海罕是天神的侄儿不能欺，	But enjoy a happy and peaceful life.
海罕是神灵的子孙要相帮。	Haihan and Sangluo descended to the earth
我也准备支援他，	And are experiencing a war there.
现在听候布领暖的吩咐，	Shouts of fighting and killing are heard every day
兵马到后即下凡。"	Because they are attacking the city of Mengjinghan.

他们两人正在谈话时，	My nephew,
只见有人牵着花母牛，	Please give them a hand!"
走到河边去饮水，	Hunwan nodded his head and quickly answered:
前后绳索一串串。	"Haihan is a nephew of the gods and should not be bullied.
阿巫戛假装倒在地，	
双手蒙眼不敢看，	Haihan is a descendant of the gods whom we should help.
躲在柱子后面把话讲，	
声音又抖又发颤：	I am willing to offer him support.
"这头牛是谁家的？	We are now waiting for Bulingnuan's order.
这是怪牛不吉祥。	We will descend to the earth as soon as we are ready."
我的侄儿啊，	While they were talking,
为何牵到这里来放养？"	They saw somebody leading the black and white cow,
混宛听了忙回答：	With reins in the front and at the back,
"阿巫戛啊，阿巫戛，	To the riverside to drink water.
这是儿媳的嫁妆，	Awu Ga pretended to fall down on the ground
我栅了二十层栅栏，	And covered his eyes as if he did not dare to look at the cow.
小心保护来喂养。	
它的左角会变银，	He hid himself behind a column and said
没有金子别人也会送到家，	In a trembling voice:
右角会变珠宝亮闪闪。	"Whose cow is this?
你怎么说它是怪牛？	It is a strange and sinister cow.
阿巫戛你莫乱讲！"	My nephew,
阿巫戛听了又回答：	Why do you graze it here?"
"我的混宛啊，	Hunwan replied:

厘俸 // Li Feng

我到人间去游玩,	"Awu Ga, oh, Awu Ga,
看见桑洛有头牛,	The cow is the dowry of my daughter-in-law.
也和这头一个样。	I built a pen with twenty circles of fences
因为他有这头牛,	To protect it and feed it there.
他的妻子被人抢,	Its left horn can change into silver.
夫妻至今仍离散。	Moreover, if you have the cow, other people will send you gold.
我又走到勐准果,	Its right horn can turn into glittering jewelry.
看见海罕也有这样一头牛,	Why do you think it is strange and sinister?
也用二十层栅栏关,	You'd better not talk so foolishly."
各路神仙每天去观看。	Awu Ga said again:
因为他有这头牛,	"Listen to me, my Hunwan.
婻崩也被俸改抢,	When I was roaming the earth,
海罕只有另寻欢。	I saw that Sangluo got a cow,
他到勐景罕,	Just like this one.
挑逗俸改的母和妻,	Just because of that cow,
白天和婻崩睡在床。	His wife was captured by others.
俸改觉察发怒火,	He and his wife have so far remained separated.
命令三千勇士把他首级砍。	When I was wandering in Mengzhunguo
婻崩命令一女仆,	I saw that Haihan also had such a cow.
背着海罕的头,	His cow was also raised in a pen of twenty fences.
来到勐准果安放。	Being so unique, it attracted gods to look at it.
因为养了这头牛,	Just because of that cow,
海罕遭厄运。	Nanbeng was captured by Fenggai.
勐准果的人就把牛杀了,	

七天七夜祭神灵。	Haihan then had to look for a new wife.
火焰冲天日夜燃，	He came to Mengjinghan,
熏得天神坐不安。	Flirting with Fenggai's mother and wife.
布法①打开天门看，	He even slept with Nanbeng in the daytime.
命令召戛拍急下凡，	Fenggai was so furious when he detected all of this
医治海罕又复活。"	And ordered three thousand warriors to cut off Haihan's head.
混宛听了以为真，	Nanbeng asked one of her maids
面对阿巫戛把话讲：	To carry Haihan's head to Mengzhunguo
"我要尽快把牛牵，	And bury it there.
牵到河源头，	Because of that cow,
让河里有鱼翻水浪。	Haihan encountered such adversity.
或者牵到田边去，	People in Mengzhunguo then killed the cow
让谷子丰收庄稼长。	And offered it to the gods seven days and seven nights.
或者牵到天上的红街或黑街，	Flames of the fire were whirling up high in the sky.
留在那里就不管！"	The smoky air made the gods feel upset and uneasy.
阿巫戛闭着一只眼，	Bufa① opened the heavenly gate and checked.
慢慢悠悠来把话说：	He ordered Zhaogapai to descend to the earth
"牵到河头鱼死光，	To bring Haihan back to life."
牵到田边谷不长。	Hunwan believed the story
牵到红街或黑街，	And said to Awu Ga:
要遭布法来指责。	"I will take the cow as soon as possible
佺儿啊，	To the source of a river
现在海罕和桑洛，	

① 布法：布领暖。

① Bufa: Bulingnuan.

厘俸 // Li Feng

正在围攻勐景罕。
艾召生也牺牲了,
还死了不少兵和将。
应该把牛牵下凡,
把它送给海罕作祭品,
把俸改的灵魂来召唤。
海罕目前正派人,
四处买花牛八方忙。
走了村寨千百个,
这种花牛实难买。
如果海罕要来买,
你就把牛卖给他。
如果海罕来讨要,
你也应无偿送给他。
我的侄儿啊,
我的话你应当记心上。"
混宛听了又回答:
  "海罕和天神是一家,
他要买我一定卖给他,
送他我也很心甘。"
阿巫戛听了心欢喜。
告别混宛出了村,
见到桑温和赛伦,
命令他俩骑上马,

So that the river will be full of fish.
Or I will lead the cow into the fields
So that the crops grow well,
Or to the Red Street or Black Street in heaven
And just leave it there!"
Awu Ga closed one of his eyes
And said in an unhurried way:
"If you lead it to the river, the fish there will die.
If you lead it into the fields, the crops there will stop
    growing.
If you lead it to the Red Street or Black Street,
You will be blamed by Bufa.
My nephew!
Haihan and Sangluo are now
Attacking Mengjinghan.
Ai Zhaosheng has lost his life in the battle.
Many other soldiers and generals have been killed as well.
You should lead the cow down to the earth
And give it to Haihan as a sacrifice
To summon Fenggai's soul.
Haihan is now sending people
To search for a black-and-white cow
In a thousand villages,
But he has still failed to find one.

随他进宫见混宛。	If Haihan comes to buy your cow,
到了宫廷下马来，	Sell it to him.
按照哈勐①把混宛来拜见。	If Haihan comes to beg for your cow,
桑温、赛伦开口说：	Give it to him.
"海罕派我们来见你，	My nephew!
因为攻不下勐景罕，	Keep in mind my words."
还损失了艾冈晓，	Hunwan then replied:
妻子婻崩也夺不回，	"Haihan and all the gods are family.
他的宝刀准备放入鞘，	I will sell the cow to him if he wants to buy it.
蹬着占拜舍往回转。	I will also be pleased to give it to him without charge."
但又怕天下人取笑，	Awu Ga was so glad to hear that.
心中犹豫思绪乱。	He said goodbye to his nephew and left the village.
听说你有一头花母牛，	He met Sangwen and Sailun again
他请求把牛送给他。	And asked them to mount their horses
他把金丝筒裙来献上，	And go with him to meet Hunwan.
作为礼品送婻勐②，	They got off their horses at the palace,
婻勐一定心欢喜。	And greeted Hunwan according to *hameng*①.
如果勐俸被攻下，	Sangwen and Sailun spoke up:
一千户的村寨归她管。"	"Haihan has sent us to visit you,
混宛开口说了话：	For we failed to capture Mengjinghan,
"勐与勐的友谊比象大，	Even at the cost of losing General Gangxiao.
要牵走花母牛，	Moreover we failed to take Nanbeng back.

① 哈勐：勐与勐之间首领相见时的礼节。
② 婻勐：混宛的儿媳。

① Hameng: etiquetle the chiefs of the *mengs* follow when they meet.

厘俸 // Li Feng

我不会阻拦。
双混啊,
我日夜惦记着海罕,
我要支援他。
大象已养得膘肥体壮,
只等布法的兵马到,
就率兵下凡去作战。
既然布法已把书信传,
枪炮刀矛已备好。
双混啊,
你们今日来相求,
我一定送牛一定帮!"
混宛接着下命令,
牵出厩中花母牛。
阿巫戛接牛心欢喜,
牵着花牛回地上。

Haihan thus is going to put his sword back into its scabbard,
And turn back on his Zhanbaishe.
With a fear of being ridiculed by his people,
He hesitated and became upset.
He heard that you have a black-and-white cow,
And would like to ask you for the cow.
Here is a straight skirt woven with golden thread
As a gift for Nanmeng[①],
Which we think she will like.
If we finally capture Mengjinghan,
We will give her a village of a thousand households."
Hunwan then said:
"The friendship between *mengs* is bigger than an elephant.
I won't say no
If you want to take the cow away.
Sangwen and Sailun,
I am always concerned about Haihan.
I will definitely give him a hand.
My elephants are well-fed and strong.
As soon as Bufa's troops come,
We will go down to the earth to fight.

---

① Nanmeng: Hunwan's daughter-in-law.

Now that Bufa has sent his messages,

I believe all kinds of weapons are ready.

Sangwen and Sailun,

You come to ask for help today.

I certainly will give you the cow and offer you help."

He then gave the order

To lead the cow out of the pen.

Awu Ga took the cow

And went back to the earth quite happily.

阿巫戛三人刚离开，	When Awu Ga, Sangwen and Sailun had just left,
婻勐已从娘家返。	Nanmeng came back from her parents' home.
回来不见花母牛，	She found her cow gone
又哭又闹把话讲：	And began to cry and scream:
"早知要把牛送人，	"If I had known you were going to give my cow to others,
我就不愿回娘家。	I would not have gone back to my parents' home.
花母牛是好嫁妆，	The cow is my lucky dowry
又能生财又吉祥。	That brings in endless wealth and treasure.
它在河头是鱼宝，	It is good for the fish in rivers.
它在田头是谷宝。	It is good for the crops in the fields.
牵它上街赶集，	When it is led to a market,
集市热闹。	The market becomes busy and prosperous.
没有珠宝，	If you lack jewelry,
会有人送上门来。	Somebody will send you some.

厘俸 // Li Feng

花牛是舅舅给我的嫁妆，	The cow is a dowry from my uncle.
它是我的财产。	It is my property.
要送也要告诉我，	You should have asked for my permission.
不打招呼就送人，	Now you have given it away without even telling me.
把我当作卡①看待。	Are you treating me as a *ka*①?
即使是卡也要告诉他，	But even a ka deserves to be informed in advance.
我却比卡还低下！	I am even more inferior than a *ka*!
失去花牛我心悲伤，	Losing the cow makes me feel so sad
如今我不愿在宫中住，	That I no longer want to live in the palace.
我要用尖刀来自杀。	I'd rather kill myself with a knife.
我的花母牛啊，	Oh my cow,
你价值千头万头象，	You are actually worth thousands of elephants.
现在已经失去你，	Now that you are gone,
我只好去死！"	I have no choice but to die!"
婻勐越说越气恼，	The more she said, the angrier she got.
就把织机上的布扯下来，	She pulled down the cloth from her loom,
织机摇摇又晃晃。	Shaking it violently.
众人个个来相劝，	People came to soothe her one after another,
把她当作娃娃哄。	Treating her like a child.
婻勐的怒气仍不消，	But Nanmeng just could not cool down.
不吃不喝乱摔打，	She refused to eat and drink and smashed things up,
如同病魔缠身上。	As if she was haunted by evil spirits of sickness.

① 卡：奴隶，地位低下之人。
　　——译者注

① Ka: inferior person. – Translator's note

阿巫戛三人急赶路，	Awu Ga, Sangwen and Sailun hurried off.
双混各人搓根茅草绳，	The two officers, Sangwen and Sailun, made two ropes out of thatch.
一人前面把牛牵，	One of them was leading the cow from the front,
一个后面把牛赶。	And the other was driving the cow from behind.
花牛小跑满身汗，	The cow trotted on
三人脸上也淌汗。	And the three men sweated.
眼看就要到远负见海罕，	When they approached Haihan's camp,
只见迎接的人群闹嚷嚷，	They saw people come out to welcome them.
绿色营帐布满路两旁。	The green tents were set up on both sides of the road.
花母牛牵到海罕前，	The cow was brought before Haihan,
他见了花牛心花放！	Who was wild with joy.
满脸笑容开了口：	He said with a smile:
"如果没有阿巫戛，	"Without you, Awu Ga,
就难得到这头牛。	It's impossible for us to have the cow.
阿巫戛啊，	Oh Awu Ga!
祝愿你长生不老又健康，	I wish you good health and longevity!
日夜有姑娘来陪伴！"	I wish you to be accompanied by beauties day and night!"
阿巫戛听后哈哈笑：	Awu Ga was delighted and said:
"如果不是我出马，	"If it were not for me,
这头牛实在难得到。"	The cow would have not been brought here."
海罕派人传命令：	Haihan then gave his order:
"千劢的召幢、召冈和召伴，	"Zhaozhuangs, Zhaogangs and Zhaobans of the one
神奇花牛已牵到。	

厘俸 // Li Feng

初一属鸡那天最吉祥,	thousand *mengs*!
只等那天一来到,	We have the magic cow now.
就用花牛祭神灵。	The first day of the month is the Day of the Rooster.
还要陪祭马一匹,	When this propitious day comes,
马背上面罩花鞍。	We will sacrifice the cow and worship the gods.
还要陪祭两姐妹,	We will also sacrifice a horse
不是少女都不要。	With a colorful saddle on its back.
一牛一马两姑娘,	At the same time we will sacrifice two sisters
杀了之后魂飞勐景罕。	Who must be virgins.
召唤俸改灵魂来吃肉,	The souls of the cow, the horse and the two sisters
让他魂离身体人死亡。	Will fly to Mengjinghan and seduce the soul of Fenggai
千勐的召幢、召冈和召伴,	To leave his body and come to eat the cow.
要通知百姓人人记,	Fenggai then will die without his soul in his body.
祭祀之日两不准:	Zhaozhuangs, Zhaogangs and Zhaobans of the one
不准下河去洗澡,	thousand *mengs*!
不准种田和种地,	Please inform all your people
否则灵魂离身把祭品吃,	That two things are not allowed on the day of the sacrifice:
误遭身亡。"	Nobody is allowed to bathe in the rivers.
	Nobody is allowed to plough and sow.
	If they do so their souls will leave their bodies
	And mistakenly eat the cow and then die."
属鸡的初一转眼到,	Very soon the Day of the Rooster came.
招魂开始人紧张。	The ritual of summoning souls made everybody nervous.

占卜师名叫莫黄罕，	The exorcist named Mohuanghan
抱着黄舍①到桌前，	Held a *huangshe*① in his hand and came to the table,
桌上还放着鸡和鱼。	On which there were chicken and fish.
莫黄罕开口叫又唱：	Mohuanghan then began to chant:
"海罕的灵魂不要离身，	"The soul of Haihan, please don't go away.
婻崩的灵魂不要走散，	The soul of Nanbeng, please don't wander away.
两人要守在祭桌旁。	You two need to stay at the ritual table,
桑本、桑洛也要来，	Along with Sangben and Sangluo,
还有千勐的召幢、召冈和召伴。"	And Zhaozhuangs, Zhaogangs and Zhaobans of the one thousand *mengs*."
占卜师说完又起身，	The exorcist then rose to his feet
来到另一处祭场。	And went to another sacrificial altar.
牵出五只角的花母牛，	He led out the five-horn cow,
面对俸改住的方向，	Facing the direction where Fenggai lived,
开始把魂招。	And began to call Fenggai's soul
声音恐怖如飞猡②，	In a voice as horrible as a *feiluo's*② shouts,
又像老虎在哀鸣。	And as plaintive as a tiger's whines.
"求勐俸的神灵来相帮，	"I am pleading for the gods in Mengfeng to help me
领着俸改的灵魂来这里。	To guide Fenggai's soul to here.
求勐俸的鬼神也跟上，	

---

① 黄舍：用竹篾编织的小笭。笭内放着海罕、召幢、召冈和召伴等人的衣服，意思是先把他们的魂招回。

② 飞猡：如蝙蝠状，体重十余斤，夜晚出没，叫声大而凄凉，使人听了感到阴森恐怖。

① Huangshe: a small bamboo basket. Inside the basket the clothes of Haihan, Zhaozhuangs, Zhaogangs and Zhaobans were put, with the purpose of calling their souls back.

② Feiluo: a bat-like animal, weighing more than ten kilos. This animal comes out usually at night. It shouts loudly and dismally, making the hearer feel gloomy and horrible.

厘俸 // Li Feng

领着千百个将领的灵魂来这里。	I am pleading for the ghosts in Mengfeng to help me
来到这里把簸箕上的牛血都吃光,	To guide the souls of thousands of the generals to here.
把树叶上粘着的马血也舔完。	Let the souls eat up the cow blood in the bamboo dustpan.
俸改的灵魂快快来,	Let the souls lick up the horse blood on the tree leaves.
领着两姐妹的灵魂做妻子。	The soul of Fenggai, come quickly!
俸改啊,	Come to take the two sisters' souls to be your wives.
你只身一人太孤单,	The soul of Fenggai,
要领着皆温的灵魂一起来,	Don't come alone!
还有身边的众将官。"	Ask the soul of Jiewen to come with you
占卜师的话刚说完,	And the souls of your generals as well."
手起刀落宰花牛,	As soon as the exorcist finished his words,
牛血喷在簸箕上,	He killed the cow with a knife.
又把马杀倒在树叶下。	The cow blood splashed and spattered into the bamboo dustpan.
可怜那姐妹俩,	Then he killed the horse and it fell down on the tree leaves.
吓得晕倒又昏死。	The poor sisters
占卜师手起刀又落,	Were so frightened and fainted.
把她俩杀死在绸缎上。	The exorcist raised his knife again and killed the two sisters
转身又杀猪一头,	Who fell down and died on a piece of silk and satin.
四只蹄子倒生长。	He then turned around and killed a pig
再把一只羊来杀,	Whose four hoofs grew in a backwards way.
脚上长有三叉蹄。	He also killed a goat
还要杀蜜蜂三百窝,	Whose hoofs were divided into three parts instead of two.
蚊子三百个。	He then killed the bees living in three hundred
还要杀簸箕般粗大的蟒蛇一	

大条，	honeycombs,
还要杀毛虫一条，	Three hundred mosquitoes,
最后又把鸡来杀，	A python as thick as a bamboo dustpan,
再把鸡血四周洒。	And a caterpillar.
该杀的都杀了，	Finally, he killed a chicken
占卜师开始施法术。	And sprayed the blood in all directions.
牛头拿来对马头，	He killed all that should be killed
瞬时天上乌云翻巨浪，	And got down to the magic spells.
风雨齐来天昏暗。	When he placed the cow head opposite the horse head,
又拿羊头对蛇头，	Rolling dark clouds began to cover the sky,
霎时天上雷电闪，	The wind blew, rain poured down, and the world was dark.
雨更猛烈风更狂。	When he placed the goat head opposite the python head,
俸改的灵魂变成马，	Lightning flashed and thunder rumbled in the sky.
随风来到祭场上。	The rain became heavier and the wind stronger.
先饮花牛的血，	Fenggai's soul, in the form of a horse,
又在两姐妹身上打了滚。	Ran to the altar,
皆温的灵魂也来到，	Drinking the cow blood first,
变成一只鹞鹰在天上，	Then rolling about on the two sisters' bodies.
围着祭场在旋转。	Jiewen's soul came, too,
千百个大将的灵魂也来到，	In the form of a sparrow hawk
变成一群花蝴蝶，	Hovering above the altar.
飞来祭场忙吸血。	And the souls of thousands of generals came,
俸改的灵魂也过来，	In the shape of a cluster of butterflies
饮血饮得吱吱响。	Flying to suck blood.

厘俸 // Li Feng

海罕一声命令下，	Fenggai's soul came to suck blood, too,
埋伏的弓弩手万箭发，	Making a slurping sound.
雨点般地射向俸改的灵魂。	At Haihan's command,
俸改的灵魂中了箭，	A ambushing bowmen shot out a rain of arrows
大家把他的灵魂变成的马头砍，	Straight at Fenggai's soul.
然后摆到祭台上！	Fenggai's soul got shot and
锣鼓齐鸣万众欢。	The head of the horse he turned into
占卜师取出鸡卦看，	Was cut off and put on the altar!
第一只鸡卦是豪没非①，	There was a deafening cheerful sound of gongs and drums!
第二只鸡卦是豪拉丁款②。	The exorcist took out the chicken bones to tell the fortune.
	The first chicken bone divination showed "*Haomofei*"①
	and
	The second chicken bone divination tells "*Haoladingkuan*"②.
第二天早晨天刚亮，	When the dawn broke the next morning,
海罕起床漱洗吃早饭，	Haihan got up, washed, and finished his breakfast.
然后传下一道令：	He then delivered an order:
"修理衣甲、兵器和象舆，	"Mend your armor, repair your weapons and howdahs.
准备进军勐景罕。"	Get ready to march towards Mengjinghan."
俸改站在转颂上，	At that time Fenggai stood on *zhuansong*.

---

① 豪没非：凡是丢失的东西，都会回到主人手里；被抢走的妻子，不论到什么地方都会回来。

② 豪拉丁款：经商的人可以得到金银财宝；打仗可以取胜。

① Haomofei: All the lost things will come back to the owners. The wife captured will return home wherever she goes.

② Haoladingkuan: Businessmen will gain a lot of gold and treasures. People will win the war.

指指点点向北望。	And looked north in the distance.
只见天空起云雾，	The whirling up mist and clouds
黑压压卷向勐景罕。	Were rolling over and moving towards Mengjinghan.
俸改睁眼仔细看，	Fenggai looked carefully and found
来的好像是天兵和天将。	They seemed to be heavenly soldiers and generals.
他自言自语把话讲：	He said to himself:
"可能是布听法①派兵来援我，	"This may be the reinforcement sent by Butingfa①
马上就要从天降。"	Coming soon from heaven to help me."
他命令两个布冈狠②，	He asked his two *buganghens*②
准备金杯和美酒，	To prepare gold cups and good wine in advance,
还有瓜果礼品放桌上，	Plus some melons and other fruit,
天神来到要慰问。	To welcome and treat the gods.
俸改又把书信写，	Fenggai then wrote a letter
把心中想法信中写：	To express himself better:
"我的布听法啊，	"My dear Butingfa,
请不要安营在城外，	You don't have to camp outside the city.
请直接来到宫廷上。"	Please come straight to my palace."
布冈狠接信迎天神，	The two *buganghens* went out to meet the gods,
见到天兵和天将，	Kneeling down and presenting the letter
急忙跪下送书信。	As soon as they met the heavenly troops.
桑勐、桑色③接书信，	Sangmeng and Sangse③ received the letter
只见信上落有俸改名，	With Fenggai's signature

---

① 布听法：天神名。
② 布冈狠：俸改的军师。
③ 桑勐、桑色：天神名。

① Butingfa: name of a heavenly god.
② Buganghen: army adviser and counselor.
③ Sangmeng and Sangse: the names of two gods.

厘俸 // Li Feng

大印盖在信中央。	And his seal in the middle.
两神看信互耳语，	The two gods whispered to each other
相对而笑忍不住，	And could not help grinning.
然后大声开了腔：	They then spoke in a loud voice:
"谢谢两位布冈狠，	"Thank you so much
远道迎接辛苦了。	For coming a long way to meet us!
现在请你们往回返，	Please return
天神旨意告俸改：	And tell Fenggai the decree from heaven:
布听法没有派兵来支援，	Butingfa did not send troops to support you.
这次派兵的是布领暖。	It was Bulingnuan who sent this force of reinforcement.
我俩率兵八十万，	We are now leading eight hundred thousand soldiers
下凡支援混海罕。	Coming to back up Hun Haihan.
你们的城池不牢固，	Your city wall is not strong enough
应该加刺围和打栅栏，	And needs more fences of thistle and thorns.
壕沟也要再加宽。	The trenches also need to be widened.
赶快去告诉俸改，	Hurry back to tell Fenggai,
做好准备打大仗。"	To ready well for a great battle."
布冈狠听完一席话，	Hearing these words,
浑身瘫软心慌乱。	The two *buganghens* were paralyzed with fear.
抖声抖气说了话：	They asked in trembling voices:
"两位天神所讲的，	"Are you telling the truth
不知是真还是假？	Or are you kidding?
如果说的是真话，	If what you say is true,
大难降临勐景罕。	Mengjinghan is facing an imminent disaster.

两位天神啊,	Dear two gods,
我们不明真假心不安!"	We will feel upset if we don't know the truth."
两位天神又回答:	The two gods replied:
"我们不会把谎说,	"We never tell lies.
布领暖派我们下凡来,	Bulingnuan sent us down
就是为了援海罕。	To support Haihan
天神的力量大又大,	With powerful and invincible forces.
请看看我们带的兵和将。	Take a look at our soldiers and generals.
两位军师啊,	You two should go back promptly
赶快去告诉俸改!"	And report to Fenggai."
布冈狠急忙往回返,	The two *buganghens* returned quickly
愁目苦脸见俸改,	And morosely reported to Fenggai
把天神旨意照实传:	The exact words of the gods:
"我们的召法勐啊,	"Our respectable Zhao Fameng!
不知天神怎么了,	We really do not know what is happening.
布听法没有派兵来,	Butingfa did not send us even a single soldier.
来的是布领暖的兵和将,	Those who come are Bulingnuan's troops.
他们不帮我们帮海罕。	They come to help Haihan, not us.
八十万天兵已下凡,	There are eight hundred thousand heavenly soldiers and generals.
前面的天兵持天斧,	In the front are sodiers holding heavenly axes
后面的拿着雷斧亮闪闪。	And at the back, soldiers holding glittering thunder axes.
看着我们恶狠狠,	Their eyes are full of hatred
好像要把天斧劈在我们脑门上!	As if they will soon split our foreheads with their axes.
我们的召法勐啊,	

厘俸 // Li Feng

如今我们怎么办？"
俸改听了吃一惊，
满脸焦愁心透凉。
顿时跺脚发怒火，
开口就骂布领暖：
"你派来天兵帮海罕，
勐景罕也不会垮。
你用天斧雷斧助海罕，
勐俸也不会烂！
布冈狠啊，
你赶快传令召巴[①]和召冈，
守好城墙和战壕，
备好弓弩和刀枪。
我们的勇士啊，
不要怕死，要战到底！"
桑勐、桑色两位神，
派出使者见海罕。
两位使者骑快马，
见到海罕把话传：
"桑勐、桑色告诉你，
布领暖派兵来支援，
八十万天兵已下凡。
海罕你就放心吧，

①召巴：百夫长。

My respectable Zhao Fameng!

What should we do now?"

Fenggai was so shocked to hear this,

Anxious and desperate.

He stamped his feet

And condemned Bulingnuan:

"Though you sent heavenly troops to help Haihan,

Mengjinghan will not be defeated.

Though you use heavenly axes and thunder axes to aid Haihan,

Mengjinghan will not be destroyed.

Oh *buganghen*,

Pass my order to Zhaoba[①] and Zhaogang,

Asking them to carefully guard the city wall and the trenches

And get a good supply of bows and swords ready.

My warriors,

Fear not death and fight till the last minute!"

Sangmeng and Sangse

Sent two messengers

Riding fast horses

To pass the word to Haihan:

"Sangmeng and Sangse would like you to know

① Zhaoba: centurion in charge of one hundred households.

不要急躁不要乱。	That Bulingnuan has come with his reinforcements
快组织兵马把城围，	Of eight hundred thousand heavenly soldiers.
天兵相助齐作战。"	So please feel relieved, Haihan.
海罕听了心喜欢，	Don't be hasty or fretful.
高高兴兴把话讲：	Reorganize your army and surround the city of Mengjinghan.
"我把天兵日夜盼，	The heavenly troops will fight with you shoulder to shoulder."
感谢亲爱的布领暖。	Haihan was pleased to hear that
派出桑勐、桑色二位神，	And spoke with joy:
率领天兵天将八十万。	"I have been expecting you day and night.
勐景罕眼看要归我，	Thank you, my dear Bulingnuan
婻崩就要回身旁。"	For sending Sangmeng and Sangse
他派人抬出象牙椅，	And their eight hundred thousand soldiers.
请二位天神坐在上。	Very soon I will conquer Mengjinghan.
他亲自端起装满美酒的金杯，	Very soon Nanbeng will be back by my side."
还有果品、茶叶和槟榔，	He had his ivory chair brought out
招待桑勐和桑色。	And asked the two gods to sit on it.
不到片刻大风起，	He himself served them
空中旗帜迎风展，	With fruit, tea, and areca nuts
天兵天将黑压压，	As well as good wine in gold cups.
哗哗降落大地上。	Soon the wind blew
万头大象也落地，	And flags waved in the air.
象舆一色火样红。	Countless heavenly soldiers and generals

厘俸 // Li Feng

胆亚巴纳①盖象头，	Swiftly descended to the earth, together with
金光晃眼亮又亮。	Ten thousand elephants.
象舆插着金幡幢，	Their howdahs were as red as fire flames.
天兵抬着天斧和雷斧。	Shiny and glittering *danyabana*①
八十万天兵到人间，	Were hung on elephant's foreheads.
如雷似雨浩浩荡荡。	Golden prayer flags were fixed on the howdahs.
	Eight hundred thousand heavenly soldiers
	Came with heavenly axes and thunder axes in their hands,
	Like lightning flashes and rain drops.
海罕骑着占拜舍，	Haihan sat on Zhanbaishe by the roadside
迎接天神天兵在路旁。	To welcome the heavenly troops.
双方战象吼又叫，	The war elephants were all howling and roaring.
兵丁闹嚷嚷。	The soldiers were hustling and bustling.
天将天兵搭篷帐，	The divine troops were busy setting up tents
绫罗绸缎金光闪。	Made of shiny silk and satin.
帐篷密麻一大片，	It was a huge camping place
四周打桩围栅栏。	With fences built
壕沟长长遍山冈，	And long trenches dug round it.
安营扎寨已停当。	Now that they were done making camp,

---

① 胆亚：漂亮的装饰物；巴纳：象头上的一块装饰物，中间有一圆镜，周围有用银子制作的泡泡。由象头披挂到脑门心上。

① Danyabana: Danya means beautiful decorations. Bana refers to the piece of decoration with a mirror in the middle and silver bubbles around the mirror. Bana is usually hung on the forehead of an elephant.

海罕叫人抬出善牙占①，	Haihan had a *shanyazhan*① taken out
再把金桌稳稳放。	And then put a golden table on it.
桑勐拿出布领暖的金铸像，	Sangmeng carefully put the gold statue
轻轻放在桌子上。	Of Bulingnuan on the table.
海罕急忙跪下来，	Haihan knelt down
恭恭敬敬来叩拜。	And worshiped the statue reverently.
然后问候桑勐和桑色，	He first greeted Sangmeng and Sangse
先表歉意开口讲：	And then expressed his apologies:
"天地之间太遥远，	"It is a long distance between heaven and earth.
二位沿途辛苦了。	It must have been toilsome all the way.
你们劳累为海罕，	All the efforts you've made are for me.
我心中不忍很不安。	I feel uneasy and I am so sorry about that.
两位敬爱的长辈啊，	Dear respectable elders,
自从攻打勐景罕，	I have been waiting for divine backup for so long
日夜盼望天兵援。	Since I began attacking Mengjinghan.
布领暖心善可怜我，	Bulingnuan is so kind-hearted
派出天兵来参战。	And sent heavenly troops to join me in the war.
天下百姓真高兴，	All the people are happy about that
人人争把这事传。	And are spreading this good news to one another.
二位尊者啊，	Dear respectable elders,
感谢你们的话说不完！"	I can never thank you enough!"
第二天早上天刚亮，	At dawn the next morning,

---

① 善牙占：象牙雕刻成的平台。　　① Shanyazhan: an ivory-carved platform.

厘俸 // Li Feng

海罕传军令：
"千个勐的召幢，
嘎西牙①那天最吉祥，
我要亲自率大军
出征攻打勐景罕。
请天神桑色攻东边，
重重包围二十层。
艾道闷鲁天②紧跟上，
与天上的战象齐攻城。
混宛道端红③与召法免④
支援城头的桑洛同作战。
桑勐负责攻城尾，
挑选的战象牙粗壮，
左右两翼共一万。
城的中部我去攻，
我要把它团团围住二十层，
我的后卫是龙王布唤罕。
一千个勐的召幢率军队，
按照原定线路向前进，
洪水般冲向城门旁。

① 嘎西牙：甲午之日，即马日。西双版纳称嘎萨牙。
② 艾道闷鲁天：天神名。
③ 混宛道端红：混宛。
④ 召法免：天神雷公。

Haihan gave his order:
"Zhaozhuangs of one thousand *mengs*,
'*Gaxiya*①' is a lucky day.
On that day I will lead my army
And head for Mengjinghan.
God Sangse will attack the east of the city,
Surrounding it in twenty rings of encirclement.
God Aidaomenlutian② should follow behind,
Leading the heavenly war elephants to fight.
Hunwandaoduanhong③ and Zhao Famian④
Will go to support Sangluo in front of the city.
Sangmeng will attack the back of the city.
His ten thousand elephants with thick tusks
Will be at his disposal on both the left and the right side.
I will go and attack the center of the city
And besiege it with twenty rings of encirclement.
My rear guard will be led by the Dragon King,
　　　Buhuanhan.
The Zhaozhuangs of one thousand *mengs* will
　　　command their soldiers

① Gaxiya: the day of Jia and Wu or the Day of the Horse. It is called Gashaya in Xishuangbanna.
② Aidaomenlutian: Name of a god.
③ Hunwandaoduanhong: Hunwan, the Sun God.
④ Zhao Famian: the Thunder God.

我亲自督阵不放松,	To proceed according to the planned route
谁往后退枷锁上。	And rush to the city gate like a flood.
谁蹬大象猛冲锋,	I will supervise all the operations in person.
不仅赐给金幡幢,	Whoever acts as deserter will be shackled.
还给一个村寨为奖赏。"	Whoever spurs their elephant forward
	Will get not only a golden prayer flag
	But also a village as a reward."
召尼率领天兵天将八十万,	Zhao Ni led eight hundred thousand heavenly troops
准备出发收营帐。	To pack up their tents and get ready to set out.
鸣炮三声轰轰响,	Three cannon shots
炮声惊动人和象。	Alerted both his soldiers and elephants.
占拜舍昂首吼叫要出发,	Zhanbaishe raised its head and gave out a roar of departure.
二十头大象①自动跑到远负正中央,	The Twenty Elephants① ran to the center of *yuanfu* on their own.
一千头象扬鼻跺脚望远方。	Another one thousand swung their trunks and stamped their feet,
士卒牵出占拜舍,	Eager to join the fight in the distance.
象舆装饰金晃晃,	Zhanbaishe was led out,
如田中稻穗迎风展。	Its howdah decoration waving like golden rice in the wind.
海罕走下宝座穿铠甲,	Haihan stepped down from his throne
铠甲上麒麟亮闪闪。	And put on his armor with a glittering kylin on it.
扣带上嵌有珠和宝,	

---

① 专为海罕提供挑选为坐骑的凶猛大象。

① The Twenty Elephants: very fierce elephants particularly chosen to be Haihan's mounts.

厘俸 // Li Feng

装宝石的背袋肩上挎，	The buckle was inlaid with pearls and precious stones.
背袋似火熊熊燃。	He held on his back a treasure bag amulet
一把宝剑挎腰上，	As red as flames of fire.
刀鞘刻着龙一条。	He had on his waist a sword
一顶莫央该①头上戴，	With a dragon engraved on its scabbard.
帽带闪亮迎风扬。	He wore a *moyanggai*① on his head,
一根金矛手中拿，	The strings of which fluttered in the wind.
占拜舍在等待，	He held a gold spear in his hand.
左边转来右边转。	Zhanbaishe waited by his side,
一顶金幡幢高高立，	Turning to the left and right impatiently.
威武的海罕幢下站。	There was a tall golden prayer flag,
亲自出征杀俸改，	Under which mighty Haihan stood.
蹬象踏平勐景罕！	He would soon lead his army to fight against Fenggai
	And drive his elephant to level the city of Mengjinghan.
一声令下大鼓响，	The drum for departure was beaten.
天兵天将上征程，	The heavenly troops as well as Haihan's troops
海罕大军也出征。	Were all ready to set out.
勇猛矛手三十万，	There were three hundred thousand spear men,
还有九十万钩矛手。	Nine hundred thousand hooked-spear men.
占拜舍昂首往前闯，	Zhanbaishe strode forward with its head high,
千名武士来保护，	Protected by thousands of soldiers

---

① 莫央该：帽子。上面缀有珠宝，亮如一把火。

① Moyanggai: a hat decorated with jewelry, shining brightly like a torch.

手中大刀要把敌来砍。	Who would kill approaching enemies.
前锋武士有万名，	There were ten thousand warriors as the vanguard,
手持长把三叉矛。	Holding long-handled trident spears.
八十万兵丁来到勐景罕，	Eight hundred thousand soldiers came
团团包围在城下。	To surround Mengjinghan at the foot of its walls.
土炮成排高高架，	The cannons were erected high;
火药引线已接上。	The fuses were affixed;
鲁非也排列，	The *lufei*s as big as spinning wheels
如簸箕大的纺车般。	Were all set and ready.
占拜舍继续在前进，	Zhanbaishe marched on.
金幡幢迎风高高扬。	The golden prayer flags flew high in the air.

桑色、桑洛抵贺勐，	Sangse and Sanghuo arrived at Hemeng,
安营扎寨忙又忙，	Busy pitching camp.
帐篷火红似太阳。	Their tents were red like the sun.
布桑勐来到腊姐看，	Busangmeng came to Lajie
只见到处是战象。	And saw war elephants everywhere.
法洪桑兰①从天空来，	God Fahongsanglan① came from heaven
与桑本同率人马来攻城，	To attack the city with Sangben.
喊声杀声震天响。	Deafening shouts of fighting were heard everywhere.
混宛和雷公召法免，	The Sun God and the God of Thunder,
还有艾道闷鲁天，	And Aidaomenlutian,
出动千头万头象，	Dispatched thousands of war elephants,

---

① 法洪桑兰：天神名。　　　　　① Fahongsanglan: The name of a god.

厘俸 // Li Feng

大象吼叫声不断。	Who howled and roared constantly.
桑温、赛伦的战象更威武，	Even more powerful were Sangwen and Sailun's elephants
长牙排列似篱笆。	With long tusks like a good shield of fence.
还有向戛和向冈，	There also came Xiangga and Xianggang,
人马多如雨点般。	Whose soldiers and horses were as numerous as rain drops.
冈庄和汉高召勐尼，	There were Gangzhuang and Hangaozhaomengni
同时并进齐向前，	Moving forward hand in hand.
象牙密如星一样。	
还有崩南宛多法，	There was Bengnanyuanduofa
马队如风奔腾上。	With his galloping horses as swift as the wind.
艾包、尼崩和桑混伦，	There were Ai Bao, Ni Beng,
波道坚混缅和赛道，	Sang Hunlun, Bodaojianhunmian and Sai Dao,
带领兵丁打头阵，	Fighting in the front with their soldiers,
象队随后往前闯。	Followed by their elephants.
还有天神布冈罕，	There was God Buganghan
率领天兵和天将，	Leading his heavenly soldiers and generals
全部金矛齐武装。	Who were equipped with golden spears.
桑海、冈罕在最后，	There were Sanghai and Ganghan at the back,
紧紧跟着海罕的坐骑占拜舍，	Following Zhanbaishe, Haihan's mount.
士卒手持锄头和红杆矛，	Their soldiers held hoes and red-handled spears,
等待占领勐景罕，	Ready to capture Mengjinghan
挖出金银和财宝。	And dig out gold, silver and other treasures from under the ground.
俸改的兵将也在忙，	Fenggai's soldiers and generals were busy, too,
日夜巡逻在城门高楼上。	

眼看城外遍人马，	Patrolling at the tower gate day and night.
急忙又敲锣鼓又吼叫：	They saw soldiers and horses everywhere outside the city
"城外兵马滚滚来，	And promptly beat the gongs and drums and shouted:
海罕的象队已经来攻城！	"There are countless soldiers and horses outside.
我们为什么不迎战？	Haihan's elephants have come to attack us!
大象为什么不出栏？	Why don't we go out to meet them head-on and fight?
我们应该像个男子汉，	Why aren't our elephants dispatched from their pens?
活捉桑洛和海罕，	We should behave like men!
把他们像牛马一样来放养。"	We should go and capture Sangluo and Haihan alive
鼓声急急四方传，	And treat them like horse and cattle."
一寨传到另一寨。	The burst of drum beats spread
士卒听到鼓声响，	From one village to another.
丢妻弃儿忙出发，	The soldiers heard the sound
脚步咚咚碗叮当，	And quickly left their wives and children and set out.
竹楼震得摇摇晃。	Their hasty and heavy footsteps
俸改见人来攻城，	Shook the bamboo houses.
稳坐转颂不慌张。	Fenggai, however, saw the enemy come to attack
摆酒设宴仍作乐，	But still sat on the *zhuansong* calmly and peacefully.
众妻紧紧围身旁。	He enjoyed the wine and the banquet as usual.
左边是娥宾，	He had his wives around him as usual.
右边是婻崩。	On his left side, there was Ebing.
用手摸摸婻崩脸，	On his right side, there was Nanbeng.
又把娥宾搂身上。	He now touched Nanbeng's face,
俸改站起拿仙笛，	Then took Ebing in his arms.

厘俸 // Li Feng

这支仙笛不离身，	He then rose to his feet and took out a magic flute,
经常把它床头放。	Which he had with him all the time,
	And often placed by his bed.

桑色、桑勐一声命令下，	At the word of command of Sangse and Sangmeng,
只见鲁非飞城中，	*Lufeis* flew across the sky
越过天空一串串。	And fell into the city of Mengjinghan.
霎时城中烟火起，	All of a sudden smoke rose and fire broke out.
天地之间迷迷茫。	Everything was hazy between the sky and the earth.
城外土炮又轰鸣，	Outside the city cannons fired again,
房屋崩裂尘土扬。	Destroying houses and raising the dust.
俸改看见这情况，	Seeing this Fenggai shouted loudly,
手扶栏杆高声喊：	With his hands holding the rails:
"该死的奴隶们，	"Damn slaves!
快快把大火来扑灭，	Hurry up and put out the fire!
谁要怕死我就把他砍！"	If you are afraid of death I will have your head cut off!"
大火连绵烧了三昼夜，	The big fire burned for three days and nights.
天空烟雾挤成团。	The smog hung over the sky and never cleared.
百姓抬水忙救火，	People were busy carrying water to put out the fire,
大火仍旧还在燃。	But it was out of control.
俸改一看势不妙，	Fenggai noticed that the situation was getting worse
急忙把弟弟皆温召，	And had to call his younger brother Jiewen
还有舅爷伴龙法。	And his grandfather Banlongfa.
然后开口把话讲：	Fenggai spoke to them:

"前次你们战冈罕，	"Last time when you fought Ganghan,
败在他矛下受了伤。	You two both were injured by his spear.
我用秘方牙窝来，	I used my secret recipe *yawolai*.
为你们医治不怠慢。	To treat your wounds immediately.
现在你俩已康复，	Now you are both cured and recovered,
身体有力又强壮。	And have become strong and vigorous again.
眼下海罕来攻城，	Haihan has now come to attack us.
赶快从栏中牵出象，	You should lead out your elephants
带领一百个召冈，	And a hundred Zhaogangs
火速奋力去迎战。	And rush to meet the enemy.
决不让对方进城来，	You should not let the enemy enter our city.
要为我拼死在沙场！	You should fight to the death in the battlefield.
伴龙法的兵丁抬着红杆矛，	Banlongfa's soldiers holding red-handled spears
兵分两路齐出发。	Should set out from two directions.
卫大罕的弟弟卫大荒，	Weidahuang, the younger brother of Weidahan!
你的人马众多如洪水，	You have an army with masses of soldiers and horses.
合力迎击勐泐的首领尼海罕。	You go fight against Nihaihan, the chief of Mengle.
巴扎哇与撒马姓，	Bazhawa and Samaxing!
布阵三层相呼应，	You go to organize three circles of soldiers
要把海罕的兵马来围困。	To besiege Haihan's troops.
皆温和贺哇仁占邦，	Jiewen and Hewarenzhanbang!
还有马门罗虎当，	And Mamenluohudang!
你们的手下兵丁抬钩矛，	Order your soldiers to hold their hooked spears
冲出城门勇猛战。	And dash out of the city gate and fight there.

厘俸 // Li Feng

我亲爱的弟弟们啊，	My dear younger brothers!
胜利回来有重赏！"	When you come back with triumph you will get generous rewards!"
俸改说完又下令，	Fenggai then ordered people
牵出大象占艾刁，	To lead out Zhan'aidiao
赠与弟弟皆温为坐骑。	And gave it to his younger brother Jiewen as his mount.
占艾刁象牙弯又弯，	Zhan'aidiao had curved tusks
一条尾巴长又长。	And a long tail.
牵出英着节，	Then Fenggai ordered people
脚上长肉包，	To lead out Yingzhuojie,
象牙红红火一样，	Which had fleshy bumps on its feet
赐给伴龙法为坐骑。	And red tusks like flames of fire.
然后又牵占艾兰，	He gave it to Banlongfa as his mount.
兵丁上前罩金舆。	Finally Zhan'ailan with a golden howdah on its back
俸改起身穿衣甲，	Was led out.
戴上头盔挎上刀，	Fenggai put on his armor
宝石袋子背身上，	And his helmet and carried his sword
金矛一根亮又亮。	And his treasure bag amulet.
珠光宝气遍全身，	His bright and shiny golden spear
金光四射晃人眼。	And the jewelry all over his body
他几步走近占艾兰，	Dazzled everyone near him.
占艾兰弯腿又低头，	He stepped towards Zhan'ailan,
乖乖让俸改来骑上。	Who bent down
千名官和将，	And obediently let Fenggai mount.
骑在象上等俸改。	

三千名哈火塔，	Thousands of officers and generals were waiting for Fenggai
三百个哈火吞，	On their elephant backs.
每天把刹生享，	Three thousand *hahuota* warriors
等待决一死战。	And three hundred *hahuotun* fighters
俸改开口把话讲：	Were enjoying delicious *duasheng* every day,
"为了保卫勐景罕，	And waiting for the decisive battle.
我精心挑选兵和将。	Fenggai said to them:
你们最忠心也最勇敢，	"In order to protect Mengjinghan,
应该为我出大力。	I have carefully selected my warriors and generals.
这次我已下决心，	You are the most loyal and the bravest ones
要活捉小混尼和他的象，	And will definitely exert yourselves vigorously.
留给后人为美谈。	This time I have made up my mind
我要带头打先锋，	To catch little Hunni and his elephant,
抬金矛的傣景罕①，	Letting my story of bravery pass to my descendants.
与我紧跟不离身。	I will fight in the front,
金矛手三十万，	Followed tightly by *daijinghans*①
拧成一根绳索齐心战。	Holding golden spears in their hands.
镖枪手共四万，	Three hundred thousand golden spear men
接近对方就镖杀。	Will fight like one man.
如果谁要往后退，	Forty thousand dart men
砍下脑袋小命丧！	Will kill every enemy they approach.
无论死伤有多少，	If anybody steps back,
往前冲杀手不软！"	

---

① 傣景罕：贴身卫队。　　① Daijinghan: private bodyguard.

厘俸 // Li Feng

话刚落音炮三响,
城门大开兵马出,
如同飞蚁密密麻,
如同风急雨又狂。

俸改从贺允东门出了城,
千军万马随后跟,
就像天上的云彩一团团。
人走象踏乱石滚滚沟踏平,
士卒跟着战象冲,
就像黑云在翻滚,
冲向艾道闷鲁天。
戴着莫纳①的兵丁,
你砍我杀不相让。
秋风卷叶人倒地,
脸上身上血斑斑。
战象咆哮声如雷,
犹如天空被撕裂。
俸改的兵丁如同无王的蜂群,
到处乱飞乱叮咬。

① 莫纳：一种防护脸部的面罩。

He will have his head cut off!
No matter how many are wounded or killed,
Just march on and never show any mercy!"
Then with the three cannon shots,
The city gate opened and the troops rushed out
Like colonies of flying ants and
Gusts of howling wind and a downpour of stormy rain.

Fenggai went out of the east gate of Heyun, the central city.
Behind him thousands of soldiers and horses followed
Like the clouds in the sky.
Crossing trenches and passing obstacles,
The soldiers behind the war elephants,
Dashed to God Aidaomenlutian
Like billowing black clouds.
Soldiers wearing *monas*①
Cut and slashed in full charge
The way autumn wind sweeps away fallen leaves.
Blood splashed on their faces and bodies.
The roaring of elephants
Tore the sky apart.
Fenggai's troops were like an army of bees with no queen

① mona: mask.

二十人结成一群，	Flying in all directions and stinging everything they saw.
拼命挥刀杀又砍。	They were organized in groups of twenty,
艾道闷鲁天势单力又薄，	Waving their swords and slashing desperately.
面对攻势难抵挡。	God Aidaomenlutian's force was too weak
只得边战边后退，	To resist the attack.
士卒伤亡已过半，	They had to retreat.
战象也掉头往回奔。	Half of his soldiers were killed and
俸改的兵马把壕沟道道占，	Their elephants turned around and ran away.
俘虏人马共四千，	Fenggai's army occupied all the trenches
全军欢腾又欢唱。	And captured more than four thousand enemies and horses.
敲起铓锣打起鼓，	Absorbed in delight,
响声震耳冲云霄。	They beat gongs and drums
俸改冷笑道：	With a deafening sound flying up high in the sky.
"这伙人哪是我的对手？"	Fenggai sneered:
说罢蹬着大象往前冲，	"These men are not my match at all!"
挥矛直取布桑色，	Then he spurred his elephant and waved his spear,
士卒挥刀紧跟上。	Rushing ahead to fight Sangse,
	With his soldiers following him closely.
桑色坐镇营寨稳如山，	Sangse sat in his camp, steady like a mountain
指挥兵将攻城正紧张。	Organizing attacks on the city.
俸改令弓弩手齐射箭，	Fenggai ordered his bowmen to shoot the enemy elephants
箭如雨点落在象身上。	With showers of arrows,

厘俸 // Li Feng

俸改又令土枪手齐发射，	While his gunmen got orders to shoot
击伤象脚鲜血淌，	The elephants' feet, which bled a lot.
大象痛叫声凄惨。	The elephants cried miserably because of the pain.
天兵也有伤和亡，	The heavenly soldiers suffered injury and death
纷纷躲避四处散。	And fled in all directions.
桑色看见心中急，	Sangse was so worried
起身蹬着占拜洪，	And left his tent for the battlefield
亲自上阵离营帐。	On the back of Zhanbaihong.
天兵手中拿天斧，	The heavenly soldiers holding axes
紧紧跟着布桑色。	Followed Sangse closely.
马队载着弓弩手，	The bowmen on horse back
利箭穿透人和象。	Shot arrows at the enemy with penetrating power.
俸改士兵纷纷倒，	Fenggai's soldiers were shot down
前面倒了后面上。	One after another.
桑色、俸改两混勐，	The two *hunmengs*, Sangse and Fenggai,
各率百万之众，	Were both leading millions of troops
两支军队急交锋。	And engaged in a fierce fight.
双方象队猛冲闯，	The elephants of both sides dashed bravely.
血肉横飞鬼神号。	Pieces of flesh flew in the air and ghosts howled.
兵器交错寒光闪，	In the clash of weapons,
血流成河尸成山。	Blood flowed like a river and dead bodies piled up.
桑色骑着大象猛冲杀，	Sangse dashed forward on his elephant.
鲁非齐放土炮响。	*Lufeis* and cannons were fired.
只见城中起大火，	Suddenly, the city center burst into flames.

俸改的兵丁无心恋战心已慌。	Fenggai's soldiers had no desire to continue fighting.
桑色乘胜向前进，	Sangse took the opportunity to push on
占拜洪象鼻腾空甩得欢。	And Zhanbaihong swung his trunk with joy.
俸改乱军之中稳住脚，	Fenggai managed to regain his footing
要想直取布桑色。	And decided to attack Sangse.
但不论他怎样蹬大象，	But no matter how hard he spurred his elephant,
也无法接近动刀枪。	He just could not approach Sangse.
他只好掉转象头找目标，	He then had to turn around and look for another target.
看见桑洛就急冲，	When he saw Sangluo, he rushed towards him
又快又猛旋风般。	As swiftly as a whirling wind.
天神布冈罕已参战，	The God Bugang Han joined the battle, too.
他放出四百头大象，	He released four hundred elephants
只见象牙如满山遍野的白花。	With tusks like white flowers all over the mountains.
天兵天将入战壕，	The heavenly soldiers and generals hid in the trenches,
战象屹立战壕旁。	And their elephants stood by the trenches.
俸改的兵丁如逗龇的马蜂，	Fenggai's troops came
蜂拥而出扑过来。	Like swarms of irritated wasps.
布冈罕蹬着大象来迎击，	Bugang Han spurred his elephant to meet him head-on.
顷刻尸体遍山冈。	In an instant, dead bodies piled up over the moutain.
俸改见了怒火上，	Seeing that,
猛蹬占艾兰，	Fenggai drove Zhan'ailan on in a rage,
冲向布冈罕。	And dashed straight at Bugang Han.
布冈罕的战象立住脚，	Bugang Han's elephant halted

厘俸 // Li Feng

昂首望天空，	And looked up at the sky, refusing to fight,
左蹬右蹬不出战。	No matter how hard its master kicked it.
然后吼叫一声往后退，	Then it withdrew with a long howl,
后退无援处境难。	Making it difficult for Buganghan to continue the battle.
兵无首领四逃散，	Even Bugang Han could not reassemble his soldiers
布冈罕也无力再呼唤，	Who ran away in all directions.
战壕失守又归勐景罕。	The trenches were lost to Mengjinghan's soldiers.
俸改冷笑一声开了口：	Fenggai sneered again:
"这伙人也不是对手，	"These men are not my rival, either.
重找一个再来战！"	Let me find another group to fight."
蹬着大象又向前，	Fenggai drove his elephant forward,
百万兵将后面跟，	Followed by millions of his soldiers and generals.
如洪水出堤泻万丈，	They rushed to Hunwan.
如马蜂离窝飞满天，	Like a flood overflowing river banks,
又如鸽群展翅	Or wasps swarming out of their hive,
在天空翱翔，	Or pigeons soaring high
顿时冲向混宛。	Up in the sky.
混宛举矛来迎击，	Hunwan came to meet them head-on with his spear,
后面跟着天兵和天将。	Followed by heavenly soldiers and generals.
放出大象二十栏，	He let out twenty herds of elephants,
还有三千铁甲兵，	Together with three thousand armored soldiers
拿着金矛冲敌方。	Who dashed at the enemy with golden spears.
只见俸改的兵丁两边闪，	Fenggai's soldiers dodged them.
死的死来逃的逃。	Some managed to flee, but others were killed.

俸改见势怒气冲，	Fenggai was so angry seeing this
传令鼓手敲响鼓。	And ordered his men to beat the drum of fighting.
兵丁听见鼓声起，	Hearing the drum beats,
纷纷聚拢又要战。	Fenggai's army reassembled.
混宛气得咬紧牙，	Hunwan ground his teeth angrily,
擒贼擒王取俸改，	Determined to kill Fenggai first, the enemy commander,
只见占艾兰牙沾鲜血滴滴淌。	Whose elephant Zhan'ailan had tusks dripping with blood.
俸改见到混宛把话讲：	Fenggai spoke to Hunwan:
"勐景罕一向很安分，	"Mengjinghan has always been harmless
未曾骚扰过何方。	And never harassed anybody.
天神为何发了怒，	For what reason are the gods irritated
派兵对我来侵犯？	And send you to invade us?
勐景罕从未得罪过天神，	Mengjinghan has never offended the gods.
天神为何调动人马和大象，	For what reason are the heavenly troops sent
四处包围勐景罕？	To surround us from all sides?
既然如此不讲理，	Now that you are so unreasonable,
今日我就来较量。	Combat is my only choice today.
我要蹬着占艾兰，	I will ride my Zhan'ailan
一比高低与你战。"	And fight you, to see who is stronger."
混宛听了就回答：	Hunwan then replied:
"你这个艾哈腊花豹子，	"You, Aihala the Leopard!
勐景罕早已丰衣又足食，	Mengjinghan is a wealthy kingdom.
为何要把桑洛的妻子娥宾抢？	Why did you go and capture Sangluo's wife Ebing?
你简直凶猛像虎狼。	You are really cruel, like wolves and tigers!

厘俸 // Li Feng

你管辖的地方宽又广，	The place you are ruling is broad and vast.
为何要把海罕的妻子婻崩抢，	Why did you go and capture Haihan's wife Nanbeng
使他们夫妻一对相离散？	And cause the couple to be separated?
你的罪恶滔天大，	You have committed the most heinous crimes
天神决不会把你饶！	And will never be forgiven by the gods.
你横行霸道太逞强，	You act tyrannously and flaunt your power.
天神个个把你恨，	The gods all hate you
人人紧握拳头要下凡把你斗。	And want to fight you with their clenched fists.
海罕是天神的侄儿应当保，	Haihan is a nephew of the gods,
他遭灾遇难应当来相帮。	And deserves our help when in trouble.
今日天神下凡来，	We descend to the earth today
就是要把你的脑袋砍！	For nothing else but cutting off your head!
艾哈腊俸改啊，	Oh, Aihala Fenggai!
你死到临头还不悔！"	Death is at hand but you still do not repent!"
说完蹬象取俸改，	Hunwan drove his elephant towards Fenggai,
俸改蹬象迎上来，	Who spurred his elephant to meet him.
双方士卒两旁让。	The soldiers of both sides had to stand back.
两强相遇猛厮杀，	Hunwan and Fenggai were engaged in a close fight
天空忽起风雨黑云飘，	When suddenly it began to rain and the wind began to blow,
不知天命注定谁先亡。	As black clouds gathered in the sky.
两头战象的牙绞得咚咚响，	Who was destined to die was still unknown.
双方士卒也交战。	The tusks of the two elephants crashed and rattled.
俸改的大象如丘陵，	The soldiers of the both sides joined the fight.
凶猛超群不一般。	

混宛的战象用尽全力拼命挑,	Fenggai's elephant was as big as a hill, unusually fierce.
占艾兰依然稳如山。	Hunwan's elephant went all out to charge with its tusks,
混宛用矛左右刺,	Zhan'ailan remained unshaken.
俸改衣甲九层厚,	Hunwan stabbed Fenggai from the left and the right
坚硬无比难刺穿。	But failed to pierce through
俸改双眼盯混宛,	The nine hard layers of Fenggai's armor.
手中长矛锋又利,	Fenggai stared at Hunwan
忽然一矛飞出去,	And thrust the long and sharp spear in his hand
混宛的衣甲被刺穿,	Towards him.
血流如注流不断。	Hunwan's armor was pierced
混宛负伤靠在象舆上,	And blood gushed from the wound.
他钩着大象往后退。	He leaned on the howdah on his elephant
俸改趁势紧追击,	And signaled his elephant to pull back.
身后百万士卒齐呐喊。	Fenggai then took the opportunity to chase after him.
混宛的大军败退逃,	The million soldiers behind him yelled and shouted in support.
一路损兵又折将。	Hunwan's army was utterly defeated,
桑洛远远已看见,	Suffering heavy casualties.
胸中怒火熊熊燃,	Sangluo watched that from far away
率领战象四百冲过来。	And was boiling with rage.
四百战象牙锋利,	He led four hundred war elephants with sharp tusks
高声吼叫斗志昂。	To rush to join the fighting.
双方诅咒又厮杀,	The fighting spirit soared aloft
天上、人间大混战。	And the two sides started another battle.
桑洛的战鼓敲不停,	

厘俸 // Li Feng

天兵四出围成圈，	It was a tangled fight between the heavenly and the earthly troops.
把混宛保护在正中央。	With constant drum beats from Sangluo's side,
远处又见尘土扬，	The heavenly soldiers attacked on all fronts
天神召法免也蹬着象，	And protected Hunwan in the middle.
赶来支援混宛。	Dust rose in the distance.
两支大军齐汇合，	It was Zhao Famian who came
犹如滚滚洪水卷巨浪，	To back up Hunwan.
冲向俸改哗哗响。	The two troops converged
双方你砍我又杀，	And rushed to attack Fenggai
杀得天昏地又暗。	Like a flood with huge billows.
三千哈火塔，	The two sides slashed and cut
三万哈火吞，	In utter disorder.
边舞大刀边弹舌，	Three thousand *hahuota* warriors
人被砍死象砍翻。	And thirty thousand *hahuotun* warriors
满身满脸是鲜血，	Waved their swords while clicking their tongues loudly,
血迹斑斑衣零乱。	Killing soldiers and elephants,
俸改下令打土炮，	Their faces and bodies spattered with blood,
桑洛的大象死又伤。	Their clothes untidy and messy.
天神召法免怒把士卒骂，	Fenggai ordered his men to fire the cannons,
拔出宝剑指向前。	Injuring and killing many of Sangluo's elephants.
士卒不敢违军令，	Zhao Famian cursed his soldiers in a rage
舍生忘死往前闯。	And pulled out his sword to force them to march forward.
发射鲁非来还击，	Not daring to defy the order,
火花四溅烈火燃，	

俸改兵丁纷纷倒。	The soldiers rushed forward disregarding the risk of death.
桑洛又令土炮轰,	They launched *lufei*s to fight back.
击中俸改的兵和将,	Sparks flew and fires blazed.
尸横遍野堆如山。	Fenggai's soldiers fell down one after another.
俸改见势不好转身逃,	Sangluo then ordered his soldiers to bombard
全军崩溃四处散。	Fenggai's soldiers and generals,
一场激战已过去,	Littering the battlefield with numerous corpses.
硝烟四散,	Under such circumstances Fenggai turned round and fled.
混宛、桑洛派兵扫战场。	All of his troops were dispersed
俘敌四千,	And the battle came to an end.
砍敌首级一万。	When the clouds of smoke dissipated,
众兵丁呜呜……齐欢呼,	Hunwan and Sangluo began to clean up the battlefield.
敲起铓锣阵阵响。	Four thousand enemy soldiers were captured
拥着混宛和桑洛,	And ten thousands enemy soldiers killed.
将士凯旋庆胜仗。	The troops were all flooded with joyful hurrahs,
	And in the victory beats of gongs and drums.
	Clustered round by their soldiers and generals,
	Hunwan and Sangluo returned triumphantly.
伴龙法和卫大荒,	Banlongfa and Weidahuang
从腊姐出城上战场。	Set out from Lajie
要想击退布桑色,	With the intention of defeating Sangse.
未能如愿又掉头,	When they failed to do so they turned around

厘俸 // Li Feng

掉转头来攻海罕。	To attack Haihan.
左攻右攻不见效，	After a few rounds of attack
海罕大军稳如山。	Haihan was still there undefeated.
伴龙法自己吹嘘最勇猛，	Banlongfa used to boast of his bravery
手下的兵丁强又壮。	And of his strong and powerful soldiers.
他两战失利怒火起，	Now losing two battles made him angry
蹬着大象攻桑勐，	And he spurred his elephant to attack Sangmeng.
后面跟着卫大荒。	Weidahuang followed him closely.
桑勐的兵丁力量弱，	Sangmeng's soldiers were so weak
节节败退难抵挡。	That they quickly lost ground.
伴龙法下令用炮击，	Banlongfa ordered his men to fire cannons
又发射鲁非一串串。	And launch *lufeis*.
桑勐的营帐起大火，	Sangmeng's tent was on fire
他拔出宝刀指天上。	And he pulled out his sword and pointed it at the sky.
天空轰轰发巨响，	The sky then responded with the rumble of thunder.
这是天上雷斧劈，	The heavenly axes were chopping
地上天斧也在砍。	And the earthly axes were cutting.
法洪桑兰呼风又唤雨，	Fahongsanglan invoked the wind and rain and
一时黑云翻滚风雨狂。	All of a sudden black clouds rolled and heavy rain fell.
道道金光落下地，	In golden flashes
雷斧劈死俸改的兵和将。	Fenggai's soldiers and generals were killed by thunder axes.
桑勐又令土炮轰，	Sangmeng gave another order to fire the cannons,
俸改的兵马又伤亡，	And Fenggai suffered more casualties.
败下阵来往回逃。	The defeated troops retreated,

人逃马跑象乱闯,	Men and animals rushed about in chaos,
如同蜂子齐回窝。	Like bees swarming back to their hives.
八百万人马退入城,	The withdrawal of eight million troops into the city
只听碗柜叮当响,	Shook the bamboo houses
竹楼踩得摇摇晃。	And the kitchen cabinets within.
桑勐蹬着占拜香,	Sangmeng urged his elephant on,
穷追不舍歼敌人,	Together with the heavenly troops,
后面还有天兵和天将。	Chasing after the enemy closely.
俸改的阵地被攻破,	Fenggai lost his position
九道壕沟都被占。	And the nine trenches on his side to the enemy.
皆温蹬着大象占艾滇,	Jiewen, riding his elephant Zhan'aidian,
旁边是贺哇仁占邦,	Together with Hewarenzhanbang,
还有马门罗虎当,	Mamenluohudang,
再一个是召冈牛仰罕,	And Zhaogang Niuyanghan,
齐头并进围桑本。	Went to attack Sangben.
又放鲁非又轰炮,	*Lufeis* and cannons were fired
炮声震天硝烟漫。	With a deafening sound and clouds of smoke.
双方交锋刀碰刀,	The swords of the two sides crashed and rattled,
刀下无数死和伤。	Causing numerous injuries and deaths.
桑温、赛伦又赶来,	Sangwen and Sailun came
支援桑本战皆温。	To join Sangben in the fight against Jiewen.
皆温的兵马多九倍,	With overwhelming military force
一心要活捉桑本领奖赏。	Jiewen determined to catch Sangben alive for a reward.

皆温下令兵丁轮番攻，	His soldiers took turns to attack,
桑本手舞长矛心不慌，	But Sangben, with a long spear in hand, was not panicked.
冲来一群死一群，	In round after round of attack
后面又冲又伤亡，	He killed group after group of enemy soldiers,
一直未能近桑本。	Making them unable to approach him.
皆温又派出马队齐齐排，	Jiewen then sent out arrays of horses
组成防线像铜墙，	As an impregnable line of defense
把桑温、赛伦来阻挡。	To stop Sangwen and Sailun's attacks.
桑本摆出大象阵，	Sangben organized his elephants
围成圆圈四面战。	To form a circle.
桑温、赛伦拼死冲，	Sangwen and Sailun went all out
靠拢桑本相互帮。	To draw close to Sangben so as to support each other.
皆温的弟弟又冲来，	Jiewen's younger brother came to join the fight,
一层一层不中断。	Starting one wave of attack after another.
桑本用力蹬大象，	Sangben violently spurred his elephant,
大象胆怯脖颤抖，	Who was trembling with fear
两根长牙插地上。	And poking tusks into the ground.
桑本处于危难中，	Sangben was in danger
如同巨流冲沙滩，	And on the brink of death
危在旦夕命难保。	Like rapid river water washing away sand.
兵马纷纷往后退，	His soldiers and horses pulled back in succession,
靠近大营向海罕。	Drawing close to the troops of Haihan.
桑温、赛伦也退下阵，	Sangwen and Sailun also retired
来到海罕大本营，	To Haihan's camp barracks,

脸色发青人发抖。	Blue in the face and trembling all over.
桑本军中一猛士，	One warrior in Sangben's army
名叫拉乱波滚叫，	Named Laluanbogunjiao
他身背宝剑一把赴战场，	Carried a sword on his back and joined the fight.
刀刃发出金绿色的寒光。	The cold blade of his sword glittered with a greenish glow.
这次战斗他勇猛异常，	He fought with extraordinary bravery
砍杀敌人头颅一千个。	And killed one thousand of the enemy.
虽然全军已退却，	When the majority of the army retreated
他却孤军一人不下阵，	He insisted on fighting all on his own
直到身负多处伤，	And did not leave his position in the trench
才跳出壕沟奔海罕。	Until he was wounded many times.
海罕见了就称赞：	Haihan praised him:
"拉乱啊，拉乱！	"Laluan, oh, Laluan!
你勇敢不怕死。	You are brave and not afraid of death.
如果人人都像你，	If every soldier was like you,
即使勐俸多坚固，	Mengjinghan would have been occupied
也早被我们攻占。	No matter how solid the city is.
你虽是个小人，	Although you are not a famous man,
我要给你重赏，	I will give you a generous reward
还要让你升官。	And promote you to be an officer.
让你有万匹马在厩中，	You will have ten thousand horses in your stable,
让年轻妻子满屋又满堂！"	And young and charming wives in your house."

厘俸 // Li Feng

桑本败退回大营，	Sangben retreated in defeat.
混勐开口就大骂：	Hunmeng shouted abuses at him:
"召桑啊，召桑！	"Zhao Sang, oh Zhao Sang!
人人都说你是我弟弟，	People all know that you are my younger brother,
你管辖下的地方宽又广，	Possessing a vast and broad land,
你的战象已成群，	And so many herds of elephants.
为什么今日打败仗？	Why were you still defeated today?
我可以把你杀，	I could have killed you
也可以把你砍，	And I could have decapitated you,
只怕众官心忧伤。	But I am afraid this may break the officers' hearts.
这次失败我饶你，	This time I will forgive you,
今后不能再这样！"	But no more failures are allowed in the future!"
桑本听了忙回答：	Sangben replied promptly:
"我的兄长召海法啊，	"My dear brother Zhao Haifa!
只怪我骑的那头象，	The blame should be put on my elephant,
蹬它它不往前走，	Who did not move forward,
弯着脖子还把牙插地上。	But bent down its head and had its tusk stab into the ground.
一边吼叫一边退，	It retreated while howling and roaring,
让我丢丑脸无光，	And made me lose face
我也无能心有愧。	And feel ashamed.
亲爱的召海法啊，	My dear Zhao Haifa!
你能否把占拜兵赐给我，	Can you give me Zhanbaibing?
如果能骑着这头象，	If I have this elephant,
我有信心攻下勐景罕。	

如果我又打败仗，	I will take Mengjinghan with complete confidence.
杀了我也心甘！"	If I am defeated again,
海罕听了下命令，	I will be most willing to be killed by you then!"
占拜兵被牵出栏，	Haihan then ordered his men
身上闪闪罩金舆。	To lead out Zhanbaibing
桑本急忙骑上去，	With a golden howdah on its back.
快如三月疾风狂。	Sangben mounted the elephant and rode it
兵将在后紧紧跟，	As fast as the wind in March.
多如江河层层浪。	Soldiers and generals, as numerous as river ripples,
拉着土炮列阵有九层，	Followed him closely.
后面是桑温和赛伦。	Behind the nine layers of cannon arrays
大军直抵勐景罕，	Were Sangwen and Sailun's troops.
分成两翼齐包抄。	The troops arrived at Mengjinghan
皆温见了桑本就大骂：	From two directions and formed a ring of encirclement.
"召桑啊，召桑！	Jiewen cursed at the sight of Sangben:
俗话你莫非忘记了？	"Zhao Sang, oh Zhao Sang!
'脑门碰树桩，	Can it be that you have forgotten the proverb?
自寻死路把命亡。'	'Strike your forehead on the tree stump,
你刚吃败仗往回退，	And you will bring about your own destruction.'
眼看就要被我砍，	You were just defeated in the last battle
幸好天神保护你，	And I was about to kill you,
现在你又来挑战。	But you were protected by the gods.
你不怕死就快蹬象，	Why do you return and challenge me again?
有胆量就来较量！"	If you are not afraid of death

厘俸 // Li Feng

桑本听了把话答：	Just come to fight me!"
"俸改的弟弟皆温啊，	Sangben replied:
俗话说得很清楚：	"Jiewen, younger brother of Fenggai!
'神灵赐战象，	There is a saying that goes:
重整旗鼓打胜仗。	'If the gods bestow you with a war elephant,
旧病怕复发，	Then rally your forces again and get ready to win the war.
复发只有等死亡。'	When an old disease comes back,
莫非你又忘记了，	There will be only one terrible result: death!'
冈罕一矛刺中你，	Can it be that you have forgotten that
如果不是士卒保，	Ganghan once stabbed you with his spear?
你早变鬼来无人样！	If your soldiers did not come to protect you,
你现在为何又出现？	You would have been killed and become a ghost.
你凭什么把口夸？	Why do you show up again?
你要和我来交战，	On what basis can you boast this way?
只怕你的象牙被绞断！	If you fight me,
你有本事就来试一试，	The tusks of your elephant will break off!
让你看看我桑本，	Do you dare to have a try?
究竟武艺强不强！"	I will let you know
话音刚落吼声起，	Whether I am skillful or not."
桑本、皆温同蹬象，	Hardly had his voice faded away
双方士卒急忙闪一旁。	When Sangben and Jiewen spurred their elephants
两象对阵头顶头，	At the same time,
拼命顶撞不相让。	Not giving in to each other.
两将交锋舞长矛，	The soldiers of both sides got out of the way.

皆温矛矛都落空。	Sangben and Jiewen fought with their spears,
桑本眼疾手又快，	But all of Jiewen's hits failed,
一矛把皆温衣甲来刺穿。	Whereas Sangben, with his quickness and his speed,
只见鲜血往外涌，	Pierced Jiewen's armor.
皆温从象舆翻身滚落在地上。	Blood gushed from the wound
桑本的兵丁涌上去，	And Jiewen fell off the howdah.
冒宰争先把头砍，	Sangben's soldiers surged forward
众士卒呜呜……齐欢呼。	And cut off Jiewen's head.
	The soldiers hailed their victory again and again.

皆温已经被杀死，	Jiewen was killed,
他的大象还不知，	But his elephant did not notice that.
仍然进攻桑本象，	It continued to fight against Sangben's elephant,
又吼又跳又冲撞。	Roaring, jumping and crashing.
士卒见了齐欢笑，	Sangben's soldiers all laughed at that.
有的偷偷爬到象脖上，	Some of them climbed on the neck of the elephant.
占艾滇乖乖被擒获，	Zhan'aidian therefore was captured without a struggle.
全军上下又欢呼。	The whole army was steeped in happiness.
呜呜……之声传四方。	Their cheerful shouts spread far and wide,
声音震动勐景罕，	Shaking the city of Mengjinghan
城内人人心胆战。	And the shocked people inside the city.
桑本把战象占艾滇，	Sangben presented Zhan'aidian
恭恭敬敬献海罕，	Respectfully to Haihan
海罕赐给金银作奖赏。	And got gold and silver as rewards.

厘俸 // Li Feng

桑本乘胜又追击，	Sangben continued his victorious pursuit
步步为营围栅栏。	And built fortifications every time he made an advance.
俘虏大官六十人，	In this battle, they captured sixty officers
还有兵丁和大象。	And a great number of soldiers and elephants.
俸改各路人马纷纷退，	Fenggai's troops quickly retreated
退到允龙城中城。	To Yunlong, the central city of Mengjinghan.
俸改见到形势很不妙，	Fenggai noticed that the situation was not good
拿出仙笛吹起来。	And took out his magic flute and blew it.
攻城兵丁顿时手脚软，	Hearing the magic flute, the soldiers attacking Mengjinghan
纷纷把手中刀矛放，	All became limp and feeble and could no longer fight,
不会杀也不会砍。	Dropping the swords in their hands.
笛声吹得震动勐景罕，	The sound of the flute also stupefied Mengjinghan.
只有天兵神志清，	Only the heavenly soldiers remained conscious.
其余的士卒全迷糊，	The rest all got confused.
有的呆立抱栅栏。	Some of them clung to the fences and stood there numbly.
如此延续两三天，	Such a situation lasted for two or three days.
烈火硝烟四弥漫。	The battlefield was full of fires and clouds of smoke.
混宛负伤回营帐，	Hunwan returned to his tent injured.
士卒把他抱下象，	When his soldiers took him down from the elephant,
已经咽气魂离体。	He was already dead.
海罕听到混宛死，	Haihan was so sorrowful
心中忧愁又悲伤，	To hear the news

泪珠流下一串串。
然后告诉阿巫戛：
"阿巫戛啊，阿巫戛！
转告混宛的儿子不要急，
父亲战死名永传。
尸体别忙往家运，
要继承父位掌幡幢。
还要把土地赐给他，
以两三个村寨为采邑。
转告他不要太悲伤，
父亲虽死还有救，
以后请戛拍①来医治。
混宛的金幢和旗帜不能倒，
要立在营帐高飘扬。"
海罕又对众将把话讲：
"混宛下凡来帮我，
现在不幸已阵亡。
今后战斗怎么办？
要请大家来商量。"

That his tears poured.
He said to Awu Ga:
"Awu Ga, oh Awu Ga!
Please tell Hunwan's son not to be heart-broken.
His father died but his great name will last forever.
Do not send the body back home immediately.
He will inherit his father's title and hold the golden prayer flag.
He will be rewarded with land,
Two or three villages as his fiefs.
Tell him not to be too grieved.
His father died but there is still hope.
I will ask *gapai*① to treat him and bring him to life again.
His golden prayer flag and banner cannot fall.
They should fly high over the tents."
Haihan then said to his generals:
"Hunwan descended from heaven to help me
But is unfortunately now dead.
How should we carry on the battle?
I would like you to give suggestions and advice."

---

① 戛拍：白鹭，一种仙鸟。

① Gapai: egret, a kind of immortal bird.

厘俸 // Li Feng

九 / IX

第二天太阳刚升起，	The next day when the sun had just risen,
只听大鼓咚咚响。	Drum beat was heard.
海罕命令所有兵和将，	Haihan ordered all his soldiers and generals,
还有天兵八十万，	Together with eight hundred thousand heavenly soldiers,
继续进攻勐景罕。	To continue to attack Mengjinghan.
千军万马又出动，	Thousands of soldiers and horses set out again
团团把允龙来包围。	And surrounded the central city Yunlong from all sides.
海罕骑着占拜舍，	Haihan rode his Zhanbaishe
亲自指挥亲临战。	And commanded his troops on site.
金幡幢插在象舆上，	The golden prayer flag with a tiger image
虎形图案雄赳赳。	Was fastened on the howdah on Zhanbaishe.
海罕的命令，	Even the heavenly troops
天兵也不敢违抗。	Dared not defy Haihan's orders.
围城兵丁战鼓催，	The soldiers beat the drum,
鼓声震动景罕城。	Shaking the city of Mengjinghan.
水中蛟龙纷纷出，	Dragons in the water were startled
出水蛟龙把江水堵。	And came out of the water and jammed the river.
所有天神都来到，	With the arrival of all the gods,
一时风云突变暴雨降。	There was a drastic weather change and a rainstorm.
海罕骑着占拜舍，	Riding his Zhanbaishe,
逼近城池要把俸改斩。	Haihan was marching towards the city to kill Fenggai.

聪明的婻崩在城中，	Inside the city, the smart Nanbeng
看见海罕亲自来作战，	Saw Haihan himself coming to fight,
她心生一计，	And hit upon an idea.
甜言蜜语向俸改，	She spoke to Fenggai with sweet words
口中含着牙万冷，	While spraying *yawanleng* in her mouth
喷向俸改把话讲：	On his face:
"兵马已团团把城围，	"The enemies have surrounded our city.
你那勇猛的兵和将，	Why don't you ask your brave and powerful soldiers
为什么不叫他们快出战？	To go out and fight?
战火已布满勐景坝，	The flames of war have reached Mengjing Basin.
为什么还不去扑灭光？	Why don't you go and put out the fires?
你应走出宫廷去，	You should go out of the court
站在转颂上仔细看，	And stand on the *zhuansong* to inspect the situation
你应该布置兵马快点将。"	And organize your troops now."
俸改听了有道理，	Fenggai listened to her
把手中仙笛放床上，	And placed the magic flute on the bed
走出宫廷到转颂，	And went out to the *zhuansong*,
然后又把将来点，	Appointing commanders
再把命令高声传：	And giving his order from there:
"如今撒马姓已战死，	"Samaxing has already fought to the death,
你们要夺回失地努力战！"	And now it's our turn to fight fiercely for the lost land."
婻崩趁俸改站在转颂点兵将，	As Fenggai stood on the *zhuansong*, giving orders,
偷偷把仙笛拿手上，	Nanbeng secretly took the magic flute

厘俸 // Li Feng

转身把它丢下楼,	And threw it down from the bamboo house.
顿时战象吼声起,	All of a sudden, the war elephants broke out in roars
你踏我踩仙笛烂。	Treading on the magic flute and breaking it into pieces.
她又把酒糟往下撒,	She then cast vinasse on the ground,
三百头公猪奔过来,	Attracting three hundred boars
你拱我挤把食抢,	To scramble for the food.
踩得仙笛破又碎,	The broken pieces of the magic flute
变成几百只花蝴蝶,	Turned into hundreds of butterflies
围着俸改飞飞扬,	Flying around Fenggai.
战象战马也在厩中吼得慌。	The war elephants and war horses were also howling in their pens.
俸改急忙回宫廷,	Fenggai hurried back to the court
一看仙笛已不在,	Only to find the magic flute gone.
心中明白怒火上,	Flames of fury ignited at the bottom of his heart,
他拔出宝剑欲杀婻崩。	And he pulled out his sword to kill Nanbeng,
婻崩吹出牙万冷,	Who blew out more *yawanleng*
吹在俸改的脸上钻进心。	On his face, which penetrated into his heart.
俸改迷迷糊糊心发软,	In a daze Fenggai's heart was softened.
伸出左手把婻崩牵,	He reached out his left hand to Nanbeng
右手把宝剑丢一旁,	And dropped the sword in his right hand.
犹如哥哥牵妹妹。	He held her hand and spoke to her
牵着婻崩把话讲:	Like a brother:
"今天我要蹬大象,	"Today I will spur my elephant
与海罕拼死决一战。	To fight with Haihan till the last moment.
两头战象阵对阵,	

不知谁的象牙会绞断？	When the two elephants fight face to face,
两把宝刀要出鞘，	Who knows whose tusks will be broken?
不知天命要谁亡？	When two swords are pulled out,
两只金矛要交锋，	Who knows who is doomed to die?
不知神灵要谁的身体被洞穿？	When two golden spears are waved,
两只大象要格斗，	Who knows whose body will be pierced through?
不知哪一头要倒在血地上？"	When two elephants wrestle and grapple,
说完牵出英耆节，	Who knows which one will drop on the blood-stained ground?"
它虽然力大但行动迟缓，	With that, he led out Yingzhejie,
俸改指象大声骂：	Who was powerful but slow in movement.
"我精心喂养你，	Fenggai pointed at his elephant and shouted:
就像养只斑鸠一个样。	"I have carefully fed you like feeding a turtledove.
喂的是雪白米饭团，	What you eat is snow-white rice balls.
象栏涂的是金粉，	Your pen is painted with gold powder.
早晚还有蔗叶和蔗秆。	You have sugarcane leaves
哪一支象牙不锐利，	And stems to eat in the morning and in the evening.
都要修整削尖如龙角。	When either of your tusks becomes blunt,
现在战火熊熊燃，	It is sharpened like a dragon horn.
我们双混①都要各自蹬大象，	Now the war has broken out,
手持金矛互交战，	And we, the two Huns①, will ride our elephants
要拼杀得血染矛杆。	And fight with golden spears
两头大象相斗时，	Till blood stains them.
你要顶住不能动。	

---

①双混：此处指俸改和海罕。

① Two Huns: Here two Huns refer to Fenggai and Haihan.

厘俸 // Li Feng

两对象牙相交时，	When you two are fighting,
你要站稳不后退，	You must resist and never move.
英着节啊，我的象！"	When two pairs of tusks collide with each other,
俸改下令敲大鼓，	You must stand firm and never retreat.
接着鸣炮响三声。	Oh, Yingzhejie, my elephant!"
各路兵马都出动，	Fenggai ordered his men to beat the drums
到处只听人马喊。	And fire three cannon shots.
象栏大开群象出，	All his troops set out
乱石踏得遍地滚，	With the war cries of soldiers and horses.
箐沟踩得平坦坦，	The stables opened and the elephants rushed out,
各色旗帜满山冈。	Kicking the stones on the road
	And making the vales flat.
	Colorful flags fluttered all over the mountain.

海罕大军紧围城，	Haihan's troops beseidged the city tightly,
重重叠叠千百层。	With layer after layer of encirclements.
只见象牙白花花，	Everywhere in sight were white tusks
只见象鼻翻腾如森林。	And rolling trunks like a forest.
天空神灵在巡视，	The gods were patrolling over the sky,
金斧银斧来保护。	Protecting Haihan with golden and silver axes.
海罕停住大象驻足看，	Haihan halted his elephant to watch for a while
只见金幡幢闪闪，	And saw golden prayer flags shining brightly.
千军万马顶烈日，	In the burning sun stood his soldiers
箭满弦紧绷，	With arrows on the bowstring,

严阵以待望前方。	Ready in full battle array.
只见俸改的大军出城来，	He saw Fenggai's troops coming out of the city.
两军相遇如云海，	The two armies encountered each other
把天地相连。	Like clouds connecting the sky and the earth,
又如两股洪流相会集，	Or two torrents converging.
杀声喊声骤然起，	Shouts and screams arose,
如同四月的风和雨。	As abruptly as April wind and rain.
四面八方土炮响，	As sounds of cannon shots came from all directions,
黑烟滚滚冲天际，	Clouds of dark smoke swirled up into the sky,
烟雾笼罩景罕城。	Shrouding the city of Mengjinghan.
鲁非串串穿空过，	*Lufei*s flew across the sky
红光闪闪如火龙。	Like fire dragons, with a red glow.
俸改的兵乱糟糟，	Fenggai's soldiers, in chaos,
成群成片如山倒。	Fell down like a flock in a landslide.
两军混战惊心动魄，	The soldiers of both sides fought in a melee,
满脸鲜血如雨淋，	With their faces bleeding
边揩边抹边死战。	But still insisted on fighting.
俸改的人马死得多，	Fenggai lost many of his soldiers and horses.
死尸密密犹如遍地攀枝花。	Dead bodies were everywhere like ceiba trees.
人血、象血四处淌，	The blood of soldiers and elephants flowed
涓涓细流汇成河。	Like confluent streams.
俸改心头冒火催战鼓，	With a flame of fury in his heart,
蹬着大象冲海罕，	Spurring on Yingzhejie, whose tusks were as sharp as dragon horns,
英着节象牙锋利如龙角。	

厘俸 // Li Feng

海罕蹬着占拜舍，	Fenggai dashed towards Haihan,
挥动长矛来迎战。	Who urged Zhanbaishe on
两头大象力相当，	And waved a long spear to meet his foe head-on.
你冲我挑猛又猛，	The two elephants were equally matched,
犹如飓风吹大树，	Grappling with each other violently.
树干摇晃树叶响。	Like a hurricane blowing big trees,
又如巨石相击撞，	Shaking the tree trunks,
砰砰巨响火花起。	And like boulders colliding with each other,
俸改开口大声骂：	Creating loud bangs and a shower of sparks.
"海罕啊，海罕！	Fenggai shouted abuse:
不是我主动找婻崩，	"Haihan! Oh, Haihan!
而是她对我献殷勤。	I didn't take the initiative to contact Nanbeng.
她早已对你变了心，	It was she who courted me.
因此我才把她抢。	She was no longer faithful to you.
她已和我成一家，	That is why I captured her.
天天坐在我身旁，	She and I am now family,
早晚和我同桌吃饭。	Staying by my side every day
美丽的婻崩属于我，	And eating with me at the same table.
每日与我共欢心，	The pretty Nanbeng belongs to me now,
已经与你不相干。	Enjoying her time with me
莫非你认为我太软？	And having nothing to do with you.
莫非你认为我无战象？	Can it be that you consider me to be softhearted?
你才带领兵马来捣乱。	Can it be that you think I have no war elephants?
你可能小看了勐景罕，	How dare you lead your army to make trouble here!

你以为这里没有男子汉，	Maybe you look down on Mengjinghan.
才带领象队来侵犯。	Maybe you lead your army to invade my kingdom
我说你是为了婻崩来送死，	Because you assume there are no tough men here.
你真是要把头放在竹箩上！	I'm sure that you are here to die for Nanbeng.
今日我们双混干戈动，	You are indeed putting your head in a bamboo basket!
为的是婻崩。	Today it's for Nanbeng
不论谁死魂升天，	That we two fight each other.
也不后悔心也甘。	Whoever goes first to heaven
海罕啊，	Should never regret.
天地作证并让后人把此事记。	Oh, Haihan!
召尼啊，	I'd like the universe to witness and our descendants to remember it.
你今日必死已无疑，	Oh, Zhao Ni!
见鬼去吧，让你永离人世！"	You are destined to die today.
海罕听了开口答：	Go to hell! Let me end your life!"
"艾哈腊俸改，	Hearing this, Haihan replied:
你这只豹子最凶残，	"Aihala Fenggai!
老象未死就拔牙，	What a brutal leopard you are!
象牙要戳你肋巴。	If you pull out the tusks of an old elephant while it is still alive,
老虎未死就拔牙，	The tusks will pierce through your ribs.
虎牙爆炸变火花，	If you pull out the teeth of an old tiger while it is still alive,
烈火燃烧勐景罕。	The teeth will explode,
我召海法还未死，	And the sparks will burn Mengjinghan.
你就把婻崩抢，	
使我夫妻不能同桌吃饭。	

厘俸 // Li Feng

我现在坐着占拜舍，	You've captured Nanbeng
率领无数兵和将，	While I am still alive,
报仇雪耻寻爱妻。	So that she and I cannot have meals together.
我的宝刀已出鞘，	Now riding my Zhanbaishe here
要把你这头豹子砍。	And commanding countless soldiers and generals,
砍了丢下河，	I've come to take revenge and look for my beloved wife.
再把肚腹剖，	I have had my sword unsheathed,
让鱼虾围上吃个光。	Determined to cut off your leopard head
艾哈腊，	And throw it into the river.
你这只豹子啊，	I will cut your stomach open,
作恶多端没有好下场！"	Making it a great meal for fish and shrimp.
话刚落音尘土扬，	Aihala!
双混交锋齐蹬象。	You are such a sinful leopard that
象牙交错象鼻甩，	You will come to no good end!"
象头相碰相顶撞。	Hardly had his voice faded away when the two Huns
天兵助战卷席来，	Urged their elephants on and started a new fight.
好像天塌把地盖。	The two elephants' tusks rattled, their trunks swung,
俸改取出通香轻摇晃，	And their heads collided with each other.
一群花蝴蝶飞起来，	The heavenly soldiers joined the battle overwhelmingly,
围着俸改四面转。	Like the sky collapsing and covering the earth.
海罕也把通香轻轻摇，	Fenggai took out his amulet bag and shook it slightly.
一时雷鸣电又闪。	A flock of colorful butterflies
俸改挥舞金矛如旋风，	Flew around him.
海罕勇猛灵活左右挡。	Haihan shook his amulet bag as well.

俸改求胜心切露破绽，	Lightning flashed and thunder rumbled.
海罕看准机会猛一矛，	Fenggai brandished his spear like a whirlwind
矛飞出正中俸改，	While Haihan warded him off dexterously.
鲜血喷流地上淌。	Fenggai's eagerness to win exposed his weakness
俸改急忙钩象往后退，	And Haihan grasped an opportunity
稳稳地靠在象舆上。	To stab right into Fenggai's body.
身后猛士三百人，	Blood gushed out from Fenggai's wound.
纷纷杀出救俸改。	Fenggai signaled his elephant to retreat
海罕乘胜追击紧不放，	But remained seated in the howdah on its back.
占拜舍胆怯不向前，	Three hundred brave warriors behind him
原来是看见俸改的坐骑，	Came promptly to save him.
象舆上插着孔雀尾。	Haihan wanted to chase him
要不是占拜舍脚步慢，	But his Zhanbaishe hesitated
海罕早已把俸改戳下象，	At the sight of the peacock feathers
亲手把他首级砍。	That decorated the howdah on Fenggai's elephant.
俸改被兵将救回城，	If it were not for the slow movement of Zhanbaishe,
败兵蜂拥逃命忙。	Haihan would have knocked Fenggai off his elephant
海罕大军齐追杀，	And cut his head off.
天兵四处俘大象。	Fenggai was escorted back into the city,
凶猛的大象难捉拿，	Clustered round by his defeated soldiers.
就用刀砍矛又刺。	Haihan's army chased them
大象受伤吼叫惨，	And captured their elephants.
乱踩乱跑又乱撞。	Elephants too fierce to be caught
	Were simply struck and killed,

厘俸 // Li Feng

俸改的贺悍①被吓坏，	Howling and shrilling with pain
纷纷忙忙跳下象，	And dashing about blindly.
拔掉象舆上的金幡幢。	Fenggai's *hehans*① were daunted.
战象无主四处窜，	They jumped off their elephants
海罕的大军穷追不舍跟在后，	And pulled away the golden prayer flags on the howdahs.
追杀到允龙一块平地上。	Without their riders, the elephants ran away in all directions.
只见矛往肋骨戳，	Haihan's army chased after them
只听惨叫声不断。	And arrived at a flat place in the central city Yunlong,
一直追杀到洪冈②的中心，	Stabbing the enemies' ribs with their spears,
老弱妇孺忙求饶，	Causing constant groaning and screaming of pain.
到处鬼哭神号人又喊。	Finally they arrived at *honggang*②, the center of the city
有的开口骂俸改：	Where the elderly, women and children all begged for mercy,
"只因俸改太霸道，	And moaning and screaming were heard everywhere.
勐景罕才遭此大难。"	Some of the people cursed Fenggai loudly:
俸改的土地宽又广，	"Just because you are too arrogant,
年轻的妻子多又多，	Our Mengjinghan has to suffer so much."
即使从早到夜晚，	Fenggai has a broad and vast territory
也难以个个轮着玩。	And so many young wives
他人心不足做坏事，	That some of them have no opportunity
又把海罕的媐崩抢，	To serve him even if they do it in turn.
使得海罕派大军，	
勐景罕因此遭祸殃。	

① 贺：首领。悍：勇猛的士卒。　　① He: chief. Han: brave warrior.
② 洪冈：城的中心地带。　　② Honggang: the central area of a city.

海罕的军队势力大,	He was so greedy that he did evil things
攻城如同在卷布,	Such as robbing Haihan of his wife Nanbeng,
围城如同栽桩打栅栏,	Forcing Haihan to send his army to take her back,
层层围困欲逃无地方。	And putting Mengjinghan in great danger.
满城百姓人心乱,	Haihan's powerful troops
绫罗绸缎遍地扔。	Attacked the city as easily as rolling up a piece of cloth,
年轻姑娘流眼泪,	And beseidged the city as easily as building a fence,
一手拿背巾,	Letting nobody flee away.
一手又把娃娃牵,	All the folks in the city were now utterly distraught,
开口求饶跪地上:	Leaving silk and satin here and there while trying to flee.
"求你海罕军,	Young women wept sadly,
十几岁的人请不要杀,	Holding baby carriers with one hand
留下为你当奴隶,	And leading children with the other,
为你割草采冬叶①,	Kneeling down and begging for mercy:
只求吃碗热米饭。	"Please, Haihan!
勐景罕归你来管,	Don't kill young kids.
留下我们不要杀,	Leave them to be your slaves
会守你在火塘边,	To cut grass and gather *dongye*① for you.
会服侍你在床旁。	They ask for only a bowl of rice in exchange.
善良的召法尼海罕啊,	Now you have become the ruler of Mengjinghan,
我们的命在你手上!"	Please leave us alive.
勐景罕的兵丁舞刀矛,	We will serve you by the fireplace

---

① 冬叶：叶宽约二十到三十公分，长约四十公分，用来包菜饭。

① Dongye: a kind of leaves used to wrap food, which are usually 20-30 cm wide and 40 cm long.

厘俸 // Li Feng

如醉如痴乱戳又乱砍，	And by the bed.
无法突围困城中，	Kindhearted Zhao Fani Haihan!
尸体成堆人叠人，	Our lives are all in your hands."
鲜血满脸难分辨，	Soldiers of Mengjinghan waved swords and spears,
哭哭叫叫阴风惨。	Stabbing and chopping insanely.
	None of them could break out of the encirclement,
	And dead bodies piled up.
	Their blood-stained faces made it hard to tell one from another.
	An evil wind blew with cries and howls.
桑洛率领兵和将，	Leading his soldiers and generals,
冲到贺允中城吼声响。	Sangluo marched loudly into the city center.
海罕另一支兵马也赶来，	Another army of Haihan also arrived
战象齐聚如森林。	With a forest of war elephants.
桑色、桑温的天兵也赶到，	Sangse and Sangwen also flooded into the city
浩浩荡荡洪水般。	With their heavenly troops.
桑温、赛伦也来到，	Sangwen and Sailun also arrived,
象牙密似秧田的篱笆。	The tusks of their elephants as dense as a rice field fence.
汉高波也随后来，	Hangaobo also arrived
身后兵马一串串。	With arrays of soldiers and horses.
混嘿南也到达，	Hun Heinan also arrived
象队排列如鱼贯。	With elephants coming in succession.
崩南宛多法也来了，	Bengnanwanduofa also came with his troops,

带领兵马到处砍。	Slaughtering their enemies on the way.
冈庄也来了，	Gangzhuang also came,
大象多又多，	With hundreds of elephants
栅栏全部被撞翻。	Knocking down the stables.
向冈、向戛也来了，	Xianggang and Xiangga also came,
象牙沾着的鲜血还未干。	Blood dripping from their elephants' tusks.
艾包、尼崩也来了，	Ai Bao and Ni Beng also came,
士兵紧握手中矛。	Their soldiers holding spears.
赛道和桑混伦也来了，	Sai Dao and Sang Hunlun also came,
象群把城中房屋撞。	Their elephants dashing against the houses.
波道坚混免也来了，	Bodaojianhunmian also came,
兵将杀人如砍瓜。	His soldiers killing people with no mercy.
天神布冈罕也来了，	God Buganghan also came,
天兵放火把房烧，	His troops burning the houses,
烟雾笼罩勐景罕。	Engulfing Mengjinghan in smoke.
艾道闷鲁天也来了，	God Aidaomenlutian also came,
带领千头好战象。	Leading a thousand war elephants.
雷公召法免也来了，	Zhao Famian, the God of Thunder, also came
天兵宝剑如星闪。	His heavenly soldiers holding shiny swords.
召桑本也来了，	Zhao Sangben also came,
蹬着大象要出战。	Riding his elephant Zhanbaibin
战象占拜兵到处冲，	And dashing here and there,
踩死俸改的兵和将。	Killing Fenggai's soldiers and generals.
冈罕和桑海也来了，	Ganghan and Sanghai also came,

厘俸 // Li Feng

手下人马遍山冈。	Their soldiers all over the mountains.
天神召法洪桑兰在天空,	God Zhaofa Hongsanglan stayed in the sky,
又是呼风又唤雨。	Busy calling up winds and summoning rains.
天兵拿着雷斧劈下来,	The heavenly soldiers struck down with axes,
只听一声霹雳响,	And, as thunder crashed,
击中俸改的金幡幢。	Split into pieces
金幡幢插在象舆上,	Fenggai's golden prayer flag
转眼散落成碎片。	Fixed on the howdah.
俸改的大象乱又乱,	Without the riders on their back,
失去主人跑四方。	Fenggai's elephant ran away in panic.
兵将撤退到允龙,	Fenggai's troops retreated to the inner city Yunlong,
海罕的大军追杀到允冈,	While Haihan's army chased them to Yungang,
允冈地处允龙城中央。	Which was in the center of Yunlong.
在允冈的洪囡①又开战,	Another battle started in Hongnan① of Yungang.
只见矛戳血溅人倒地,	There were again in the battlefield flying spears,
尸首分家各一方。	Splashing blood, and dead bodies without heads.
杀到俸改住地洪允坚,	Haihan's army reached Hongyunjian, Fenggai's palace,
此处有二十层防御大栅栏,	Which was protected by twenty layers of strong fences
内有精锐兵马和战象。	And crack troops and elephants.
俸改坚守洪允坚,	Fenggai retreated to hold his ground in Hongyunjian.
翻身一跃下了象。	When he jumped off his elephant,
妻妾全都围上来,	His wife and concubines all came and surrounded him,
拉着衣服问长又问短。	Making inquiries and showing concern.

---

① 洪：衙门。囡：小。

① Hongnan: Hong: the administration building. Nan: small.

嬭崩看见俸改已受伤，	Seeing Fenggai was wounded,
躲在后面暗自笑。	Nanbeng laughed behind their backs.
娥宾拿出牙窝莱，	Ebing took out some *yawolai*
给俸改止血医创伤。	To stop the wound from bleeding.
海罕命令阿巫戛：	Haihan ordered Awu Ga:
"阿巫戛啊，阿巫戛，	"Awu Ga, oh Awu Ga!
请你快把嬭崩看！"	Please go to look for Nanbeng immediately!"
阿巫戛拿出万拉纳①，	Awu Ga took out *wanlana*①,
朝自己身上一涂抹，	And smeared his body with it.
马上变成一个黑奴隶，	He then turned into a slave
全身黑黑如烧炭。	With skin as black as charcoal.
又把身子轻轻摇，	Swaying his body gently,
转眼就到俸改的宫廷中。	He soon got to Fenggai's palace.
他到处寻找到处看，	Being invisible,
别人却不能看见他。	He searched all around.
他看见嬭崩仍安在，	Seeing Nanbeng was safe and sound,
急忙回营报海罕。	He hurried back to report to Haihan.
雷公继续劈天斧，	The God of Thunder kept slashing with his axe,
劈中洪允坚北面，	Hitting the north side of Hongyunjian
城墙轰然倒地响。	And destroying the city walls there.
劈中洪允坚南面，	He then struck the south side of Hongyunjian,

---

① 万拉纳：一种药，涂上这种药，人会改变脸型。 ① Wanlana: a kind of medicine. When it is applied, people may change their appearance.

厘俸 // Li Feng

城墙哗哗齐倒塌。	Toppling down the city walls there.
海罕率领各路军,	Haihan led all of his troops
直捣勐景罕城心脏。	To march straight to the heart of Mengjinghan.
俸改走投无路心中急,	Finding nowhere to flee,
如同野火在燃烧,	Fenggai was desperate,
大火已烧到身旁。	As if a wild fire was approaching him.
他知死难已临头,	Knowing that death was near,
面对众妻妾把话讲:	He spoke to his wives and concubines:
"我的城池将被占,	"My city is going to be occupied,
大象将被俘来又被砍。	And my elephants are to be captured and killed.
我只好骑着飞马找叶金,	I have to ride my flying horse to ask Yejin,
她是我的大姐会帮忙。	My elder sister, for help.
她管辖下的地方宽又广,	Her territory is vast and broad,
靠近天边望不断。	Extending to the horizon.
我这个落难的大官,	I, a defeated king,
只有靠她躲灾难!	Can only seek asylum there.
她住的地方远又远,	Her place is so remote,
除了我谁也走不到。	That no one except me can reach there.
众妻妾啊, 莫悲伤,	My dear wives and concubines, don't be sad!
你们取出我的宝剑和宝袋,	Take out my sword and treasure bag for me.
宝袋挎肩上,	With the treasure bag amulet on my back
手持宝剑先往东面看,	And my sword in my hand, I look to the east first,
东面长矛闪闪映阳光。	And see long spears flashing in the sunlight.
再朝北面看,	I look to the north

桑洛的象队到处是。	And see Sangluo's elephants everywhere.
再往南面瞧，	I then look to the south,
红杆金矛看不断。	Finding red-handled golden spears everywhere.
又朝西面看，	Then I look to the west,
海罕的象队排成串，	Seeing Haihan's elephants in arrays,
象牙如秧田间的篱笆。	With tusks as dense as fences around a rice field.
形势危急我先走，	I have to go first due to the critical situation,
离开你们时间不会长！"	But won't leave you alone very long."
俸改刚把话说完，	As soon as Fenggai finished his words,
只听北面咚的一声巨响，	With a loud sound from the north,
二十路人马冲杀来。	Twenty columns of soldiers dashed out.
又听南面咚的一声响，	With another loud sound from the south,
俸改的兵丁哭又喊。	Fenggai' soldiers cried and moaned loudly.
占艾兰呆立不吃草，	Zhan'ailan stood numb and did not graze,
英着节也一样。	So did Yingzhejie.
眼看主人要远走，	Noticing their master was leaving,
两头大象呜咽身打战。	The two elephants sobbed and trembled.
满屋妻妾急又慌，	His wives and concubines gathered in the palace,
宫廷中央团团转。	Upset and panicked.
全都拉着俸改的手，	They all held Fenggai's hands,
哭哭啼啼声凄凉。	Weeping and wailing sorrowfully.
婻崩也假装在流泪，	Nanbeng pretended to be sad as well,
手揩眼睛无泪珠。	Wiping her tearless eyes.
娥宾搂着俸改腰，	Ebing put her arms around Fenggai's waist,

厘俸 // Li Feng

哭得晕倒在地上。	Crying and fainting on the ground.
咪埃汪把俸改搂，	Miaiwang held Fenggai's waist,
哭得像个醉人样，	Wailing like a drunken person.
边哭边对俸改说：	She spoke to Fenggai:
"亲爱的召法勐俸罕啊，	"Dear respectful Zhao Famengfenghan!
请你拔出宝刀来，	Please pull out your sword
先把我们都杀光！"	And kill us all before you leave!"
妻妾中有人又开口：	One of the wives and the concubines said:
"召法勐俸罕啊，	"Our Zhao Famengfenghan !
请你把毒药给我们，	Please give us some poison!
别把我们留在世，	Don't leave us alive.
做人家的奴隶命太惨！"	It is miserable to become people' slaves."
有的妻妾又开口：	Another said:
"自从我们来到宫廷中，	"Since we came to your palace,
早晚只知摆桌椅，	We know only how to arrange tables and chairs
小心侍奉送酒又送饭。	And serve you wine and food.
不知你心中想些啥，	We don't know what is in your mind actually,
一年才同我们玩一次，	For you come to stay with each of us just once a year.
好像把我们关在厩里养，	We are encaged in the palace like horses shut up in a stable!
太阳一落门上闩，	Every day at sunset the door is closed,
有人守卫在门旁。"	Guarded by the soldiers."
有的妻妾互相说：	The wives and concubines continued to complain:
"一年到头长又长，	"All the year round,
只有一二天才能床头见，	We can sleep with Hunfeng Fenggai for just one or two days.

现在混俸要逃了，	Now that he is running away,
我们应该放声笑，	We should laugh happily.
为什么还要空悲伤？	Why are we sorrowful?
海罕来攻勐景罕，	Haihan has come to Mengjinghan
要夺走占艾兰，	To capture Zhan'ailan,
还有山包样高大的英着节。	The mountainlike Yingzhejie,
还要夺走妻子和姑娘，	And wives and maids.
决不会把我们一刀杀。	He won't kill us at all.
勐景哈的伙子见我们，	When the young soldiers of Mengjingha meet us,
眼睛就会斜着看。	They will steal a glance at us,
我们生得白又嫩，	Who are fair and young,
就像十七八岁的少女一个样。	Like maids of seventeen or eighteen.
等着勐景哈的伙子来，	When the young soldiers of Mengjingha come,
我们和他们随心玩。	We'll have as much fun with them as we like.
你们不要再哭了，	So stop crying!
应该欢笑开心肠！"	We should all laugh with joy instead!"
俸改手持宝刀肩背宝石袋，	Sword in his hand and treasure bag amulet on his shoulder,
到处观察到处看。	Fenggai looked around and observed the situation.
只见大小城门烟雾漫，	Seeing all the city wall gates were engulfed in smoke,
他乘机翻身骑飞马，	He mounted his flying horse,
飞往空中去逃亡。	And flew into the sky.
勐景罕城内一片乱，	His city was in a mess,
俸改的兵马死的死，	With soldiers either dead or injured.

厘俸 // Li Feng

受伤的忙找地方藏,	The injured were trying to find a hiding place
不受伤的四处逃。	While the uninjured were fleeing.
海罕的大军一直冲,	Haihan's troops kept marching forward
冲到俸改的宫廷墙院下,	Till they reached the foot of Fenggai's palace wall,
有的守兵还抵抗,	Where some of Fenggai's soldiers were still
人少力单怎能挡?	Resisting in vain.
勐景罕的城内和城外,	Those inside and outside the city of Mengjinghan,
都是海罕的兵和将。	Were all Haihan's soldiers.
俸改的军队越战人越少,	Fenggai's troops were decreasing fast.
海罕的兵丁忙着抢大象。	Haihan's soldiers were busy catching elephants.
有的兵丁被大象踩伤了,	Some of them were trodden on
勇猛的武士骑在象身上,	And wounded by the elephants
把踩伤的兵丁来嘲笑,	And were laughed at by those riding the elephants.
笑声哭声传四方。	The laughter and cries were heard everywhere.
有的一人俘虏大象两三头,	Some of them each captured several elephants,
有的牵着俘虏一串串。	And others each led a line of captives.
弱小的兵丁眼巴巴,	The short and weak soldiers helplessly watched
看着别人把战利品抢,	Others plundering and looting
边看边把眼泪揩,	And wiped their tears,
自骂无能不像样。	Blaming their own incompetence.
海罕坐着占拜舍,	Haihan urged Zhanbaishe forward,
冲进俸改的宫廷四处看。	And dashed into Fenggai's palace and looked around.

贺纳^①不见婻崩影，	He couldn't find Nanbeng in Hena①,
又转过大象到贺得^②，	Then he came to Hede②,
贺得不见婻崩面。	But still did not see Nanbeng there.
占拜舍又鼻指贺干^③，	Zhanbaishe pointed its trunk at Hegan③,
海罕急忙蹬大象。	And Haihan spurred it in a hurry,
婻崩果然在那里，	And finally found Nanbeng there,
坐在金堆银堆上。	Sitting on piles of gold and silver.
婻崩一见海罕忙起身，	She rose to her feet at the sight of Haihan,
频频招手口中喊。	And motioned and spoke to him.
大象知情地下跪，	Haihan's elephant knowingly knelt down
海罕急忙跳下象。	And Haihan quickly got off.
夫妻二人紧拥抱，	The husband and wife embraced each other tightly.
婻崩呜咽把话讲：	Nanbeng sobbed and said:
"自从离开你以后，	"Ever since I left you,
日子苦似黄连般。	My life has been as bitter as goldthread.
每天求神保佑我，	Every day, I pray to the gods to bless me
与你早日相见偎身旁。	So that I will be united with you.
自从与你分别后，	Ever since I left you,
就像跳入火坑中，	It is like falling into a fire pit.
梦中团圆夜夜想。	Every night I dreamed of us getting together.
我的召海法啊，	My respectable Zhao Haifa!
我几次打算去死掉，	Several times I have intended to kill myself

---

① 贺纳：北面官廷。
② 贺得：南面官廷。
③ 贺干：中间的官廷。

① Hena: the northern palace.
② Hede: the southern palace.
③ Hegan: the center palace.

厘俸 // Li Feng

又怕你心中太悲伤。	But feared that you would be very much aggrieved.
我知道你会来救我，	I knew you would come to attack this place
有朝一日打进来，	To rescue me one day,
站在俸改的八层高楼上，	And you and I would stand on Fenggai's eight-storey building
你我两人同喜又共欢。	And enjoy our happy reunion.
想到这些我咬紧牙，	Thinking about all of this, I gritted my teeth
忍受侮辱活下来，	And lived with disgrace and humiliation.
终于乌云消散见太阳！"	At last, the dark clouds dissipated and the sun came out!"
婻崩牵着海罕的手，	Nanbeng held Haihan's hand,
坐在宫廷正中央，	Sitting in the center of the court
面对众人开口讲：	And spoke to the people present:
"亲爱的众将官啊，	"My dear officers and generals!
我的弟弟们①！	My dear younger brothers[①]!
你们为我太辛苦，	You have endured so much hardship because of me
我当姐姐的太惭愧，	And I feel so sorry for that.
没有衣物来送上。	I don't have clothes to send you as gifts.
我要请求混海罕，	Rather I'd like to beg Hun Haihan
挑选出最美丽的姑娘，	To choose some beautiful maids for you
送给你们做妻子。	As your wives.
我为你们拴线祝美满，	I wish you good marriages and happy family life!
亲爱的弟弟们啊！"	My dear younger brothers!"
众将让出一条路，	

---

① 婻崩出生在王族家庭，等级比她小的人，不论年龄大小，都称为弟妹。

① Nanbeng was born in a royal family. People who are inferior in class than her, no matter younger or older, are called "younger brother or sister".

桑本走上前，	The officers and generals made way
向嫂嫂婻崩叩拜，	For Sangben, who stepped forward
桑温穿着龙袍也跟上。	And kowtowed to his sister-in-law Nanbeng,
召冈、召伴也叩拜，	Followed by Sangwen in his dragon robe,
一千个勐的首领，	Zhaogang and Zhaoban,
所有的俸混，	The chiefs of the one thousand *mengs*,
齐来叩拜婻崩和海罕。	And all the officers.
海罕一一来扶起，	Haihan stepped forward to help them up one by one,
让大家坐在金椅上。	And asked them to be seated on the golden chairs.
娥宾心术很不正，	Ebing was not a faithful wife.
心中还把俸改想，	She still missed Fenggai
蒙头盖被哭得慌。	And cried in her bedroom.
阿巫戛闻声走进房，	Awu Ga entered the room
把她牵出见桑洛。	And took her out to see Sangluo.
她一手揩眼泪，	She wiped her tears with one hand,
一手牵着女儿一小双。	And held her two daughters with another.
桑洛看见怒火起，	Sangluo was furious.
拔出宝刀杀娥宾，	He pulled out his sword to kill Ebing.
海罕急忙来劝告：	Haihan stopped him and said:
"当混的不能把妻砍，	"You, as a Hun, an officer, shouldn't kill your wife,
命运让你们结成双。	As fate has united you two as a couple.
当召的不能把妻砍，	You, as a Zhao, a leader, shouldn't kill your wife.
杀妻有罪不应当。	It's a sin that you should not commit.

厘俸 // Li Feng

亲爱的召桑洛弟弟啊,	My dear brother Zhao Sangluo!
你要冷静细思量。"	You should calm down and think it over."
桑洛把宝刀插入鞘,	Sangluo put the sword back into the sheath,
心中暗暗在想:	Thinking:
当众杀妻不太好,	It is not appropriate to kill my wife in public.
还会得罪混海罕。	And it may offend Hun Haihan.
我只好息怒,	I have to calm my anger
拿出好心肠。	And show my mercy and forgiveness instead.
他想到这里大声说:	He then spoke loudly:
"我奋力来攻勐景罕,	"I fought Mengjinghan with all my might,
一心想着爱妻不变心。	Expecting my wife to be faithful.
拼命作战不怕死,	I fought with courage, never afraid of death,
肋巴骨挣得痛又痛,	And endured all the pain and hardship
为的是爱妻回身旁。	So that I could take back my beloved wife.
海罕也为婻崩来,	Haihan, too, fought for his Nanbeng.
婻崩梳妆又打扮,	She dressed herself up
坐在金堆银堆上,	And sat on the gold and silver,
把郎君等待和盼望。	Waiting for her husband to come and rescue her.
娥宾你却不像她,	You, Ebing, however,
哭哭啼啼恋俸改,	Still love Fenggai and even cry for him.
不知羞耻我心伤。	Your shamelessness hurts me so much.
娥宾啊,	Oh Ebing!
你完全变了一个样!"	You have changed completely!"
桑洛愤怒又迷茫,	Sangluo felt angry and perplexed,

就像山中云雾一团团。	As if his sight was blurred by a mountain fog.
要不是海罕在劝阻，	If Haihan had not stopped him,
他真想了结此事，	He would have severed his relationship with Ebing
和娥宾一刀成两段。	Once and for all.
海罕获胜分姑娘，	Haihan, as winner of the war, began to distribute captive girls.
俸改的小女儿曾出嫁，	Fenggai's youngest daughter, who had been
嫁给腊姐的首领作妻子，	Married to the chief of Lajie,
现在分配给混桑洛，	Was now given to Hun Sangluo
服侍桑洛不离他身旁。	To serve him all her life.
另一个女儿分配给桑本，	Another daughter of Fenggai was given to Sangben
早晚为他把衣服穿。	To help him get dressed every day.
俸改所有的妻妾全分完，	All of Fenggai's wives and concubines
分给海罕手下的众将官。	Were distributed to Haihan's generals and officers.
第二天海罕早起床，	Haihan got up early the next day,
命令打扫宫廷设酒宴。	Ordering people to clean the palace and hold a banquet.
各勐的官员都来齐，	The chiefs of each *meng* were all present,
海罕拿出金银和财宝，	And were rewarded with
分给大家作奖赏。	Gold, silver, and jewelry.
牵出战马和战象，	Haihan led out horses and elephants
分给桑色和桑勐。	And gave them to Sangse and Sangmeng,
两位天神不接受，	But the two gods declined the offer

厘俸 // Li Feng

齐声开口把话讲：	And spoke together:
"树虽砍倒根未挖，	"Although the tree is cut down,
将来还会重发芽。	The root remains and will sprout someday.
俸改逃亡在他乡.	Fenggai has fled
恐怕战争不会断。	And may come back for more wars.
金银财宝我们有，	We have enough gold and jewelry,
你们拿去作战费，	These rewards should be used
建设地方蓄力量。	To build up your military forces.
亲爱的海法侄儿啊，	Dear Haihan, our nephew!
你的心意我们记心上！"	We will remember your kindness!"
海罕摇头又回答：	Haihan shook his head and said:
"你两老率领天兵和天将，	"You two led heavenly soldiers and generals
支援我们打胜仗。	To help me win the war.
为什么不接受金银和财宝，	You deserve the gold and the silver and the jewelry,
亲爱的长辈双混啊，	My two respectable seniors!
这样做我心中很不安！"	Your refusal makes me uneasy!"
海罕转身问阿巫戛：	Haihan then turned to Awu Ga and asked:
"阿巫戛啊，阿巫戛，	"Awu Ga! Oh, Awu Ga!
我们已占领了勐景罕，	We have now occupied Mengjinghan,
可是俸改逃跑了，	But unfortunately Fenggai has fled.
不知现在在何方？	We have no idea where he has gone.
你行走如飞似斑鸠，	You can run as fast as a turtledove flies,
请你快快去察看。	So please go to search for him.
找到之后快回来，	Come back when you find him,

我们率军再征战，	Then we will go and fight him again.
不捉回俸改心不甘！"	I won't give up if Fenggai is not caught!"
阿巫戛接令离宫廷，	Awu Ga followed the order and left the palace.
站在高处放眼望，	When he looked around from a high position,
他身上长有千只眼，	He could see everything,
能看到一切毫不放。	As he had one thousand eyes on his body.
他行走如风云，	He walked swiftly like the wind,
看见俸改在前方，	And saw that Fenggai was ahead
那是勐龙拍郎林，	In remote Menglongpailanglin,
那里人走不到有魔王。	Where only devils lived and no people trod.
阿巫戛回营急报告，	Awu Ga turned back to report promptly.
海罕命令艾冈罕：	Haihan then ordered general Ai Ganghan:
"艾冈罕啊，艾冈罕，	"Ai Ganghan! Oh, Ai Ganghan!
俗话说得好，	As the saying goes,
胜利者才能当道①，	Only the winner can become a *dao*①,
勤奋者才能当混，	Only the hard-working man can become a *Hun*.
有福者才能坐大象，	Only the lucky man can ride an elephant,
倾家荡产者臭名传千里。	And only the bankrupt man becomes notorious.
冈罕啊，	Oh, Ganghan,
你要把俸改活捉拿，	You must go and capture Fenggai alive,
立功回来我重赏。	And return with honor and receive my rewards.
哪里的土地最宽广，	I will grant you
我就把它封给你。	The vastest fief in our kingdom.

---

① 道：官职，勐以上的官员。　　① Dao: high official.

厘俸 // Li Feng

众婳满室又满堂，	I will fill your house with many ladies,
由你挑选随你占，	Who will be selected by you.
还要赐给你大象。"	And I will give you elephants."
冈罕跪下忙叩拜：	Ganghan knelt down and said:
"我的召海法啊，	"My respectable Zhao Haifa!
我冈罕是奴臣，	Ganghan is under your leadership
你的吩咐重如山，	And will always obey you
怎敢不听来违抗？	And never defy you.
我冈罕是孤儿，	I am an orphan,
无牵无挂身胆壮，	Free of care but full of courage.
混勐让我捉俸改，	I will set out without hesitation
我立即出发不停留。	At your command to catch Fenggai.
我的召海法啊，	My respectable Zhao Haifa!
不捉到俸改我不回来！"	I will not come back until I capture Fenggai!"

冈罕回营敲金鼓，	Ganghan went back to his camp,
鼓声咚咚命令传。	And with the boom of drums,
全军整装齐出发，	The troops were ready to set out.
日夜兼程蹬大象。	They urged their elephants forward day and night
来到一条大江边，	And came to a large river with rapid currents.
水流湍急无人烟。	No people lived there.
渡口拴着几只船，	There were several ferries
只见一只大螃蟹，	And a gaint crab
大如箩笆一个样。	As big as a bamboo fence.

冈罕下令快渡江,	Ganghan ordered his men to cross the river quickly,
大象吼叫往回退,	But the elephants cried and moved back,
原来是螃蟹把大象腿夹伤。	For their feet were gripped by crab claws.
冈罕急得没办法,	Anxious Ganghan had no choice
只好把大象紧紧拉,	But to fasten the elephants tightly
拴在竹筏和船上。	To the bamboo rafts and boats.
螃蟹又来夹竹筏,	The crab then pinched the bamboo rafts,
竹筏在水中摇摇晃。	Making them wobbling on the water.
冈罕只好不渡江,	Ganghan had to give up
扎起大营在江岸。	And encamped beside the river temporarily.
派人到山中砍藤条,	He sent his men to get some rattan on the mountains.
又将藤条搓成绳,	They twisted them into ropes,
再把绳子织成网,	Wove the ropes into nets,
然后把网水中放,	Put them into the river,
捉住螃蟹甩岸上。	Caught the crabs, and threw them on the shore.
从此以后传下来,	Ever since then this tradition of fishing with nets
人们织网来捕鱼。	Has been passed down from generation to generation.
冈罕的人马渡过江,	Ganghan and his men got across the river,
到达勐龙拍郎林。	And arrived at Menglongpailanglin.
一座城池在前方,	Seeing a city in the distance,
冈罕的人马不停蹄,	They went on quickly
立即把城团团围。	And surrounded it tightly.
城中住着魔鬼群,	Inside the city there lived
上天入地不费力,	Groups of fierce and terrible demons who could fly in

厘俸 // Li Feng

凶猛可怕不一般。
见到冈罕来围城，
他们派人把话讲：
"俸改有难来投奔，
我们怎能把他捆，
轻而易举送你们？
你们赶快骑上象，
空跑一趟把家回。"
冈罕几次派使者，
面对魔鬼把话传：
"俸改的领土那么大，
已经陷落不归他。
你们孤城一座势力单，
为什么留下俸改还不放？
如果我们要攻城，
你们无人支援无人帮。
你们快把俸改来捆绑，
交给我们送海罕。
只有这样做，
你们才能得平安。"
魔王名叫布皮拍，
冷笑一声来回答：
"海罕攻下勐景罕，
算他撞在好运上。

the sky
And burrow into the earth with ease
They saw Ganghan come to surround their city
And sent messages to him:
"Fenggai turned to us for help.
How can we bind him
And let you take him away easily?
You'd better get on your elephants,
And go back home empty-handed."
Ganghan sent messengers several times
To deliver his words to the devils:
"As vast Fenggai's territory was,
He has lost it now.
Your city is weak and small.
Why do you insist on keeping Fenggai there?
If we attack you,
No one will support or rescue you.
You'd better tie him up
And hand him over to Haihan.
Only in this way
Can you stay safe and live in peace."
The King of the demons, named Bupipai,
Replied with a sneer:
"Occupying Mengjinghan successfully

如果事前俸改通知我，	Was just a fluke for Haihan.
我会带着魔鬼皮来里，	If I had been informed earlier by Fenggai,
他手拿长刀会钻地，	I would have sent the devil Pilaili,
把海罕大军搅得天昏又地暗，	Who holds a long knife and can disappear underground,
他就攻不下勐景罕。	To stir Haihan's troops into a mess.
现在派来你冈罕，	And Haihan wouldn't have occupied Mengjinghan.
人少马少象也少，	Now you are sent here.
要想攻城是梦想！	With a few soldiers and horses and elephants,
你未免过分小看人，	It is impossible for you to take our city!
好像天下只有你是男子汉！"	Don't look down upon me!
话刚落音下命令，	You are not the only hero in the world!"
城中敲锣又打鼓。	As soon as Pupipai's voice faded away,
魔鬼纷纷跑出来，	The drum and gongs were beaten in the city
又吼又叫战冈罕。	And the devils all came out, roaring and shouting,
冈罕的兵马久经战，	To fight Ganghan.
人人武艺都高强，	Ganghan had an army of experienced soldiers
同魔鬼作战手不软。	Very skillful in military tactics
冈罕下令放土炮，	Who showed no mercy while fighting.
魔鬼密密满城墙。	Ganghan ordered his men to fire cannons
射出鲁非一串串，	At the numerous devils standing on the city wall.
有的魔鬼钻进地，	As the *lufei*s were fired,
城中空空无一人，	The devils disappeared underground for protection,
后面包抄围冈罕。	Leaving the whole city empty and deserted.
冈罕人马只顾前，	

厘俸 // Li Feng

忽听后面吼声响,	But they went on to attack Ganghan from behind.
魔鬼从地下钻出来,	Absorbed in the situation ahead,
前后左右齐冲上。	Ganghan's troops suddenly heard roars coming from behind
冈罕的兵丁难招架,	And saw devils coming out of the ground,
死伤成堆难计算,	Dashing forward from all directions.
犹如满山木柴遍地放。	Ganghan's soldiers could not resist
活着的只好互相掩护往后退,	And countless numbers of them were injured and killed,
败回营中气还喘。	Scattered on the ground like firewood in the mountains.
勐龙拍郎林攻不下,	Those who were still alive, covering each other,
冈罕心中似火燃。	Retreated to their camps out of breath.
阿巫戛想出一妙计,	Menglongpailanglin remained intact,
派兵上山把竹砍,	Making Ganghan flare with anger.
做成达了①一个个,	Awu Ga suddenly came up with a good idea.
魔鬼必经之路全放上。	He sent some soldiers to cut bamboo on the mountain
	And make some *dales*①
	To be put on the road the devils must take.
第二天天刚蒙蒙亮,	The next day when dawn was just breaking,
冈罕下令敲起鼓。	Ganghan ordered his men to beat drums.

---

① 达了：用竹篾编成菱形的篱笆，用木棍插在路上，表示外勐的人不能进入村寨，如果用艾草绳穿挂在家门口，能克制魔鬼。

① Dale: diamond-shaped bamboo fence. When it stands on the road, it indicates that people from other *mengs* can not enter the village. If it is hung on the door of a house with wormwood, it has the power of driving away evil spirits.

兵丁纷纷去攻城，	The soldiers all went to attack the city,
城中魔鬼又钻入地。	Forcing the devils to go underground again.
当从地下钻出来，	When they came up,
头脖正好卡在达了上。	Their heads were trapped by the *dales*.
冈罕的兵丁返回身，	Ganghan's soldiers turned around
把魔鬼脑袋全部砍，	And cut off their heads
如砍南瓜一个样。	As easily as cutting pumpkins.
魔鬼伤亡惨又重，	The devils suffered heavy losses
血迹斑斑映泥塘。	And their blood stained the mires.
达了的功劳实在大，	*Dales* contributed so much
用它来把魔鬼克，	In defeating the devils
世世代代后人传。	That this story has been passed down from generation to generation.
俸改失去依靠心发慌，	Fenggai then had nobody to rely on and began to panic.
骑上飞马穿云层。	He rode on a flying horse across the sky
到达遥远天边勐乜缅，	And arrived at remote Mengmiemian
他大姐住在这地方。	Where his elder sister lived.

冈罕派人送书信，	Ganghan sent a letter to Haihan
把详情告诉海罕：	To inform him of everything in detail:
"到了勐龙拍郎林，	"When we got to Menglongpailanglin,
我们准备把俸改来捉拿。	We were all ready to capture Fenggai alive.
魔鬼保护俸改又作乱，	But the devils protected Fenggai and made things difficult.
现在我们已把城攻破，	Now we have occupied the city

厘俸 // Li Feng

攻城伤亡一千五。	At the cost of one thousand and five hundred soldiers' lives.
俸改无处再躲藏，	Fenggai could find no place to hide
骑着飞马上天际。	And had to flee into the sky on a flying horse.
我们带着兵马去追赶，	We are now chasing after him
不捉到俸改心不甘。	And will not give up until we seize him.
我的混勐啊，	My respectable Hunmeng!
等着胜利消息传！"	Wait for our news of victory!"
第二天冈罕又起程，	Ganghan set off again the next day,
大军滚滚如波浪。	With his troops marching like rolling waves.
到达天边勐乜缅，	When they arrived at remote Mengmiemian,
一封书信射城中，	They shot a letter into the city,
要求尽快把俸改交，	Requiring people there to hand over Fenggai promptly.
如果不交就攻城。	If not, the city would be attacked.
城中派出使者来，	Then a messenger came out
提出问题问冈罕：	To ask Ganghan some questions:
"勐景罕已经被攻下，	"Mengjinghan has been occupied.
海罕的人马到底有多少？	How many troops does Haihan actually have?
勐景罕已成灰烬！	Mengjinghan has been burned to ashes!
海罕的战象到底有多少？	How many elephants does Haihan actually have?
冈罕啊！	Oh Ganghan!
请你回答别隐瞒。"	Please tell me and don't conceal the fact."
冈罕连忙来回答：	Ganghan quickly replied:
"海罕的战象数不清，	"Haihan has countless war elephants,
天兵就有八十万。	And eight hundred thousand heavenly soldiers.

我带的人马多又多，	I have a great number of soldiers,
他们在途中放大象，	Who are feeding their elephants on the way
让我冈罕打先锋。	And I come first as the vanguard.
我紧跟俸改足迹来，	I followed Fenggai's footsteps here
大队人马在后面，	And behind me is our main force
浩浩荡荡云雾般。	With great strength and vigour.
战象到处在吃草，	Our war elephants graze everywhere,
足足遍布十个勐。	Dotting the land of ten *mengs*.
如果海罕的大军到，	When Haihan's troops all arrive,
勐乜缅很快也要丢！	Mengmiemian will soon be defeated!
如果你们想和好，	If you want to make peace,
就把俸改反绑胳膊交给我，	Tie Fenggai's arms behind his back
我要用一个大颈枷，	And hand him over to me.
卡在他的脖子上，	I will put a chain on his neck,
押回营中送海罕。	And take him to Haihan's camp.
我的陶姐冈俸勐①啊，	My taojiegangfengmeng①,
请你认真考虑仔细想！"	Please think it over!"
使者传话回城中，	The messenger took the word back to the city,
大家忙把事商量。	And the people consulted in a hurry.
有的说：	Some said:
俸改遇难来投靠，	Fenggai came to us for refuge,
不应把他交对方。	And shouldn't be handed over to Ganghan.

---

① 陶姐：民主选举的有威望的老人。冈：官名。俸勐：管理勐的事务的头人。

① Taojie: an old man with high reputation selected by the local people. Gang: an official title. Fengmeng: chief of a *meng*.

厘俸 // Li Feng

有的说：	Others said:
海罕的兵马多如沙，	Haihan has troops as numerous as grains of sand!
海罕的战象多如草，	Haihan's war elephants are as numerous as blades of grass!
我们只有兵马三十万，	We have only three hundred thousand soldiers.
怎么能抵挡！	How can we resist them!
如果不把俸改交，	If we don't hand over Fenggai to Haihan,
全城百姓要遭殃！	Our city and people will suffer!
有的说：	Still others said:
俸改只是一个人，	Fenggai is just one person,
却把灾祸带全城。	But he brings disaster to all the people in our city.
应该把他送出去，	We should send him out
才能保住全城得安宁。	So as to keep the city safe.
大家最后下决心，	Finally they made up their minds
决定把俸改交海罕。	And all agreed to hand Fenggai over to Haihan.
于是就去捆俸改，	Then they went to bind him,
边捆边把他安慰。	And tried to comfort him at the same time.
俸改拉着姐姐不肯去，	Fenggai held his sister's hands and refused to go,
失声痛哭开口讲：	Crying and saying:
"亲爱的姐姐啊，	"My dear sister,
从此不能来相见，	We will neve meet again henceforth!
亲人分离太悲伤！"	Separation makes me feel so sad!"
姐姐流泪说了话：	His sister spoke in tears:
"我孤身一人到这里，	"I came here alone,
无骨肉在身旁，	Accompanied by no relatives or friends,

好像一根细芦苇，	Like a thin reed
夹在苦竹丛中央。	Among groves of bitter bamboo,
姐姐我啊有难处，	I have my own difficulties,
不能救你免灾难。	And cannot help you out.
你回去应该快求情，	You should beg Haihan for mercy
说尽好话求海罕。	With good words.
他一定会发慈悲心，	He is sure to show mercy,
最后把你来饶放。	And finally forgive you.
我的弟弟啊，	My younger brother!
可怜的召法勐俸罕！"	My poor Zhao Famengfenghan!"
姐弟二人抱头哭，	They cried on each other's shoulder
姐姐挥泪转身去。	And the tearful sister had to leave.
兵丁带着俸改出，	As the city gate opened, the soldiers brought Fenggai out
打开城门交冈罕。	And handed him over to Ganghan.
冈罕拿出金颈枷，	Ganghan took out a golden neck chain,
卡在俸改脖子上。	And put it on Fenggai's neck.
然后开口把话讲：	Then Ganghan said:
"因为路途太遥远，	"There is a long way to go.
我怕你半路逃脱找麻烦，	I am afraid you may escape halfway and make trouble,
因此把你的手脚捆，	So I will bind your hands and feet,
脖上套个大颈枷。	And put big chains round your neck.
你的死期还未到，	Your doom hasn't come yet.
还要把你交海罕。	You will be handed over to Haihan.
见了海罕要下跪，	When you see him, kneel down,

厘俸 // Li Feng

叩拜求饶不杀你,	Beg him not to kill you
还会赏你一口饭。"	And give you a mouthful of rice."
冈罕的人马凯旋,	Ganghan's troops returned in triumph.
马放南山象入栏,	The horses cheerfully grazed on the mountains
马欢跳来象把耳朵扇。	And the elephants happily stayed in the stables.
冈罕拉着俸改进宫廷,	Ganghan dragged Fenggai into the court,
人群蜂拥来围观。	Attracting the crowd to flock over and watch.
俸改到了八层高楼上,	Fenggai was taken to the eight-storey building,
只见到处金光闪,	Where his former Dragon Throne was still
昔日的宝座仍然在,	Shining in the whole palace,
如今已被海罕占。	But it was now occupied by Haihan.
他想起往事两眼直流泪,	Tears streamed down his cheeks as he recalled the past.
喉头哽咽拜海罕。	He kowtowed to Haihan and almost choked with sobs.
海罕端坐眯眯笑,	Haihan sat up smiling,
拿起金杯把酒饮,	Took up the golden cup for some drink,
然后叫俸改坐下来。	And asked Fenggai to be seated.
海罕开口把话讲:	Haihan said:
"艾俸温你啊罪该杀,	"Oh Aifengwen Fenggai! You deserve to be killed!
为了给勐景罕留情面,	In order not to embarrass Mengjinghan,
我饶你不死活世上。	I will forgive you and let your live.
让你作为奴隶去养马,	As a slave, you will feed horses
让你割草喂大象!"	And cut grass for elephants!"
俸改直起脖子来回答:	Fenggai straightened his neck and answered:
"我不怕杀来不怕砍,	"I am not afraid of being killed or beheaded.

只求你杀我不要把脸伤,	Kill me, but do not deform my face.
我的脸要留下来,	My face should be left to Nanbeng
留给婻崩亲个够。	For her to kiss as much as she likes.
只求你砍我莫砍脖,	Kill me, but do not cut off my head.
脖子要留给娥宾搂。	I want to leave my neck to Ebing.
要砍只能砍背脊,	You can only hack my back,
那里跳蚤咬了就发痒,	Where it is itchy after being bitten by a flea,
又是手抓不到的地方。	But I just can't scratch it.
海罕啊,	Oh Haihan!
快快动手莫心慌!"	Kill me now and don't be flustered!"
海罕听了怒火上,	Haihan flew into a rage when he heard that.
俸改死到临头还逞强,	Fenggai still taunted him when death was falling.
怎能留他当奴隶?	How could he leave him alive as a slave?
于是下令把他斩。	So Haihan ordered him to be beheaded.
只见俸改脸变色,	Fenggai's face
忽黑忽绿忽发黄。	Turned black, green and yellow.
皮哇豪①拉着他往外走,	He was paralyzed with fright
俸改吓得全身软。	As the executioner dragged him out.
走啊走啊向前走,	They walked on and on
走到太阳落山的阴地方。	Till they got to a shady place where the sun set.
俸改的胡须迎风飘,	Fenggai's beard fluttered in the wind,
两眼暗淡无神光。	And his eyes were dim and lifeless.
走到丛林深处停下来,	They walked into the forest

---

① 皮哇豪:行刑官。

厘俸 // Li Feng

前面一个大凹坑，	And stopped in front of a huge pit,
俸改将要被埋葬。	Where Fenggai was to be buried.
兵丁拿出绳索来，	The soldiers took out a rope,
套住他的脖子就要拉。	Put it around his neck and pulled.
俸改顿时脸发紫，	His face turned purple immediately,
哆哆嗦嗦弯腰站。	And he began to shiver and fall over.
前面的士兵猛一拉，	When the soldier in front gave a sharp pull on the rope,
俸改咚的一声往前倒。	He fell forward with a thud.
后面的士兵猛一拉，	When the soldier in the back gave sharp pull on the rope,
俸改咚的一声往后翻。	He fell backward with a thud.
皮哇豪阵阵发吼声，	With a blast of roar of the *piwahao*①,
俸改咽气蹬脚命已亡。	Fenggai breathed his last breath and died.
全城敲起铓锣和大鼓，	All over the city gongs and drums were beaten
欢呼声震动勐景罕。	And cheerful shouts shook Mengjinghan.

俸改已经被杀死，	The news of Fenggai's death,
消息传到天宫中。	Spread to the palace of heaven.
天神传话到人间：	The gods sent this message:
"做人不要像俸改，	"Do not behave like Fenggai,
作恶多端无好死，	Who did evil deeds and died like a dog,
死后埋葬烂泥塘。	And was buried in a muddy pond.
海罕把此事详细记，	Haihan should write everyting down
俸改的恶行一一写，	To record Fenggai's evil deeds

① Piwahao: executioner.

留给后人天下传。"	To remind and warn future generations."
召尼二月开始攻打俸改，	Zhao Ni started to attack Fenggai in February.
野花开落已七次，	From then on wild flowers had bloomed and faded seven times.
秋雨绵绵已七载，	From then on autumn rain had fallen seven years.
终于才攻下勐景罕。	Mengjinghan at last was conquered.
杀了俸改，	Having killed Fenggai,
海罕坐镇勐景罕。	Haihan stayed at Mengjinghan.
从此嫡崩回身旁，	From then on his wife was returned to him.
二人共把美酒饮，	Together they drank wine,
二人同桌共吃饭，	Together they had meals, and
快乐度日情意长。	They lived happily ever after.
海罕称召是道勐俸，	Haihan claimed to be Zhao of Mengjinghan
消息传遍四面和八方，	And the news spread everywhere,
村村寨寨心喜欢。	Making people in the villages all delighted.
内地汉族的君王知道了，	Even the emperor of the Han people praised Haihan
也齐声把他来称赞。	When he realized the end of the war.
海罕称召力量大，	Haihan was now a Zhao with greater strength and power,
攻下的村寨有一万，	Ruling ten thousand villages as his fiefdom.
成为食邑的好地方。	
海罕已经得天下，	As the ruler of the kingdom,
对部将分封又赐赏，	Haihan granted his generals enfeoffment and rewards,
每年用象、马、金、银作贡纳。	And in return, they paid him yearly tribute
海罕心善良，	In the form of elephants, horses, gold and silver.
美名天下扬！	The kind-hearted Haihan

厘俸 // Li Feng

| | Became prestigious all over the world! |

海罕写信给天宫，	Haihan sent a letter to the heavenly palace,
请求布领暖赐仙丹，	Asking Bulingnuan for an elixir
救活冈晓回人间。	To bring Gangxiao back to life.
布领暖派遣召戛拍，	Bulingnuan then sent Zhaogapai
拿着仙丹就下凡。	To the earth with an elixir.
冈晓的身子仍然在，	Gangxiao's body was still there,
冈晓的头被婻崩藏。	And his head was well kept by Nanbeng.
召戛拍拿过头来脖上连，	Zhaogapai connected the head with the body,
又喂冈晓牙布老①。	And feed him *yabulao*①.
冈晓身子渐渐暖，	Gangxiao's body warmed up gradually,
睁开眼睛复活了。	And he opened his eyes and came to life again.
他起身叩拜召戛拍，	Then he rose and kowtowed to Zhaogapai,
高兴得手舞足蹈胡须扬！	Kicking up his heels with his beard fluttering!
好像睡了几十年，	It seemed that he had been asleep for decades
如今一梦醒来了。	And now he had woken up.
他走向海罕去叩拜，	He went to kowtow to Haihan,
又去问候众将官。	And greeted the generals as well.
人们纷纷围上来，	A crowd gathered around him,
看望冈晓房摇晃。	Their hustle and bustle shaking the house.
这乐坏了召冈和召伴，	The scene made Zhaogang and Zhaoban go wild with joy.

---

① 牙布老：仙草，能使人起死回生。

① Yabulao: a kind of magic grass which can make dead people revive.

二人开口把话讲：	They said:
"自从你战死在战场，	"Ever since you were killed on the battlefield,
日夜都在思念你。	We have been missing you day and night.
现在勐景罕已属我们管，	Now that Mengjinghan belongs to us,
你的英名人人传。"	Everyone is talking about your wisdom and talent."
冈晓捋起手袖说了话：	Gangxiao rolled up his sleeves and said:
"我死又复生不容易，	"It's really not easy for me to be revived after death.
要与各位有福同享有难同当，	You and I should share our joy and sorrow,
白头到老不变心，	Live together till old age with heart unchanged,
保住天下永平安！	And keep the world safe forever!
亲爱的混贺信勐①啊，	Dear hunhexinmengs①!
所有的陶姐冈混俸②，	All my taojieganghunfengs②!
咱们同心有力量！"	We work with one heart and are so powerful!"
海罕命令摆金桌，	Haihan ordered people to set the golden table.
冈晓坐在金椅上，	Gangxiao sat on a golden chair,
只见胡须两边飞，	His beard fluttering from side to side.
冈罕、冈庄坐在旁。	Ganghan and Gangzhuang sat next to him.
海罕也已坐下来，	Haihan was also seated,
两边是布冈戈和布冈伴，	With Bugang Ge and Bugang Ban,
还有桑本和桑温。	Sangben and Sangwen
鼓乐齐鸣歌声扬，	Sitting on both sides,
群群宫女把口弦弹。	There were drum beats, music, and melodious songs,

---

① 混贺信勐：千勐的召幢。
② 陶姐冈混俸：将官，老的布冈等。

① Hunhexinmeng: a chief who governs one thousand *mengs*.
② Taojieganghunfeng: generals and high officers.

厘俸 // Li Feng

众人边饮美酒边谈笑，
海罕和冈晓干杯忙。
酒宴快要结束时，
海罕微笑把令传：
"从栏中牵出占拜舍，
罩上一个好金舆。
所有的召兰闷①，
备齐礼品骑上象，
欢送混宛回家乡。
送到遥远的天边皆法，
那是混宛住的好地方。"
宴会一散众人忙，
欢送的人马排成队，
渡过美丽的勐卯江，
江水哗哗波浪翻。
海罕日夜兼程把路赶，
终于平安到家乡。
锣鼓齐鸣人欢腾，
只见允罕②映阳光，
顿觉眼睛明又亮。
海罕把混宛送进宫，
混宛又把酒宴设。

And groups of maids playing mouth organs.
People drank and laughed and talked.
Haihan and Gangxiao were busy drinking toasts.
When the banquet came to a close,
Haihan gave an order with a smile:
"Lead Zhanbaishe out of the stall,
And put a good howdah on its back.
All my *zhaolanmens*①
Should prepare gifts and mount your elephants,
And go to see Hunwan off.
He will return to remote Jiefa,
Where he used to live."
When the feast was over,
People saw Hunwan off in lines.
Having crossed the beautiful Mengmao river
With quick currents and swirling water,
And having hurried on with his journey day and night,
Haihan reached Hunwan hometown safe and sound.
The cheers of the jubilant crowds were mingled with drum beats.
Yunhan② city shone in the bright sun light,
Making everyone's eyes brighter.

---

① 召兰闷：参加宴会的官员。
② 允罕：混宛住的金子城。

① Zhaolanmen: the offials attending the banquet.
② Yunhan: the gold city where Hunwan lived.

海罕与混宛相告辞,	Haihan accompanied Hunwan back to his palace
蹬着大象往回返。	And Hunwan treated him to a banquet in return.
	Having said goodbye to Hunwan,
	Haihan returned home on his elephant.

婻崩见海罕回来了,	Nanbeng saw Haihan coming back,
骑着花牛迎路旁。	And rode the black-and-white cow to meet him on the road side.
耳坠上的宝石多又多,	She wore beautiful ear rings with lots of diamonds,
映得两颊真漂亮。	Looking even more beautiful.
左右侍女高举金幡幢,	Beside her, two ladies were holding golden prayer flags.
彩色旗帜迎风展。	The colorful banners fluttered high in the wind.
混勐缓缓入宫廷,	Hunmeng walked slowly into his palace
坐上金椅把召当。	And sat on his gold throne as Zhao.
庆贺的人群来来往,	People came to congratulate him.
到处挂满金幡幢,	Golden prayer flags were hung everywhere.
宫中金碧映辉煌!	The palace was splendid and magnificent!

译后记

傣族是一个历史悠久的民族。傣族文学内容丰富多彩、别具一格,十分引人注目。傣族书面文学有1000多年的历史,但仍保留有口头创作的基本特征。手抄本中经书统称为"坦",而历史、地理、法规、医药卫生以及文学创作则统称为"厘"。

《厘俸》讲述了两个古代傣族部落之间的战争,起因是勐景哈国王海罕的美丽王后嫡崩被勐景罕国王俸改掠走。海罕联合其他部落发动了对俸改的征讨,经过旷日持久的战争,终于在天神的帮助下夺回妻子,班师回朝。

《厘俸》从叙事内容到叙事结构和世界上其他民族的许多英雄史诗有很多共同之处。内容方面与《伊利亚特》和《罗摩衍那》一样,战争都是由于抢劫妇女诱发的。在《厘俸》中,海罕因为其妻被俸改抢走而发动了对俸改的战争。叙事结构方面,《厘俸》和《伊利亚特》《罗摩衍那》的叙事空间都涉及天界、人世间和冥界。都有"外出征战""英雄凯旋""死而复生"的由本及末、顺时连贯的叙事方式。在世界民族史诗宝库里,具有重要的文学价值和民族学、民俗学、宗教学研究价值。

和其他各民族的史诗一样，《厘俸》在相当长的时期内通过口头传承的方式而得以保存，因此整个史诗在艺术上保留了口传文学的特点，简单、易听、易记。故事朗朗上口，生动形象地表现了傣族地区特有的自然风貌和生活习俗。故事中还大量使用拟人、夸张、排比的修辞手法，故事情节丰富，人物形象鲜明，结构完整，是一部不可多得的民族史诗。

杨　燕

Translator's Afterword

The Dai people have a long history. They have a rich, colorful and remarkable literature with a unique style of their own. Their literature has a history of more than one thousand years but still preserves the basic characteristics of oral literature. Among the ancient manuscripts, the sacred books are usually classified as "tan", meaning "classics", while history, geography, law, medicine, and folklore and literature are categorized as "li", which means "story".

Li Feng is about the war between two ancient Dai tribes. It was started by Fenggai, the king of Mengjinghan, who kidnapped Nanbeng, the queen of Mengjingha, and took her back to his kingdom. Haihan, the king of Mengjingha, gathering together the chiefs of neighboring tribes, launched an expedition to punish Fenggai. After a long and arduous war, Haihan, assisted by the gods, defeated Fenggai and returned triumphantly to his kingdom with his queen.

Li Feng has much in common with other epics in the world in terms of its plot and narrative structure. The story of *Li Feng*, like those of *The Iliad* and *Ramayana*, is about a war which breaks out because a woman has been kidnapped. In *Li Feng*, Haihan declares war on Fenggai, who has kidnapped his queen. As for narrative structure, *Li Feng*, *The Iliad* and *Ramayana* all involve the narrative space of heaven, the earth and the underworld. The development of the story from "going on an expedition" to "triumphant return" to "hero resurrection" follow a chronological and coherent order. In the treasure house of world epics, *Li Feng*, as an important ethnic epic, plays an important role in ethnology, folklore and religious studies.

Like other ethnic epics, the story of *Li Feng* has long been passed down from generation to generation by means of oral inheritance. The story thus has the characteristics of oral literature, such as being "simple, easy to tell, and easy to remember". The story is reader-friendly, describing vividly the unique natural landscape and living customs in the Dai areas. Many rhetorical devices, such as personification, hyperbole and parallelism, are used. The well-developed plots, the vividly portrayed characters, and the complete story structure make the epic extraordinary.

Yang Yan

译者简介

杨燕，云南师范大学外国语学院副教授。从事英语专业教学工作31年。曾赴新加坡、加拿大、澳大利亚学习和访学。主要从事英语教学研究和多元文化教师教育研究。译者本人上大学之前一直在西双版纳学习和生活，对傣族人民和傣族文化有着非常深厚的感情，对傣族民俗、宗教、文学和艺术均有丰富的了解和体验，希望通过对《厘俸》的翻译，在民族文化尤其是傣族文化外译方面尽自己微薄而真诚的努力。

About the Translator

Yang Yan is an associate professor of English in the School of Foreign Languages and Literature at Yunnan Normal University. She has been teaching English for 31 years and has been to Singapore, Australia and Canada as an trainee, a student, and a visiting scholar respectively. Her research interests are English language teaching and multicultural teacher education. The translator had been living and studying in Xishuangbanna Dai Autonomous Prefecture before she went to university. She loves the Dai people and Dai culture, and has had a rich experience of local customs, religion, literature and arts. Through the translation of *Li Feng*, she feels quite happy that she can make some small but sincere effort in introducing the culture of the Dai ethnic group to the English world.